MAYAN SUNSET

J.G. NADEAU

This is a work of fiction. All of the characters, organizations, and events portrayed in this novel are either products of the author's imagination or are used fictitiously.

MAYAN SUNSET
Copyright © 2015 J.G. Nadeau
All rights reserved.

ISBN: 978-0-9948847-0-1
Printed by CreateSpace, An Amazon.com Company

For Zachary,
who never ceases
to amaze me.

And for Trudy,
who always supports me,
no matter how crazy
my endeavors.

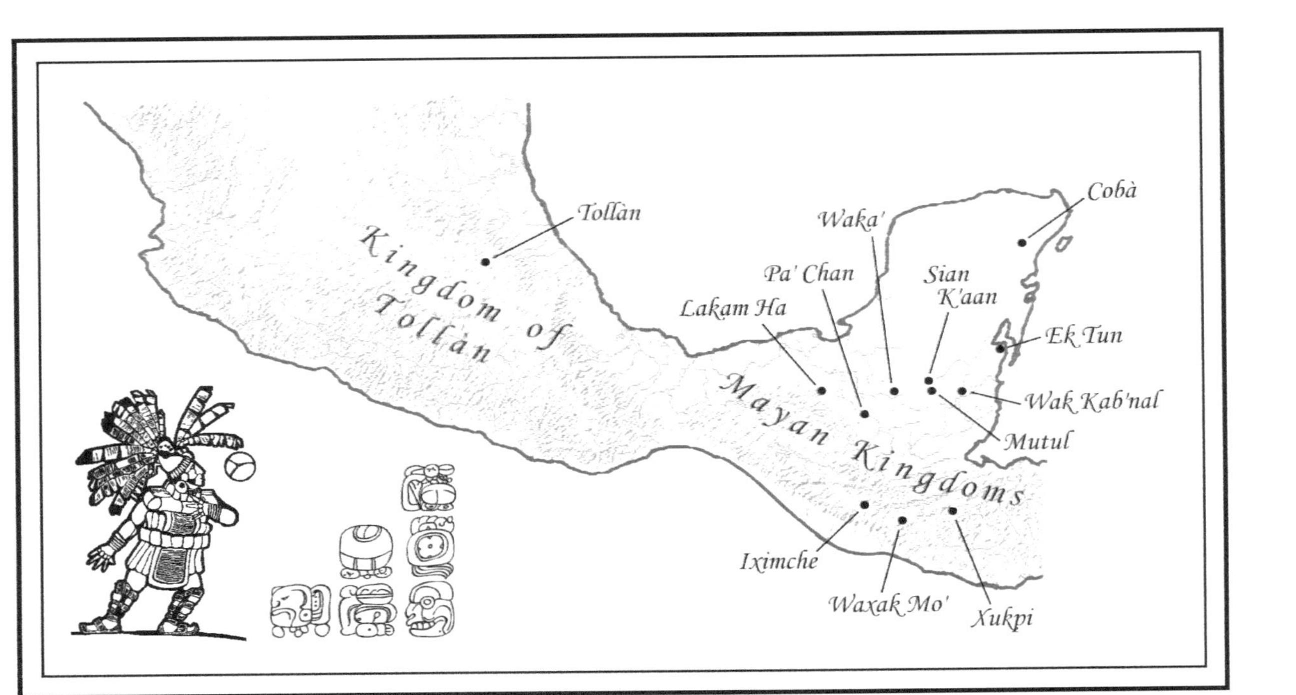

Kingdom of Tollàn
Tollàn
Mayan Kingdoms
Waka'
Pa' Chan
Lakam Ha
Sian K'aan
Cobà
Ek Tun
Wak Kab'nal
Mutul
Iximche
Waxak Mo'
Xukpi

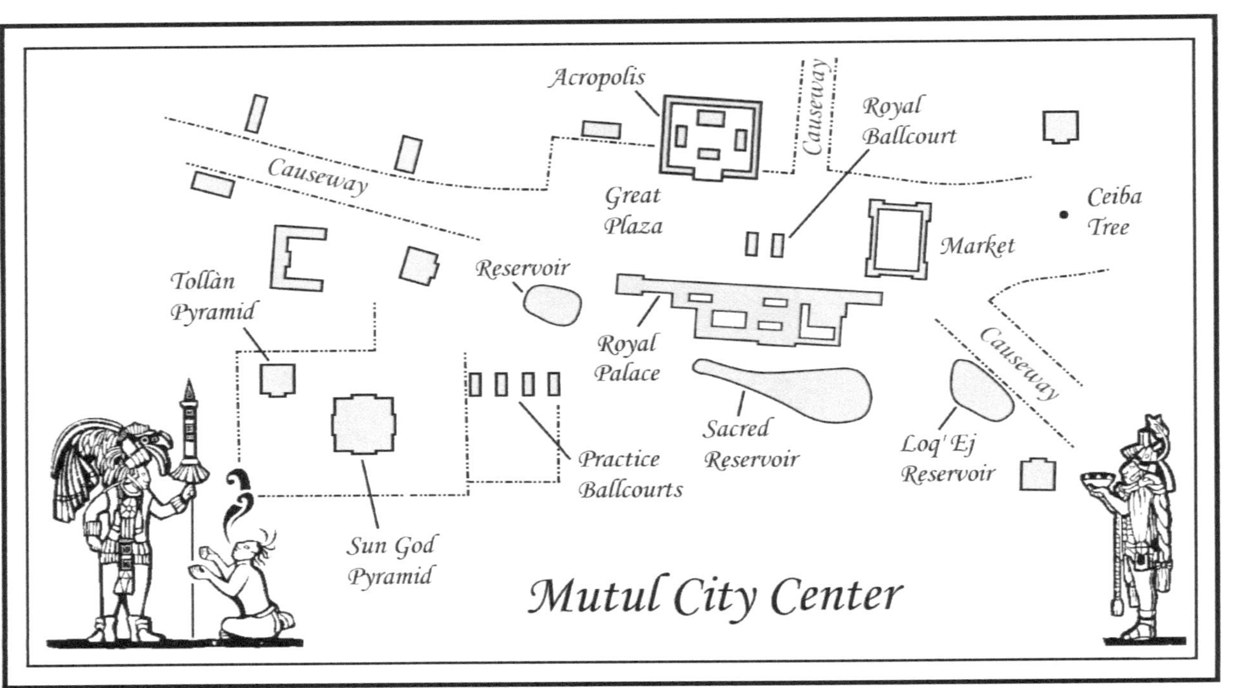

Acropolis
Causeway
Royal
Ballcourt
Causeway
Great
Plaza
Market
Ceiba
Tree
Tollán
Pyramid
Reservoir
Royal
Palace
Causeway
Sacred
Reservoir
Loq'Ej
Reservoir
Practice
Ballcourts
Sun God
Pyramid
Mutul City Center

THE END
OF A K'ATUN

Okib' slowly raised his chin toward the deep blue sky. His skin was glistening with sweat. The air was thick and heavy. The warm breeze caressing his face provided little relief against the scorching midday sun.

He longed for water, but the priests had already prepared his body. They had already given him the sacred drink. There would be no relief now, no rescue from the upcoming ordeal. From now on, there would only be heat.

Soon, there would also be pain.

Patiently waiting for the ritual to begin he concentrated on his own breathing, helpless to prevent his own thoughts from morphing into nightmarish images of the upcoming ceremony and of the dreaded stingray spine.

Struggling to maintain control of himself he channeled all of his inner strength and successfully fought the urge to run away from the approaching ordeal. To run away from the blood and pain.

He closed his eyes.

In his mind he saw his own grandfather performing the same sacred ceremony so many years ago. He was only a child at the time yet he clearly remembered the aging man sitting atop the acropolis wearing a prestigious black obsidian necklace, heavy jade ear spools, and an elaborate green feathered headdress. While a westerly wind had blown thick black clouds over the city, the darkened sky did little in bereaving the man from his magnificence.

To his own credit, he'd never once looked away as the ceremony had unfolded. He stood watching, proud and strong until the end, although he'd been glad for his mother's reassuring touch when his grandfather had pierced his own skin. Then, exactly twenty years later, his late father had performed the exact same ritual. Atop the very same acropolis, he had shed his own blood for them.

For the past thirteen generations, his ancestors had successfully performed the k'atun ending ceremony, the ritualistic sacrifice marking the end of a twenty year period and the beginning of a new cycle. Today, the task was his. On his own shoulders now rested the responsibility of opening a portal to the otherworld. Of communicating with the gods. Of sustaining them, in the hope of allowing the sun to complete its daily cycle above their heads for another twenty years.

Out of nowhere, a drumbeat suddenly pulled him out of his thoughts. The ceremony was about to begin. Okib' took a deep breath, and tried to focus on the prayer spoken by the priest.

"... we beg you, Itzamnà, almighty creator god, to please receive our sacrifice. Feed from the blood of your devoted children and grant us your divine blessing. Allow us to honor you again and again for another twenty years. Please receive this offering with open arms. Share it with K'inich Ahau, the mighty sun god who restlessly travels our skies, and who generously provides us with..."

The rest was lost to him. No longer able to bear the infernal heat, his head became foggy. Dizziness slowly overcame him.

There was no telling for how long he drifted in and out of consciousness. As he came back to himself, he noticed that silence now surrounded him. There were no more prayers. No more drums. There was only the subtle sound of the feathers adorning his headdress gently flowing in the breeze.

It was time.

He opened his eyes, and was immediately blinded by the day's brightness. As his pupils adjusted to the light he first noticed the black smoke clouds rising towards the heavens. His eyes wandered towards the mattress of dried maize leaves at his side, and to the small pottery bowl filled with rolls of bark paper. His chest tightened with anxiety as he finally rested his gaze upon the stingray spine.

Aware of the many eyes now fixed upon him, he ceremoniously picked up the spine and held it before him. His vision blurred. The glyphs engraved on the spine slowly faded away. He felt nauseous, the smell of burning incense strongly disagreeing with the aftertaste of the fermented maize and mushroom beverage he'd been given to alter his perception of reality.

He would have to act quickly. His fingers reached for his mouth, and pulled out his tongue.

Now, he thought. *Do it. Now!*

Without any further hesitation, he promptly stabbed himself through the tongue. A sharp pain immediately shot throughout his entire body and tears flowed from his eyes as the barbed sting perforated his flesh.

He waited for what seemed like an eternity. When he could bear the pain no more, he pulled the pointy spine out of his tongue and gasped for air. Thick, warm blood filled his mouth as the bowl was brought to his lips, the paper rolls quickly turning red with blood.

Despite the heat, his body started shivering. His eyes burned from the surrounding smoke. He felt lightheaded and weak, the intense throbbing pain quickly draining all of his strength away.

With blood pouring from his tongue he stood up, took a hesitant step forward, and almost faltered. Fortunately, a strong arm supportively grabbed him and carried him towards the fire pit.

With a shaky hand he threw the blood soaked rolls into the burning embers. The paper hissed as the sacrificed blood turned to smoke, becoming one with the dark smoke clouds, dematerializing from this plane of existence and passing into the realm of the gods.

Immediately, a conch shell horn was blown and silence was broken as the thirty thousand people gathered before him on the great plaza acclaimed him loud and strong in a deafening ovation.

His birth name was Okib', but he was now known throughout the land as Chak Tok Ich'aak, Great Jaguar Paw, fourteenth king of Mutul. He was the K'uhul Ahau, the Holy Lord and ruler of the greatest Mayan city-state of his time. Once again, he was about to demonstrate his ability to interact with the otherworld.

From atop the royal acropolis where he stood, Great Jaguar Paw raised his arms towards the heavens as blood and sweat mingled all over his painted body. Black clouds of smoke swirled around him in a dizzying dance. The air was unbreathable. The heat, suffocating.

Then, emerging from the smoke, he saw them. One by one, his ancestors materialized into the air, joining him into this plane of existence.

His spirit soared as he recognized his father and his grandfather. Then came all of the others who'd ruled before them, the ones whose stories and legends were carved on the many stelas displayed throughout the city. The ancient kings of Mutul had answered his call. His ancestors had returned from the realm of death and pledged him their support. In their wake would follow Itzamnà, Chaak, K'awiil, and the many other deities inhabiting the heavens.

Great Jaguar Paw smiled. He had successfully opened a portal to the otherworld.

Once again, the drummers lined up at the bottom of the acropolis started striking their instruments, their furious rolling beat echoing far past the reaches of the city, across the maize fields, and deep into the surrounding jungle. Priests recited prayers, praising the king who, through his own bloodletting sacrifice, had before them established contact with the divine realm, and the crowd chanted in a ground shaking clamor.

All of a sudden, Great Jaguar Paw reached towards his priest for support. Just as he was about to collapse he noticed the bearded prisoner lying at the bottom of the stairs. His hands were tied behind his back. His clothes, torn to shreds. Standing next to him was the nacom, the executioner, his arms resting over a large broad flint ax.

The king's own blood had been sacrificed to open a portal to the otherworld.

Now, the prisoner's life would be sacrificed to nourish the gods that were summoned through it.

THE IGUANA
TATTOOED WARRIOR

"Sian K'aan, our neighboring city. For several generations we've both cohabited peacefully. We've shared goods and resources. We've united our strengths against common foes. A true partnership, with Mutul in the south and Sian K'aan in the north. Close enough to one another that a man could easily walk the distance between both cities in a single day."

"Ultimately, that proximity between us would become our doom. The armies which used to stand back to back against invading forces now faced each other, weapons in hand. Legends would blame an ancient feud between our kings, a failed arranged marriage, or a treacherous assassination attempt. It is now all irrelevant."

"Regardless of the reason, tensions steadily grew over time as Mutul opened its markets to newcomers and embraced commerce and economy while Sian K'aan, in a desperate effort to maintain a traditional way of self-sustainment, chose to enclose themselves from outside influences. Within a few generations, Mutul had expanded to the point where we became the most influential trade center of the region, commercially involved with all other great Mayan states. As for Sian K'aan, they struggled for food and farmland. Their people suffered."

"It all started with remote altercations. Isolated skirmishes. The theft of a few crops. Over the past generations, the conflict has quickly escalated. The attacks gradually became more frequent, more violent, and several Mutul peasants are now killed every year as enemy warriors cross into our land to steal our food and goods."

Excerpt from "The Sian K'aan Conflict"
Mutul library, Wars and Conquests section
Dated 5 K'an, 12 Ch'en

Kabrak'an woke up before dawn and headed straight into town, taking the time to look around, to breathe the air. He always relished that magical short-lived moment before sunrise when the misty fog left by the night's dampness still lingered around the city. In the coolness of the early morning he passed before the acropolis and made his way across the great plaza where, already, hundreds of workers were gathering in preparation for the day's many chores. As he walked through the crowd, people fell silent and stepped aside, acknowledging his presence, respectfully nodding at his passage.

Just as the sun rose above the horizon and burned out the last remnants of misty puffs lying over the ground, Kabrak'an entered the already busy market alleys, where he was immediately assailed by an incredible variety of smells and colors. Maize, squash, beans, chili peppers, sweet potatoes, and freshly prepared tortilla bread brightened the stalls with various shades of green and yellow and red, while the air carried the strong smell of spices. It was a feast for the nose and the eyes.

He slowly made his way down the street, looking left and right for anything that might suit his taste to break the morning fast before eventually stopping before a table covered with a mountain of avocados. With an expert eye he carefully chose a fruit, delicately pressed the dark skin between his fingers, and smelled it's aroma. Satisfied, he nodded towards the merchant.

"One kakaw please, ahau," asked the man with an accent betraying a northern origin.

Ahau meant *lord* in the Mayan language.

Kabrak'an handed the man a dried cocoa bean and resumed his walk down the busy narrow street.

"Balché! Balché!" yelled another merchant. "Freshly brewed balché made from the sweetest honey there is! Nowhere else in Mutul will you find a better mead!"

He hesitated a moment, tempted by the tasty alcoholic beverage.

"Isn't it a bit early for a drink?" called out a friendly voice.

"Winaq, old friend!" he said as a familiar stooped figure slowly approached him through the crowd. "How are you doing this morning?"

"Me? Surprisingly well, actually," Winaq answered as both men grabbed each other's forearm for the traditional arm shake. "Apparently, the gods have granted me another day amongst you young fools."

"Better get used to it. I expect you to have many more years ahead of you!"

"Then I have been cursed, for my trip to the otherworld is long overdue."

Winaq was indeed very old, long past the average life expectancy of any normal man. His hair had long ago turned white, and his deeply wrinkled face was marked by a toothless smile. However, he'd been gifted with a strong health, a little luck, and a despicable sense of humor. All of which, according to him, contributed to his longevity.

"Tell me," Kabrak'an said, "what brings you here so early?"

"The fresh air," answered the old man, looking straight ahead. "I always fancy a breath of fresh air before shutting myself up inside our cold and humid palace. I always hated that place you know, but I must confess that it feels even worse lately."

The old man moved in closer.

"The dampness makes my joints hurt, and my bladder go," he whispered.

Kabrak'an laughed. With his simple unadorned cotton robe and poor manners, very few people would have guessed Winaq to be one of the most influential men in the state.

"It has been hot lately," the old man added.

"Mm mmm," acknowledged the other with tight lips.

"Mind you, with the passing years, I find myself less and less tolerant to colder nights, so I welcome the warmer spell. Come. Let's walk together for a while."

They both walked for a very long time in silent.

"Great Jaguar Paw is expecting you," Winaq eventually added.

"I know," answered Kabrak'an. "I was also heading to the palace. With the harvest approaching and the thousands of workers soon to be spread across the fields, the king will be expecting details regarding the deployment of our troops, and my plan to ensure the safety of our people."

"He does not take the lives of his people lightly."

"Neither do I."

"Of course," murmured the old man. "Is that what's been bothering you?"

Kabrak'an stopped abruptly and looked at his friend with a surprised look. "What do you mean?" he asked.

"Your forehead always wrinkles when something's on your mind. It gives your iguana a strange look."

Unconsciously, Kabrak'an raised a hand towards his

head, touching the imposing iguana tattoo covering the entire right half of his face. It was a beautiful work of art where the reptile's head rested above his left eyebrow, and its scaly body arched around his right eye while a long twisting tail extended all the way down to his neck.

All Mayans wore tattoos, especially warriors, but Kabrak'an was the most decorated man in Mutul. Scenes of great victories and mythical beings were permanently imprinted all over his body.

He was Mutul's warlord, commander of king Great Jaguar Paw's armies. His body was a testament of many battles and achievements. The iguana covering his face represented Itzamnà, the creator god, and he proudly wore it as a dual sign of supremacy and benevolence. Amongst his own warriors, the famous tattoo had earned Kabrak'an the title of o'on nimal, the Iguana Leader, while his enemies mostly knew him as o'on kamikal, the Iguana of Death.

"Nothing gets past your wisdom, does it?" Kabrak'an said, resuming his walk. "The harvest season will soon begin. Most of the city's workforce will be scattered across the land, gathering maize and squash. You know what that means."

"The raids will start again."

Kabrak'an looked at the sky. Birds where circling above their heads in search of food. "Once again, Sian K'aan warriors will cross our borders. They will murder our workers. Steal our crops. And..." He stopped himself just in time. *And this year will be worse,* he almost said, but there would be time later for Winaq to learn the truth. "And ... many will die," he simply whispered.

Winaq nodded.

"My soldiers are the only men available to patrol the border." Kabrak'an added. "We are too few."

"I thought you spent the rainy season training more

men?"

"I did. Three hundred new warriors will join my troops tomorrow."

They walked by a table covered with freshly prepared tamales, and the smell of venison meat opened Kabrak'an's appetite. He pulled out an obsidian dagger and cut his avocado in two. "Unfortunately, I would need at least five times as much!"

He offered half the avocado to Winaq, who silently refused. "Hopefully, most will survive the season. They say the harvest might barely meet our needs for food this year," Kabrak'an added.

"I've heard. At least the water reservoirs are already filled at maximum capacity. No one will grow thirsty during the dry season. Besides, the king has just successfully completed the k'atun ritual. How long has it been since the ceremony? Six days? People are still talking about the event. Everyone is confident that Great Jaguar Paw has successfully warranted our ancestor's protection for the years ahead."

The warrior smirked.

"You know religious highlights are always short-lived. People are happy and optimistic for a while. Then comes the next drought. Or plague. Or war. All of a sudden, the gods have abandoned us and we're once again doomed."

"Then the king comes out and calls upon the gods once again! The population returns to their daily activities with renewed confidence. The king has performed his duty, and the cycle continues. It's all a matter of cycles. Life and death. Peace and war. Abundance. Drought. Health, sickness. Days. Years."

Kabrak'an chuckled. "I prefer to focus on the more tangible issues. The ones I can do something about."

"Spoken like a true warrior!" laughed Winaq. "You've never been particularly religious. That's because you are a practical man. Unfortunately, most people are not like you. They need someone above themselves to govern their lives. They rely on authority for direction. I believe the proper..."

Their conversation was abruptly interrupted as shouting and brawling sounds suddenly erupted from further down the street, in an area of the market where traders sold wares and commodities such as tools, fabric and pottery.

Without saying a word, Kabrak'an instinctively reached for his spear only to realize he was completely unarmed except for the small dagger hanging at his waist.

Damn, he thought.

They both hastened the pace towards the commotion.

NEW FRIENDS

The heat quickly settled in as the sun rose high above the horizon and casted its rays upon the land. In Mutul, the working class citizens were long gone out in the fields, warriors were either training or patrolling the streets, and merchants were busy tending to their businesses. As for the nobles, they were most likely gathered somewhere out of sight, discussing philosophical matters and sharing the burdens of nobility.

For a few fortunate ones, however, the beautiful day was an opportunity to unwind, and one of the favorite place to do so was under the giant ceiba tree growing in the middle of the city.

Of course, the people lying there were all wealthy, most of them children of rich merchants and highly positioned nobles. Before midday, many had already gathered in the tree's soothing shade, overindulging in balché and other alcoholic beverages in the company of friends.

One young man, however, was standing there alone, leaning against the smooth bark of the imposing trunk, peacefully savoring a fresh papaya. A stranger, as made obvious by his attire.

Tupac had been in the Mayan city for less than two days. Yet, as he observed the people around him, the young man knew he would be happy in Mutul. The temperature was warmer than in Tollàn, his home city. The food was good, and the local mead was excellent. It was fortunate that he liked Mutul so much since he planned on staying for a very long time.

He was eating the last bits of flesh off the fruit when he finally saw Balam, his new friend, approaching with a large bag hung over his shoulder. Both of them were about the same age, in their late teens. Both were young and strong although, even in the distance, Tupac could see how the heavily overfilled bag threatened to crush the young Mayan to the ground, the thought of which drew a smile over his face.

The two boys had met at the palace on the previous day. Tupac and his uncle had been standing before the corbelled arch leading inside the thick stone walls, the latter loudly arguing with the two warriors standing guard at the entrance when Balam had finally walked out of the palace.

"What is the matter here?" he'd asked. "What is all this commotion about?"

"This stranger has been relentlessly requesting an audience with the king," answered one of the guards as he pointed a finger towards the older man while holding his spear in a non-threatening way, although his face was flushed and his voice betrayed his exasperation.

"We repeatedly told him the king is unavailable at the moment. He does not understand," added the other.

"Finally, someone!" interjected the older stranger in perfect Mayan. "I certainly hope you are less stubborn than this big oaf!"

The warrior grimaced at the insult.

"I am a lord of Tollàn, sent here on behalf of my king. I request to be introduced to K'uhul Ahau Great Jaguar Paw immediately!"

Balam looked at him with a calm look. The man, who was old enough to be his father, was dressed in plain travel clothes. His face was dirty and his sandals were covered with dust, but there was an assurance about him. Something in the way he acted definitely marked him as a man of higher status. The boy had no reason to doubt his claim.

"May I have your name please, ahau?" he respectfully asked.

"I am Atlatl Cauac Tlacatl," answered the Tollàn. "You may address me as lord Spearthrower Owl."

Balam nodded.

"I understand your request, ahau. Unfortunately, the king is indisposed at the moment. I am afraid you will have to schedule a proper audience when he is better."

"This is outrageous, you insolent young man!" raged the man. "I must see him at once!"

"I regret," answered Balam with a firm voice. "The king has not seen anyone in five days. You will have to come back later."

As the foreigner moved forward, the guards subtly raised their sharp spear blades towards him, a reaction which did not go unnoticed by Spearthrower Owl.

The man took a step back, red with fury. His nostrils flared as he breathed deeply.

"This delay is unacceptable! Your authorities will hear about this!" he finally said before turning around and storming away, leaving his nephew behind.

They all watched him disappear down the street.

"I must apologize for my uncle," said the young man. Unlike his relative, he spoke with a heavy foreign accent. "The trip here was long and..." he searched for the proper word, "...arduous. He will be better in the morning, after a decent meal and a good night's sleep. My name is Tupac."

"You can call me Balam," the Mayan answered, offering his right arm.

Tupac reached out, and they shook arms.

Now, a day later, Balam was hurrying towards his new friend with the heavy burden on his back.

"Good morning," he said, embarrassed as he dropped

the bag to the ground. The bag fell with a heavy thud. "I apologize for being late. I had to stop by the barracks to find some equipment for you."

"No worries," replied Tupac. He spat one of the papaya's black seeds on the ground. "I was enjoying the scenery."

The Tollàn boy nodded towards a young woman sitting nearby in the company of friends. Her rich green dress covered with obsidian ornaments and quetzal feathers undoubtedly marked her as a woman of higher status. As she looked in their direction Tupac gave her a smile. She smiled back, revealing a series of filed teeth imbedded with round jade beads on their front face. Tupac shrugged.

"What's with the teeth?" he asked.

Balam must have looked confused as Tupac understood the need to clarify himself.

"The filing and the jewels?"

"All young girls dream of shaped teeth and jade implants. Is it not the same in your land?"

"No," replied Tupac with a frown. "They dream of being fortunate enough not to lose them to decay or other diseases."

Balam smiled.

"Your Mayan is very good," he complimented. "Where did you learn our language?"

"In Tollàn. My father insisted, so an old Mayan named Ch'akan taught me. He claimed that with the increasing trade between our people, both of our worlds would cross each other, and great opportunities would come to those who could communicate with your people. Your language is very different from mine. I am still learning."

"You will learn quickly here. Your vocabulary is already quite impressive. I only wish I could speak Tollàn that well."

"You speak Tollàn?"

"Only a few words."

"I could teach you, if you want."

Balam nodded. He had always been fascinated by the many foreign languages spoken around the city.

"I would very much like that, thank you!"

"Your name," Tupac continued, "it means *jaguar*, right?"

"Yes, it does."

"How did that name come to you?"

"I was rescued from the jungle when I was a child. One of the king's servants found me hiding between bushes like a jaguar stalking its prey, or so he said. It couldn't have been very long after my parents, or anyone, had actually abandoned me there. I suppose I was fortunate, as I could never have survived more than a day alone. Anyway, he took me with him to the palace and named me Hun Balam. Shortly after, I was adopted by one of the nobleman whose wife couldn't bear any children."

"Your full name is Hun Balam?"

"Hun Balam Ku'x actually, the Jaguar's Heart. My friends simply call me Balam."

"So you now live with your adoptive parents?"

"No, I live at the palace with the servants."

Tupac raised his eyebrows in surprise.

"My adoptive parents passed away years ago," Balam explained. "They left me a few valuable possessions and a well-respected name. I am Hun Balam Ku'x Na-Chaan Tilij Ka'ab, the son of Tilij Ka'ab Ahau, and so I was allowed to stay at the palace. Today, I remain at the king's service."

"Then you are not a noble," Tupac remarked.

Balam lowered his head.

"No, although they pretend to treat me like one of their own. I am often entrusted with several responsibilities and administrative duties around the palace, but I am simply too different from them. Most of these nobles are mainly driven by wealth, ambition, and politics while I, on the other hand, aspire to a much simpler life."

"Tell me, what is it that you want?" asked Tupac. "What do you like?"

"Hunting, music, and of course, playing ball. I would also like to travel. To see the world."

"Noble deeds, all of them, although travelling isn't as fulfilling as it may seem."

"Have you travelled a lot?"

"It is my first time. I had never left my city before."

"Please, tell me about your journey from Tollàn!"

"There isn't much to say," replied Tupac. "It was a rather uneventful trip. The road is quite busy, and we've crossed many travelers and merchants. Overall, not a particularly unpleasant journey. Still, after two months of walking through mountains and valleys, I am quite happy to be here."

"Two months? Please, tell me more!"

So Tupac went on, explaining in great detail all aspects of his long journey from Tollàn to Mutul. Balam was all ears, avidly listening to every detail when, suddenly, his attention shifted towards the market.

Tupac looked in the same direction. At first, his saw nothing unusual. Tarps of various colors were hung above the street, shielding the wealthy customers from the sun, while a few heavily built strongmen ensured the area remained clear of anyone who obviously couldn't afford the luxurious goods sold by the merchants.

Then, he noticed the two men casually walking along the streets. The first was quite old. The other, middle-aged. One of them had obviously caught Balam's attention.

The younger one was indeed physically impressive. Not as strongly built as the bullies guarding the market perimeter, he, however, looked much more agile, more athletic. More deadly.

Definitely a warrior, he thought.

His hair was fashioned in what Tupac would later learn was the official Mutul style. Long hair attached with a knot at the back of the head. The vast array of tattoos covering the man's body was impressive, but the most outstanding thing was the way people acted around him. It was as if a mystical aura surrounded him. The man was either strongly feared or highly respected.

"Who is he?" asked Tupac.

"Who he is?" Balam replied, surprised. "He is Ch'o'j Ahau Kabrak'an, Aj Waxaklajun Baak! The o'on nimal!"

Tupac looked at him with a confused face.

"Warlord Kabrak'an, he of eighteen prisoners! The iguana warlord!" Balam explained, proud to introduce the famous soldier. "He is the greatest warrior of Mutul!"

"Mmmm," Tupac replied, somewhat uninterested. Most of the *great* warriors he'd met in Tollàn were little more than the product of either gross exaggeration or sheer luck in battle.

"Eighteen prisoners?"

"Eighteen," Balam proudly confirmed with a nod.

"Doesn't seem like much."

"No? You try capturing a man willing to fight to the death. We'll see how well you fare."

Tupac gave out a smirk.

"It is said that Lord Kabrak'an is the son of an ancient forgotten deity. That he was born from the Great River of Blood flowing through the underworld. He is also single-handedly responsible for Mutul's victory at the battle of Pa' Chan!"

Balam raised his arms, animating with great gestures the story known to every child.

"It was a particularly bloody battle. Men were fighting on the ground while, amidst thunder and lightning, the summoned spirits of ancestors battled each other in the sky. They fought for three entire days and nights, without sleep nor rest, but the enemy was too powerful. One by one, our men were falling. In the moment of despair, when everything seemed lost, Kabrak'an emerged from the clouds, riding the breathing avatar of Itzamnà himself. Carried through the sky by the creator god, he fearlessly wielded his terrible spear, mercilessly slaying any foe standing in his path. As the lifeless bodies of his victims piled up higher than the royal acropolis itself, victory was ours, and the earth turned red with the blood of sacrificed prisoners!"

Tupac laughed, applauding the passionate story-telling.

"I see he is quite the hero!" he said, and gave one last look towards the warlord.

"He is indeed," answered Balam with admiration.

"What about the other one? Never seen a man so old."

"Winaq Ahau," answered Balam. "Our most respected elder, and a personal counselor to the king."

Tupac registered the names and faces into his mind and watched as the pair suddenly hurried away. Once they were out of sight, he turned back towards his friend.

"I need some exercise," he said, nodding towards the bag lying on the ground. "I am anxious to see this ball game of yours. Shall we go?" he asked with a defiant look.

"I thought you'd never ask," Balam replied with a huge smile.

He picked up the heavy bag. Together, they left the coolness of the giant tree's shade and headed towards the ball court.

SHORTAGES

"Obsidian, an absolute necessity for all Mayans from the common worker to the highest noble. Crafted into cutting tools of all sorts, this volcanic glass is used for a variety of domestic tasks and ritualistic purposes. Unfortunately, obsidian is not found in our part of the world, so we must rely on importation to supply Mutul's markets and citizens with this vital resource."

"To the best of our knowledge, there are only two obsidian-producing mountain ranges in the entire world. The first, located faraway along the southern coast, is under the dominion of the southern Mayan states. With the local kings and warlords relentlessly disputing themselves the rights to the many quarries and mining sites of the region, it is a land torn by war and grief."

"The other source lies even further away, far beyond the outer reaches of the Mayan land in the western kingdom of Tollàn."

"There was a time, not so long ago, when the only Tollàn goods found in our cities were imported by the rare, isolated merchants who dared travel the long and treacherous path between both territories. The few pieces of obsidian jewelry they brought with them were usually sold to rich nobles at an exuberant price."

"Eventually, the Tollàns realized the extent and potential of the Mayan markets. They saw our richness, and they understood our need for obsidian. At the expense of the southern Mayan kings, Tollàn obsidian slowly started appearing in our markets."

"Nowadays, Tollàn has gained a significant share of the fiercely disputed market, and one can now easily purchase Tollàn obsidian or, for that matter, any other products exported from the foreign capital. The rich wear their clothes and jewelry. Their pottery is found on every street corner. In exchange, Mayan cocoa seeds and prized quetzal feathers are regularly exported towards the faraway land."

Excerpt from "The Emergence of Tollàn Obsidian"
Mutul library, Commerce and Economy section
Dated 3 Muluk, 17 Mol

The fighting was quickly dying down as a patrol of three warriors forcefully interposed themselves between the rowdy market crowd and the merchant. They were busy ordering the mob back to their daily business when Kabrak'an arrived, closely followed by Winaq. As he saw them approaching, one of the warriors immediately straightened up and held his head up high.

"Ch'o'j Ahau Kabrak'an Aj Waxaklajun Baak," he yelled loud and clear, using Kabrak'an's formal title. The crowd immediately went silent at the announcement of the warlord's presence.

Purposely taking his time, Kabrak'an looked at the young warrior. He was wearing a red loincloth, leather sandals, and a cotton mantle cloak as protection against the sun. In his left hand was the warrior's traditional weapon, a short spear tipped with a lethally sharp flint blade. He then looked at the crowd in silence. People were standing around him, a few paces away. No one dared move or say anything. The warlord was well known throughout the city, and he was particularly well respected.

The soldier offered an explanation.

"Obsidian shortage, Kabrak'an ahau," he said. "The merchant claims his merchandise was not delivered this morning. These people were arguing over the last available obsidian blades."

Kabrak'an turned towards the merchant. The short, overweight man was wearing an expensive jade ear spool in his left ear, a mark of high status. The warlord stared at him for several seconds until a trickle of sweat appeared over the merchant's forehead. Satisfied, he finally nodded towards the empty table.

"Your shipment was not delivered?" he asked.

"No, ahau. As your warrior told you." The man had an annoying, nosy voice. "I was expecting a full shipment of blades from Xukpi, but nothing has arrived. Nothing except rumors about the caravan being attacked on its way here. Apparently, the entire merchandise was stolen."

The crowd murmured. Kabrak'an felt Winaq's eyes falling upon him. He chose to ignore his friend's silent enquiry.

"Rumors," he replied.

The merchant smiled.

"Maybe," he defiantly acknowledged. The man reached deep inside a small bag attached to his waist. "My sources are, however, rarely mistaken. In any case, I've almost nothing left to sell."

He pulled out his hand and slowly opened his fist, revealing half a dozen obsidian blades.

"Is this truly all you have left?"

"As far as I know, it might be all that remains in the whole market," he said loudly, as if challenging the warlord's authority.

The crowd grumbled.

Kabrak'an reached out, grabbed one of the blades, and

held it before his eyes. The sun reflected brightly on the glassy pitch black surface.

The blade was relatively short, about the length of his middle finger. He turned it around and examined its longer face, which had been skillfully worked into a razor sharp edge.

"How much do you ask for this one?" Kabrak'an asked.

The man hesitated slightly before answering.

"Fifty kakaw, ahau."

The crowd erupted in protest. Fifty kakaw was an aberrant price for the small tool. Without a doubt, the merchant was seeking to take advantage of the situation by making an indecent profit. Kabrak'an looked into the man's eyes, who stood his gaze for a few seconds and then looked away. The warlord silenced the crowd with a gesture, and then spoke softly.

"This is nothing more than a standard common tool produced by an averagely skilled craftsman." He turned the blade between his fingers, cautious to avoid the razor-sharp edge. "How much did you sell them for a few days ago? Ten? Fifteen kakaw?"

The man did not protest.

"When is your next shipment expected to arrive?" he immediately asked.

"In fifteen days, ahau." He paused. "*If* it arrives..."

Kabrak'an ignored the sarcasm, and turned back towards the crowd. There were at least three dozen people gathered around the stall, hoping to buy one of the precious few remaining tools from the Mayan seller.

"Very well," he announced. "I know for a fact that a shipment of Tollàn obsidian is due here in about three days. We will make certain it is sold at a fair price. I will see to it. Personally."

Without even looking back, he could sense the anger in the salesman behind him. "In the meantime, I suggest you all go back to your daily business. As for you," he turned back towards the merchant, and lowered his voice. "Since you will be out of business for several days, you will report to the city's magistrate for harvest duty. There is plenty of work to be done in the fields."

"Ahau, I cannot! I own a business! There are things to manage, stock distribution to plan, shipments to…"

"There is nothing to plan. Until your next shipment arrives, you have nothing left to sell."

"I am a respected member of Mutul's nobility!" The merchant was whispering, but there was fury in his voice and venom in his eyes. "I come from a rich obsidian-selling family, and I will not be treated as a vulgar peasant!"

"You are a vulture, that's what you are!" roared Kabrak'an as he loudly slammed both hands on the table before him. The merchant stepped back.

"Now listen carefully. You will report to the magistrate tomorrow morning at sunrise, or I will have my men search your tent, your house, and all of your family's properties. You better hope, for your own sake, that we do not find a single hidden obsidian blade amongst your belongings, or I will put you out of business for a very long time!"

The man was about to protest, then wisely decided it was probably better for him to remain silent. He could not afford the patrols to find his hidden stash of obsidian. Besides, arguing with the warlord was useless.

Satisfied that his threat had succeeded, Kabrak'an walked away under the approving smiles of the crowd. Winaq quickly caught up to him.

"A lucky guess," he said.

Kabrak'an smiled. "Maybe."

"Was it wise, standing against him? Was it not provocation enough to send his customers to his rivals?"

"You think he could have challenged me?"

"Not him personally but the nobles might hear about it."

"The nobles will soon have a much bigger problem on their hands."

Winaq looked at him with a concerned look. "What do you mean? What do you know?"

Kabrak'an sighed. "The merchant was not entirely dishonest. A major shipment coming from the south was in fact attacked two days ago."

"What!" Winaq stopped, grabbing his friend by the arm.

"The whole merchandise was lost. Flint, serpentine, jadeite, and obsidian. Most of these goods were destined to neighboring states. The obsidian was for us." Kabrak'an lowered his voice to a barely audible whisper. "Only a handful of witnesses escaped. The others were mercilessly massacred. They did not even take prisoners."

"Why was I not made aware of this? Does the king even know?"

"I have only received the report late last night. I was on my way now to personally inform him."

"Do we at least know who is responsible?" Winaq asked anxiously.

Kabrak'an looked at him. "Their faces were painted in red," he said.

The old man gasped.

"And they wore macaw tattoos."

Winaq could hardly believe what he was hearing.

"Sian K'aan warriors," he said in disbelief. "But their city is in the north! Didn't you say the shipment was attacked in the south?"

Kabrak'an nodded. "I suppose they must have traveled around our perimeter, evading our patrols by staying west of the Great Marshes."

"An armed party traveling south? For what purpose? It is rumored they have no men to spare. Besides, if true, why foolishly reveal their presence by attacking one of the shipments? It makes no sense!"

"It does make sense if attacking the merchandise was their intent all along."

Winaq thought for an instant.

"Blessed gods, it must be true! The war party left Sian K'aan with the predetermined intent of attacking the shipment!"

The old counselor paused, absorbing the full implication of what he'd just learned. He now knew what had been bothering his friend all morning, and it was very bad news indeed. Up to this day, the conflict between both cities had been limited to local raids and skirmishes for crops along the northern border. Apparently, the enemy had now increased the scale of their attacks.

As a major trade center, Mutul's economy was highly dependent on the import and export of the various merchandises regularly passing through its borders. If Sian K'aan had decided to strike Mutul's commercial activities, it could seriously affect the city's relations with other surrounding states.

It could send Mutul into war.

ICOQUIH

The hawk was circling high above the palace, quickly gaining altitude in the warm ascending current. Suddenly, the bird broke left. It soared northwards across the great plaza and towards the acropolis where Great Jaguar Paw, king of Mutul, had pierced his own tongue only a few days ago.

The sacred acropolis, the very heart of the city's ceremonial center. A massive stone platform upon which stood four smaller temples. Built on the very emplacement where Mutul's founders had first established themselves generations ago, it was a place entirely dedicated to one single purpose; communicating with the gods.

From his vantage point atop his own palace, Great Jaguar Paw stared at the monument for an instant. A shiver ran down his spine at the sight of the structure. More than a group of temples, the acropolis was also the burial ground of ancient kings. Continuously built over and remodeled, the structure was a huge funeral monument for the revered ancestors of the king's unbroken lineage. One day, it would become his own final resting place as well.

After his death, his body would be set to rest inside a small chamber hidden under the southern temple, and the entrance would be sealed forever. His descendants would then build over the grave, burying the temple under a new layer of brick and mortar, bringing the platform ever closer to the heavens for the glory of future rulers.

Hopefully, that would have to wait.

"K'uhul Ahau, the ahauob is ready," suddenly called a young, delicate voice.

Great Jaguar Paw smiled before turning towards his daughter, who was standing barefoot in the sun, only a few steps away. She was wearing a simple white huipil, the common Mayan long dress. Around her neck, a delicate obsidian necklace was barely visible between her loose hair. So deeply buried in his own thoughts he had never heard her approaching.

"Thank you Icoquih," he said, immediately wincing at the pain in his mouth. Although still swollen, the wounded tongue was healing properly, thankfully without any infection. Still, it would probably be several weeks before his next decent meal. In the meantime, the king was condemned to a diet of maize gruel, mashed vegetables, and soft fruits.

At least, there was balché to dull the pain.

"Remind me to pierce an ear next time," he murmured. "Or my nose."

"Then your sacrifice wouldn't have the same significance, father. The twenty-year ritual is a very sacred ceremony."

"In this case, let us hope I do not live to see the next one."

Icoquih looked down.

"Is there anything else I can do for you, K'uhul Ahau?" she asked.

"Yes. Please see that Winaq's grandchildren do find their way to the temple today. He would not want them to miss the afternoon blessings once again. And please make sure they do not forget their incense this time."

"Of course, father."

It was customary for the nobleman's children to assist the priests in their ceremonial functions, so as to learn the ways of the gods and of the world, but while Winaq's grandchildren were still only learning the basic elements of their religious ceremonies, Icoquih had been fully initiated to their divine secrets, to the art of reading the subtle signs and omens presented by the gods.

Normally, that would have been the duty of the eldest son. The king to be. The royal heir, just as the young Okib' had spent his entire youth training, learning to interact with their ancestors and divinities, preparing for the day when he would replace his own father and take the name of Great Jaguar Paw.

Unfortunately, the gods had not blessed him with a son yet. With the passing of his wife, there was little hope for one in sight.

"Tewiq'nel speaks highly of you," the king added proudly. "Apparently, your preparation for the k'atun ceremony was exemplary. He greatly values your assistance."

"I only wish to make you proud, father."

"He also says you are gifted in the art of communicating with the otherworld."

Icoquih remained silent.

"Does that surprise you?" added the father.

"I only see an unpleasant, grumpy old man who spends most of his time complaining about such things as the incompetence of young priests, the rapid changes in the weather, or the ever increasing amount of immigrants found within the city."

The king laughed and immediately grimaced, his hand reaching for his mouth.

"Unpleasant he is," Great Jaguar Paw said after the pain had passed away. "However, Tewiq'nel is the high priest of Mutul, and he is deeply competent in anything regarding the ways of our gods. For him to praise you is a testament to your many skills and talents."

The king rested his hands over his daughter's shoulders.

"You've become a fine woman Icoquih." He sighed, then added "You know, every day you look more and more like your mother."

She looked aside, unable to hold back a tear.

The queen had died almost exactly three years ago. One night, she had awakened with labored breathing, vomiting blood. Within days she'd lost weight and became incoherent. Shamans had spent entire days and nights by her side, trying to conjure healing spirits, surrounding her with incense and tobacco smoke. Tewiq'nel had never left her bedside, relentlessly invoking Itzamnà and Ixchel, the curers of diseases. They'd bathed her in medicinal herbs. They'd even sacrificed a jaguar in her name.

It was all in vain.

As her last breath drew away, an overwhelming feeling of emptiness had engulfed Great Jaguar Paw, a feeling which remained with him ever since.

He looked at his daughter.

"She loved you so much father," Icoquih told him. "Her only regret was that she never gave you a son."

"She gave me years of happiness," the king said. "She gave me a beautiful daughter to cherish."

"You seem to forget the kingdom needs an heir, ahau. You cannot mourn forever."

"There will be plenty of years ahead for me to solve this problem. Let me worry about the heir," he whispered, as he kissed her forehead. "And please let me mourn a little longer."

Icoquih bowed her head one last time and walked away.

In spite of his apparent dismissal of the matter, Great Jaguar Paw often thought about the heir issue. As the fourteenth direct ruler of his family he was not about to let his dynasty end, but he was not yet ready to take another wife.

Besides, he had more urgent matters on his mind,

duties requiring his immediate attention.

He turned back towards the landscape where, all around the palace, the city stretched as far as the eye could see. An uneven mixture of stone and wood houses regrouped in living quarters of various social standings. Scattered throughout the city he saw several red temples protruding above the city line, every single one of them standing atop its own stepped pyramid.

It was the custom for all Mayan temples to be plastered with a thick layer of stucco and covered with a red coating. Red, the sacred color of the gods. Symbol of the rising sun. Symbol of blood.

Symbol of life.

All within his sight was his. The temples. The houses. The fields. The surrounding villages. The people. It was all his to rule. His responsibility to protect against danger and evil. As a child, Great Jaguar Paw often came here, on the highest roof of the palace, to run away from his governess and flee his chores. Nowadays, he came here to remind himself of his duties. Tens of thousands of people lived under his rule, their wellbeing lying within his own hands. From inside the palace's dark walls, it was too easy to forget the true burden of kingship.

Yes, there would be plenty of time to worry about a son later. For now, the city was on the brink of war. At his own request the ahauob, the council of nobles, had been assembled for an emergency meeting.

The king looked up to the sky one last time where the hawk flew effortlessly above the acropolis's four red temples and disappeared over the eastern horizon.

This was a good omen.

He then walked back inside the palace, and headed straight for the council meeting room.

BALL PLAYERS

"Ah, finally! Here we are!" exclaimed Balam as he and Tupac reached the practice ball court area. "Have you ever been on a Mayan ball court before?"

"Never even seen one," answered Tupac, impressed with the sight.

Before him were three rectangular stone courts built side-by-side, each of them consisting of an open-ended playing surface bordered on their longest sides by waist-high embankments. From these embankments, side walls steeply sloped away from the court center. A stone ring was vertically mounted on top of each side wall.

The first court was already occupied by four players.

"So, this is the game everyone is talking about?" enquired Tupac, as he observed the players before him. All four men were intensely competing for possession of a rubber ball.

"To us, it is much more than a game. It's our passion. Our way of life. Mind you, it's not only played for pleasure. Our leaders sometimes use it to settle important political matters. The priests rely on it for certain rituals. Every respectable city in our land has at least one stone court, the greatest having many more."

"Religious rituals are practiced here?" asked Tupac suspiciously.

"Oh no, never," reassured Balam. "Not here. Those are merely practice courts, where you risk little more than losing your pride to your friends. On the other hand, I certainly wouldn't advise you to play on the royal court. That one is reserved for sacred religious matters. It is guarded by powerful gods."

Tupac silently stared down in the direction pointed by his friend with an anxious look on his face.

Balam laughed.

"Come! Let me show you how it works!"

The young man walked down to the next available court and spilled the content of his bag to the ground, unveiling several pieces of equipment.

First, Tupac was handed a thick, sleeveless cotton jacket. "Padding," explained Balam. "It will dampen the blows. You wear it under this heavy leather chest armor, and use this leather belt to tighten everything around your waist."

Balam then strapped stiff leather pads over his friend's legs, knees and forearms as additional protection against the ball, and he also gave him a thick leather helmet.

The Tollàn boy looked at himself with an astonished look. There was a strong and highly unpleasant perspiration smell about the cotton shirt, which was heavily stained with blood and yellow sweat marks. The bulky armor was battered, discolored and cracked, while the helmet was hot and sticky.

The gear had obviously seen many games.

"Deer hide," explained Balam as he finished tightening the straps. "I borrowed it from the soldiers' supply. It might not look good, but the stiffness of the leather helps in returning the ball. It will also keep you from harm."

"What will keep me from the smell?" mumbled Tupac. "I feel as if I was going to war. I've seen warriors less equipped for battle. And how come your gear looks so much better than mine?" he asked.

"This gear belonged to my adoptive father," answered Balam. "Ball gear is very precious here, and is often passed through generations. Despite being old, this equipment is well made."

Tupac watched in disbelief as Balam quickly stepped into his own armor without any apparent effort.

"How is it you can move so freely? My equipment is so bulky I can barely raise my arms! Do I really need all of this?"

"Absolutely," answered Balam. "Trust me, injuries do happen, despite all the protection." He pointed towards his crooked nose, which had obviously been broken at some point in the past.

"Besides," he added, "you'll quickly get used to it."

The young Mayan then unveiled his most highly prized possession, his very own rubber ball, which he immediately threw towards his friend.

The hard rubber mass made a dull *'thump'* as it struck Tupac's protective gear. The Tollàn stepped back, thrown out of balance by the weight of the impact.

"Meet your new best friend," Balam said with a smirk as he walked towards the court center.

"First, you must learn to control the ball. Get used to its weight. Understand how it reacts. Figure out the amount of force required to send it flying to a certain height. Learn how to bounce it off the side walls," he added, as he sprinkled the field surface with dried maize kernels.

"What are you doing?" asked Tupac with a frown.

"The sound of a bouncing ball disturbs the death lords who live in the underworld," he explained. "Listen."

On the adjacent court, the thumping of the ball against the walls could almost be felt through the ground.

Thump, thump-thump.

Thump.

"The bouncing angers them. These kernels will ensure the maize god's protection from their wrath."

He threw the last kernels into the air and started

explaining the rules.

"Very well, listen carefully. The object of the game is to send the ball through any one of these two rings." He pointed at the vertical rings mounted atop each sloped side wall. "Every time you hit the stone ring itself, you score one point. The first player to score three points wins the match."

Tupac nodded.

"If you send the ball through the ring, the game ends immediately. You win. Now, you can hit the ball with any part of your body except the hands or feet. If you do so, you lose possession. If the ball hits the ground, you lose possession. You can, however, bounce it off the side walls or the bordering embankments for as long as you want. You only lose possession if the ball hits the ground itself. Otherwise, the game is on as long as the ball is in play."

"What does it mean to lose possession?"

"In a one-on-one match, your opponent regains the ball at the closest end of the field."

"It can never touch the ground?"

"No, although a single bounce on the ground is often allowed for children."

"What about contact between players? These guys next to us seem to be playing it a little rough." There was a smirk of anticipation on Tupac's face. The young Tollàn was looking forward to the challenge of the game, and a little physical roughness could only make victory more satisfying.

"It is a physical sport. Your equipment will not only protect you from the ball, but also from your opponents. When you do not have the ball, your goal is obviously to steal it from the other team, or at least to prevent them from marking a point. A reasonable level of roughness is usually tolerated, and even expected. For now, however, you should concentrate on learning the basics."

"What about multi-player rules? How does that work?"

"It's up to the players. Usually, two or three men will play individually, one against the others. Four or six players could play in teams of two or three. I have seen the game played with up to ten players on bigger courts. Official tournaments usually play three against three. Ritualistic matches are always one-on-one. There are many variants, but the basic rules generally apply for all. Here, let me show you."

Balam threw the ball above his head and repeatedly bounced it off his knees a few times. He then sent it flying high into the air, jumped on one of the narrow side embankment and, with a powerful hip movement, redirected the ball straight through the nearest ring.

"Game over!" he smiled.

"That looked easy," replied Tupac, impressed.

"You will find it much more difficult with someone playing against you!"

"I imagine. Why not simply jam the ball between your waist and elbow, and then walk straight up to the ring?"

"The ball has to be free at all times," explained Balam. "While you can bounce it off your body, you may never hold it or jam it between any limbs. Here, give it a try."

He threw the ball to Tupac, who awkwardly bounced it off his forearm padding and sent it flying far out of reach. He ran after it and started again.

At first, the bulkiness of the equipment seriously restricted his movements, and he doubted he would ever succeed in sending the ball through the rings, let alone control the damned thing, as the heavy rubber ball kept flying in all directions.

Yet, the more he practiced, the more he managed to control the ball, and the more he overcame his initial frustrations. He attempted to bounce it off various parts of his body, exploring the different possibilities and searching for different successful combinations. He eventually managed a few decent sequences where he kept the ball airborne by repeatedly bouncing it off the side walls. It took him several more tries before he finally succeeded in touching the edge of the stone ring and scoring a point.

"Excellent!" exclaimed Balam. "Well done! You can practice scoring points on your own later. Now, I want you to focus on keeping control of the ball, no matter what. So try again. This time, I will be nearby, trying to take the ball away from you."

Tupac acknowledged. Once again, he practiced for a long time as Balam turned around him, staying close, trying to disturb him.

"So," asked Balam after a while, looking for different ways to distract his student. "You said your uncle is responsible for all of Tollàn's trade?"

"He is in charge of all commerce to and from the Mayan world," Tupac answered, bouncing the ball high off his thighs as he slowly approached a ring.

Balam was carefully observing his friend, counteracting his every moves. "You trade with all Mayan states?"

"Our products are distributed throughout most of your land, but our primary trade partner is Mutul. You are a major trade center amongst the Mayan nation, are you not?" replied Tupac, who was finding it hard to control the ball while having a discussion.

Balam smiled.

"Mutul is in fact centrally located. We do have trade routes leaving in every direction towards the far reaches of our land."

"Which is precisely why we are here," he said, looking for a breach in Balam's coverage. "From Mutul, we can monitor the trade between both of our cities, and oversee the distribution of our goods across your entire territory."

"So I assume this commerce is beneficial to you?"

"The profits are... reasonable," answered Tupac with a grin, his eyes never leaving the bouncing rubber mass. "Besides, we also benefit from your exported products."

"Do you plan on increasing your presence here then?" Balam asked. The arrival of the Tollàn representatives in Mutul had generated much gossip within the city, and although no one at the palace openly admitted it, there were many who secretly disapproved of the growing relationship with these foreigners.

"My king rules a great empire. We trade with all who wish to do so." Tupac stumbled, then skillfully managed to send the ball against the sloped side wall with enough strength to bounce it off high above him, thereby giving him enough time to regain his footing. "We are an economic society. Tollàn is home to over two hundred thousand people you know."

Balam gasped at the number. "Two hundred thousand?"

"Yes. Our citizens are entirely dependent on the importation of food to nourish their families. Besides, our people have come to appreciate high quality foreign goods. Nowadays, there isn't a decent meal served amongst the Tollàn nobility which doesn't include your famous cocoa, and Mayan honey now sweetens our greatest dishes."

"I see," Balam answered, as he swiftly stole the ball from his opponent. Before Tupac could react, Balam had turned around and scored in the ring behind him.

Tupac stood straight, out of breath. The equipment was uncomfortable and heavy, while the sun was getting crushingly unbearable. Already, his cotton under armor was soaked with sweat.

"This game is difficult," he protested, panting. "I think I'm in for some serious bruising tomorrow."

"Here. Sit in the shade for an instant. You are already quite good," he answered truthfully as he handed his friend a gourd of water. "You learn quickly. Before long, you will be a feared opponent."

The Tollàn boy smiled as he massaged his aching hip.

Balam sat next to Tupac and took a sip from the gourd. The water was warm, and not particularly refreshing.

"You told me why your uncle is here. What about you? Why are you so far away from home?"

"My father wanted me to learn all there is to know about commerce and economy. So when my uncle was assigned here, he saw the perfect opportunity for me to broaden my experience. Besides, he believes it would do me good to travel the world and see for myself what is out there."

"How long do you plan on staying?"

"I don't know. Two, maybe three years."

"Oh, that sounds like a long time."

"It is hardly worth traveling two months for a shorter stay. Besides, I am sure it will go by rapidly."

"Mmmm. Then we'd better hurry up if we want to turn you into a great ballplayer," Balam said, as he stood up. "Come. Now I have the ball, and you try to take it away from me."

Tupac nodded as Balam walked back towards the sun bathed playing surface.

And so they played ball for most of the day.

A FOREIGN LORD

The ahauob meeting hadn't even started that, already, tempers were flaring amongst the council members.

"I am sorry. I cannot afford to lose any more men."

"You know the harvest has priority over other tasks. You know the directive; all able bodied workforce shall be assigned to the fields!"

"I am telling you, I cannot spare any more people! I need the few remaining workers I still have for city chores and maintenance!"

"You can have the entire workforce you want in three months from now! There will be plenty of time for renovations and repairs during the dry season!"

"Of course... Year after year you hold the same speech. But when the harvest is over, the men are re-assigned to the defensive wall construction or to the acropolis upgrade. Before soon, planting season is back, and our temples fall into ruins!"

"Ruins? Aren't you exaggerating a little?"

"Have you walked through the city lately? Half of the irrigation canals are clogged with filth and debris. The Ek Chuaj temple has never been reopened since the collapse of its roof, and I haven't even begun speaking of the terrible state of the roads yet!"

The two nobles were standing in the middle of the palace's inner-courtyard, practically shouting in each other's face as another half a dozen men vigorously joined in the debate after it was suggested using their people to compensate for someone else's needs. The discussion was intense, but it was not unusual for the ahauob members to fight this way. Politics, it seemed, was a never ending battle of intimidation and arguments for supremacy and power.

Sitting on the side, the iguana tattooed warlord Kabrak'an silently watched as the nobles argued between themselves, and he thought of how pointless all this controversy would seem in a few days when he would finally leave for the border outpost.

Soon enough, he would be far from all the political issues and meaningless debates. Soon enough, he would be amongst his fellow warriors, fighting for his life and the lives of Mutul's workers.

He sighed heavily as he looked around.

Winaq, the old advisor, was calmly sitting next to him, obviously lost in his own thoughts. Tewiq'nel, the high priest, was standing to one side, watching the heated conversation with an amused smile on his face. His was the realm of the gods, and so he had little business with the problems of men.

Also present was the ah'tsib, the royal scribe. The man was patiently waiting, completely oblivious to the commotion around him, ready to record and formalize any of the council's decisions. Kabrak'an was staring at the man who, for the hundredth time, obsessively readjusted the position of his many brushes between a blank sheet of bark paper and a pot of ink. The warrior had met a few scribes in his lifetime, and he always found them intriguing. Somehow, they all seemed to share the same learned-man appearance. Calm, reserved, knowledgeable, and annoyingly obsessed with irrelevant details.

The complete opposite of his harsh and rude warriors.

The warlord looked back towards the arguing administrators, who all wore finely tailored robes dyed with the brightest colors. They adorned themselves with expensive jade jewelry. They even fashioned their hair in the same hairstyle; tied in a knot at the back of the head. Their bodies, however, were marked with very few tattoos. An abstract symbol marking a belonging to some prestigious group or fellowship, or a family glyph highlighting a noble ascendance. No sign of any truly honorable achievement.

Not from a warrior's point of view anyway.

Unlike the king himself who, in his youth, had participated in several battles and took his share of enemy lives, these politicians seemed more inclined towards the less glorious and undoubtedly safer administrative responsibilities. It was their choice.

It was not his.

Yes, they all looked the same. The politicians. The administrators. The noble ahauob members. Even the high priest was starting to look like a rich man with his expensive jewelry and fancy sandals. Yet, there was one individual in the ahauob who differed significantly from the others, someone who would never blend into any crowd.

Not that he could even if he wanted to.

Slowly, almost resentfully, the warlord's eyes moved towards the last person present in the courtyard.

Siyah Kak.

The man was sitting in a shadowy corner, harboring a dark look on his face. He hadn't spoken a single word since his arrival, his soulless eyes absently staring before him. As Kabrak'an, he was a deadly warrior whose reputation reached far beyond the regional borders of their city-state.

There ended the extent of their similarities. Contrary to Kabrak'an, most people deeply feared him, for a permanently gloomy aura surrounded the man. He always wore a black loincloth. The many tattoos covering his body were either disturbingly violent or made little sense, and wherever he went, he was always accompanied by the skeletal rattle of the human bones intertwined within his careless hair, trophies attesting of past victories and defeated enemies.

He was also the nacom, the ceremonial executioner appointed by the high priest to sacrifice human victims whenever deemed necessary. Although seldom required, it was a duty generally despised throughout the Mayan land, one for which it was usually difficult to find a volunteer. It was a duty strangely well suited to Siyah Kak.

However, it was not his attire nor his duties that made him the scariest and most intimidating man in the city, but the severe burn marks scarring most of his body. Badly disfiguring him, the scars made Siyah Kak a creature of nightmares.

On cold dark nights, when people gathered around campfires, elders would sometimes tell of a young boy, of the unwanted son spawned from the cursed union between a demon and an evil witch. It is said the child was born from a great pyre lit by the gods themselves, scarred for life in penitence for the many sufferings caused by his parents.

Legends, folk tales, and stories no doubt nourished by the name the boy had chosen for himself as he'd reached adulthood.

Siyah Kak.

Born in fire.

The nobles were still arguing over the workforce assignments when Great Jaguar Paw finally appeared in the courtyard.

"K'uhul Ahau Chak Tok Ich'aak," announced Winaq, the old counselor. There was an immediate silence as everyone stood straight.

Without saying a word, Great Jaguar Paw walked towards his seat. The king stood up for several seconds, watching each member of his ahauob council attentively. He then exchanged the slightest nod with Winaq and sat down. Silently, the ahauob members did the same.

"My friends," he said. "Although not unexpected, I regret to see that some of the issues regarding the harvest are still being disputed amongst yourselves." He looked at the administrators who'd been arguing only moments ago with a reproachful look.

"May I remind you," Great Jaguar Paw added, "that beside the security of our own people, the harvest shall be our first priority, for there will be no one left to pray in our freshly painted temples unless we can first feed ourselves."

Great Jaguar Paw noticed how one of the nobles lowered his eyes, a defeated look on his face.

"I do, however, understand and share Kawak's concerns," he added, not wanting to openly discredit any one of them. "Therefore, I wish to see a detailed listing of all outstanding maintenance tasks, which shall be tackled as soon as the harvest is over. Now, I trust you are all more than capable of solving the details amongst yourselves without any further intervention from my part. For now, we have a more urgent matter before us. I have requested this meeting to discuss Sian K'aan's attack on the obsidian shipment."

All members of the council listened carefully as the king explained in details the events reported earlier by his warlord.

"It appears that Sian K'aan is now targeting our merchandise. Our borders are threatened, our crops are threatened, and now our commerce is threatened. I am waiting for your suggestions. How do we protect ourselves, and how do we guarantee the safety of the several merchants coming in and out of the city?"

The noblemen looked at each other. Except for Winaq and Kabrak'an, this was news to them. Devastating news coming at the worst of time, right before the harvest, the busiest season of the year. After a long moment of silence, one of the administrators voiced his opinion.

"We need to complete the wall, K'uhul Ahau. Only with adequate protection can we guarantee the safety of our city. Permanently guarded, a continuous stone structure running along Sian K'aan's border would provide a significant deterrent against incoming invaders."

"The wall project was undertaken years ago," argued another. "Unfortunately, the wall is still several seasons from completion. Even if we'd double or triple the workforce assigned to its construction, we'd never complete it within an acceptable timeframe. Sian K'aan would have plenty of time to run through our defenses and inflict us considerable damages. There is simply not enough time to build a suitable defensive structure!"

"Especially if we must now also defend the southern borders," added a third man. "We never planned on extending the wall that far south in the first place."

"What exactly is the status of this project?" asked the king.

"We started building the wall in areas considered most at risk along the northern and eastern borders," explained Kabrak'an. "Efforts were concentrated in areas lying between the seasonal marshes. Being impassable during the wet season, the swamps do provide some additional natural defense against any incursion. However, with the dry season fast approaching, the marshes will soon dry up, opening the passage to the enemy."

He looked around.

"Currently, all we have is a fence full of holes. And may I remind you all that even if we had a completed wall today, I simply do not have enough warriors to efficiently guard this huge perimeter."

The king nodded.

"So, what is your suggestion?" he asked.

The warrior was about to admit he had none when, for

the first time, Siyah Kak's raspy voice was heard.

"Maybe it is finally time to retaliate, ahau."

Everyone looked at him in surprise. The man was notorious for remaining silent during meetings, usually preferring to keep his opinions to himself, but the indulgence granted to the enemy had been bothering him for quite a while now.

"If an acceptable defense cannot be raised, then we must change our tactic. I suggest we move to offence."

He was looking around the courtyard, as though searching for approval. "We must strike them fast and hard. They attack our people? Then we should attack theirs. They threaten our trade? They steal our crops? Then I say we plunder their meagre harvest and burn whatever we leave behind. Starve them before the dry season! Next time, they will think twice before crossing our border, assuming they survive the year at all."

There were some discreet murmurs of agreement within the council when Great Jaguar Paw raised his hand.

"We all know your feelings on this issue, Siyah Kak ahau," he slowly replied. "Deep inside, I suppose most of us do share them, at least up to a certain extent. I also believe everyone here is aware of my position on this subject."

He looked around. "Are there any other suggestions?" he asked, hoping for a wiser course of action.

"My king, I must insist! How long before our trade partners abandon us to our fate if we cannot guarantee their safety? How much longer will we let the enemy cross our borders and steal our crops! How much longer will we endure and leave them unpunished! I believe an immediate and merciless attack to be the only solution!"

Siyah Kak turned once again towards the ahauob, surprising most of them with this sudden burst of enthusiasm and emotion. "What do you all say? Are you with me? Let's attack the enemy without any further hesitation!"

"I will not go," answered Kabrak'an. "I will not lead this butchery."

The nacom stood on his feet. "If the warlord and his valiant troops will not join me, then I shall go alone," he threatened, hammering his wrist into his open palm. "I will raise a militia, and we will raid Sian K'aan once and for all!"

"Then you would most certainly condemn hundreds of good men," replied the warlord. "Fathers, and sons. For death is all that would await them."

"Coward! We can win this battle!" His scarred face looked even more terrifying under the strain of anger.

"Then tell me, what will…"

Great Jaguar Paw did not let Kabrak'an finish his protest. From a swift gesture of the hand he commanded immediate silence. Once everyone was silent he spoke very slowly, leaving no doubt about this being his final decision.

"I know we can win, Siyah Kak. Truly, I do believe we could face the enemy and emerge victorious. But have you thought of what would happen next? After we have victoriously walked into Sian K'aan? After the soil has turned red with the blood of our warriors? And of theirs? For, regardless of the outcome, casualties will be significant on both sides. So tell me who, then, would protect our borders after the destruction of our armies? Who would see to the safety of our children? Siyah Kak, as noble as they are, your actions can only lead to a bloodbath, and I will not let both armies fight until mutual extermination. While I want to solve this conflict, a full scale attack would likely prove much too costly. I refuse to consider that option unless it is the last resort to protect our city. For now the situation is nowhere near that critical, nor is it desperate enough to warrant such drastic measures."

Siyah Kak sat down with a disgusted look.

"So, once again, are there any other suggestions?" asked

the king.

Several seconds elapsed before Winaq finally stood up. He'd thought the situation through several times since Kabrak'an had first informed him of the attack, and only one solution seemed acceptable to him at the moment.

"Ahau, maybe we should approach the problem differently. Maybe we should focus on managing the threat instead of trying to eliminate it."

The king looked at him. "Explain yourself, old friend."

"Currently, our warlord Kabrak'an and his troops are efficiently limiting casualties to what can be considered as acceptable losses along the border."

"No loss of life or resources is acceptable Winaq."

"Of course, ahau. Considering the situation, we could hardly do better for now. These are difficult times for all of us. If the problem is the attacks on our merchandise, then maybe we should concentrate on protecting the shipments." He looked around. "While we cannot get rid of the enemy, we can certainly limit our exposure to their spears!"

Kabrak'an sat straight and replied. "I also thought about that, but how do we protect all of them? Shipments come in and out of our land from every direction. We cannot escort them all, we simply do not have enough men!"

"No. We cannot. Instead of sending many warriors to protect many shipments on many routes, why not concentrate all of our strengths over one single road? Then, there would be no need for accompanying the caravans. All we have to do is station guards all along the road at a reasonable distance. With a minimal manpower investment, we could significantly increase the protection over this single route! I believe this to be our best option."

The warlord thought for a while. "A great suggestion indeed. With at least one safe passage, a constant flow of merchandise coming in and out of the city could definitely be assured."

"But merchants arrive from all directions," remarked one of the administrators. "Cotton and textiles arrive from the north. Jade and obsidian from the south. Salt and other coastal products come from the east, and Tollàn lies in the west. Our trade partners are scattered all around us."

"We choose a single route," answered Winaq. "I propose the main southern road. It is the one furthest away from the enemy."

"That would imply significant detours for all other merchants. We simply cannot impose such action!"

"We impose nothing. The choice will be theirs," replied the king. "So far, only one shipment has been attacked, and there is no evidence leading me to believe there will be more. Although we might be overreacting, I shall wait no further. Mutul will guarantee their safety and the safety of their cargo if merchants use the southern road. I believe most will realize the incurred delays are far more desirable than the loss of merchandise."

Most of the ahauob nodded approvingly at Winaq's suggestion. Most, but not Siyah Kak.

"Ahau, I still firmly believe offence to be the best..."

"I know what you believe Siyah Kak," interrupted Great Jaguar Paw, visibly annoyed. "I feel the thunder growling inside you, and I respect that. For now, *I* believe Winaq's proposal to be more appropriate than any harsh actions we might later regret." There was an unmistakable emphasis on the word *I*.

"Now, if that doesn't prove to be the right decision, we shall once again reconvene to reconsider all options." The king always appreciated any form of constructive argumentation. Today, however, he was anxious to end the meeting. He felt tired, and his tongue was throbbing with pain.

Siyah Kak looked down, an obvious look of disbelief and

anger on his face. *Sian K'aan has taunted us for too long*, he taught. *Why do you not see it is time for concrete action? Why not get rid of them once and for all?*

"Kabrak'an," the king was now looking at his warlord. "Select men from your troops and organize a safe route towards the south. We will then inform our trade partners of these new measures. They may use the southern route if they wish our protection."

All council members nodded, and the scribe recorded the king's instructions.

"Now, the solstice ceremony and celebrations are quickly approaching, and I would like to review all preparations for the..."

Great Jaguar Paw was interrupted as a guard stormed inside the courtyard. The warrior walked straight to him, and whispered something in his ear.

"No. Tell him I will see him another day."

More whispers.

"This is a private meeting, internal to the state's affairs. He can wait within the palace if he wishes to do so."

Again, the guard whispered something. The king closed his eyes and lowered his head, sighing.

"Fine, allow him in."

Without another word the soldier left, leaving behind a crowd silently wondering at the nature of the intrusion. Their curiosity was quickly satisfied as the armed man promptly returned accompanied by a foreigner. The stranger was middle-aged. His skin was dark. His tiny eyes, piercing. Long black hair hung straight against his back, partially covering a white cloak covered with spiders and butterfly diagrams.

Tollàn symbols.

"Atlatl Cauac Tlacatl," the guard announced.

One of the city's administrators raised his eyebrows with an inquisitive look on his face.

"Lord Spearthrower Owl," Winaq whispered. "From Tollàn. Their newly appointed administrator in charge of all trade in the Mayan land."

The ahauob greeted the stranger with suspicious yet curious faces, and Great Jaguar Paw discretely signaled his guard to remain in the room. As he looked at the man, he had the strange feeling of having met him before, although he couldn't say where or when. He disregarded the thought and addressed the man with the usual greetings.

Spearthrower Owl quickly dismissed the civilities.

"Please, spare me the politeness, lord," he said in a flawless Mayan. "Since my arrival I have sought an audience, and only now do you receive me. This is unfit for an official representative of your most important trade partner!"

Great Jaguar Paw disliked him at once.

"Excuse the delay, lord Cauac. As you might have heard, I am still recovering from a serious wound. Since I have barely begun recovering the ability of speech, I am sure you will understand my reluctance to engage myself in official business. Please accept my apologies. The state of Mutul welcomes you amongst us. I was told you were provided with suitable accommodations. I trust they are to your liking?"

"I was just informed that one of my obsidian shipment was attacked this morning," he added furiously, ignoring the question. "It happened on your territory, under your watch. Only a few of our men escaped with their lives."

"You mean two days ago," said Kabrak'an. "It was my understanding the shipment was not from Tollàn, but from the southern Mayan states. You claim it was yours?"

"I do mean this morning," the foreigner answered angrily with a side look towards the warlord. "And yes, it was one of our shipments coming directly from the west."

The ahauob looked at each other. If this was true, it was

the second attack in three days. Murmurs erupted amongst the nobles.

Great Jaguar Paw silenced them with a gesture of the hand.

"I was not yet informed of these events. We are sorry about the unfortunate attack on your people and merchandise. Though we cannot replace human lives, we will do our best to assist you and your survivors in any possible way. In the meantime, you will be happy to learn we have just established additional safety measures for our trade partners."

He explained the details regarding the implementation of the guarded southern route. To the king's surprise, Spearthrower Owl looked offended.

"This is totally unacceptable," he said. "Why only guard the southern route? This detour will cause us significant delays, adding several days to our delivery time. This will undoubtedly incur additional costs for Tollàn. We will be forced to raise our prices, while Xukpi and the southern merchants will profit from the unfair advantage of their route being the one protected!" He paused for a few seconds, and took a defiant look.

"We formally request that Mutul also provides military protection over the western route going through Lakam Ha and towards Tollàn!"

Great Jaguar Paw sat back to organize his thoughts, silently cursing at his foolish decision to meet the foreigner unprepared and before his entire council. The king was walking along a thin edge.

"Unfortunately, we do not have sufficient manpower to adequately guard both routes," he finally said. "While the western road is preferable to you for obvious reasons, I believe the southern road to be a better solution. For one, being farthest away from our enemy, it will grant you the safest possible passage to our city. You will acknowledge that a few days are insignificant compared to the long journey from Tollàn."

West was also a dark, unlucky direction. *When in doubt, never choose west,* had once told him an old priest. Somehow, he doubted the foreigner would share his superstitious beliefs.

"I understand you point completely, king Great Jaguar Paw," replied Spearthrower Owl, a deceptive smirk on his face. "Therefore, Tollàn would be happy to provide the state of Mutul with the necessary warriors to also guard the western trade route. We will send our men to your assistance. Temporarily, of course, until your conflict with Sian K'aan is resolved. Rest assured, however, that our soldiers do not necessarily need to reside inside your city. If you prefer, you could assign us a territory near the border and arrangements will be made to build a ..."

The king interrupted him, knowing exactly where the conversation was heading. He had anticipated Tollàn's proposal for such a course of action. Still, he was deeply troubled at the rapidity with which it was suggested. "I apologize, lord Cauac. Your offer, although generous, cannot be accepted."

Spearthrower Owl frowned.

"Forgive me," he replied. "I do not understand."

"I cannot accept your offer." The truth was that Great Jaguar Paw did not trust the man. Nor his nation. With their history of conquest, Tollàn would be too happy to establish any kind of military foothold inside the Mayan realm. Too often in the past had they use deceptive tactics to invade neighboring lands, turning entire populations into slavery. He would not give them the slightest possibility to do the same to his people.

Spearthrower Owl, however, was not a man who easily abandoned. "If Mutul will not offer us protection," he said "I will have no choice but to find myself under the obligation of requesting all of our goods to be escorted by our own warriors, and we will not hesitate to post Tollàn spearmen on every road between here and Tollàn!"

The nobles all looked at each other anxiously, not knowing how to react to this sudden escalation of tension. Kabrak'an stiffened in his seat while Great Jaguar Paw, against his own better judgment, stood straight up before the menace.

"Be warned!" he shouted, ignoring the pain in his mouth. He would not let anyone threaten the safety or sovereignty of his land, and especially not a guest inside his own palace. "We will tolerate absolutely no foreign military incursion over our land! If a single Tollàn warrior is seen passed our borders, I will personally rally every Mayan state against you, and Tollàn will face the consequences!"

There was a long, tangible silence as the aging king and the Tollàn lord stared at each other. Tension was high. Had the king gone too far? Even Great Jaguar Paw was surprised at his own sudden burst of anger. Threatening an ally was never wise, especially a powerful one, but he couldn't see any other solution. He had to leave no doubt as to his position on the subject matter. Whatever the price, he would never allow Tollàn troops to enter his realm.

"Very well," snarled Spearthrower Owl in a conceding tone. "Let's not compromise our exemplary diplomatic relation over a simple suggestion, as I am certain we will eventually come to a mutually acceptable arrangement satisfying both parties."

People relaxed in their seat as the king sat down.

"You do have a very serious problem here though," pursued the Tollàn. "It is a problem for us all, and you would better solve it before we do." Again, there was a threatening tone in his voice. "Our armies can help you with that, if you so desire."

The king smiled. "Again, we speak of conflict," he said.

"I do not believe war to be the way for the well-being of my people."

Spearthrower Owl bent his head low in feigned resignation. "In time, ahau, I trust you will come to see the logic and good sense in our proposal. On that day, I will be available to provide you with complete assistance, but I would advise you not to test our patience. In the meantime, Tollàn will be grateful for the protection of your southern route. As a demonstration of our good faith, there will be no price increase for your people. For the time being, at least."

Without another word, he turned around and walked away. Apparently, Great Jaguar Paw would be more difficult to manipulate than he had anticipated.

But Spearthrower Owl was a resourceful man.

SUNRISE

As always, the whole city had been anxiously looking forward to the solstice celebrations. The shortest day of the year not only announced the approaching end of the rainy season, but after a month of hard work in the fields the population would finally get a day to pause and celebrate before getting through the last stage of the harvest, which had been surprisingly productive after all. Despite an early dry spell in the season, the rain god had finally answered the king's prayers and the city's underground storage pits were now rapidly filling up with provisions. Every day, workers were returning from the fields with baskets full of freshly harvested maize, beans and sweet potatoes.

As for Kabrak'an and his warriors, the season was particularly busy. Sian K'aan had been relentless in their attacks, regularly raiding villages and temporary storage depots along the border. The warlord and his troops did their best in patrolling the area as tightly as possible. Nonetheless, the attacks were usually so swift that by the time the alarm was given and warriors dispatched on location, there was usually little left to find other than scattered bodies.

It didn't help that Kabrak'an also needed to shift part of his attention away from the border, as several more attacks were perpetrated against merchants travelling in and out of the city. Fortunately, Winaq's strategy to implement a safe passage in the south was proving successful. Despite the general displeasure caused by the incurred delays, even the most stubborn traders gradually came to adopt the protected southern route. For the moment, at least.

Great Jaguar Paw knew the solution was only temporary. Eventually, the merchants' patience would run out, and he would have to solve the conflict once and for all. But today was a day for celebration and Mutul's population, now gathered at the base of the sun god's pyramid, intended to do just that.

Located in the center of a large open plaza, the pyramid was part of the most ancient ceremonial complex of the city. After fourteen generations, it still held the exact same purpose it did on the day it was built – to honor K'inich, the sun god.

It was still dark when Great Jaguar Paw climbed up the steep pyramid stairs, closely followed by his daughter Icoquih and Tewiq'nel, the high priest. Pine torches on both sides of the stairway lit their path as they slowly made their way towards the summit platform, where copal incense had burnt all night long in support of the sun during its longest overnight trip through the underworld.

Great Jaguar Paw looked flamboyant. He was wearing an elaborate headdress decorated with quetzal feathers and animal bones. His face was mostly covered by a massive jade nosepiece, while imposing green obsidian ear spools dangled from his ears. He was also wearing a large seashell pectoral and, in his hands, he carried the K'inich scepter; a long staff ended by an intricately shaped flint ornament representing the sun god.

For a long moment the king stood still at the top, meditating in silence. He then raised his arms and presented the staff towards the dark heavens. Meanwhile, Icoquih's voice suddenly broke the silence and started reciting the many legends and sagas of K'inich who, every evening, fearlessly plunged into the underworld and fought his way back towards the eastern horizon. As her lonely voice echoed across the plaza, the high priest danced frantically atop the summit platform. Slowly, the eastern sky turned from a light blue to a yellow color, and an increasing sense of excitement emanated from the anticipating crowd gathered on the ground.

Soon, the sun would rise.

Standing on the outskirts of the plaza Kabrak'an was silently watching, bored by the lengthy ceremony, when he noticed a familiar figure hurrying towards him. Even in the darkness, the grin displayed on his face was plain to see.

"Wak Xook!" he called out happily.

Wak Xook, one of Kabrak'an's most trusted patrol commanders. Most of the war tattoos they both carried were gained while fighting side-by-side and, naturally, they had both developed a close relationship after so many years of battle and shared hardship.

"Kabrak'an," replied the slightly younger man as they hugged in a friendly embrace. "I'm happy to see you!"

"Not as much as I am, my friend. Sian K'aan has been ruthless in their attacks, and we are in desperate needs of warriors such as you!"

"Then hand me a spear and show me the fight!" They laughed. "Tell me, how have you been?"

"Better than you, apparently," answered Kabrak'an. "You look like you could use some rest, a steam bath, and a gourd of manioc beer. And not necessarily in that order!"

"I've been longing for Ichik's brewed marvels for the past month and a half. After spending so many days on the road, one grows tired of maize gruel and flatbread. I really wanted to be back for the festivities so I hurried back home as fast as I could, stopping neither for rest nor bath!"

"You came directly from Lakam Ha?"

"I left eight days ago."

"How was your trip?"

"Unexceptional, really. Other than a few altercations

with their surrounding tribes, all is well in the western states."

"And? Any good news to report?" the warlord asked expectantly. Wak Xook lowered his eyes.

"Unfortunately, both Pa' Chan and Lakam Ha respectfully regret to inform us they have no troops to spare, as they are both engaged in their own skirmishes with neighboring forces."

"Well, I suppose that was to be expected," said the warlord, obviously disappointed. With the prospect of a war against Sian K'aan, Kabrak'an had hoped for a few experienced warriors from their allies to complement his troops.

"However, they do send us their support. And Lakam Ha did give me two hundred flint spearheads as a contribution to our war effort."

"Then it hasn't all been in vain!" cheered Kabrak'an as he grabbed his friend by the shoulders. "I am happy you are back! Come. What other news have you gathered during your travels?"

"No news more exciting than the rumors spreading from Mutul. I hear there is a new Tollàn in town?"

The warlord threw him a surprised look.

"News of a Tollàn lord's arrival in Mutul has reached the western states."

"Unfortunately, what you heard is true," Kabrak'an confirmed. "For once, it is not their priests who worry me the most. It is that Owl Lord himself." The commander chuckled at the mention of the Tollàn lord's nickname.

"Since his arrival, the man has been going here and there throughout the city, and his wanderings haven't gone unnoticed. It is not unusual to see him talking to merchants, soldiers, and even common folks. Most people have gotten accustomed to the foreigner's presence, although many are still suspicious of his activities. I, for one, have the distinct impression he is surveying our capabilities. I've heard troubling reports of Spearthrower Owl asking questions about food production, manpower, and even military defenses. That cannot be good."

"It is disturbing," admitted Wak Xook. "Maybe he is only curious."

Kabrak'an looked at him with raised eyebrows.

"His reputation does precede him," admitted the warrior. "This Owl man is well known in the west. Rumor says he is a religious fanatic. I heard he requested the right to perform human sacrifices inside his temple."

"You heard right. The king refused, of course."

"He did? That can't be helping the situation."

"You seem surprised."

"I have always considered the king to be relatively tolerant of foreign religions. Aren't Mayans, Teeneks, Be'ena'a, and Tollàns usually permitted to pray their gods in whatever way they see fit?"

"We are talking about human sacrifice here. Not prayers and incense burning."

"We've sacrificed a prisoner during the k'atun ceremony, heven't we?" Wak Xook reminded him. "And we sacrifice prisoners regularly along the border!"

"Enemy warriors caught trespassing our borders, criminals roaming our land with the sole intent of killing and plundering."

"Then what about that boy, two years ago?"

Kabrak'an looked at his friend.

"I see you do not understand," he said. "That young man died to save us all from the plague. He was honored to give his life, knowing his sacrifice would save thousands of us. As for the k'atun ceremony prisoner, he died so the sun could rise for another twenty years!"

He waved his arm towards the crowd still waiting for the sunrise.

"Soon, the solstice sun will rise, people will shed a few drops of their own blood, and that will be sufficient. That will be enough blood to nourish the gods and show thankfulness for all we have been provided with. Only in desperate cases of drought, famine or disease do we offer a human life."

The commander nodded in agreement, and Kabrak'an continued his explanation.

"Tollàn, however, has the most bloodthirsty gods I have ever seen. They sacrifice people every single day! I was there once, long ago. I have seen their priests, forcefully dragging people up their temples, butchering them by the dozen in a single morning, and still they requested more blood just to make it to sunset!"

Wak Xook looked at him in awe. "You've seen this for yourself?"

"It is the most terrifying thing I have ever witnessed. Rivers of blood flowing down the pyramid stairs. Bodies piling up as more screaming victims were coercively laid over the sacrificial altar. These foreign rituals are not well known around here. We are only starting to know these westerly strangers. I am telling you, the Tollàns would sacrifice life on a daily basis just to keep their gods happy. So maybe there is a good reason why Great Jaguar Paw refuses them the right to do so. Can you imagine the amount of bodies we would have to deal with if every priest of every nation started performing sacrifices at such a rate? Would merchants line up at the border with a fresh supply of new victims for the daily ceremony? How long until surrounding villages are decimated by prisoner-hunters? How long until people live in constant fear of seeing their children kidnapped? For that is the fate awaiting the people conquered by Tollàn; fear and death."

The commander was shocked by the extent of the truth, yet he silently nodded towards the only other monument in the sun god's plaza, a strange looking pyramid with a small temple at its summit.

"So, what do you think is happening up there?" he asked.

Kabrak'an turned his head and stared at the foreign-looking structure. He looked at the series of platforms built over sloped embankments, and he remembered seeing similar pyramids a long time ago, in a distant city.

It was Great Jaguar Paw's father who'd granted Tollàn the right to build a pyramid of their own in Mutul, a place to worship their gods. A gesture of good faith, in anticipation of the trade deal. It stood there ever since, a foreign structure adorned with the images of foreign deities.

At the time, it might have seemed like a good idea, an innocent gesture of friendship. Now, this pyramid stood in their city like a foreign stronghold in the Mayan heartland, while the Tollàn culture only seemed to implant itself deeper and deeper into their world.

"I don't know what is happening inside that temple," he admitted, finally answering Wak Xook's question. "Somehow, I don't believe their priests have any respect for our laws. Maybe it's time to see for ourselves."

In the last moments of darkness, he noticed a shadow slowly climbing up the stairs towards the modest Tollàn temple. No doubt their priests would now be gathering up there, also preparing to celebrate the solstice.

The two warriors spent what little was left of the night in silence.

As the eastern sky turned to a bright orange color and sunrise became imminent, priests stopped their prayers and countless drummers started striking their drums. The sound of rubber-coated sticks beating the hollowed trunks submerged the plaza with a rhythm reminiscent of a heartbeat.

Bom-bom, Bom-bom, Bom-bom.

The crowd anxiously waited. All eyes were now turned towards the east in anticipation of the upcoming event.

After a long wait, the bright orange crescent of the sun finally appeared over the horizon. People closed their eyes before the intense morning brightness and chanted in joy. Many pulled obsidian blades and stingray spines out of their clothes. They pierced their ears and lips, and smeared blood all over their faces as a personal sacrifice. Then, the whole population of Mutul raised their arms, honoring the sun god in their presence.

The longest night of the year was over.

Trays of food were brought to the pyramid summit. Freshly harvested loads of maize, squash and beans were set ablaze as an offering to the god who'd risen from its longest journey through the underworld. As the crops were burnt, Great Jaguar Paw walked to the edge of the platform, his eyes squinted almost shut before the morning sun. He stared at the thousands surrounding the pyramid, and he spoke loudly.

"Citizens of Mutul, the gods have blessed us with another sunrise! Witness the sacrifice of our crops as we thank them for another plentiful harvest. Thanks to their generosity, our children will not go hungry during the dry season!"

The crowd erupted in cheers as the burnt offerings turned to smoke and crossed into the realm of the divine.

"Today," pursued the king, "we thank K'inich for the warmth of the sun. We thank Chaak for the rain allowing the crops to grow. And we thank Itzamnà, the benevolent creator, for all kindnesses bestowed upon us!"

Once again, the crowd cheered, praising their king's name.

"Today is a day for celebration. Now go. Feast on the product of your labor and enjoy this blessed day!"

So started the solstice festival.

All around the plaza, tables were covered with heady drinks and flavorsome meals such as venison stew, salted fish, fresh fruits, vegetables, honey, maguey beer and many more delicacies, while the smell of cinnamon, vanilla and allspice seasoning filled the air. People feasted and celebrated. Musicians played cheerful songs on their instruments. From sunrise to sunset, everyone ate, drank and danced aplenty at the sounds of flutes and drums.

As for Balam, along with most young men, he barely grabbed something to eat before hurrying towards the ball court for the solstice tournament.

On this special occasion, trios from all social levels would compete for the prestigious honor of triumphing in front of the whole city. Not only nobles, merchants and warriors but also commoners, stone workers, carpenters and farmers would face each other in friendly ball matches. As usual, Balam teamed up with two of his friends, Chava and Kinan, warriors from the king's personal guard with whom he'd been playing for years.

By midday, they had already secured two victories, overall allowing only two points to their opponents.

Their third match was even easier. Barely a few moments in, Balam jumped on the embankment and redirected a pass from Chava directly through the center of the ring, instantly winning the game. People cheered his name as they celebrated him.

Balam! Balam! Hun Balam Ku'x!

They were barely off the field when a group of youngsters huddled around them, excited at meeting their star players, apparently unbothered that all three were covered in sweat and dust. Balam did his best to answer a few questions before being eventually rescued by Kinan who, in a not so subtle way, grabbed him by the arm and pulled him away.

"Sorry lads! Got to go. We have another match later."

The three players laughed as they walked away, and suddenly came face to face with the warlord.

"Kabrak'an ahau," immediately greeted Balam, straightening up. "It is an honor to see you here."

The warlord stared at them for a moment.

"I hear you three are doing well," he finally said.

"Yes, o'on nimal ahau," replied Chava using the warlord's iguana leader title. "Three victories already."

"Have you come to watch the tournament?" asked Balam.

"Unfortunately, no. I must return to the border immediately. There is no rest for the warriors." It was only then that Balam noticed the spear in Kabrak'an's hand. "However, I do need a favor from you, young man. There is something you could help me with before my departure."

Balam bowed his head.

"Anything you need, ahau."

"Good. Come with me."

"Kabrak'an ahau, Balam is our best player," interrupted Kinan. "We need him for the tournament!"

He regretted speaking the words the instant they came out of his mouth.

The warlord snapped his head around and looked at Kinan straight in the eyes. Unable to withstand the intensity of the gaze, the man slightly shifted his eyes to the side, instead choosing to stare at the imposing iguana tattoo covering the warlord's face.

To his immediate relief, Kabrak'an only smiled.

"Don't worry," he answered with a wink. "He will be back before your next match."

XOCHITL

Atop the Tollàn pyramid, well concealed within the temple's shadows, Spearthrower Owl discretely watched as the Mayans celebrated and feasted on the grounds below him. Dressed in flamboyant colors they danced and drank aplenty. Joyful music reached his ears, and the smell of cooked meat filled his nostrils.

It all made him feel nauseous.

"They are celebrating," he scorned furiously. "Today, out of all days, they are enjoying themselves, indulging in food, drinks and games!"

He turned towards the Tollàn priest, who was standing deep inside the temple.

"Today should be a day of prayer! A day of humble worship! A day without food, for only in fasting can our sacrifices reach the gods! They are fools, ignorants who believe their meaningless bloodletting acts sufficient to nourish the sun into its daily journey! As if a few drops of blood ever changed anything!"

The priest simply nodded in approval of his lord's comments as Spearthrower Owl paced back and forth inside the small inner chamber, accompanying his speech with great hand gestures to emphasize the anger in his voice.

"Twice, I have requested that proper sacrifice be allowed. Twice, that heretic king refused me! May his bones burn to ashes and his flesh rot in the swamps of Xacoatl!"

"They value human life," the priest answered in a serene tone.

"So do the gods! It is exactly because life is so valuable that they demand it!"

The priest stepped out of the shadow and walked into the flickering light of a small burning fire. His face was entirely painted in black, his white robe covered with dark red stains. At his feet was the body of a young eviscerated man, lying in a pool of his own blood. The fear accompanying his death could still be seen in his lifeless eyes, the terror forever imprinted on his pale, rigid face.

In his last living moments, the man had seen his still beating heart ripped out of his chest and burnt as an offering.

"You cannot blame the Mayans and their kings, my lord. They have such a poor understanding of the ways of this world. Their gods are weak. Their ceremonies, purposeless. Thanks to us, the sun will rise again in the morning."

Spearthrower Owl nodded. "Hopefully it will. Hopefully."

"Let us not despair. Soon, this land will be ours. Then, we shall impose our ways to these savages! You will dictate the rules, and we will sacrifice aplenty to show our gratitude!"

"Great Jaguar Paw might be a fool, but he is highly respected amongst his people. We must not forget that Mutul is still his territory. He controls everything here. The warriors. The workforce. The trade. With the city's artificial basins, he even controls water distribution during the dry season!"

"You could take their land by force, my lord!"

"Imbecile! This is not just another small neighboring kingship. Their land is twice as big as ours. Tollàn's entire armed forces wouldn't be sufficient to maintain control over all of them! We are used to war and conquest. Here, we must act differently. I have another plan."

"A plan, my lord?"

"If we are to establish our dominance over this land, we must first control their resources."

"Control? You think you can control their water? Or their obsidian? Their jadeite? Their salt, their cocoa, their cotton? The production of these goods is spread throughout their land, each under the dominion of several different states. Not with a single city could you control them all!"

"I do not wish to control their production, priest, but their distribution! All we need is a significant influence over one key location, over one single main trade center. Then we can infiltrate ourselves into the system."

"Mutul! That's why you want Mutul!"

Spearthrower Owl looked at him with a smile.

"We cannot do it alone. Before we take control of this city, we need to ensure ourselves the support of sufficient neighboring Mayan kings. As you have so brilliantly remarked, they are already divided into various states, whose kings are more often than not at war against each other. Let us use that to our advantage. Let us keep them separated. Let us make certain they do not regroup against us. Then, it will only be a matter of making a few allies within the lot. Only then can we replace Great Jaguar Paw and put a new king on the throne."

"Tell me, who would side with us? How do you expect to find allies here my lord, when we are nothing more than foreigners to them?"

"Their trade is their weakness," he answered with a grin. "Trust me, I have already taken the first steps."

He looked back outside, and his thoughts suddenly wandered towards Tollàn. He wondered if he would ever see his own land again.

Spearthrower Owl closed his eyes. He missed his native

city. He missed the great painted murals. He missed the food, the milder climate, the fresh mountain air, the language, the music. He missed everything.

He despised this foreign land of lush jungles filled with swarms of insects. He hated the crushing humidity, the exacerbating heat. Yet, it was his destiny to contribute to the grandeur of his king.

And to his own.

"I believe I can secure an alliance with one of Great Jaguar Paw's council members," he finally said. "This should give me a direct access to all the information and leverage we need."

The priest's eyes glowed in wonder.

"Who, my lord?"

"Patience. Soon enough, you will find out. In the meantime, I must leave for a few months. I have learned a lot here, and there are now many people I wish to discuss with. In my absence, your orders are to proceed exactly as planned."

The priest bowed his head.

"As you wish, my lord."

Spearthrower smiled. Things were now slowly developing as he'd hoped.

Balam was walking steadily across the plaza, oblivious to all the happiness and festivities surrounding him. Despite the joyful atmosphere inhabiting the crowded court, he was now entirely focused on his destination.

The pyramid of Tollàn.

Built in the far corner of the ancient ceremonial center, the strange monument waited, silently scoffing him, openly challenging his courage.

Damn you Kabrak'an. Damn you, he thought. It was reluctantly, and only after a long persuasive speech, that the young man had finally accepted the warlord's request to climb to the summit of the Tollàn monument. At the time, it had seemed like a bad idea to defy their gods over their own ground.

Now that the pyramid was rapidly approaching, the idea seemed even worse.

"Why not go yourself?" he had asked Kabrak'an. "You could pretend to carry the invitation. Then you could have a look for yourself! See if they really do kill people in there!"

"I cannot go because he knows who I am."

"Then why me? Why not one of your own men?"

"You mean one of my scarred battle-hardened warriors? That wouldn't be very subtle... No, your young and sweet innocent look is exactly what I need to avoid raising suspicions."

So apparently it was his look that got him the assignment. Balam grimaced for he hated his look, especially since the accident which had left his nose broken and leaning sideways in the middle of his face. For the umpteenth time, he cursed at his appearance.

And at the warlord.

And at the bad fate suddenly befalling him.

He was still silently cursing when a young woman wearing a bright yellow huipil suddenly appeared before him, grabbed him by the waist, and started jumping around with him in her arms. There was a foul, alcoholic stench about her. Startled, Balam looked aside and politely danced a few steps with her before swiftly escaping her grasp, leaving her behind, laughing.

He never was an adept of large celebrations. For some reason, he always felt out of place when surrounded by drunken people stumbling all around him. For once, he wished he could have just stood there with the others and enjoyed the festivities.

He wished he could be back on the ball court.

He wished he would be heading anywhere but where he was heading now.

"My lord, someone is approaching!" warned the priestess.

"What! Who?"

"A young man, my lord. A Mayan, by the looks of it. He is climbing up the stairs."

Without hesitation, Spearthrower Owl hurried towards the temple's entrance, careful to remain concealed behind the young woman who was standing guard. Looking above her shoulder he saw a boy who was barely a man, dressed in dirty ball gear, steadily climbing his pyramid towards the summit.

The Tollàn lord held his breath for a second, and looked back inside. *What does he think he is doing?* he thought. Then he saw the sacrificed man lying on the floor. *The Mayan must not see the body, and he must especially not see me in here!* His eyes quickly scanned around him. The one-roomed chamber had but a single entrance, and time was running out.

He stepped back and looked at the priest, who was praying in the shadows, kneeling by the body.

"The body. There is nowhere to hide the body," he whispered nervously. "Kill the fire, and do not let him in. Make sure he stays out of the temple!"

The priestess nodded.

As Balam climbed up the steep stairway, he once again wondered what he had gotten himself into. For the first time in his life he was trespassing onto a Tollàn pyramid.

He was openly violating the sacred ground of a foreign temple, and he simply had no idea how their gods would react to such insolence.

The sounds of the festivities beneath him slowly faded in the distance with every step he took. He shivered, truly frightened at the impertinence and thoughtlessness of his actions. A trickle of sweat ran down his spine, and his legs started shaking. In his mind, he silently repeated the same prayer, on and on.

> *Ô benevolent maize god,*
> *Keeper of our crops,*
> *Guardian of our souls,*
> *Please listen to our prayers,*
> *Grant us your protection,*
> *And let us honor you once again.*

The words had little effect in calming his fears. Again, he silently cursed at the warlord for sending him there.

It was then that he raised his head and noticed the young woman standing in the temple's archway above him.

At first, he only saw her white dress gently flowing in the wind. As he moved closer, his fear slowly disappeared and he was overwhelmed by a troubling sensation of awe and elation for, despite the brightness of the day, she somehow seemed to outshine everything in sight. He noticed her beautiful hazel eyes, her delicate figure, and her long raven hair. For an instant, time stood still, and as she smiled to him his legs suddenly felt weak.

He tripped.

His heart stopped. Reality came rushing back to him.

The pyramid was steep. Very steep. Too steep to ever hope recovering from a fall.

For an instant, he saw himself tumbling down, heading straight towards the ground, breaking his neck and every other bone inside his body along the way.

Luckily, his ballplayer instincts kicked in. He barely managed to shift his weight forward and came to a stop with both hands resting on the stairs before him.

"Why do they build them so steep?" he mumbled, looking down at the faraway ground below him, pale faced. He took a deep breath and looked back up, almost expecting the woman to be gone, a vision sent by a malevolent Tollàn gods as a punishment for his presence on their sacred monument.

Fortunately she was still there, apparently real. For a split second, he thought he saw a concerned look on her face, but the concern quickly faded away as she realized he would be all right.

The shamed ballplayer resumed his climb, feeling foolish at the extreme carefulness he now exercised with every step, his heart still pounding in his chest from the scare. He'd forgotten all about the Tollàn deities now, as he was strangely inhabited by both anticipation and apprehension at the thought of reaching her. A small part of him felt like running towards the young woman though he mostly wished he could disappear.

Balam finally reached the top, where the priestess greeted him with another soft smile.

His mind raced, desperately searching for something to say. He opened his mouth. No words came out, and so they both stood at the pyramid's summit, silently staring at each other, sharing a short moment of silence.

"Kwalli Tonalli," she finally greeted him in her native tongue.

"Good day to you," Balam replied.

She tilted her head slightly, still smiling.

"How may I help you?" she asked in Mayan.

"Hum? Oh, yes. I ... euh," he felt like a fool. Balam had forgotten all about why he was there.

"My name is Balam. Hun Balam Ku'x. You can call me Balam," he quickly added. "And you are?"

He didn't know why but he immediately regretted asking for her name, thinking he should have just moved ahead with the delivery of his message. To his great relief and surprise, she seemed pleased to answer him.

"Xochitl," she said. "My name is Xochitl."

Balam raised his eyebrows.

"Xo..." he started, as equally confused by her strong foreign accent as by her great beauty.

She gently laughed at his ill-attempt to pronounce her name, and it was the purest laugh Balam had ever heard.

"It is pronounced Sho-Cheet," she explained, slowly articulating every syllable in her name. "Xochitl. It means flower. I was named after my grandmother."

"Xochitl! What a beautiful name! You speak our language very well," he complimented.

In truth, her Mayan was horrible. She spoke very slowly, confusing most of her verb tenses. Every word was punctuated by a strong Tollàn accent.

Xochitl smiled at the obvious lie.

"Thank you," she simply answered. The priestess gestured to her side. "Have you come to offer prayers to Tlaloc and Quetzalcoátl on this beautiful solstice day?"

Up to that point, Balam had completely forgotten where he was. That was until he noticed the two wooden idols standing guard on each side of the archway. The first was a deity he'd never seen before, some sort of a humanoid figure with large goggled eyes and menacing fangs.

The second, the one she referred to as Quetzalcoátl, was better known amongst his people as the feathered serpent. Always represented as a snake covered with feathers, the Tollàn god of the sky was feared by any warrior opposing him in battle.

Both idols were stained with fresh blood.

The young man jumped at their sight and immediately took a step back, fearing one of the statues would come to life and drag him deep into the Tollàn underworld if he dared approach the dark temple chamber.

The priestess raised her hands, sensing his insecurity. "Do not worry if you are not here to offer a sacrifice," she said. "Our gods will take no offense. I assure you, no harm will come to you here today. Please, tell me, why have you come?"

Balam took a deep breath before answering.

"I have an invitation for Spearth... for lord Atlatl Cauac."

The priestess frowned.

"Maybe you could allow me to step inside so that I could transmit my message?" he added reluctantly.

Xochitl shook her head.

"Access to the temple is strictly restricted to our priests," she answered, and Balam relaxed a little. "Lord Atlatl Cauac is not here at the moment. If you give me your message, I will make certain it is delivered to him properly."

Balam was about to insist but changed his mind at the last moment. He found it strange that Spearthrower Owl was not in the temple. Kabrak'an did tell him he personally saw the shadow of the Tollàn lord climbing up the pyramid earlier in the morning.

Obviously, the warlord was mistaken. Or, maybe the man had simply left since then. Nonetheless, he was only too happy strangers were forbidden inside the temple, and decided on delivering the message to her where she stood. After all, he wasn't too eager on entering the sacred structure, although he did try to sneak a peek inside.

As his eyes glanced above her shoulder she cleverly shifted her weight on the other foot to hide his view, and while it might have only been his imagination, something in the young woman's eyes told him he should not insist any further, although he did perceive the warning more as a friendly advice than as a threat.

"Well," he said, resigned, "please tell your lord that my king, Chak Tok Ich'aak, K'uhul Ahau of Mutul, wishes to invite him to tonight's feast which will be held inside the palace in honor of the solstice. Please tell him it would be a great pleasure to receive him on this occasion."

Xochitl nodded.

"For us, the solstice is a day to be spent in prayer and, how do you say, in fasting."

Balam opened his mouth to say something.

"I will nonetheless transmit your message, Balam," she quickly added. He shivered as she spoke his name. "And I will make sure the answer finds its way to you. Personally."

That last comment came with another smile and this time, he was certain it was not only his imagination.

"Maybe I could come back later for your lord's answer? I'm playing in the ball tournament, maybe I could return after my next match?" he said, excited at the prospect of seeing her again.

Xochitl blushed. Before she could answer, a tall priest appeared behind her. There was a menacing look on his black, painted face.

The young boy took a step back, startled, and the smile instantly disappeared from the priestess's face. There was an obvious disdain in the high priest's voice as he addressed the Mayan.

"I am sure my lord Cauac will be honored by your invitation. However, I speak for him when I tell you that, unfortunately, he will not be able to attend the event."

Balam nodded, sensing tension in the young woman. Undoubtedly, the priest scared her. He raised his head slightly, not wanting to look intimidated in front of her.

"The invitation is addressed to lord Cauac," he

answered with a new found sense of defiance. "It is him who should answer my king."

The priest's lips curled in a strange smile attempt.

"Don't be foolish boy. Tell your king lord Cauac sends him his greetings on this holiday," the priest continued. "Now, if there is nothing else, you may leave."

Not wanting to tempt the foreigner's patience Balam looked one last time at Xochitl, whose eyes were locked on the ground, and headed straight down the stairs. Once at the bottom, he quickly turned around, hoping to get a final glimpse of the young woman.

There was no one in sight. There was nothing other than the dark vacant temple opening, and he wondered if it had all been a dream.

As he slowly walked away, he was once again surrounded by his people celebrating all over the plaza, happily drinking and dancing to the sound of music. There was no time for him to feast. He had a ballgame to play.

His thoughts were split between the beautiful priestess and the report he would soon deliver to the warlord. Although somewhat happy he was denied access to the temple, Kabrak'an would certainly be disappointed he could not get past the doorway to see for himself what was going on inside.

Anyhow, his mission had not been entirely fruitless. There was fresh blood everywhere, although it would be difficult to tell if it was human or animal without seeing a body.

One thing was certain though, there had been a sacrifice in there. The whole temple stank of death.

But she smelled of vanilla.

A SECRET MESSAGE

It was late at night, and while most people had long gone to bed after a full day of feasting, a few drunken roisterers well intended on continuing the solstice celebrations by themselves if they had to. They randomly wandered throughout the city, cheering and bellowing for more balché and music with little regard for those who tried to sleep. Eventually, a patrol was dispatched on location, and the noisy drunks were quickly sent home under the threat of flint spearheads and extra labor shifts in the morning. Soon enough, silence returned to the dark city streets.

Things were also calm and quiet inside the palace's walls, where there wasn't a single sound other than the discreet footsteps of the two guards tirelessly patrolling the corridors, walking from one dark room to another, surrounded only by the dim light of their pine torches. That is, until one of them could no longer contain his frustrations.

"I still cannot believe we've lost!"

"Get over it."

"I can't…"

"Try."

"I've already tried."

"Then try harder!"

"Arghhh! We should have won!"

"For the last time, will you please shut up!" Chava turned around, barely resisting the urge to grab Kinan by the shoulders to shake him senseless. "You sound like my little brother! Honestly, all this whining makes me miss the days when I was patrolling with the old commander. By far the worst year of my life!"

"Couldn't have been worse than standing in the middle of the ball court today! Couldn't have been worse than being humiliated in front of the whole city!"

"Not again..."

"What can I say? This year was supposed to be our year!"

"Well I won't stand you complaining all night about this tournament!"

"And could you please tell me what was wrong with Balam? His missed at least three open rings in the afternoon. Three! And I haven't started talking about his poor defensive play yet," Kinan added in an outburst of disbelief. "I've never seen him so absent-minded! Did Kabrak'an cast a spell on him or what?"

"Enough!" Chava pressed on, exasperated by his partner. "I will hear about this no more!"

They'd started the tournament with three decisive victories but in the afternoon, after Balam's return from his secret assignment, the team had suffered two straight losses, preventing them from accessing to the finale.

Chava was accepting the whole outcome quite well, while Kinan, obviously, had difficulties coping with both defeats. Balam, however, had seemed strangely unaffected by the result. After the game, he'd simply returned to his quarters without saying or eating anything, which was quite out of character for him. Everyone knew the young man was extremely proud and competitive, especially when it came down to his ball game.

"Fine," finally conceded Kinan. "I tell you, he's been bewitched! He would've never missed such a perfectly executed pass after the..."

"Stop!" interrupted Chava, an alarmed look on his face.

Kinan looked at him disapprovingly.

"Don't change the subject. That play could have changed the outcome of the game!"

Chava grimaced and pushed him aside.

"Seriously," he said, as he stared through the dark opening leading into one of the palace's many room. "Do you see that flickering orange glow in the back? There's a fire burning in there!"

"It's the library," said Kinan with a concerned face.

Fire was always a serious threat in a city, especially in the palace's bark-paper filled library, where fire could rapidly spread towards the living quarters and endanger the king's life.

"Let's sound the alarm!"

"No, wait," hushed Chava. "It might only be a torch. We should check it out first."

"Very well. Patrol!" he announced loudly. "If someone is in there, identify yourself!"

No answer.

"Is anyone supposed to be here tonight?"

"Only the scribe is allowed in there," answered Kinan. "Even he must be sleeping at this time. That little son of a demon would never..."

Chava silenced him with a commanding look and carefully took a step inside. The musty smell of old paper immediately filled his nostrils.

"Maybe we shouldn't walk in here carrying torches," remarked Kinan. "It might not look good for us if *we* were the ones who actually started a fire."

Chava pretended not to hear.

"Then again, how would they know," he murmured to himself. "We could simply pretend the fire was already burning when we got here. Or maybe I would blame it all on you."

The other guard simply walked ahead, preferring to remain silent. As he walked deeper into the room, the dim light of his torch revealed thousands of paper codices carefully disposed upon shelves from the floor to the roof. Curious, he brought his torch closer to a shelf. Several glyphs were carved into the wood. The symbols spelled *astronomical charts*, *wars and conquests*, *population surveys*, *historical facts* and many more, but the warrior wouldn't have known that.

"What's all this?" he asked, amazed.

"Who knows," answered Kinan. "I can't read."

"Neither can I."

As they reached the back, they both realized the light they'd first seen was coming from a smaller room off to their left. In the dead of the night, the flickering glow added a gloomy ambiance to the already ghastly-looking place.

Chava stopped and listened. Everything was dead quiet. He tightened his grip over his spear shaft, took a few steps forward, and carefully looked inside the adjoining room.

There was no one in sight.

A single torch, barely sufficient to lit the small apartment, was well secured to the opposite wall. Smoke rose from the flame and merged into the shadows of the high vaulted roof, escaping through a single window well above arm's reach.

A few dozen codices were piled up on a small table in the corner, while an old dusty mat covered with blank paper sheets, empty ink pots, and a series of brushes of different sizes laid on the floor. Apparently, they had stumbled inside the scribe's working room.

"There is no one in here," remarked Kinan.

Chava looked at him and rolled his eyes.

"I admire your observation skills," he said.

The comment was answered by a mocking grimace.

"The torch couldn't have been burning for long. I

suppose we should take it out and search the palace for the ah'tsib. The scribe must be here somewhere," he simply said with an annoyed tone.

Before he could proceed, they were both startled by footsteps coming from behind.

Both men jumped in surprise and immediately turned around to face the approaching threat, spears leveled before them.

"Easy! Easy!" pleaded a voice as its owner took a step back, arms thrown up in the air. "I do not wish to be killed tonight!"

"Scribe? Is that you?" asked Chava, still holding his spear in a menacing way.

"Of course it's me," came a nervous answer. "Who else do you expect to find in here? Now could you please lower your weapons before someone gets hurt?"

Both guards looked at themselves and eventually obliged as the scribe slowly walked into the light.

"What are you doing here so late?" asked Kinan, recovering from the surprise. "We were told no one would be present in this area tonight."

The scribe took a shallow breath before answering.

"I didn't think I had to justify my presence here," he said.

"Who's asking for any justification?" asked Chava.

"We're only talking," added Kinan.

"I wanted to record the day's events while they were still fresh in my mind," lied the scribe. "I was out of black ink."

He pointed to the large piece of black charcoal at the bottom of the pottery bowl in his hand.

Chava suspiciously looked inside the orange vessel and hesitated a moment before finally deciding that nothing there warranted any further attention from their part.

"Very well, then. I shall wish you a good night," he said condescendingly. "Next time, please refrain from leaving a burning torch unattended inside the palace. You wouldn't want to be responsible for burning all of your predecessor's lifetime achievements."

Kinan smiled and the scribe nodded, relieved.

"And please record your presence with the guards on duty. You also wouldn't want to be speared by mistake in the middle of the night."

They both turned around and walked away without waiting for an answer.

As their footsteps faded down the corridor, the scribe heard one of them complaining about some unsportsmanlike strategy supposedly used by another team during a ballgame, a comment which was immediately answered by his obviously annoyed colleague asking him to once again change the subject.

He waited until the arguing voices completely disappeared in the distance before returning to his workroom, unpleased at himself for having been so careless.

Not that he cared about the warning. In his opinion, the torch was perfectly well secured to the wall in a safe and responsible manner. He was, however, feeling foolish for the lack of secrecy surrounding his own whereabouts, as he would have much preferred his presence inside the palace so late at night to remain unnoticed. On the other hand, he didn't expect the two guards to think anything special about it. Apparently, they'd bought his story. This was, after all, his personal working apartment. Still, he would have to exercise more caution in the future.

He lit a stick of copal incense for his own protection against the mischievous spirits lurking in the dark, and sat down on the mat, legs crossed, his mind not yet fully concentrated on the task before him.

In the silence of the night, the scribe reached for a small basalt mortar lying in the dark and started crushing the charcoal piece at the bottom of the pottery bowl. As his experienced hands skillfully reduced the content into a fine black powder, he recalled the instructions he'd received earlier in the day.

"I need to discuss the attacks against merchants along the trade routes leading in and out of Mutul."

"Do you really think that wise?" he'd asked.

"I have a strange feeling about this. I fear this situation could send the conflict into an unrecoverable escalation, maybe even into a large scale war."

"I thought the attacks had basically stopped."

"They did, for the moment, although the warlord expects a re-occurrence of ambushes immediately after the harvest season. Frankly, I tend to agree with him. Tell them Sian K'aan is being held responsible for the attacks."

"As you wish. Is there anything else?"

"No, it will be all for now. Let's see what they have to say, but I can already guess their answer. If I am right, and I believe I am, many things could soon change. Obviously, this would be considered as treason, so it is imperative that you are not caught carrying this message. Proceed very cautiously, and personally deliver it as planned. Everything will be fine. All you have to do is leave it in the designated location, and your contact will ensure it reaches its final destination."

"My contact?"

"If all goes according to plan, you will never meet him. Leave the message and return immediately. Avoid patrols at all costs." There was a strong emphasis on the last sentence.

And for good reasons.

The scribe shrugged at the thought of being caught by one of Kabrak'an's patrol. Without any good reason for being out of the city so late, he would obviously be searched. If the message was found on him, he could be executed straight away.

The risk had to be taken.

He lifted the mortar and inspected the finely crushed coal dust. Satisfied, he added a little water to the powdery substance and mixed thoroughly before reaching for a new piece of bark paper. He dipped a brush into the freshly stirred ink, and started writing.

The brush glided smoothly over the sheet, leaving behind a trail of black lines and curves which slowly took the form of readable glyphic images. Before long, the paper was entirely covered with perfectly aligned columns of symbols. The message was complete.

The scribe sat straight and started reviewing his text. As his eyes carefully moved from one glyph to another, they suddenly came to rest upon one particular symbol. A glyph representing the back side of a head with a knot tied across, the famous knotted hairstyle worn by all nobles.

The Mutul glyph.

His eyes then quickly jumped to another symbol; an imposing feline paw out of which protruded a series of menacing talons.

Great Jaguar Paw's name glyph.

As the scribe contemplated both symbols, he was suddenly overwhelmed with concern regarding the fate of his beloved city. Silently, he wondered if his current actions were the right ones. For an instant, he felt as if he was betraying all he'd ever stood for. Deep inside, doubt blossomed within his heart, but he had given his oath. He would honor his word until the end, be it right or wrong.

The scribe completed his review and re-read the entire text one last time. Satisfied the message was complete and accurate, he quickly folded the bark paper sheet into the customary accordion style and buried it deep into his clothes.

There was only a few hours left before sunrise, leaving

him with very little time to deliver the message and return to the safety of the city. It was absolutely necessary to take advantage of the cover of darkness if he wanted to come back without raising any more suspicions.

He blew out the torch and headed outside. The night was dark and moonless, which greatly helped his cause. In the silence of the night, he passed through the city suburbs and walked into the partially harvested fields.

Up ahead, hidden in the jungle, was a small forgotten shrine.

And an obscure courier waiting for a secret delivery.

WARRIORS

Wak Xook was running hurriedly across the now fully harvested field. Sweat was pouring down his forehead. His heart was pounding inside his chest. His lungs were burning. His throat screamed for water, but he could not afford to stop. If the information they'd received was accurate, absolutely no time could be wasted.

He concentrated on breathing deeply, on keeping his balance as his feet frantically sprinted over the rugged terrain, careful not to sprain an ankle as every step landed over the uneven surface of upturned earth and hacked down plants.

Closely following behind him was the sound of his fellow patrolmen's own footsteps falling upon the dry earth with a cacophonic thumping sound reminiscent of a herd on the run. Every now and then, the loud cracking sound of a sandaled foot heavily landing on one of the thick maize stalks left to dry in the sun thundered above their racket, a sound inevitably followed by some sort of swearing from an exhausted man pushed to the limit.

All around them was a desolate and lifeless scenery of dried earth scorched by the burning dry season sun.

The harvest was over. The city's storage pits were now filled with food and the dry season had started. In a few months Chaak, the rain god, would rip the sky open with his great ax and the rain, returning as suddenly as it had stopped, would once again fall from the heavens. A lush vegetation would then cover the land and crops would grow in most Mayan fields.

Most, but not in this one.

A few years ago, the green jungle covering this patch of land had been burnt to the ground and farmed to satisfy the hunger of Mutul's ever increasing population. Unfortunately, this earth was poor. Despite the frequent weeding or usual intercropping techniques, the soil had quickly depleted and the yield was deemed insufficient. Overall, the gods were generous over the past months as Mutul's harvest had proved to be more than satisfactory, but this particular field was now a barren land which would have to be left to replenish itself. Nothing would grow there for several years.

As Wak Xook ran forward he focused straight ahead on the only visible sign of life in the area. Standing before him like a surviving island of vegetation amongst a sea of dry earth was a patch of jungle harboring a lonely village. If the traveler's information was true, that was where the next attack would happen.

There was their destination.

Behind him, the commander could hear his comrades slowly losing ground. His men were tired, exhausted by the long run under the harsh midday sun. The heat was almost unbearable. He knew the young soldiers would not abandon, at least not as long as he kept going.

"Come on!" he yelled. "We are almost there. We cannot let these people down!"

There was no answer other than exhausted breaths and labored breathing.

"Balché's on me tonight for any man who kills an enemy warrior!" he added.

Still no answer, although he felt a slightly more energetic beat in the steps trailing behind him.

The tree line lying ahead slowly got closer and after what seemed like an eternity they finally reached the first bushes. The warriors blessed the gods as they headed into the cooling shade of the jungle. Wak Xook didn't slow his pace. He jumped on the narrow trail he knew led straight to the village. Having regained some energy at the thought of approaching their goal the three men following him were now closely following their leader.

"Do you think we're too late?" asked one of them, panting.

"I don't know," replied another. "I suppose we'll soon find out."

"Silence!" ordered Wak Xook in a hushed voice as he raised his fist above his head. All four men stopped. The soldiers remained motionless, waiting for their commander's orders, firmly holding their short spears.

Wak Xook scanned the area as his eyes slowly adjusted to the shadowy undergrowth. Everything was surprisingly calm. No leaves brushed by the wind. No birds chirping in the trees. Yet, if he remembered correctly, the village was close ahead. Doubt suddenly filled his mind. Were they too late?

The warrior recovered his breath and proceeded cautiously, his eyes scanning the thick foliage for any sign of enemy ambush. Insects buzzed around them, attracted by their sweaty skin.

He signaled his men forward. Following their commander's lead, the warriors resumed their walk through the jungle, silently fearing the gruesome confirmation of their failure at every turn in the path.

Suddenly, a scream echoed through the air. Somewhere ahead of them, birds flew off a tree, panicked by the sound. Without hesitation Wak Xook started running again.

Branches flew by his face, whipping his cheeks as he pushed his dehydrated muscles to their limit. His fingers were tensely gripped around his spear, ready for combat.

In that instant he emerged into the clearing and stopped

dead in his tracks.

Before him, four children were tossing around the remains of a shredded cotton doll while the obvious owner of the dismembered toy stood by, screaming at her tormentors.

As the soldiers arrived the boys all ran away, laughing mischievously, leaving the little girl in tears behind them.

"That's it? Children playing?" asked one of the warriors in disbelief. The sobbing girl slowly walked away.

Wak Xook looked around. "I don't suppose we've missed anything," he said. "False alarm."

"Then we ran all the way here for nothing!" complained the youngest one of them, who was bent over with his hands over his knees.

"Stop whining," answered another as he punched him on the shoulder. "A little running is only good for you. It's not as if you..."

"Hey don't start..."

"Silence!" interrupted Wak Xook with an authoritarian tone. "All of you! Enough!"

The mocking soldier displayed a large grin across his face, a grin which grew even larger as the young panting warrior turned around and vomited into the jungle after devoting so much effort to the run. His smile quickly disappeared though as the commander stared him in the eyes for a few seconds.

"Now move on, towards the village," he ordered.

There were discreet mocking laughs behind him. Although his soldiers were usually quite disciplined, the long run under the scorching sun's heat combined with the stress created by the constant war threat with Sian K'aan was obviously taking its toll on the young men. The dry season had barely started that, already, many friends had been lost to enemy ambushes. For most, it was their first look at death.

Kabrak'an was right. It would be a deadly season.

Despite the previous scoffing, all were now silent as they walked into the small village, where they were mostly met with suspicious looks by the few villagers surrounding them. Women, for the most part, and a few children. Strangely, there were no men in sight.

They walked by a few modest houses and quickly came to the village center, a small open patch of dusty ground covered by fallen leaves. Three rabbits and a small peccary were skewed over a fire burning in the middle of the place. The smell of cooking meat reminded Wak Xook he hadn't eaten anything since early morning. His stomach rumbled.

To his right, half a dozen women sat in the shade next to large basalt stones. All were busy grinding maize kernels into a thick paste which would eventually be flattened and cooked into a bread, or mixed with water and eaten as a gruel in the morning.

Wak Xook approached them.

The women did not look at him.

"Good day," said the commander after a while.

No answer. The warriors looked at each other.

"Everything seems to be very calm here," he added, looking around. He noticed the four boys they'd met earlier were now standing in the doorway of a nearby wood and thatch house, staring at them.

"Should it not be so?" asked an older woman, her eyes still fixed on the wet kernels being crushed under her pestle. "You were expected something different, perhaps?"

Wak Xook hesitated, surprised by the inhospitality.

"Where are the rest of the villagers?" he asked. "Where are all the men?"

One of the younger women raised her eyes wearily, and then quickly stared back at her work.

"In Mutul," bitterly replied the old woman. "The men are all in Mutul. Warriors came here, three days ago. Men dressed just like you. They were accompanied by a nobleman wearing jade jewelry who proclaimed all men to be thereby enrolled by the king. They took them to work on the acropolis renovation."

"All of them?"

The old women nodded. "Up to the eldest one."

"If the hunters are all in the city, then who killed the wild pig?" he asked, nodding towards the carcasses roasting above the burning embers.

"The young man," she replied, nodding somewhere behind her. "He will be a great hunter. Just like his father once was."

Wak Xook looked in the direction indicated by the old woman, and came eye to eye with a young boy not yet at the age of manhood. The boy was proudly leaning on his blowgun. On his chest was a single tattoo depicting a hunter and its prey.

The old woman finally raised her eyes and looked at him. She was blind in one eye, and a deep scar marked her left cheek. "Is there anything else we can do for you, warrior?"

Wak Xook shifted uncomfortably on his feet. He looked around. There must have been about two dozen families living in the village. Everything seemed fine.

"No. Thank you," he said before walking back to his men.

"What is wrong with them?" murmured one of the warriors.

The commander looked back. "These people live on the border, close to our enemies. For years now, they've suffered the anxiety of war and raiding parties. Can you blame them for being nervous at the sight of warriors, especially when all their men are absent? For all they know, we could be here to rampage the place. Who would prevent us from taking whatever we want here? That underage kid standing over there?" He nodded towards the young hunter.

"Still, they could have offered us some of that meat cooking on the fire. I am starving!"

"So am I," added another.

"You can eat your saksa' on the way back," replied the commander. "There is no reason to remain here any longer."

The young men complained at the thought of eating their maize and water drink on the road.

Wak Xook quickly silenced them.

"We will check the area for any sign of enemy presence," he added. "Then we return to camp."

"I wonder what happened," asked one of the soldiers as they headed down the path they came from. "They should have been here already."

"Sian K'aan?" replied another.

"Yes."

"Maybe the information was wrong. Maybe they were talking about another village. They are so many settlements like this one around Mutul. Our source could have easily been mistaken."

"The location was clear; the small village east of Ixchel's shrine. We should've met them on our way here."

"Maybe they got intercepted by another patrol. Who knows? I suppose we'll learn more when we return to camp. After this long run, I am looking forward to a decent meal."

As they all walked away, Wak Xook also wondered why the enemy was nowhere to be found. They were in the right village, he was sure of it. Guilt rose within him, and he wondered if his decision to leave hadn't been premature. Should they have stayed longer? Then again, how much longer? Half a day? A day? Maybe they could've spent the night there, just in case. And then what?

He was debating whether or not to turn around when the answer came by itself. At a turn in the narrow, winding path he suddenly found himself face to face with a large, heavily built man.

Then everything happened very fast.

In an instant, Wak Xook's eyes jumped from the man's spear to his heavily tattooed face to his red painted body. He immediately recognized the symbol on his skin. The macaw tattoo left no doubt as to their provenance.

Sian K'aan warriors.

Without hesitation, his actions driven by pure instinct, he thrusted his spear forward in a single, powerful movement. Before the enemy warrior could recover from his surprise, the Mutul commander had earned his first victory of the day.

It would not be his last.

As he felt the weight of the dying man over his spear, several other warriors came screaming into their direction. The jungle, which had been so peacefully silent just an instant before, suddenly became the theater of another massacre filled with the screams of dying men.

"Sian K'aan!" yelled someone as Wak Xook and his warriors quickly assumed a defensive position. Within a few seconds the enemy had surrounded them. The commander counted five enemy soldiers.

They attacked without showing any sign of fear.

Two men jumped towards him, hoping to grab the honor of killing a highly ranked enemy. Mayan leaders always made certain they could be easily recognizable on the battlefield, their flamboyant appearance meant as a challenge to anyone opposing them. Wak Xook was no exception. The richly decorated loincloth hanging from his waist and the rare green quetzal feathers attached to his spear marked him as a target of high prestige.

Before he could realize what was happening, the

commander was tightly engaged in a deadly spear fight. Adrenaline rushed through his body, immediately raising his awareness to a higher level as all of his senses were now dedicated towards one single goal; his own survival.

It wasn't long before he realized the inexperience of the two warriors facing him. The first one was slow and clumsy, while the other one's attacks were childishly basic and totally predictable.

With a quick sidestep he threw the clumsy one off balance. He then spun around and dodged in anticipation of the obvious attack he knew would come from the second one. As a spear whistled past his head, he lunged forward with all of his weight. The quetzal feathers decorating his spear turned red as the sharp flint spearhead buried itself deeply into his enemy's chest.

Around him his ears picked up the sounds of other warriors fighting each other, but his own battle was not yet over. His hands quickly let go off the spear and reached for his obsidian dagger. The remaining warrior facing him took a step back. A trickle of sweat ran down his forehead, his inexperienced knuckles turning white under the excessive strain of his grasp over his own spear shaft.

Wak Xook did not let the man think twice about his next move. He threw himself towards the red-painted warrior who, panicked, swung his spear before him. The blade sliced through thin air, leaving the man's right side totally exposed.

The opening was more than the commander's blade needed to reach his enemy's throat.

With blood still dripping from his dagger, Wak Xook turned around to assess the situation. Already, the fighting was almost over. One of his men was lying on the ground, mortally wounded. Another was crouched over an enemy body, breathing heavily. The fourth Sian K'aan soldier also laid dead a few steps away.

Only two men were still facing each other. The commander was about to join the fight when he realized the battle was already won. The enemy warrior was crouching low, tightly grabbing his right shoulder as blood flowed from a deep wound and mixed with the red paint covering his body. His mouth was wide open, gasping for air.

It was the look in his eyes that captured the commander's attention. It was a look Wak Xook had seen so many times before.

The look of defeat.

Standing before him, firmly holding his short spear with both hands, was the young recruit who'd been mocked earlier for being sick. Although breathing heavily, the young man appeared surprisingly calm.

As the enemy soldier jumped forward in a desperate attempt to strike, the young Mutul warrior stepped sideways and smashed him on the back of the head with the butt end of his spear.

The man fell to the ground with a heavy thud.

HE OF ONE PRISONER

"Warlord! Warlord! O'on Nimal Ahau!"

Kabrak'an turned around as he heard the warrior running in his direction.

"You have been looking for me ahau?" the man asked, exhausted.

"Yes. Any news from Wak Xook and his patrol?"

"Nothing yet, unfortunately."

"Are you certain?"

"I just checked ahau. Every sentry is on the lookout for them. You will be warned as soon as they are reported back into camp."

Kabrak'an swore. It was already getting dark. Soon, night would fall and still there was no news of his friend.

"They should have returned by now," he said. "They should have been back a long time ago."

"There are a hundred reasons that could explain their delay," replied the seasoned warrior. "How trustworthy was the information on the enemy's whereabouts?"

"Doubtful at best," conceded Kabrak'an. "Two travelers claimed to have overheard a Sian K'aan party after almost being surprised in the jungle. Their recollection of the event was very vague and confused."

"Then perhaps Wak Xook hasn't encountered anyone, or maybe the commander decided to patrol the area a little further. With darkness approaching, it is also possible he chose to spend the night in the safety of the village."

Kabrak'an smirked. "Maybe," he whispered, not

believing it. He raised a hand to the iguana tattoo covering his face. As his fingers landed on a wrinkle across his forehead, he regretted not sending more men with Wak Xook.

"What about the other patrols?" he asked.

"All are now safely back inside the camp and probably enjoying a well-deserved meal as we speak," the warrior reported. "Except for the overnight patrols who, of course, won't be back until tomorrow. There were no enemy sightings today. No wounded, and no deaths."

The warlord smiled at the news. Too often in the past month had the late day report been much gloomier with some of his men losing their lives on duty.

"It gets better," continued the warrior. "One patrol accidently stumbled across the missing cotton shipment. They were found a full day west of here. Apparently, they got lost trying to go around the city."

"So the northerners have finally agreed to stay clear of the war zone?"

"Maybe not all of them, but at least this merchant will be safe."

"Good," he said. "What about tomorrow?"

"All patrol leaders have already been briefed, ahau. Routine patrols will basically proceed as usual, although the defensive wall situation has forced us to make minor adjustments."

"I've stopped by the western construction site two days ago. The workers have been busy."

"Yes. Several trees have been brought down," replied the warrior. "Unfortunately, the heat has significantly slowed their progress. If I may," he said, pulling a folded bark paper sheet out of his cloak.

Kabrak'an silently watched as the man unfolded a map of the region before him. In the lower half he recognized the city's outline and suburbs, as well as major roads leading towards surrounding villages and other major cities. The top part of the map was mostly covered by the outlines of bajos, the seasonal swamps that would soon evaporate under the dry season sun. An 'X' marked the location of their camp along the border, while several lines representing wall sections were drafted between the swamps.

It was the same map that had been shown to him every day for the past two years, the only difference being the random addition of new 'wall' lines suddenly appearing over the jungle from time to time. Although Kabrak'an was in no position to judge the construction's progress, he did feel that lines appeared at an atrociously slow rate.

The process, after all, didn't seem particularly complicated to him. After the wall's projected path was marked in the jungle, all trees along the line were cut down and sent to the city for burning or as construction material. Workers then dug a deep trench through the soft rock along the treeless line, carefully packing the rubbles along the Mutul side of the excavation.

The net result was a solid rock wall surrounded on the exterior side by a trench twice as deep as a man's height, a formidable obstacle for any approaching enemy parties. A simple construction that would definitely prove efficient once completed, provided it could be manned with a sufficient quantity of soldiers. For the moment, though, it was nothing more than palisade segments linked together by gaping holes, and the situation would only worsen as the bajos would gradually dry up.

"Right now, the workers are still concentrated here, here, and there," the warrior said, pointing at three different areas. He dragged his finger to a long, straight line. "While they are still applying the finishing touches on this section, the construction coordinator informs me we could man the wall right away should you wish to do so."

Kabrak'an nodded. They both knew no men could be spent to guard the completed sections, as his warriors were already too few in numbers to efficiently patrol their territory. Any soldier assigned to a fix sentinel location would be a waste of manpower. As long as the wall would not be entirely completed, enemies could simply walk unchallenged through the breeches. It was useless to point that out to the construction crew.

"Tomorrow, people will start working here." He pointed to a shorter line next to a bajo. "The deforestation has been completed, and the digging of the trench can start. I've reorganized the patrols to increase our protection in the area."

"You mentioned delays caused by the heat?" the warlord enquired.

The warrior shifted his finger to a different area.

"The past few days have been particularly hot, enough to significantly slow the work. The coordinator has ordered all men to start their work day before dawn to benefit from the morning's coolness, and he gives them a longer pause at midday. However, the nights haven't been much cooler lately. They had to assign additional resources to water distribution. Overall, the situation has improved slightly, but just about everywhere men will be working longer than expected before shifting to a new location. We will, of course, maintain tight patrols in the area as long as required."

Kabrak'an mentally recorded the information. "Anything else?"

"Nothing ahau," responded the warrior as he folded the bark paper map and stuffed it back under his cloak.

"Tell me, how are the men?" asked the warlord.

"Well fed, well trained, and always prepared for combat. As usual, ahau."

"And their motivation?"

The warrior hesitated an instant.

"It has been difficult lately," he admitted. "Especially for the younger ones. They are hanging on."

With the dry season now well settled in, the camp was staffed to its maximum capacity. Over eight hundred warriors would spend the next few months along the border, in the middle of the jungle, protecting the city from Sian K'aan's attacks. Out of those hundreds, half were farmers or field workers, and several had not yet seen their first k'atun celebration, the twenty years mark. Before the end of the season, most would face combat. Many had already died.

Hopefully, the majority would live to see the next crop.

Kabrak'an dismissed the warrior and headed towards the main gate, anxious to see if Wak Xook was back.

Warriors saluted him as he made his way between the many fires lit here and there throughout the camp. Warriors spent most of their free time training, playing ball, scrounging for food or enjoying themselves around campfires and, as he walked amongst his men, Kabrak'an thought about how life at the outpost camp was not at all unpleasant, quite the opposite.

Abhorring the ever present political aspects of Mutul's palace, the aging warlord openly admitted his preference for spending time amongst his fellow warriors, regardless of his status as an ahauob member. In his own opinion, the companionship of soldiers combined with a well dosed supply of maguey beer largely compensated for the deficiencies of living with the ever-constant pressure of enemies lying in the shadows. Besides, it was a warrior's fate to die in battle, and he hoped for no less of an end to his own life.

He walked by the armory, the food storage house, the training areas and the makeshift ball court before he finally reached the camp sentinel, who informed him that no word had been heard from the commander since his departure earlier in the afternoon.

Kabrak'an sighed and looked towards the western horizon where a faint trace of blue, the last remnant of the sun's presence in the world, was slowly blending into the darkness of the night. High above his head, stars were brilliantly shining amongst a pitch black sky.

Since he could do nothing more than wait, he headed towards the kitchen and looked for something to eat. In the morning, he decided, he would personally go to the village and find out what fate had befallen his friend.

That would prove unnecessary.

It was much later that he heard shouting coming from somewhere within the camp. How much later he couldn't tell for he'd fallen asleep soon after finding some leftover stew, but a quick look at the stars later confirmed a long time had passed and dawn was near.

Kabrak'an abruptly woke up and instinctively reacted to the noise. His left hand reached for his spear while the right one jumped to his waist, searching for the only weapon Kabrak'an carried at all times. His fingers quickly found the short obsidian dagger and wrapped themselves around the hemp covered handle which provided a more reliable grip when the weapon was soaked in sweat and blood.

Without hesitation, he walked out of his hut and hurried towards the screaming voices. All around him men rapidly awoke, startled by the commotion. Far ahead, a group of warriors had gathered together. Kabrak'an nervously quickened the pace as, all over camp, the glowing ambers of abandoned fires were quickly stirred back to life.

Relief filled him as he got closer and saw Wak Xook, standing in the middle of the crowd, smiling. They headed straight towards each other and shook arms.

"You are late!" Kabrak'an said. "I was beginning to

wonder if this assignment would turn out to be more than you could handle!"

Wak Xook laughed.

"How easily do I seem to lose your trust these days! Maybe I should resign as commander of your troops before you officially have me challenged in the Kik' tz'enem!"

"Nonsense," he replied. "I would never allow you the honor of the warrior's challenge! Besides, there is no one else in whom I have more faith than you!"

"The village is safe, ahau," proudly reported the commander. "The information was accurate. We've managed to stop the enemy party before they could attack our people."

"Tell me everything," asked Kabrak'an. Around them, warriors were now chanting an old battle song in honor of Wak Xook's victory.

"There were six of them. We've stumbled against each other by surprise." His smile disappeared, as he recalled the encounter and its outcome. "I lost one man, a good and promising warrior. It was his second season with me."

Kabrak'an grabbed him by the shoulder.

"I left the body in the care of the villagers, much to their dismay, with the promise of sending someone for him as soon as I return to camp. I also promised to send back a few warriors while their men are absent. And I have a wounded man. Luckily, we did manage to capture one of Sian K'aan's warriors alive," he added, gesturing behind him.

The warlord looked behind his friend, and saw a Mutul soldier barely older than a boy. Too young, he thought, to witness the horrors of battle. The young man was nonetheless displaying a large grin across his face. Around him, everyone was cheering, clasping him in the back, congratulating him.

At his feet was the defeated enemy warrior. Lying on his

knees, hands bound together with only a torn and dirty loincloth to cover his genitals, the prisoner had been stripped of all his possessions. He carried no weapons. His ear spools had been ripped out of their cartilaginous sockets, leaving bloody earlobes hanging loose next to his sunken cheeks. His hair had been carelessly shaven, revealing a large crust of dried blood over his scalp where the spear had struck him. Even his tattoos had been taken from him, as shallow cuts in his flesh now rendered them unrecognizable. At the sight of his bleeding knees, it was obvious the man had been pitilessly dragged behind his captors over a significant distance.

When an enemy warrior was taken alive, it was their way to strip them of their pride, to dishonor them to the utmost level, to deny them their humanity. For that reason, Mayans always fought to the death, for there was no worst punishment than capture and humiliation. There was a somber look of hopelessness and despair in the prisoner's face as he waited for his undeniable fate.

"Pa'k!" called Wak Xook, introducing the young man loud and clear for all to hear. "Pa'k, a warrior of Mutul who, from now on, shall be known as Pa'k the captor, he of one prisoner!"

The assembled warriors cheered as Wak Xook congratulated the young man, who proudly took a step forward and stared at the large iguana tattoo covering Kabrak'an's face.

"It is an honor for me to present you with this enemy warrior, warlord Kabrak'an ahau, he of eighteen prisoners. He is yours. May I, one day, also count as many victims as you do."

To his surprise, the warlord shook his head.

"He is your prisoner, young man. You've earned the right to take him to the shaman."

Pa'k smiled, and nodded. "Thank you, ahau."

The other warriors massed around him. He was offered food. He was offered beer. He was offered all sorts of presents. Together, they all made their way towards the center of the camp, singing and chanting while Pa'k dragged his victim behind him.

"Fourteen," whispered Kabrak'an as he watched them walk away. "It should be fourteen prisoners. Not eighteen."

Wak Xook looked at him with an inquisitive look as the others disappeared in the distance.

"One was wrongly attributed to me," explained the warlord. "Another actually surrendered, which is rather unheard of. And two died of their wounds shortly after their capture, so I really should be known as *he of fourteen prisoners*, not eighteen."

The commander nudged him in the ribs with a smirk on his face.

"Fourteen. Eighteen. What difference does it make? Your name is legend. Your warriors look up to you."

"Do I deserve it Wak Xook? I am just a man," he said, his eyes staring at the darkness.

"You give them something to aspire to. You give them the promise of a greater purpose."

The commander waived his hand towards the singing warriors. "These men, they will never be gods. None of us will ever wield lightning bolts or cast rain from a thunderous sky. And yes, you are a just man, just like them, but listen to the legends surrounding you! You give them something to strive for!"

Kabrak'an thought about Wak Xook's words for an instant and then laughed at the absurdity of it all.

"Come," he said. "I need something to drink. You look thirsty."

"I am," replied the commander. "First, I need to stop by the medical barrack to check on my wounded warrior."

"How is he?"

"His arm was severely mangled. I fear he will never again be able to wield a spear."

For the seriously wounded, life was often a curse more terrible than death. Many spent days under the cares of the medicine-men, often standing between life and death. Most of those who survived would never again be soldiers, and were returned to Mutul as soon as they were fit to travel. The luckiest ones usually ended up limping across the city, hoping to be employed in the market or for any other task fit to their condition. As for the others, the amputated and sometimes disfigured ones, they were usually forced into a life of begging with the endless mockeries of children as their only reward for their service in his troops.

"Fine. I will go with you," answered the warlord.

Kabrak'an's stomach reeked as he thought of the medical barrack and its ever present stench of blood and festering wounds, but it was his duty to give these men one last touch of humanity before sending them back to a life of pain and suffering.

"Behold the ancient gods of Mutul!" cried the odd looking man standing in the middle of the camp. His back was turned against the raging fire burning behind him, his arms raised towards the pitch black sky, his crouched body an unnatural shadow quivering before the dancing flames.

"Behold the forgotten earth and sky deities, and fear the jaguar spirit, for they have joined us tonight to witness the fate of this man!" he said, pointing a long, bony finger towards the prisoner.

He was a shaman. A healer. A caster of dark spells. A cursed being whose flesh belonged to the world of men. Whose soul, capable of crossing to the realm of spirits, continuously wandered between the various planes of existence, searching for the truth in places inaccessible to others.

The nameless man, who could go without food for days while his soul traveled to the spiritual world, looked dangerously thin. Bones showed through his skin. His long, drawn face was dried by the sun, making him look much older than he actually was. His dark skin was covered with mystical tattoos of meaningless shapes and symbols whose true significance could only be understood by a man touched by the spirits. His fingernails were long and dirty, and a foul smelling deer head, not so freshly cut off its own body, sat on top of his wild, unkempt hair.

"Spirits of the forest, spirits of the night, tell me, what shall become of this poor soul?" he asked aloud, his eyes turned over inside his head with only the white showing.

"Sacrifice him!" chanted the warriors massed around the scene. "Sacrifice him! Sacrifice his life to Itzamnà!"

The shaman stood still for an instant, muttering inaudible words. He then started shivering, and life returned to his eyes.

"Pray to your gods!" he said, dancing around the prisoner. "Pray, for the spirits have spoken." With every step he took, the many animal bones attached to his dirty rags stuck each other in a skeletal sound, adding to the eeriness of the scene. "Pray that your soul finds its way to your ancestors before the underworld demons claim it for eternity!"

The warriors watched as the unwilling prisoner was coercively laid over the dark-stained altar, his pleas for mercy drowned in a sea of cheers. A thick mixture of balché and mushrooms was forced down his throat while red and black symbols were promptly drawn on his chest.

Copal incense was lit, dried tobacco leaves were thrown into the fires, and a thick smoke cloud covered the camp. A warrior approached. A large, bulky man carrying a heavy flint axe over his shoulder. The shaman's prayer ended, and with the prisoner still forcefully held onto the sacrificial stone, the axe was raised and dropped in one swift movement.

The crowd started singing as the severed head rolled into the dust. Pa'k, the young Mutul soldier, did not take the life of an enemy on that day. Nor did he slay an opponent in single combat.

No, he had accomplished something much more remarkable.

He had captured a Sian K'aan warrior.

And he had offered his life to the gods.

TOLLÀN

The sun was slowly disappearing behind the temples, casting long shadows over Tollàn's main avenue where two hundred thousand people had gathered, waiting for their king to arrive. Most were tired, completely worn out after a long day of work, and although children were restless there was no whining for all had been severely warned by their parents to remain calm and silent. No lack of discipline would be tolerated by the temple's guards, who cared little whether or not it was long past their bedtime.

The entire population of Tollàn wearily watched as the procession finally appeared down the avenue, slowly making its way towards the pyramid of the moon. As priests walked through the crowd, people politely clapped and unconvincingly cheered for the king.

"Look at them Temictzin!" exclaimed Motecumatl, king of Tollàn. He majestically waved at his subjects, his exaggerated smile exhibiting a full row of yellowed, unusually crooked teeth.

"Listen to them! They love me!"

"They certainly do, my lord," responded the old man limping next to the royal palanquin.

The liquor he'd ingested earlier had initially reduced the pain in his lower back. Yet, barely halfway through this long ceremonial walk, the pain and stiffness was slowly coming back. The old man shifted more weight over his walking stick, hoping to relieve some of the discomfort.

It would be a long night.

"They certainly do," he simply said once again, making no effort to hide the total lack of enthusiasm in his voice.

The king laughed forcefully. "Don't be so sarcastic Temictzin. One day, I shall have you beaten for so shamefully lying to my face! Of course they don't like me. They hate me. Even from up here, I can feel their disdain. I smell their fear. Can you not?"

The old man nodded silently. After so many years, he had grown accustomed to hearing the same pretentious speech over and over again.

"They fear me," he continued. "And fear is the only true form of control. Forget the ideologist theories of my grandfather. Forget his great ideas of nations allied together for the benefit of all men. Conquest is what will make our empire grow. Fear is what will keep it together!"

Temictzin looked at the king as he discussed his philosophy about rulership. He certainly looked majestic with his fists raised up in the air, sitting high on the litter carried by six nameless slaves who'd been captured somewhere in the faraway northern deserts. The king was wearing a black coat, an imposing headdress, and hundreds of expensive quetzal feathers imported from the Mayan land adorned the elaborate canopy shielding him from the sun.

Yes, he looked kingly indeed, but Temictzin knew better.

Enjoy your glory while it lasts, thought the old man. *Your grandfather was a great man. He built this kingdom with his own sweat. He gave it the grandness we now enjoy. History teaches us that tyrants like you usually meet a violent and precipitated fate. Let's only hope your folly does not bring this kingdom down with you.*

The elder raised his head and squinted his eyes. His eyesight had gotten noticeably worse since the last ceremony. Still, he clearly recognized the outline of their destination, the world's tallest pyramid. As always, he marveled at the monument's striking resemblance with the mountainous background.

A mountain within a mountain, he thought. *Let us hope the Goddess can protect us from your madness.*

Home of Coyolxauqui, the moon goddess, the tallest mountain beyond the city's outskirts was strictly forbidden to all men. Anyone who dared set foot on its slopes would immediately be put to death. It was to offer proper rituals to the goddess and symbolically allow men access to its summit that the giant pyramid mimicking the sacred mountain's outline had been built at the end of the sacred alley.

"How is you son?" asked the king unexpectedly as the procession slowly moved forward.

The question almost sent the old man tumbling over his own walking stick.

"My lord?" replied Temictzin, awestruck. It was totally unlike the king to enquire about his subject's well-being.

"Your son, Huemac. I do not remember seeing him during our last banquet."

"Huemac, of course. He was ill, my lord. Please accept my apologies for his absence."

"I see. Many fell sick during the past few months. I, myself, suffered a fever for a day or two. It was most unpleasant. He is now better, I hope?"

"He is, my lord," answered Temictzin, still puzzled by the questioning. "Thank you for your interest."

"Don't flatter yourself," replied the king as he waved condescendingly towards the unresponsive crowd. "I have a task for him."

The old man looked up towards the king. Having suddenly inherited the kingdom after his father's untimely death, many had questioned the wisdom of having such a young ruler on the throne. Youth, power, and ambition often proved to be a dangerous combination, and most would have preferred to see the kingdom ruled by a committee until the young prince would mature a little more.

With the people opposing him mysteriously disappearing or suddenly found murdered, Motecumatl had quickly managed to silence any opposition to what he'd considered his birth right. By the time he was officially proclaimed king a score of the city's most respected and influent elders had already been buried, and although most of the remaining nobles who'd survived the political onslaught still silently disagreed with his policies, no one dared challenge him openly.

Not everyone in the city, however, was opposed to the king. The military, whose support was crucial in his accession, were quite content with his warlike, invasive policies. Most of the young men in the nation saw him as a symbol of strength under whom they could finally rally, someone who would show the outside world the superiority of Tollàn.

Apparently, foolishness and rash actions were also traits of youth and inexperience.

Unfortunately, Temictzin's middle son had also fallen under the spell of Motecumatl, and, as a father, he was concerned about Huemac having already managed to grab the king's attention.

"I hear your son is an excellent soldier," pursued the king, gently wobbling under his carrying slave's constant pace. "My war chief praises his abilities, not only as a warrior, but also as a leader. Apparently, your son lead his own men to victory on several occasions."

"He lives only to serve you, my lord."

May he live long enough to realize his mistake, he thought.

"Perfect," said the king. "Then have him brought to me

after the ceremony. I shall discuss with him."

The old man silently nodded, and the king proudly looked ahead.

Before him, ceremonial dancers jumped and twirled under the music of many flutes, nonetheless failing to uplift the mood of the crowd who, except for sudden surges of faked excitement whenever priests or guards would pass by, remained mostly silent.

As the procession slowly progressed towards the pyramid, Temictzin could only wonder what doom would soon befall his son.

The water in the ceramic bowl turned red as the king of Tollàn washed his own hands.

"I am certain the Goddess accepted your gift my lord," said the priest reluctantly, his face still covered by a thick layer of the black ceremonial makeup.

"Fool!" angrily answered the king as he sent the bowl flying across the room with the back of his hand. The pottery vessel shattered in pieces as it landed hard on the ground close to where Temictzin was silently standing.

"The moon did not rise tonight! The goddess did not attend!" he pursued furiously. "You swore she would be present!"

"The clouds veiled her face, my lord, but Coyolxauqui was definitely amongst us!" The priest trembled as he spoke. "It is not uncommon for Tlaloc, god of rain, to send clouds into the sky on the night of the moon ceremony. The goddess is his wife, after all. Are they not entitled to some private time together?"

"I should have you executed!" shouted Motecumatl as he dried his hands on a cotton towel. "The ceremony will be performed again tomorrow. You'd better make certain all citizens are present. All of them!"

He looked at the priest with a venomous look. "And make sure they at least pretend to be happy this time! No wonder the goddess refuses to show herself if only to be greeted by the sorrow-faced scum living in this city! Now leave!"

The priest nodded and hurried out of the room.

It was almost dawn by then. The king had waited a long time atop the pyramid, hoping for a glimpse of the moon. The embrace of Tlaloc was strong, the clouds were thick. The goddess never came. Usually, they would've still proceeded with the ceremony and think nothing more of it. Tonight, for some unknown reason, the king had insisted that everyone should wait for the moon to appear.

Eventually, people got tired. Children fell asleep. In the end, he nonetheless decided to perform the sacrifice before sending his people home for some rest before another hard day of work, but the blood did not calm his bad mood.

"The goddess will show up tomorrow," said Temictzin, hoping to calm the king's temper. "When she does, she will most certainly recognize and reward your perseverance."

"Maybe she will," answered Motecumatl with an absent-minded look. His face changed to a frown. "Then again, maybe she won't. I shall make it up to her."

He turned around and walked straight to his throne. "I understand your son is here. Let him in," he ordered, making himself comfortable amongst the expensive cushions.

Temictzin bowed his head and walked out.

Very few people were ever allowed past the heavily guarded door leading into the king's apartments. Motecumatl was much too conscious of his unpopularity to let anyone near his private quarters, let alone a young warrior trained to kill with his bare hands if necessary. Huemac had never even seen the inside of the palace and as he nervously waited outside, he meticulously reviewed his Tollàn warrior uniform, making sure everything was impeccable.

From the look on the priest's face who'd walked out a few moments ago, it was clear the king was in no mood to be displeased.

He made certain the deer hide armor protecting his legs and torso was properly adjusted. He polished the many obsidian fragments incrusted into his chest plate, proud of the stones which marked him as a leader. He straightened the thick leather helmet over his head, tightened the straps covering his cheeks, and removed a hair from his red loincloth.

"The king is waiting Huemac," said Temictzin as he came out of the room. "Follow me."

Huemac silently acknowledged his father and followed him in.

His eyes widened in astonishment as he walked through the royal door for the first time in his life. The room, lit by a series of torches, was bigger than he had expected. Magnificent colorful murals depicting wild animals and hunting scenes were painted on the walls, while censors hanging from the ceiling gave off a pleasant aroma. He barely noticed the broken vessel and the splattered water in the nearby corner.

Huemac's eyes looked around the room before finally falling upon the king. The man was sitting on his throne, silently staring at him.

He'd never seen Motecumatl from so close before, and

the dark glitter in his eyes suddenly awakened Huemac's warrior instincts. *This is a dangerous man,* he thought. A cold shiver ran down the young warrior's spine as he held the stare back, fighting the urge to look down for fear it might have been interpreted as a sign of weakness. And so, as he felt the man's heavy stare studying him, he did the only thing he could do. He proudly straightened his back, raised his head, and waited for the king to break the silence.

After what seemed like an eternity, the slightest smirk appeared on Motecumatl's lips.

"Good evening, young Huemac."

"Good evening, my lord," replied the young man with assurance.

"Approach," gestured the king. "You must be wondering why I've summoned you here, so late in the night," he added, jumping straight to the point.

The king was not a man who enjoyed casual conversations, especially with subordinate military personnel. He had hopes that Temictzin's son would become an important member of his governing military staff, and from the way the boy had looked at him, Motecumatl immediately knew he was not a spineless toad.

Spearthrower Owl is right, he thought. *This one might be worth something. If, of course, he survives long enough.*

Huemac was in fact wondering why his presence had been requested. He nonetheless decided to simply walk towards the throne in silence, guessing Motecumatl was not really expecting an answer to his question.

"Have you met lord Cauac?" asked the king, as the soldier was signaled to stop.

"I did, my lord."

"Then I suppose you've been made aware of his mission?"

"I had the pleasure of discussing with him a few days before he left for the Mayan lands. He told me about his mission, and about the strategy he plans to use, my lord."

The young man immediately regretted his answer.

Temictzin subtly cleared his throat as Huemac bit his lower lip. It was well known that the king hated two things above anything else; weakness, and unnecessarily long answers. A simple *yes* would have sufficed.

The king shifted in his seat, obviously annoyed.

"He speaks highly of you. How many soldiers do you have under your command?" asked the king after several seconds.

"I command twenty men, my lord."

"Twenty! No more?" exclaimed Motecumatl, surprised. "I was told you led over a hundred men into combat during our last campaign."

"I did. They were lord Quilaztli's warriors, my king." Huemac hesitated, then risked a longer answer before the king's inquisitive glare. "He entrusted me with a hundred men after splitting his troops for an ambush. I believe he must have appreciated my leadership for he left twenty of those warriors with me after that day. They are the same twenty I still command today my lord. I have lost no one."

"He recognized your abilities as a leader, as well as the calm with which you took decisions under combat pressure."

Huemac lowered his head, and managed to suppress a smile.

"I have recently received news from lord Cauac. His plan is progressing well, and he now believes we should proceed to the next step."

The young man was all ears.

"As expected, he now needs support. I want you to lead our troops. Unfortunately, I cannot spare many of our current soldiers. You can keep your twenty men. I will give you an additional eighty seasoned warriors, as well as two hundred recruits. Three hundred men in all. They are yours, for as long as you can keep them alive. Starting tomorrow, you will have three months to train them."

Huemac swallowed, honored and excited about this opportunity.

"Once your men are ready," pursued the king, "you will take them straight into the heart of the Mayan realm. Lord Atlatl Cauac's plan cannot fail."

He leaned forward.

"You and your warriors will bring honor to the nation of Tollàn!"

THE BURNT LORD

"Pass! Pass!" bellowed Wak Xook, frantically waving his arms in the hope of grabbing his teammate's attention.

"Kabrak'an! Pass!"

On the opposite end of the court, the warlord had long noticed that Wak Xook had successfully created a little separation with his opponent. He was, however, barely in control of the ball, and the larger than average warrior facing him was particularly efficient at matching his every move. The warlord was tiring fast.

No matter how much he tried, every single sidestep and feint always seemed to end up to the other man's advantage. Slowly but surely, he was now being forced into the corner. His thighs were burning, his lungs were dry, and his eyes were itchy with sweat. It was now or never.

He took a quick breath, jumped to one side, and skillfully sent the ball flying towards the opposite wall.

His timing was perfect.

Under his opponent's awed look, the rubber ball flew high into the air, struck the makeshift sloped wall with a dull *thump* and bounced off towards Wak Xook, who focused on the ball as he crisped his muscles. From the corner of his eyes he spotted the unguarded ring.

Victory was within his grasp.

He bent his knees and prepared for the shot. Just as he positioned himself in the path of the flying rubber ball, he was severely knocked aside by a firm blow. Completely taken by surprise, the commander fell flat on the dusty ground as another particularly large warrior intercepted the pass. Alone and unchallenged, the man easily directed the ball straight through the closest ring before Kabrak'an could do anything.

"Victory!" celebrated the two soldiers as they raised their arms. The small crowd gathered around the field immediately cheered and applauded the victors. It had been a good, entertaining match.

"Well played," encouraged a visibly disappointed Kabrak'an as he offered Wak Xook a helping hand. The commander was still lying in the dust, dumbfounded at what had just happened. Concentrating on the ball, he had never seen the other man coming straight at him. He'd never anticipated the interception, nor did he expect the hit.

"I think I bit my tongue," he mumbled as the warlord helped him to his feet. "I shouldn't have called for that pass. I wasn't careful enough."

"You were well unmarked when I saw you. Besides, the other one gave me no choice. He would've crushed me to the wall had I not gotten rid of the ball. I must admit, these two move surprisingly fast for big guys."

"We'll get them next time," added Wak Xook with a smile. He knew the other two warriors were still well within ear's reach.

"In your dreams, commander!" laughed one of their opponents.

"Go nurse that tongue," mockingly replied the other as he grabbed Wak Xook around the neck. "The medical barrack is in that direction. Then, we'll accept a rematch anytime!"

"Enjoy your victory Xakiq. Next time will be different," answered Wak Xook. He pushed the soldier away and walked off the court. The matches were friendly and Xakiq was one of the many warriors under his command. Still, he hated losing.

"Now out of my sight, before I assign you extra patrol duties for tomorrow."

The two warriors walked away laughing, not wanting to test the seriousness of their commander's threat.

While a beaten down Wak Xook sat in the shade to remove his heavy equipment, four other players took place on the court under the still cheering crowd of off-duty warriors. The surface was sprinkled with the customary maize kernels and, without any further delay, the heavy rubber ball once again started bouncing off the walls.

Kabrak'an approached Wak Xook and offered him a gourd of balché. The commander gratefully accepted. The evening was hot and humid.

"Thank you," he said after quenching his thirst. The alcoholic beverage took away the taste of blood in his mouth.

He looked at the calabash gourd with a smirk. "Now I know why we've lost. If you've been drinking this all day, then it's no wonder..."

"Kabrak'an ahau!" interrupted someone.

They both turned their heads. A warrior was running in their direction.

"Ahau," said the young man, panting. "I've been looking for you."

Kabrak'an sat straight.

"Calm down," he said. "What's the hurry?"

"The nacom. Siyah Kak ahau." The young man, visibly out of breath, was speaking spasmodically.

"Siyah Kak? What about him?" Kabrak'an hadn't heard about the burnt lord since his last meeting in Mutul.

"He is here, O'on Nimal. He is looking for you."

"Siyah Kak is in the camp?" asked Wak Xook with a serious look. "Are you sure it's him?"

The warrior looked at the commander with raised

eyebrows. "I could hardly be mistaken ahau," he said. "He doesn't exactly blend into the crowd."

"No. I suppose he doesn't. I wonder what he wants. Let's find out!" said Wak Xook.

Before the commander could jump back to his feet, the nacom was upon them, seemingly out of nowhere.

"Warlord," called the sinister voice. "Finally, I find you."

Kabrak'an turned around as the young warrior who'd reported the nacom's arrival discretely took a few steps away.

Siyah Kak was fully dressed in battle gear and armed with his usual complement of weapons; a short spear strapped across his back, a pair of obsidian daggers, and a large wooden club hanging at his waist.

It should have seemed odd for any war leader to carry such a primitive weapon, but just as Siyah Kak was no ordinary man, his club was no ordinary weapon. Covered with a score of razor-sharp obsidian insets, the weapon's bulged end was not only capable of crushing skulls to pieces; it also ripped skin to shreds. It was a terrifying weapon, a prestigious and deadly instrument of war.

Of course, prestige had its cost. Almost every time the weapon was used, shards of obsidian would remain lodged into his enemy's body, and the empty indentations constantly had to be replenished with new blades.

Kabrak'an stared at the weapon for an instant. He noticed several empty slots on the bulged end of the club.

The nacom had been busy.

"Siyah Kak ahau, greetings. You are welcome amongst us," greeted Kabrak'an unenthusiastically. "I was not informed of your presence here, ahau. Had I known, I would have invited you to share our evening meal."

"Spare me the politeness," replied the nacom with a gloomy frown. His heavily scarred face seemed even more terrifying in the fading evening light. "I come unannounced, having spent the better part of the month deep into the jungle hunting down the criminals who roam unchallenged throughout our territory."

The warlord chose not to act upon Siyah Kak's insult.

"The fresh finger bones in your hair tell me you've been successful. What brings you here today?"

The nacom sniffed, observing Kabrak'an from head to toe before resting his eyes upon the famous iguana tattoo covering his face.

"Our city is at war. Our people are being murdered. Our crops, stolen. I can't remember the last time I have eaten or slept decently and yet, here I find you. Fully rested, leisurely walking around with your belly full, drinking balché while your men are enjoying themselves on the ball court!"

As if to prove his point, the crowd gathered around the court suddenly cheered as one of the team scored a point.

"They are enjoying a well-deserved break after spending the last three months shedding their own sweat and blood," replied Kabrak'an. "Giving them a rest once in a while improves their morale, their efficiency and, most of all, their survival rate."

"You treat your men as a father would his daughters!" There was despise in Siyah Kak's last words. "A true warrior would be out there, hunting down his enemies until ultimate victory or until his own death!"

Kabrak'an breathed deeply, and felt Wak Xook stiffen beside him. He really hated the man. He always did.

No, not always, he corrected himself. There was a time when Siyah Kak was not so despicable, a time when his heart was not filled with so much hatred for the world. Most who didn't know him only saw the burn marks as a reflection of his true nature, of the monster living inside.

Kabrak'an knew his scars were nothing more than the eternal reminder of an unfortunate childhood accident, as he himself clearly recalled the events deeply engraved within his own mind.

It was many years ago. They were all children at the time. Four boys playing in the fields on a hot day. He remembered the black clouds rolling in. The strong winds suddenly picking up. The run for cover. It was raining hard by the time they'd all found shelter in a small abandoned house, laughing at themselves for being soaking wet.

The misadventure quickly turned into a nightmare as the unusually strong storm picked up even more strength. The afternoon turned dark as night, sporadically illuminated by flashes of lightning. To this day, Kabrak'an had never again witnessed such a fierce display of wrath from K'awiil, the lightning god.

Then came a sudden flash of light. Thunder. They all held their breath as the dry thatch roof suddenly collapsed over their heads. At first there was only darkness. A faint smell of smoke. Incandescent embers. Screams.

Luckily, three of them managed to escape the collapsed structure virtually unscathed. They tried to run back inside for their missing friend, but as flames started to appear fear filled their young hearts. Black smoke choked their lungs. So they knelt, and cried for help.

Farmers came from the fields. They braved the fire, and finally pulled a writhed, mangled form out of the burning remains. It had taken him a moment to realize that the black moaning shape in their arms was his friend. As the smell of burnt flesh and hair filled his nostrils, the young Kabrak'an turned around and vomited.

Against all odds, the boy who later became known as Siyah Kak had survived. The charred skin healed but his spirit never fully recovered, and he never was the same after. Years passed and Siyah Kak grew apart from the rest of the world. He became dark and distant, dedicating all of his strength in learning the only skill that could somehow make sense of what he had become.

He learned how to kill, and he became exceedingly good at it.

Now, standing face to face, Kabrak'an only felt pity for him.

"You obviously came here to see me," he said bluntly. "What do you want?"

The nacom smiled at the crude attitude. His fingers reached for a hemp rope attached over his chest. He untied the knot, grabbed a bag from behind his back, and threw it at Kabrak'an's feet. Several items shifted inside as the bag landed heavily on the ground.

With an almost imperceptible nod, Siyah Kak invited Kabrak'an to look inside.

The warlord hesitated, then slowly kneeled to inspect the content, fearful of what he would find. He looked, and breathed a discrete sigh of relief.

The bag was filled with several obsidian items of various shapes. He randomly chose a blade, and carefully observed it in the fading daylight. The pitch black vitreous material had been skillfully crafted into a sturdy, razor sharp weapon.

Careful not to cut himself, he quickly rummaged through the rest of the content. He found several other blades, jewels, household tools, flakes, beads, and random objects of various value.

"You've recovered part of a stolen shipment?" he guessed.

"No," answered Siyah Kak. "We caught this in the hands of Lakam Ha smugglers wandering beyond our borders."

Kabrak'an raised his head.

"Smugglers? Outside our borders? Exactly where did you find these?" he asked sharply.

"Never mind. The point is you are looking at contraband

material destined to the black market of Mutul," replied the nacom.

The warlord rose to his feet.

"I seriously doubt that," he answered. "These are excellent quality products, all of great craftsmanship. Smugglers always sell cheap, poorly manufactured tools."

"Things change, my friend. We are catching more and more smugglers around the city, and the quality of their material has been steadily increasing since the beginning of the season. The war with Sian K'aan is definitely impacting our trade. Prices are going up. An increase of black market activities is only the first sign of a population's dissatisfaction as people turn towards other sources to acquire their goods. Sources willing to sell at more reasonable prices."

He took a step closer to the warlord and lowered his voice. "Ask yourself, why is there a sudden surge of good quality obsidian available on the city streets? It certainly didn't appear out of nowhere. Who is providing this raw material?"

He paused an instant to let the thought sink in.

"Our own stolen obsidian is being sold back to us through criminal hands! The king is slowly losing control over his own land. His influence amongst the other states is decreasing. Soon, the population will lose faith. They will no longer believe he can support their own needs. It is inevitable."

Kabrak'an threw the blade back into the bag. "You are grossly exaggerating ahau." It was his turn to use a despiteful tone.

"Am I?" challenged the nacom. "Do you not see this is where we are heading? We are holding back, passively defending our territory while the enemy is slowly tightening its grasp on us. They are hitting us where it hurts the most, on our economy. Eventually, the south will realize our little conflict is costing them more and more profit. Neighboring states will be alerted. Great Jaguar Paw will be held accountable!"

"What do you expect from me?" Kabrak'an asked again. "Tell me why you are here!"

"Join me," he answered. "I will raise a militia. I will gather men ready to fight for their land. Let's unite our strengths and destroy Sian K'aan. Together we will easily defeat them. Join me, and we will rid the Mayan land of this threat once and for all!"

Kabrak'an lowered his head and took a deep breath. The nacom was not entirely wrong. Mutul was not respecting the regional economic treaties, and the king was the one who would be held responsible. Great Jaguar Paw, however, insisted on not attacking Sian K'aan, and the warlord fully trusted his king.

"I believe there is a better way to use a militia," the warlord finally said. "We could integrate them with the regular troops. That way, they could gain some combat experience, and with them as a dissuasive force, we could more efficiently defend our borders."

"Integrate them in the regular troops? Never! They would be much more useful under my command!"

"Would they? You have no business patrolling beyond our land. You are careless and irrational!"

"I do what has to be done, which is more than what you can say for yourself! I have slaughtered enemies as far as the marshes of death. I have patrolled from the Kamikal Paxq'ol to the Ek Sayisaj for the purpose of keeping our people safe!"

"You serve your own purpose, and refuse to follow the instructions of your king. You should protect our borders, not seek trouble beyond them!"

"Kabrak'an, I beg you. One last time. Attack Sian K'aan with me!"

"The king will never allow it."

"Why do you care about the king? He is already lost anyway!"

"This is seditious!" interjected Wak Xook, no longer able to contain himself. "We are nowhere near the point where Mutul no longer supports his king!"

"Fools!" yelled Siyah Kak.

Kabrak'an was about to reply when he noticed the deep silence now surrounding them. There were no more cheerings, no more ball bouncing against the walls. The game had come to a stop, and the warriors no longer engaged in their evening activities. The warlord felt the weight of hundreds of eyes staring at them.

"Your diseased flesh will rot into the underworld. Insects will crawl into your eye sockets, and wild pigs will grind your bones to dust!" added the nacom. "Do you not see we are all doomed unless we act now?"

The warlord opened his mouth and looked around. Most of the warriors in the vicinity had gathered around them, with many more quickly approaching as news of the confrontation quickly spreaded to the camp's outskirts. No matter how much he would have liked to reply, Kabrak'an wisely elected to remain silent. The argument had degenerated beyond common civilities, and no good would now come from such a conversation.

The burnt man stared at Kabrak'an for an instant, and finally understood he would get no answer. He spat on the ground.

"Fine," he added. "Then please pay my greetings to our king." With these words, Siyah Kak turned around and walked away.

Kabrak'an crossed his arms and prepared himself to order his men back to their business. Before he could react, the commander took a step forward and addressed the burnt warrior.

"The king will hear about this!" warned Wak Xook.

The nacom abruptly stopped and looked back, harboring a threatening look on an already frightening face.

"You dare threaten me? You? Do you think I fear you? Look at yourself! Filthy, sweaty, face bloodied and breath reeking of alcohol! You look more like a diseased beggar out of a drunken brawl than a respectable warrior. Your men should follow me instead of you!"

Wak Xook was about to go after him when Kabrak'an grabbed his friend by the arm, holding him back.

Siyah Kak sneered and walked away.

"You disloyal... pretentious... motherless... son of a demon whore!" screamed Wak Xook infuriated, unable to find an insult strong enough to express his emotions.

Kabrak'an watched the nacom disappear in the distance then looked at his friend with a smile.

"Motherless son of a whore?" he repeated mockingly.

Wak Xook simply waived his arms up in the air under the discreet laughter of his companion and took a step away.

"What shall we do now?" he finally asked.

"I must return to Mutul immediately," the warlord answered. "I need to inform the council as soon as possible. The emergence of black market activities is indeed troubling, assuming it is true. Winaq will know what to do."

"What shall we do about Siyah Kak?"

"You know him. You know how he is. Let him be. He will soon calm down and return to his senses. I will nonetheless inform Great Jaguar Paw of what happened here, though I doubt it will do any good. Siyah Kak is as temperamental as a child."

Wak Xook nodded. "You will miss Pa'k's ceremony. His juch'um is tonight. He was looking forward to the honor of having you as his witness."

The juch'um. The warrior's tattooing ceremony. Kabrak'an smiled, remembering his first capture. Of the actual encounter itself he recalled very little. Whistling blades. Blood. Sweat. A wounded enemy lying on the ground under his own body, struggling for his life. The elation of victory. Yet, he clearly remembered his own juch'um celebration afterwards. The burning sensation of the balché going down his throat, and his nervous apprehension as the shaman had walked up to him.

His own witness, a promising patrol leader who long ago fell under enemy blades, had been there beside him all along. He was there when the old medicine man had drawn the tattoo's outline on his skin. When he had pulled out a sharp obsidian blade from a dirty sheath. It was a blade as dark as the night.

"The honor will be yours my friend," Kabrak'an said. "You will support him throughout the ordeal."

Wak Xook nodded.

Unconsciously, the warlord touched his right shoulder. He remembered the intense pain he'd felt as the blade had cut through his skin, again and again along the drawn pattern. He remembered the burning sensation of the shaman rubbing ashes into the wound, smearing dirt and blood all over his arm under the watchful eyes of his fellow warriors. And he remembered the pride he'd felt after managing to keep a straight face through it all.

Eventually the wound had healed, leaving the dark outline of a spear point permanently etched into his skin.

His first prisoner tattoo. His first victory.

It now seemed like so many years ago.

THE HONEY GOD

Balam's renovation project had been going perfectly well. The materials were of good quality. The workers were efficient and competent. Even the weather had been cooperating, although anything other than clear blue sky would have been quite unusual in the middle of the dry season. Yes, everything had been going as planned, and the renovation was on schedule.

Then everything changed.

After a sudden series of unforeseen problems, progress suddenly came to a halt, and Balam now felt the pressure of his new assignment.

The Mayan boy was used to being given responsibilities. A few months ago, the ahauob had offered him the opportunity to manage and lead his own project. A few of the nobles had initially protested the assignment, arguing his youth and inexperience to be an unnecessary risk, although Balam had guessed the true nature of their protest to simply be jealousy.

At first, he'd been reluctant to accept, uncertain of his own competence in leading such a task. Most of all, he was unsure as to why he'd been selected without showing any prior interest in the matter. It was Winaq who'd finally convinced him to take on the project after explaining how Great Jaguar Paw himself had suggested his name, expressing the desire that Balam be given more important duties within the city.

"The K'uhul Ahau wants me to carry this task? But why

would the king himself specifically request me? Why the sudden interest?"

"The king has long had his eyes on you, young man," answered Winaq. "You learned a lot at the palace, more than you think. Most of all, you are not corrupted by the greed of politicians. The king wants to know what you are capable of as a leader."

"Why now? Why this? Why not ask me to organize a ball tournament or something I would be more comfortable with?"

"Because, for once, it would be a good opportunity for you to show your skills other than on a ball court. Consider it as a challenge, and as an honor. These appointments are usually reserved for nobles."

"Exactly! Nobles! Not me. This is a task for people who aspire to climb higher on society's political ladder. The ones who want to make a name for themselves. The ones who want to be recognized by their peers. The ones who see themselves amongst the council. No offense, but I have no desire to mingle with the political crowd."

"Then don't do it to impress the wealthy. Do it to help the people who would pray there every day. They need your help."

It had been enough to convince him.

A small temple located on the outskirt of the city had long been in need of repairs. It was a modest shrine dedicated to Ah Mucen Cab, patron god of honey and beekeeping, a deity of whom Balam had never been particularly knowledgeable. As one of the several dozen minor deities in the Mayan pantheon, Ah Mucen Cab was mostly popular in the northern states where the majority of honey producers lived.

For years now, northerners living in the neighborhood had been complaining about the lack of proper facilities where they could conduct offerings to the honey god, claiming the old temple no longer suited their needs. After postponing the issue several times, the council had finally agreed not only to repair the shrine but, to the delight of all worshippers, to also add an adjoining altar.

When Balam first visited the site, he was surprised at how badly the temple was indeed in desperate need of repairs. Years of wind, rain and storms had left their mark on the old structure. The bright crimson walls had lost their color. The once magnificent bee god mural adorning the roof comb was now faded and unreadable. Birds took dominion over the place, building nests within the roof beams. The floors were littered with excrements and the irrigation trench surrounding the building was filled with dirt and muck, preventing proper drainage during the wet season. As a result, nasty yellow marks now stained the bottom of the walls while a foul moldy smell had settled inside the chamber.

Anxious to help the local worshippers, Balam had quickly devised a project schedule covering everything from the temple renovation to the altar construction. The assignment was fairly simple. Still, with the latest problems befalling him, he was once again wondering if he was the right person for the job.

He was silently walking across the site, thinking about how he could re-organize and optimize his efforts when a familiar voice interrupted his thoughts.

"Well, well, well! Here you are!"

"Tupac!" he answered with a big smile as he saw the Tollàn young man approaching. "What brings you out so far away from the city center?"

"I wanted to see for myself why my friend has been neglecting me for the past month," he replied in Mayan, looking around. "No one has seen you at the palace lately."

Balam nodded and marveled at how Tupac's vocabulary had improved since his arrival, a few months ago. Up until the renovation assignment, the two boys made a point of seeing each other practically every day for language lessons and ball game practices. The immersion had been beneficial. Tupac was now perfectly fluent in Mayan and speaking without any noticeable accent, while Balam, although struggling with the more complicated words, was comfortably functional in Tollàn.

"I am sorry," apologized the Mayan. "Every day, I wake up before sunrise and hurry here, only to get back to my apartment long after dark, usually exhausted. Sometimes I don't even make it back home. Two nights ago I ended up sleeping here, lying against the outside wall. Unfortunately, I don't have time to hang around friends or play ball anymore."

Tupac looked at him with a reproachful look.

"So, your little project has been keeping you busy?"

"You could say that."

"You look tired."

"I am overwhelmed!" replied Balam with a slightly raised voice. "I must plan the work, order materials, find workers who are not only competent but also available, dispatch the various tasks, and oversee the whole process!"

"You must find your own workers?"

"It's part of my duties since I am the one who schedules the various jobs requiring different specialties. And then I must deal with all of the unexpected situations," continued Balam. "For example, one of my workers has been sick for a few days, and the limestone blocks delivery I was expecting three days ago has been delayed. In the meantime, the stucco artisan is scheduled to start before the end of the month. Now, that might not be possible anymore since the structure won't be ready for him. So I'll probably have to reschedule him later. However, another coordinator also needs him for the Chaak temple and his project has priority over mine. My window of opportunity is rapidly vanishing.

If I lose him, I'll have to find someone else. It's absolutely mind boggling!"

Balam stopped, exhausted after having spoken all of his frustrations in a single breath. He looked at Tupac in search of some sort of approval or support.

Instead, his friend only started laughing.

"What?" asked Balam in Tollàn, shocked by the unexpected reaction. "What's so funny?"

"You sound so important!" laughed Tupac, who also switched to his own native language.

Balam looked at him for an instant, startled. A smile suddenly appeared on his face, baring his teeth. Then they both laughed together.

"Now please, show me everything," asked the young Tollàn.

Balam wiped the tears off his face and turned around towards the modest temple built atop a low platform. As much as he had laughed just an instant ago, he now suddenly felt completely discouraged. The site seemed worse now than it did before he started the renovations.

"First, we got rid of all the bushes and plants growing all over the grounds. Next, we cleaned the water drainage trench and exposed the pyramid's foundations. Fortunately, it was still in fairly good condition. You can see the exterior walls have been stripped down to the stucco layer. Eventually, a new coat of red paint will be applied everywhere but first, we must repair the damages," he explained, pointing at a section where the underlying limestone structure was exposed through the flaking stucco.

"I have two men currently performing repairs on the exterior." He nodded towards two workers dressed in plain cotton loin cloths and worn out sandals. Both were patching holes and resurfacing the southern wall with a fresh mixture of stucco.

"Look at this wall here," he said, as he slid his fingers along the impeccable surface. "It is basically ready for the final coating."

"Mmmm," said Tupac, as he admired the smooth wall surface. "I thought you said the stucco artisan was only scheduled to start much later?"

"He is," replied Balam, lowering his voice. "These two are plain workers, sufficiently skilled for patching walls but for delicate work, well... you know."

He grimaced.

"The artisan I was referring to is a real sculptor, a talented artist who will carve elaborate masks on each side of the entrance."

Tupac nodded, curiously looking around. "What about the interior walls?"

Balam moved towards the entrance.

"Fortunately, the roof has never leaked so the painted murals covering the inside surfaces remained well protected from the weather. The stain marks and mold spots on the bottom have been cleaned out. Only minimal touch ups on the murals are now required. I have someone coming today for their restoration." A look of concern appeared on his face. "Actually, he should have been here by now."

"I see. Apparently, things are going fairly well. So what's all the panic about?"

Balam let out a sigh and switched back to Mayan.

"The temple is progressing very well indeed. It's with the altar platform that I have some problems."

"You're building a platform for the altar?"

"Yes, although not a big one. No more than three steps high. Still, I wanted to give the altar some importance." He pointed beside the temple towards an unfinished limestone foundation.

"We had to bring down two large trees to clear the area.

The stumps were much more difficult to remove than expected. We've finally managed to pull them out. Then we leveled off the ground, filled the area with gravel, and started working on the altar's foundation. You can see that part of the first stone layer is already in place. Unfortunately, I had to put everything on hold and return my workers home because I have no more limestone blocks."

"You miscalculated?"

"No, they stopped being delivered!"

"Really? Do you know why?"

"Apparently, there has been an epidemic amongst the quarry workers. I was told several fell very ill, and a few even died. While things are supposedly better now, all orders have been delayed, and the most prestigious projects have taken priority over minor upgrades. Still, I was promised I would receive the necessary blocks soon. I only have two other layers to put down."

Tupac was walking around the site, looking at everything around him.

"When is this project due?"

"I must have everything completed before the planting season, otherwise I will lose the entire workforce and the temple will stay as it stands for another year."

Tupac wandered around a little more, genuinely intrigued by the construction techniques. "This is a great project," he finally said. "And I thought you were avoiding me because you were spending all of your free time with our priestess. What's here name again? Xochitl?"

Balam blushed at the mention of her name, and he looked away.

"Come on! Tell me about her!" he asked in Tollàn.

"There really isn't much to say. We bumped into each other a few times since our first meeting. Nothing more."

"Nothing more? Then why do your eyes lit up every time

someone mentions her name?" Tupac asked teasingly.

Balam smiled, but did not answer. He really liked the young woman. Since the day they'd met, her beautiful face was always on his mind. Now and then he would find himself smiling for no reason, wondering where she was, what she was doing. He spent the better part of his time thinking about her, looking for an excuse to walk past the Tollàn pyramid in the hope of seeing her.

Usually she would be nowhere in sight, and he would feel like an idiot for wasting his time. Sometimes, luck would be on his side, and their paths would cross. His heart then bursted with joy and a simple smile from her would fill him with happiness for an entire day. There were times when she would even stop long enough to exchange a few words, or even walk with him a little. Unfortunately, those were always fleeting moments, irremediably too short and leaving him hoping for more.

"What?" asked Tupac, sensing his friend was hiding something from him. "What is it?"

"She agreed to meet me at the ceiba tree," Balam answered shyly. "Tomorrow evening."

"Congratulations!" Tupac gently punched him on the shoulder. "You must be so nervous!"

"I'm terrified. What if she doesn't like me? Or what if she's so bored she never wants to see me again?"

"How is it like when you two talk together?"

Balam absently stared before him and smiled.

"It's like nothing I've ever felt. It's as if we could talk for entire days and always we'd have something more to say, like we have some sort of connection I can't explain. Like time could stop and still it would pass too quickly."

"Then you should be fine. Worst case, it will be the longest evening of her life, and you will never see her again. There are plenty of girls out there you know!"

Somehow, Balam did not find that thought very

comforting. He'd never met anyone like Xochitl. He so wanted to impress her. So wanted her to see who he really was. So wanted her to find him interesting.

"Is there anything I should know?" he asked.

Tupac looked at him with a puzzled look.

"I mean, she is Tollàn. She is a priestess of your feathered god. What should I expect? The only other Tollàn I know is you. She seems so..." He looked down as he searched for the proper word. "She seems so surreal to me. So out of reach. Are Tollàn priestesses even allowed this kind of relationship?"

Tupac laughed at his friend's obviously enamored state. "You are so pathetic Balam! Xochitl's heart and blood might belong to Quetzalcoátl, but her flesh and soul belong to her, and her only. Otherwise, what would be the value of sacrifice if life already belonged to the divine? Rest assured, and enjoy your date. She is free to go as she pleases. Tollàn gods will not strike you down."

Balam shuddered.

"Hey, listen! Join me on the ball court later!" proposed Tupac enthusiastically. "That would put your mind on something else!"

"I can't!" answered Balam, shaking his head in disappointment. "I have too many things to do here!"

"Come on! I've improved so much since last month! You really have to see me! I bet I might even stand a chance to win for once!"

"I wish I could. I so wish I could!"

He really did. Unfortunately, he had so little time on his hands to practice lately, unlike Tupac who, besides having a natural talent for the game, had been playing every single day. Since his arrival, the Tollàn young man had become a fierce player, a feared opponent worthy of respect. At this rate, Balam wondered how much longer it would be before Tupac truly outshined him.

"Too bad," answered the Tollàn boy as he raised his shoulders. "I really wanted to show you my new moves."

"Maybe in a couple of days. If the limestone blocks don't arrive, I'll be idle anyway."

"As you wish. In the meantime, I suppose I'll just have to hang around the practice courts and find another partner. There is usually always someone waiting there for a match, although they are rarely as good as you are. Not much of a challenge anymore."

"Enjoy yourself," Balam replied with a little jealousy. "Will you have something to eat before you go? I should have some bread and honey somewhere."

"With pleasure."

"Make yourself at ease. I'll be back in a moment."

Tupac looked for a comfortable place to wait in the shade. As he sat on the ground, resting against the temple's wall, the Tollàn was startled by a voice calling him.

"Tupac!"

He jumped straight back to his feet, surprised, as Spearthrower Owl walked onto the renovation site.

"Uncle! Lord! We haven't seen you in two months. Since when have you been back in Mutul?"

"I just returned late last night," answered the man in the language of Tollàn.

"How was your trip?"

A grin appeared on the foreigner's face.

"Productive, my young nephew," he answered. "Very productive. Come with me. There is a lot to discuss."

DEMONS OF THE DEEP

Great Jaguar Paw silently stared at his own reflection over the reservoir's surface. He raised his hand towards his creased forehead, slowly ran a finger over his drooping eyelids, and realized just how much he'd aged lately. Apparently, years of kingship and worries had taken its toll on his body.

As if to test himself, he clenched his fingers into a fist and squeezed until his shortly trimmed fingernails painfully dug into the flesh. There was still strength in his forearms, but while his hands could still hold a spear, his shoulders had lost some of their former bulkiness, and his belly had gone limp. Unlike his old friend Kabrak'an, he did not manage to stay physically fit during the past seasons, and he silently cursed the many obligations which kept him closer to the acropolis than to the ball court or even to the border.

In his youth he'd often been sent into battle, and he'd even managed to bring a few enemy warriors back to the sacrificial stone. His body still carried the captor's tattoos he was awarded for his accomplishments, although he often wondered if his combat experience was genuine, or if it was somehow arranged to heighten his reputation before the population. It was important for a king to be seen as a strong man, both in battle and on the ball court.

As his reputation as a great leader grew stronger, the council had allowed him less and less direct exposure to danger, and he now often silently envied the freedom enjoyed by his warrior friend.

As the king dwelled upon his past a bird flew right by him, came to rest over the water, and flapped its wings frantically for a moment. The furious beating sent water droplets flying in all directions. Refreshed from the day's heat, it then abruptly took off, leaving a series of concentric ripples traveling along the reservoir's surface.

Great Jaguar Paw followed the bird as it faded in the distance, marveling at the wonder of flight. He then refocused his attention to the recipients next to him. A simple, unadorned orange pottery bowl containing dried maize kernels, and a calabash gourd filled with a dark and thick liquid.

With a wave of the hand he brushed away an insect buzzing around the gourd and slowly grabbed a handful of maize kernels, which he randomly sprinkled all around him to create an invisible protective barrier. He then picked up the calabash gourd and raised it towards the sky. With the hot rays of the midday sun caressing his face, he recited a prayer, brought the gourd to his lips and took a sip.

The king cringed as the thick liquid ran down his throat. With the bitter taste still present in his mouth, he ceremoniously poured the remaining sacred beverage of balché, cocoa and honey into the water. In a swift movement, he then picked up a stingray spine, pierced his elbow, and spilled a few drops of his own blood into the reservoir. With an intense curiosity he watched as the blood droplets blended into the dark waters, slowly dissipating into nothingness, forever becoming an indissociable part of the basin itself.

Great Jaguar Paw suddenly recalled a time when Icoquih, his daughter, was no more than four or five years old.

"Please," she had begged. "May I please witness your ceremony father? I promise I will sit and remain silent. I promise I won't say a single word!"

He'd agreed to let her watch the small offering as long as she promised, once again, to remain perfectly still and silent. It was time, after all, for her to start learning about religious matters, although he should have known that a four year old's curiosity overcame almost anything, and especially promises forgotten the instant they were spoken.

"Why do you sacrifice your blood to the reservoir?" she'd asked in her sweet innocent voice, to which Great Jaguar Paw could not help but smile. "Is it because of the demons living in the deep?"

"Do you know what lies down there, below the water's surface?"

There was no hesitation in her voice.

"The underworld," she immediately answered.

"This basin is a portal to the watery lower levels of the world. It leads directly to the domain of the death lords and their demons. Anyone foolish enough to jump in would inevitably reach their realm of death and suffering."

"Father, if we can travel down there, what prevents them from using the same passage to reach us?"

"Nothing at all, which is exactly why I regularly come here to perform this ceremony."

"So you sacrifice your blood to keep the death lords from hurting us?"

"I sacrifice my blood to sustain them, to prevent them from crossing over to our plane of existence for nourishment. Yes, I sacrifice my blood to keep all of us safe."

She looked at the dark water with a pensive look.

"Then we must fill the basin with earth!" she proclaimed. "We must block the passage!"

Great Jaguar Paw laughed, and gently caressed her cheek with the back of his hand.

"There are several passages in this world they could use

to reach us," he explained. "If we block this one, they will only come through another. Like it or not, the gods are part of this world, so we must learn to coexist with them. If you regularly say your prayers, perform your sacrifices, and show thankfulness and gratitude for all that has been given to us, then even the most evil ones will not harm you. They might even help you. Do not fear this reservoir, child. While it links us to the underworld, it also provides our people with water during the dry season, and so we should be grateful."

She nodded in understanding.

After that day, and at her own request, the young princess started spending a lot of time with the priests, everyday becoming more and more knowledgeable of their religious teachings.

Today, Icoquih was a grown woman, ready to take his place.

If only she could have been a boy.

Great Jaguar Paw returned his attention to the reservoir, and realized just how much the water level had gone down since the beginning of the dry season.

"It has been particularly hot lately," said Winaq, guessing the king's thoughts. The old counselor was standing in the shade, a few steps behind, with his hands behind his back. "Fortunately, there is still plenty of water left. Soon, the afternoon skies will darken, and rain will pour from the heavens, marking the beginning of a new cycle. The fields will be irrigated, the bajos will swell with water, and the basins will once again fill in preparation for next year."

"Blessed are these sacred pools which keep us from thirst."

Winaq nodded silently.

"I hear lord Spearthrower Owl is back in Mutul," added Great Jaguar Paw after a long moment.

"He has reappeared amongst us as swiftly as he had disappeared barely a few months ago. Sometime around the solstice, if I remember correctly."

"He might come and go without being seen, but his absence did not go unnoticed. Apparently, neither did his return."

"Nor his whereabouts, K'uhul Ahau. He was seen in several southern states. Iximche. Xukpi. Waxak Mo'."

"Obsidian traders," said Great Jaguar Paw.

"All of them. He was reported meeting with several influent members of the south. We know he was received in private by K'inich Wuk Muwaan, king of Waxak Mo'."

"It is as you feared, old friend. Spearthrower Owl is most displeased at our situation with Sian K'aan. He has traveled to our most important suppliers. He has likely shared his discontent with them, and who knows what else."

"He is a foreigner ahau. Their competition. It is surprising they've even received him at all."

"Still, I understand why they would talk to him. With our little neighborly war, we've given them a common cause. We've made them allies against the Mutul problem. Now that black market is on the rise, matters will only get worse."

Winaq raised his eyebrows.

"Kabrak'an came back from the border. Apparently, Siyah Kak has paid him a visit after recovering stolen goods in the jungle. Not only are merchants attacked, but now our customers themselves are driven away towards smugglers who re-sell them the very goods destined to our market stalls, depriving our trade partners of their rightful profits."

The king explained every detail of the encounter between the warlord and the nacom.

"Siyah Kak is a dangerous animal," replied Winaq.

"While he does have a fiery temper, he acts on my

command. I am the one who asked him to patrol beyond our land. He will track down the smugglers."

"Shouldn't Kabrak'an take care of this matter?"

"Kabrak'an's duty is to keep our borders safe, and he is already severely undermanned. I cannot lay this additional burden over his shoulders. No, Siyah Kak will do it. Besides, he has the perfect temper for this kind of duty."

"Track down the enemy? Perhaps. But can we control him? He is a wild beast!" exclaimed Winaq.

"He has always served us well, has he not? I'll admit to be sometimes torn as to what I should do," he added. "I argue with myself during entire nights, for I do not always entirely approve of his methods, but what else can we do? War is coming to us on all fronts."

He lowered his voice.

"Winaq, the southern states are losing money. Their kings are losing profit. So tell me, why wouldn't they support Spearthrower Owl? Or worse. Why wouldn't they join their forces and attack us?"

The king took a deep breath, and looked at his counselor in the eyes.

"Am I losing control Winaq? Will this war become my downfall?"

"You are not alone, K'uhul Ahau. The northern and eastern states support you."

"I know, it is the western states that worry me. Lakam Ha should side with me, but Pa' Chan? I do not know. And what about my people? Who will they support?"

"The population supports you, K'uhul Ahau. They know you will do everything possible to protect them."

"Do they? Are my actions really aimed at stopping this war? Am I truly dedicated to restoring peace and stability in this region? What is the role of a king if not to protect his land and his people from harm?"

The king closed his fist.

"I could crush Sian K'aan in a single day if I wanted to. I could listen to Siyah Kak and to most of my ahauob. I could send Kabrak'an and his troops against our foe. Most of them would return with prisoners and fresh tattoos, leaving nothing but ashes and graves behind them. I could end it all right now and my people would love me for it, but that would mean denying all that I believe in, and all that my ancestors have always fought for. It would deny the very essence of what makes me the K'uhul Ahau, the Divine Ruler."

He leaned back.

"Four times the gods have created and destroyed humanity. It took them four trials before finally managing to create the perfect world. If I destroy Sian K'aan today, I upset the delicate balance so carefully established by the gods, and who knows where that could send us. I have no right to do so. Do you understand my conflict?"

"It doesn't have to end with a heap of decapitated bodies," replied Winaq. "Defeat their army. Overtake their king. Bring an end to their royal lineage, and rule over both kingdoms."

"Rule over their defeated people as a tyrant?"

"Rule over them as a victorious king! They attack our people, they steal our crops. Do they really deserve any better?"

Great Jaguar Paw stared him in the eyes.

"You feel this way because you are only seeing this conflict from our point of view. Did it ever occur to you that in fact, *we* might be the ones who are condemnable?"

"Ahau?"

"For generations, both of our cities have lived in peace. There was plenty of food for everyone, and modest trading provided us with basic necessities such as salt and cotton. Then outsiders came with their faraway goods and riches and while Sian K'aan opted to keep to their traditional ways, we started trading with the foreigners. We prospered as our people slowly grew accustomed to luxurious items. We grew beyond our borders, ever appropriating ourselves more and more farmland. Every year we harvest deeper into their ancestral hunting grounds, driving the animals further away. Slowly but surely, we are chocking our neighbors, strangling their traditional society with our modern ways. Today, we ask ourselves why they must pillage our borders to ensure their survival? Did we not force them down this inevitable path?"

He looked at the deep blue sky.

"You see, I cannot convince myself they deserve anything less than a fair chance."

Winaq nodded. "In that case, what option do we have left, K'uhul Ahau?"

The king turned back towards the reservoir. He stared at the black water, and wondered what demons lurked in the depths.

"There is one last hope, my friend. There is one last course of action upon which I put all my faith to end this war peacefully."

And if I fail, he thought, *then and only then will I take the necessary actions to protect my people and destroy their city. The blood of Sian K'aan would then be on my hands and for that, surely, the demons will come and drag me down to my doom.*

FLOWERS ON
THE GROUND

Balam's nervousness was rapidly increasing as he made his way towards the giant ceiba tree. His stomach was so tight he hadn't been able to eat anything all day, and his heart was pounding faster and harder than it had ever done before. It was all nonsense, he thought, how she had totally bewitched him. Ever since that day when they first met at the pyramid's summit he didn't sleep well, he ate very little, and he often lacked concentration as his mind was constantly focused on one single thing.

Her.

He barely knew the young priestess yet, for some reason, he felt like he could tell her anything. He wanted to tell her everything about him as much as he wanted to know everything about her. He wanted to share his dreams with her, his feelings, and the desires buried deep within him, although he was debating whether or not it was wise to let her know how he felt, how he wanted to spend time with her.

Is it too early? he thought. *Would it only scare her away? Maybe I should wait and give her the chance to know me better, let things follow their course. But then, would she think I am not interested? What if she meets someone else, not knowing how much I care for her?*

He'd spent the entire day trying to imagine different conversation topics, struggling to come up with subjects that would make him look interesting in her eyes. She had agreed to this date and now he felt as if it was his only chance to impress her, to make her want to see him again.

Unfortunately, he had no idea how.

You want to know the secret to a girl's heart? You must make her laugh, Tupac had once told him. *Once you make a girl laugh, she's pretty much yours!*

Somehow, he doubted his friend's wisdom. Besides, he was never one to be funny.

He washed himself clean and put on his most beautiful clothes, along with a brand new pair of sandals. He also wore his nicest jade pendant, and cleverly attached his long dark hair in a fancy way subtly letting his ballplayer tattoo show. He was particularly proud of the tattoo he'd been awarded after a well-deserved victory over the visiting champion of Pa' Chan. Located on his neck, below his right ear, the tattoo marked him as one of the greatest ballplayers of the region.

Unable to further contain himself he finally headed out, still undecided whether or not to tell her how he felt, hoping she might give him a hint that would make his decision obvious in one way or the other. At least, after hours of struggling and rephrasing, he came up with what he believed was a great opening line.

As he approached the sacred tree, all of his thoughts suddenly got confused. His mind went totally blank, and he couldn't remember anything of the perfect speech he'd composed. He unconsciously slowed down, desperately trying to remember the words and ideas he wanted to discuss.

Nothing came forth.

Facing this total absentmindedness his heart sunk and his legs felt weak as he came to realize the only logical conclusion.

He would soon look like a complete idiot.

There was barely anyone under the tree when Balam arrived. He quickly scanned around for her and settled under the tree's lengthening shade after realizing she hadn't arrived yet. He was, after all, a little early. So he sat down, terribly excited and frightened at the same time. Deep within, part of him almost wished she wouldn't show up to let him better prepare himself.

As he finally saw her approaching in the distance, all fear disappeared and happiness filled him. She was wearing her simple and unadorned priestess robe. Her hair, hanging loose, was gently flowing in the wind. Her pace looked relaxed. There was a peaceful orange glow about her in the evening light of the setting sun.

She is so beautiful, Balam thought, and he immediately forgot about everything that was not her.

"Good evening," Xochitl said with a smile as she walked up to him.

"Good evening," replied Balam with the slightest stutter. He subtly cleared his throat. "You look ... very pretty."

He almost said gorgeous.

"Thank you. You look very nice yourself."

Balam blushed at the compliment.

"So this is the famous ceiba tree," she added looking around. "I don't believe I have ever seen a tree so big in my entire life!"

"This is it. Our most popular meeting point. We usually regroup here before heading out. Or sometimes we just sit in the shade and let the day go by, although I haven't had much time for that lately."

"Your project is still keeping you very busy?"

Balam smiled. He loved her foreign accent, and he found the subtle scent of vanilla accompanying her intoxicating.

"It is. We had a few problems with materials delivery, but we've managed to work around them. Things are now moving back into place. Hopefully, we will complete the renovation in time, before the planting season."

"Please, tell me all about it!"

She seemed genuinely interested so Balam gave her all the latest developments, although he feared boring her with mundane discussions. If she was bored she hid it well, for she listened intently and smiled all along.

"And you? How was your day?" he then asked clumsily.

"Oh, me?" she said, trying to hide her disappointment. She needed a change of mind, and would have much preferred not to discuss the temple activities. Still, she answered the question.

"Well, you know. Pretty much the usual. Rituals. Prayers. Offerings. The gods are accustomed to certain protocols, so we do the necessary to keep them happy. Our gods do not enjoy originality."

In fact, life at the temple was horrible. The high priest gave her very little liberty with regards to her whereabouts and activities. She was kept to a very strict code of conduct, and constantly reminded about the severe consequences of endangering the secret of the illegal human sacrifices they were forced to perform under Spearthrower Owl's orders. Unfortunately, she could not tell him that.

Balam sensed her discomfort, and immediately changed the subject.

"Would you like to see some of our finest art?" he asked. "The temple of the goddess Ixchel is reputed for being one of the most beautiful in the entire Mayan land. I thought, maybe, we could visit it together?"

"I heard about the temple. I would very much like to see it," she answered happily. Xochitl then opened her arms. "All I own is this priestess robe. As a foreigner, I fear insulting your goddess."

"Rest assured, Ixchel welcomes everyone. Mothers, fathers, children, rich, poor, and even Tollàn priestesses.

She will not be offended by your presence nor by your attire."

They left the tree and its colonies of chattering birds, and slowly started walking towards the temple. On their way, they talked about their youths, their hopes, their dreams. Despite Balam's earlier fears conversation came very easily, naturally flowing from one subject to another. The more they talked, the more he realized just how much they had in common.

Xochitl was born in a small village near Tollàn. After the tragic death of her parents, she was brought to the temple and raised by the priests, who provided her with food and shelter. Since then, she'd devoted her life to the Tollàn deities.

She had no say in the decision which sent her in Mutul, although she welcomed the opportunity to see different cultures and meet new people. So far, reality hadn't met her expectations as her life was now, more than ever, mostly one of seclusion and disappointment. Meeting Balam, however, was the proof that one must never lose hope. Now that she had someone to share her thoughts with, she was once again hopeful about the future.

Before they knew it, they had traveled halfway across the city and reached their destination.

Not unlike the great majority of temples in the Mayan world, the Ixchel temple consisted of a small, four-sided crimson structure mounted atop a small stepped pyramid. One thing, however, immediately surprised Xochitl at their arrival. The grounds surrounding the temple were covered with countless offerings of food, clothes and flowers, bringing an indescribable variety of colors and smells to the otherwise common sight.

"This place is beautiful," she exclaimed.

"Ixchel the Benevolent has many faces," Balam explained. "First and foremost, she is a goddess of healing.

She is also the nurturing goddess of birth, watching over women during pregnancy and child birth. Every day people come here to offer prayers, food, and incense. She is beloved above all other deities."

Balam looked at Xochitl.

"Come, let's get closer."

He shyly offered his hand. To his astonishment, she reached out to him, and interlaced her fingers within his. He marveled at how her hand felt so light and delicate. Hand in hand, they made their way towards the temple, jumping from one bare spot of earth to another, taking care to avoid the many offerings on the ground.

"This place smells wonderful," she remarked.

"It's the flowers. Here, wait."

He bent down and grabbed a beautiful orchid, which he carefully set in her hair.

"Are you not stealing from your goddess?"

"She will understand. Besides, there are way too many flowers out here for one single woman."

Her eyes glowed, and they both moved forward. As they reached the pyramid, Balam dropped a few kakaw into a small pottery vessel lying on the first stair. The cocoa beans joined a few others at the bottom of the bowl.

"An offering to the goddess?" she asked.

"An offering to the poor."

He gestured all around.

"How long do you think all of this will stay here? As soon as night falls, the poor will come and grab everything. For most, it will be their only meal of the day. Hopefully, this money can help someone."

"They take from the temple without punishment?"

"Officially, these goods are offerings to the goddess, but since Ixchel gives back to the people the thefts are overlooked. In a way, it all comes down to the same thing, does it not? Besides, it keeps the grounds clean. This place will once again be packed with food and flowers by midday tomorrow."

She smiled at the wisdom of the custom.

They climbed the six stairs leading to the summit and walked inside the temple. There, Xochitl stopped in awe at the beauty of the murals surrounding her.

The four walls were entirely covered, from floor to ceiling, with a series of beautiful red and black paintings depicting the various legends of Ixchel.

In the first scene on the left she was shown with her husband K'inich Ahau, the sun god. In another, this one bordered by skulls and symbols of death, she was the mighty warrior goddess, depicted with a serpent on her head and holding a spear within her clawed fingers while heaps of defeated enemies surrounded her.

In the center she was once again the beloved mother of medicine and healing while on the right she was represented with Chaak, the rain god, providing water to the world. Always, the goddess was beautifully dressed in an elaborate arrangement of feathers and jewelry.

Open minded to this foreign culture, Xochitl listened to every description provided by her companion, thoroughly enjoying Balam's company. She listened as he talked about Itzamnà and the creation of the world, and as he described how Chaak, accompanied by Ixchel, had descended from the sky to split the earth with his mighty axe, thereby allowing maize to grow from the land.

After the visit was completed they both walked to the Loq' Ej reservoir where, earlier, Balam had carefully hidden a meal of beans and rabbit stew sweetened in a honey sauce. The rabbit was fresh, for he had hunted it himself on the very same morning.

They ate while once again sharing numerous stories, although he later couldn't remember the subjects they had discussed. In fact, he couldn't recall anything other than having a great time, and when the meal was over, they both laid on their backs, bellies full, staring at the heavens.

The sky was totally black by then. Before their eyes shined thousands of stars, their beauty only outmatched by the purity and brightness of the moon silently ruling over the night.

"There rests Ixchel tonight," said Balam. "Comfortably sitting on the crescent of the moon. She is watching over us. Watching over a world who will soon fall asleep below her."

"The moon goddess," whispered Xochitl. "To us, she is Coyolxauqui."

"Coyolxauqui," he repeated. "Tell me, do you also see the moon and the stars from your home?"

The priestess laughed, and Balam thought about Tupac's earlier comment.

"Do we also see the moon in Tollàn? Of course we do!"

"But Tollàn is so far away. Does she look the same, or is she different?"

"I see what you mean," she said, still giggling. "You know, I was also afraid she would look different here, far away from home. Fortunately, she is exactly the same. Majestic amongst the stars. In our stories, Coyolxauqui was killed and decapitated by Huitzilopochtli, the sun god, who then threw her head high up in the sky. And so she became the moon, the guardian of the night."

She paused a few seconds. "Whenever I feel lonely, I come out at night so we can both share in our loneliness."

Balam looked at the moon, and he could only guess at how lonely it must really feel to slowly travel across the sky, night after night, for eternity.

"This evening is perfect," Xochitl added.

Balam simply smiled, without answering. There was no need for words now as, sometimes, there could be no greater complicity than the one experienced during a comfortable moment of silence. He'd never experienced such a feeling before, and he simply wished this instant could last forever.

"The month ends in two days," he finally added in the most serious tone. "The Wayeb will soon be here."

"The Wayeb, you mean the five unlucky days at the end of your calendar?"

"Yes. It is a dark period during which the spirits of the dead roam the land, looking for innocent souls to bring back with them."

"I heard the stories. Is it really that dangerous?"

"Most of us barely leave our homes out of fear for our lives. You must be careful."

"You need not to worry for me. I am a priestess of Quetzalcoátl. He will protect me from harm, if he so desires."

"Forgive me, but I do not trust your feathered snake god. He is not familiar with the treacheries and maliciousness of our death lords."

"He is a great warrior god," she answered, grabbing his hand in an effort to ease his concerns. "I trust him with my life."

"Still," Balam said, unsure. "Stay away from water. It connects to the underworld. Refrain from long, unnecessary outings. And take this."

He handed her a small wooden idol pendant.

"It will protect you."

Xochitl took the idol in her hand and observed it carefully. It seemed to be carved in the image of a man with a large ear of corn over his head, although it was hard to tell since the pendant's surfaces were almost worn smooth after years of handling.

"Who is he?"

"Ah Mun, my patron god. He is the god of maize. He is also a great ballplayer. This pendant has been with me since my childhood. All of these years, it kept me from harm. It will do the same for you.”

“And why should your god protect me? A Tollàn?”

Balam showed her the fresh bloodletting wound on his own elbow.

“Because I asked him to,” he answered.

Without another word, she carefully attached the pendant around her neck, and rewarded him with the most beautiful smile he’d ever seen.

A smile that would haunt him for the rest of his life.

TREASON

"Lasting only five days, Wayeb is the shortest of the nineteen Mayan months. They are five nameless days of fear. A time when all barriers between the realm of death and our plane of existence are shattered, allowing evil-intended spirits and long deceased ancestors to roam the land in search of revenge or redemption for past injustices. A time of terror, during which every sensible Mayan barricaded himself within the relative safety of his home, surrounded by protective charms and idols representing benevolent deities."

"There are rules to keep one's family safe, guidelines to improve the odds of surviving these five days. For all who can endure it, fasting is the safest way to keep evil spirits at bay. For the others, only bread and maize gruel is allowed, as all other food will turn tasteless. Alcoholic beverages are strictly forbidden, and so are bathing and cleaning. Generally speaking, any forms of contact with water shall be religiously avoided in the fear of providing the dark spirits with a means of accessing one's soul."

Excerpt from "The Wayeb"
Mutul library, Calendar and Festivals section
Dated 10 Chuwen, 20 Kumk'u

Mutul was eerily silent and lifeless on this third day of the nineteenth and last month of the year, the unlucky month of Wayeb. The streets were deserted. The temples were empty. Even the usually crowded marketplace now bathed in a strange and desolate silence. There were no vibrantly colored textiles displayed over the stands. No patrons in search of goods, and the air was devoid of the heartwarming smell of cooking meals. It was as though the entire city had suddenly been abandoned by its people, as if the world had inexplicably returned to a time before the creation of mankind.

But the market was not totally lifeless.

There were still birds singing in the trees, monkeys wandering around tables in search of discarded leftovers, and a single cloaked figure slowly moving throughout the abandoned streets, cautiously making its way between the empty stalls. The dark hood covering the man's head hid all facial features from the light.

Anyone foolish enough to be outside would have easily guessed him to be an accomplished hunter. Or, more likely, a warrior. The stealth in his step told a lot about his nature. There was, however, no need to watch his demeanor to bring the list of this man's potential identity down to a handful of people. Very few Mayans were that tall. Even fewer were that strongly built.

The cloaked individual furtively made his way through the market, his eyes frantically looking around for any threat. His ears were in search of any unusual sound. His nose, on the lookout for the putrefying smell usually accompanying the underworld demons.

So when he picked up the sounds of approaching footsteps, the man immediately jumped behind an empty stand and crouched between two large hemp baskets. There, very much aware of his precarious concealment, he mentally prepared to fight for his own life as his hand slowly reached for a dagger.

His heartbeat shot up in anticipation of the nearby danger, although his own experience quickly overcame the anxiety. Consciously, he slowed his breathing down and relaxed his muscles, preparing for the kill. Then, suddenly, he breathed a sigh of relief as human voices reached his ears.

"I still don't see what I did wrong," complained a man.

"What do you mean?" asked another.

"This is the third year in a row I am selected for Wayeb patrol duties. Obviously the commander hates me for some reason!"

Someone chuckled.

Damn! A patrol, thought the dark figure, silently cursing his ill-fated luck. *Better them than demons I suppose. Still, there are barely any patrols out here today, and I had to stumble across one. If they find me here, I could be in deep trouble. How unlucky!*

He sneered at the irony. *Bad luck during the Wayeb unlucky days. Something to be expected, I suppose.*

He attempted a glance towards the soldiers, only to realize he couldn't possibly get a decent look without compromising his position. By the sounds of their footsteps he counted three men. All of them were most likely armed.

Three against one. With the element of surprise, I could easily overcome them. Their deaths would be blamed on the demons with no one the wiser. If anyone sees me, though, I am good for the sacrificial stone.

His presence in the marketplace was by no means illegal. There was no curfew during the Wayeb, no rules to keep anyone off the streets. Fear was all that kept the Mayans hidden inside their houses. His presence, however, would undoubtedly be considered as highly unusual. Why would someone his rank be outside today, exposing himself to such danger? Above all, why would he be hiding under a cloak? Considering his destination, and more particularly whom he was about to meet with, he much rather preferred his presence to remain unnoticed.

His fingers tightened around the dagger's hilt. As the footsteps inched closer he considered his options, and decided it would definitely be better for him if nobody knew of his whereabouts.

He unsheathed the weapon.

"Maybe the gods would bring you better luck if you performed your sacrifices more regularly," laughed one of the voices.

"Really! You think?" replied another. "Then what about Junam? He never burns any copal incense, let alone pray the gods, and I've never seen him on Wayeb patrol! He is home with his family while I am out here, walking the empty streets, an innocent prey for the first ill-intended spirit to cross our path! No, I tell you, the commander hates me for some reason. I would very much like to know why!"

"I truly couldn't care less about your problems with authority," answered the first man in a more serious tone. "But you are right about one thing. Junam is home with his family while I, also, am out here. I want to stop by my house to check on my wife and children. I want to make sure everyone is safe!"

"Enough!" commanded the third man, who was obviously the patrol leader. "I told you we'd stop by each of your houses later in the day," he said firmly. "We all have families. In the meantime, no matter how scared out of reason you both are, we will do what we are sworn to do, and we will patrol the city streets!"

"Easy for you to say. You have no children!" called one of the other two.

The leader suddenly stopped and turned around, the whistling sound of a spear point answering the challenge.

The patrolmen were arguing barely a few steps away from the cloaked figure who, again, swore under his breath at his misfortune.

Must they really fight here? At this moment?

All this bickering only increased the chances of him being discovered. The hidden man took a shallow breath and risked a discreet look.

From where he was, he could see the legs and torso of the warriors, who were standing much too close to him for comfort. As he'd rightfully guessed, it was a standard three men patrol equipped with regular short spears and daggers, with nothing unusual about them other than the extravagant protective charms they all carried at their waist and around their necks. Maize leaves, basalt amulets, wooden idols, all supposed to protect the men wearing them but in this very instant, the most immediate threat to the two warriors came from their own patrol leader, more specifically from his spear now pointed directly at them.

There was a long moment of silence during which the cloaked man repositioned his fingers around his dagger's hilt. Although he couldn't see much of what was happening, he'd seen more than enough to plan his attack. With their little argument unresolved, now could be the perfect opportunity to jump out and slit their throats.

"You will listen to me very carefully," said the leader to the other two, his spear still pointed towards their faces. "Tell me, without us patrolling the city, how long would it be before our temples and food storages are looted? Or worse. With all the incense-burning going around, what do you suppose would happen should a house catch fire? Especially now, at the end of the dry season? Half the city could burn down before anyone would even raise the alarm!"

The two men looked down.

"We will complete our morning patrol," added the

leader. "Then I promise we will visit your homes and families."

"I still think they should hire foreigners, people who wouldn't mind patrolling the streets during Wayeb," said one of the two others.

The patrol leader sighed and turned around.

"You two would better stop arguing," he added, walking away. "If you think the commander hates you, I have also earned patrol duties for tomorrow, and I just might put in a special request for you two to join me."

There were no more complaints as the steps faded in the distance.

The cloaked man pushed a sigh of relief and waited for the patrol to be long gone before leaving his hiding place. After making certain no one was in the vicinity, he walked out from behind the stand and hurried towards his destination.

Although the near encounter had delayed him a little, he was confident his contact would wait.

Laughter echoed from within the sweat bath's stone walls as members of the Tollàn community enjoyed a good time, totally oblivious to the general sentiment of fear inhabiting the Mayan people.

"The steam is gone! Will someone pour water over the stones!" demanded Spearthrower Owl, comfortably sitting in a corner with a towel wrapped around his hips.

Out of the dozen men surrounding him someone stood up and poured a large cup of water over the burning hearth. A hissing sound accompanied by a thick cloud of steam immediately filled the room as water instantly evaporated on contact with the red hot stones, and everyone expressed a feeling of contentment.

It was a rare treat to be allowed inside the baths. A rare pleasure to sweat out all of the filth and grime which had inevitably accumulated over the body after a long day in the sun, a privilege strictly reserved to the Mayan nobles and, occasionally, to their foreign counterparts.

However, not unlike the rest of the city, the baths were unsurprisingly empty at this particular time of year. Upon their arrival the previous morning, Spearthrower Owl and his Tollàn mob had fired up the hearth and claimed ownership of the complex for the rest of the Wayeb. With two guards posted outside, he had turned the usually restricted area into a nice little private resort for him and his surroundings. All were now sprawled over the benches, enjoying the luxuries of the facilities and exchanging vulgarities while drinking aplenty and although it was still fairly early in the day, most had already consumed more than their fair share of alcohol.

"Ah, nephew!" greeted Spearthrower Owl as the young Tupac suddenly walked in. "Grab a gourd of pulque and come sit next to me!"

The young man stepped inside the room, resisting the urge to pinch his nose under the stench of body odor mixed with alcohol.

"Here you are boy! Prove us you're a man!" said a barely articulate voice as a calabash gourd was forcefully shoved to his face, spilling most of the milk-colored content all over the floor in the process.

The room erupted in laughter.

Tupac stepped back, cautious not to step on any of the obnoxious mobsters lying on the stone floor. He grabbed the drink and headed towards his uncle, all along despising the people around him. They were mostly merchants and traders, all of them ambitious followers, unscrupulous rats who spent most of their time around his uncle in the hope of gaining any little favor which might come their way. He'd talked about this with Spearthrower Owl once. His uncle understood only too well what kind of people they were.

"They are the type who would kneel before me if it suited their personal agenda," he had told him. "Hypocrite bastards, all of them. They would not hesitate to backstab me, or any other man who stands in their way for that matter. They are the type of people you can never trust. Never. They are insects. Parasites."

"So why keep them around?" he'd asked.

"Because even insects can sometimes be useful. There are two things you must learn about insects. How to use them to your advantage. And how to get rid of them when they become a nuisance. Or when they outlive their usefulness. Or when they become a threat."

Tupac had remembered the lesson well. There was a time when he used to admire people who could rule and lead by example, people who could acquire devotion and loyalty through respect and friendship. There were very few such men. Great Jaguar Paw was one of them.

Trust, Tupac quickly realized, was also a major weakness. Loyalties could be changed. Confidence could be misplaced. Besides, friendship would never overcome sheer strength and power in battle. The Mayan king's trust in his followers would soon be his doom, for Great Jaguar Paw's days were now numbered.

Despite laughing earlier, people lying on the floor silently nodded as Tupac reached his uncle. They all knew Spearthrower Owl had the greatest respect for his nephew, and while none of them knew the extent of his plans, many suspected the young man would hold a key role in the events about to happen. Who knew from whose hands the crumbs would fall next? As such, most of them treated the young man with some respect, potentially positioning themselves favorably for a near or far future.

"So?" asked Spearthrower Owl as Tupac sat close to him. "How are things?"

"Quite uneventful," replied Tupac. "Boring, actually. The streets are absolutely deserted. Other than a few foreigners hanging out here and there, everyone is sheltered inside. There is nowhere to buy decent food. Even the ball courts are empty!"

"Good. Learn from their fears; they will serve you well in the future. Above all, enjoy these days of peace and quiet. The upcoming months will be tiring for us all."

"We are moving ahead with our plan then?"

"The events are already in motion, the pieces are slowly falling into place. If all goes well, we'll have another major alliance secured by the end of the morning."

Tupac took a sip of the white, viscous liquid, and made a grimace. Pulque was a fermented beverage made from the sap of a large spiny plant growing in the mountains near Tollàn. The taste reminded him of home, but the drink had obviously spent too much time sitting in the hot air of the sweat baths, a fact most of the noisy drunks around him didn't seem to care about.

"He hasn't shown up yet?" asked the young man as he dismissively placed the gourd on the ground next to him.

"Not yet. Fear not, he will come." Spearthrower Owl rested an arm over his nephew's shoulders. "Tell me. What have you learned from this Balam boy?"

"A lot, uncle. He is teaching me a lot about their culture and their ways. Truly, I have learned a great deal about the Mayans since we've arrived here. He is even helping me with my ball game skills!"

Steam rose from the hissing hearth as someone poured more water over the hot stones. Spearthrower Owl looked at Tupac and started speaking in the Mayan language.

"How is your Mayan?" he asked. His own mastery of the

foreign tongue was flawless.

"Improving, as you can hear. But their writing is so elusive I don't think I can ever learn how to read it!"

"Maybe you could put a little more effort on your reading skills, and a little less on the ball game?"

"Uncle," replied Tupac, still in Mayan. "You know how important the game is to them, much more than it is to us. For religious *and* political reasons. You must believe me on this. Balam is regarded as one of the best at it. If I could master the game, it would bring me both respect and popularity."

"Very well. Still, I really want you to also concentrate on learning as much as you can about every other aspect of their beliefs and society. It is absolutely critical. There is very little time left."

"What about Balam? He has become very fond of one of our priestess. I fear she could tell him a lot about us. Maybe too much."

"It is all irrelevant, young man. In time, we will take care of them. Soon, Great Jaguar Paw will be totally helpless against us. At that point, it won't matter what the boy knows."

He moved closer to him, and whispered into his ear. "Listen, you will soon be king of both Mutul *and* Sian K'aan. Only by thoroughly knowing them will you be able to truly dominate them."

"I still don't understand why you shouldn't rule both kingdoms yourself?"

"The Mayan land is wide, my dear nephew. There will be much to be done after Mutul is ours to fulfill our king's thirst for power, more kingdoms to subdue. Having you in control here will give me the perfect foothold to anchor our invasion. We are years away from our goal. In the meantime, do not despair. The day will come. We will play our part, and so is the man coming here today."

Tupac nodded, as drops of sweat slowly trickled down his back. He found the humidity terribly uncomfortable.

"My lord," interrupted a guard standing at the entrance.

Spearthrower Owl looked at him.

"He has arrived."

Silence immediately fell inside the room.

"Excellent! Let him in," he ordered in Tollàn.

"My lord," replied the guard. "He won't let me search him."

The Tollàn lord grinned. "Of course he won't, he is no fool. It is why people like me and him survive. Let him in, but stay within arm's reach."

"As you wish."

"And open your eyes," he added. "This man could kill you in a heartbeat."

The guard nodded, and walked out.

"Finally," murmured Spearthrower Owl. "Another piece falls into place."

Tupac anxiously straightened up. He did not share his uncle's confidence in the outcome of this little meeting. He, also, knew the reputation of the man who was about to walk in.

An instant later, the room darkened as a large shadow appeared in the middle of the archway's bright opening, blocking all sunlight from coming in.

Despite the heat, Tupac felt a shiver run down his spine. Everyone nervously watched as the mysterious cloaked figure slowly approached Spearthrower Owl's position. There was no more laughter amongst the intoxicated crowd. Only a revered silence.

The Tollàn lord let the man reach the center of the room and raised his hand, clearly implying the newcomer had come close enough. The guard accompanying him stopped a single step behind. One did not reach Spearthrower Owl's position without being cautious, so he judged it was probably wiser to keep the man out of immediate striking distance, no matter how confident he was. The guard, standing much too close, was obviously doomed should the cloaked figure decide to strike, but the delay might give Spearthrower Owl enough time to save his own life.

Maybe.

The man stopped in the middle of the room as ordered, a misty cloud of steam suspended around him. In an attempt to establish a friendly mood, Spearthrower Owl initiated the conversation.

"Greetings, ahau," he confidently said in Mayan. "I thank you for being here, as your very presence in this room represents your people's greatest hope for peace and prosperity."

"I will be the judge of that," answered the deep voice emanating from the cloak. "But do not make the mistake of misjudging me. I will not bow to you."

Spearthrower Owl smiled. Unlike all of the weaklings who constantly sucked up to him, this man would constitute a formidable ally at his side.

"Please, let's discuss openly."

Everyone held their breath as a strong pair of hands emerged from the cloak and slowly reached up to the hood. Bones clashed and rattled, and many gasped as the badly burnt face was revealed.

"Welcome, Siyah Kak ahau," said Spearthrower Owl.

NEW YEAR

The immense sense of relief was immediately palpable as the sun finally rose on the first day of the month of Pop. People let their censers burn out, and they opened their doors and shutters to the outside world. For the first time in days the sun was allowed to brighten the inside of their house. The stuffy smell of mold and humidity was washed away by clean, fresh air, and a welcomed breeze finally blew out the smoke which had lingered inside every home since the beginning of the unlucky days.

The Wayeb was finally over, and life returned to Mutul. People washed their hair and bodies of the accumulated filth. They put on fresh clothes with vibrant colors. They walked out onto the streets. Those who'd lost loved ones during these past five days of ordeal would soon mourn their loss, but not today.

Today was New Year's Day. Today was a day for festivities. Today, everyone celebrated their blessings and exchanged wishes of hope and well-being for the coming year.

As the first rays of light appeared over the horizon, Balam quickly washed himself clean and headed out. He had spent the Wayeb inside the palace along with the royal family, where a few priests had relentlessly relayed themselves day and night, offering prayers and sacrifices to protect the king and his family. Apparently, their efforts had been successful. Everyone inside the royal apartments had escaped unharmed from the terrifying month, as did most of the nobles who'd elected to keep their own families within the safety of the palace.

As for Kabrak'an, his usual sense of duty had unsurprisingly guided his judgment. He'd elected to spend the Wayeb at the frontier with a few volunteers in case some foolish or desperate enemy soldiers would have attempted to take advantage of the abandoned outpost to strike. Although there was no news of him yet, Balam did not fear for the warlord. The old warrior had stared death directly in the eyes too many times to fall into the traps of the Wayeb. No, he'd never feared for Kabrak'an's safety, as he'd never feared for his own, but he was concerned for the sake of a young priestess who had little knowledge of the dangers present around her during these days of terror.

So he hurried away, hoping the maize god did not let him down, praying that he would find her safe and sound. He wanted to run to her, anxious to know she was all right.

Progress was difficult as people emerged from every house, flooding the streets and celebrating. He jumped left and right, unsuccessfully trying to get around everyone.

"Sorry! Sorry!" he apologized as he went bumping against folks here and there, frustrated by his lack of progress. Fortunately, people did not take offense to his rudeness. Everyone was happy. They all expressed signs of relief as they realized their friends were safe. They enquired about the well-being of neighboring families, they exchanged tales of fear and hardship.

By the time he reached his destination, Balam had overheard countless stories of demons howling into the night, of spirits trying to force their way inside houses, and of heroic fathers running outside, armed only with incense and maize to scare away the lost souls wandering the streets.

He felt relieved for a brief moment as he finally reached his destination but there, at the base of the Tollàn pyramid, fear once again flooded his heart. He felt as if a giant hand had suddenly crushed the air out of his lungs.

Xochitl was nowhere to be seen.

This is the right place, he thought, exhausted. *This is where we'd agreed to meet. Maybe she is late. Or maybe she is up there, unable to come out.*

He looked up the cold and intimidating Tollàn monument. For an instant he wanted to climb up, to enquire about her safety even though the Tollàn high priest scared him. He was always there, inside the temple, looking around with his evil eye. Balam couldn't remember his name. He only remembered the coldness surrounding him.

"Blood and death are his only companions," Xochitl had once told him. "He has no respect for human life. You should never again come up this pyramid, and stay as far away from him as possible. Especially when his face is painted in black."

"In black? Why?"

"I cannot tell, but you must trust me!" she'd pleaded. "Fear the black face, and please stay away from him! Stay away from this place!"

So Balam stayed on the ground, pacing back and forth, anxiously waiting for her while constantly looking around. In the distance, he saw scores of people coming from all corners of the city, heading towards the sacred acropolis where the king would soon perform the bloodletting ritual launching the New Year festivities. He did not join them. Instead, he waited at the base of the foreign structure for what seemed like an eternity. He waited, until he finally saw her.

She was standing at the top of the pyramid, leaning against the temple archway, looking at him with her usual smile as if to say "See, I am safe. There is nothing to be concerned about. You worried for nothing."

She discretely waved at him, turned around, and

walked back into the temple's dark portal.

She is fine, he thought. *Thank you, maize lord.*

An overwhelming sense of relief and happiness filled him, and he suddenly realized he was starving after leaving in a hurry, without eating a single bite. He hadn't eaten anything in five days, and his stomach screamed for nourishment.

The ceremony was over by the time he caught up to everyone. Still, he did not go in vain. Before him, hundreds of tables were set up in the plaza and various dishes of meat, bread and vegetables coming directly from the city's storage pits were being prepared by the servants and generously offered to the population. He hurried to the closest table and grabbed whatever fell under his hand, happy to finally eat something.

"Balam!" called a friendly voice.

"Hogging all the food as usual!" added another.

"Chava! Kinan!" he answered with his mouth full, greeting the king's guards. "Why am I not surprised to find you two here?"

"You know us," answered Chava. "Where there's food, there's pleasure! I am surprised to find you alive though."

"Why? You had the shaman put a spell on me?"

"Me? No. I bet Kinan did, though. He still hasn't forgiven you for our loss during the solstice tournament."

"Bah," mumbled Kinan as he stuffed himself with salted rabbit meat. "We'll win next year."

Balam laughed. "I see you two are off duty," he said. Members of Great Jaguar Paw's personal guard usually wore the distinctive jaguar hide and carried the short spear whenever they were on assignment. At this moment, both were dressed in civilian clothes and carried no visible weapons, although Balam knew them well enough to know an obsidian blade was probably concealed somewhere within their clothes. They'd both pledged to protect the king with their lives, and the need to do so could arise anytime, even while on personal time.

"We are free for the morning," confirmed Kinan.

"We must report to the palace this afternoon," added Chava. "As usual, the king will be receiving citizens, and every member of the guard is requested to attend. One can never be too cautious."

"No, I suppose not. Especially in time of war."

"Right. You never know who could show up. How about you?"

"Not much. I basically spent the whole Wayeb locked up inside the palace. I need some fresh air. And you? I trust your past few days were as uneventful as mine?"

"On the contrary," answered Kinan.

Chava chuckled.

"It is not funny! You two know I was never the one to believe in such tales! I always thought New Year horror stories were embellished to impress the neighbors or to frighten children. Honestly, I wouldn't have believed this myself if I hadn't witnessed it with my own eyes!"

He took a deep breath and stepped closer to Balam as if to share a secret, but he made no effort to lower his voice so that everyone standing nearby could overhear what he had to say.

"It was on the fourth day, during the evening. I went outside for a few moments. You see, I planned on fasting but my mother was home with me, and you know old people. They need to eat! I planned things a little poorly and was out of food. So, I needed to get to my chultùn, which is right next to the house."

"To get food for her, of course. Not for you?"

"What? No! I mean yes, of course for her. Stop interrupting! Anyway, as I took the cover off the underground storage pit, an old woman crossed the street. She was all by herself. I heard her footsteps echoing in the quiet evening. And I knew! I just knew something bad was about to happen. She almost made it across. Almost! Then, suddenly, she faltered and fell to the ground. At first, I thought she might have just tripped on something. She was, after all, very old. Then I swear she started convulsing. She started vomiting blood! Demons were all over her, fighting for her soul!"

"So you helped her?" asked Balam.

"Me? Fight an underworld creature? What could I do against a spirit? I ran back inside my house as fast as I could. They tried to catch me! One of them actually tripped me and I landed straight on my face. I was lucky enough to reach my doorway alive! I slammed the door shut, lit some incense, and crouched in a corner. I didn't sleep the whole night!"

"Terrifying," said Balam in a slightly mocking tone. "What about the old lady?"

"Dead before I reached the house. They picked up her lifeless body this morning."

"Then we can only hope you will act with more bravery when our king's life is endangered."

"Hey, I would have liked to see you two in my place!"

Chava and Balam started laughing, and they were soon joined by their companion.

"Did you say you two are free until midday?" asked Balam.

"Mmmm mmm," replied Chava, guessing his thoughts. "You want to hit the court?"

"After being sheltered for five days, I need to stretch my legs!"

All three of them ran to get their ball gear.

ON THEIR WAY

Huemac climbed to the top of the ridge and turned towards the west. He stood there, silently staring at the horizon, for a very long time.

Tollàn was long gone behind them, a speck within the faraway mountains no longer visible in the distance. Still he looked, as if the city would somehow reveal itself to him one last time.

It didn't.

They had left Tollàn exactly one month ago on this day. Three hundred warriors sent out on a faraway mission. Three hundred men seeking honor and glory in the Mayan land. The will to do his king's bidding still burned fiercely within Huemac, but regardless of all the pride he felt, there was still a pang in his heart.

Never before had he been so far away from home.

"Commander!" interrupted a voice.

Huemac slightly turned his head, his eyes still fixed on the horizon.

"The camp is set commander. The troops are ready for the night."

He looked down the ridge.

His men had settled a short distance away from a crossroad where, with military efficiency, they'd opened a small clearing within the jungle and prepared camp. Wood was being piled up and, already, a fire was burning.

"Thank you Axehotl," he answered. "What about food?"

"I sent two dozen men hunting in all directions. These

jungles are lush with animals. They should soon bring something back to eat."

Huemac slapped his neck, and looked at the dead bug in his palm.

"These jungles would indeed be a blessing Axehotl, if it wouldn't be for the intolerable swarms of insects."

"It seems to be getting worse with every step we take. The undergrowth grows thicker. The air feels hot and humid. We are getting close, are we not?"

"Yes, we are approaching. The Mayan border is less than five days ahead of us."

"Finally, we will be in their land."

"Not yet, my friend. Not yet."

"What? What do you mean?"

"Tomorrow, we change our route. We must now go south."

"South? Lord Huemac, isn't our target east of here? Why head south?"

"The eastern road would take us directly through Lakam Ha. Their king is a friend of Great Jaguar Paw. His borders are well guarded. We would never make it through unnoticed."

"Then my lord, if I may ask, what is our way?"

"We head south until we reach the mountains. We will enter the Mayan land from their southern states."

"Their southern states? How would that be easier?"

Huemac grinned.

"Because Spearthrower Owl has arranged free passage for us. From there, we can more easily travel to our destination without being seen."

The warrior nodded.

Cheers were suddenly heard coming from the clearing below. As Huemac looked down he saw three men returning to camp. They were carrying a deer over their shoulders.

"Food, my lord. Come eat."

"Later. I would like to stay here a little longer, alone."

"As you wish."

The warrior bowed and left.

"Axehotl!" bellowed Huemac.

The warrior stopped and turned around.

"Assemble a small group of men. Send them to that village we see in the distance."

He nodded towards a plume of smoke rising above the jungle canopy.

"My lord?"

"They are to capture a prisoner. Bring him back alive. It is time to offer a sacrifice to the goddess."

"It will be done, lord Huemac."

HUNTERS

The sun had barely risen above the horizon when, already, Balam was knocking on Tupac's door. The young man took a step back, waited anxiously for a few seconds, and then knocked once again, impatiently waiving his long blowgun before the window.

He heard muffled footsteps inside the house. As the wooden door slowly opened with a creak, Tupac's face appeared through a widening crack. His eyes were red and puffy. He yawned deeply.

"What's up?" asked Balam in disbelief. "I told you I'd be here by sunrise!"

"Yeah, yeah," replied the Tollàn boy with a raspy voice. "I'm ready, we're leaving. Just give me a moment."

Without any further consideration he slammed the door shut. Balam stood wordless and astonished as the wooden planks stopped barely a few inches from his crooked nose.

Now that his renovation project was over, it was finally time for Balam to take a well-deserved break. It had been a hard challenge to meet the deadline. His people had been working on the altar structure right up to the very last day before planting was scheduled to begin. In the end, it was all well worth the effort as the final result was amazing.

The local population was so proud and happy of their newly renovated temple that they had invited Balam to a humble feast of beans and maize. It was a poor man's meal, but they had little more to offer. Balam, generous of his person, had gratefully accepted regardless of how anxious he was to leave for the jungle. It was a decision he never regretted; seeing the smiles on the worshipper's faces was priceless.

Normally, he would have now left for several days at a time, alone, taking barely any food with him and trusting only his skills as a hunter to keep his belly full. Hunting had always been an occasion for him to escape, to detach himself from the city life. In his experience, two hunters made way too much noise, or gave off too strong of a scent. Being two, it was also much easier to get carried away, to engage in conversation, or to lose focus on the task at hand.

Today however, he was happy to share the experience with a friend. He had neglected Tupac these past few months, and felt like he owed him some of his time. Besides, Tupac had promised to teach him the Tollàn way of hunting deer, which he was really looking forward to. It would be nice to learn some new techniques while being out of the city for a few days.

It was a short while before the Tollàn boy finally reappeared through the door, still yawning. He stepped out wearing travel clothes. There was a gourd at his waist, and a leather bag over his shoulder. He yawned one last time.

"So?" Tupac said. "Shall we go?"

"What's that?" asked Balam, pointing at the package strapped over Tupac's back. "It's too short to be a blowgun."

"It's my atlatl."

"Never heard of an atlatl before. What is it?"

"You'll soon find out. I don't hunt with a blowgun." He looked around. "Where are we going?"

"Towards the west. Plenty of small game this time of year. And lots of deer."

"Perfect. Free drink to whoever catches the largest prey!"

"Deal!"

So the two young men walked out of the city and entered the vast agricultural fields where, as far as the eye could see, hundreds of workers were busy planting what would soon grow into the next crop.

Tupac slowed down and watched intensely as the path took them right next to a man busy planting seeds. With a sharp movement of the wrist, the man opened a hole in the ground using a long, pointed stick. With the other hand he dropped a handful of seeds in the hole. Then, in one continuous movement, he pressed the earth back into place with his foot while already preparing the next hole with his stick.

While Tupac had been told about the Mayan's agricultural techniques, it was the first time he actually saw the planters in action for himself. He immediately admired the efficiency of their organization and the fluidity of their movement as they effortlessly planted their fields.

"Amazing," admitted the Tollàn. "Are they planting maize?"

"They are intercropping various plants, actually. By planting maize, beans and squash together, we achieve a higher yield as the three plants positively interact together. The beans climb along the maize stalks, the ground covering squash reduces weed progression, and the taller maize plants protect the other two from the harsh rays of the sun."

"I see. Interesting. Truly interesting..."

It was past midday by the time they finally reached the jungle and headed down Balam's favorite hunting path.

"Besides deer, what can we expect to hunt around here?" asked Tupac.

"Oh, there are plenty of rabbits, peccaries, monkeys, tapirs. We might even see a few pacas, small mammals. They are a real delicacy when stewed with sweet potatoes and squash seeds! Of course, there are also several species of game birds. Quails, curassows, chachalacas. And turkey!"

"Chachalacas?"

"Small dark birds. Not my favorite, but they'll keep you fed when there is nothing else to eat."

"Wow, so many animals. The land around here is so rich with wildlife compared to the dry mountains surrounding Tollàn!"

"Yes," agreed Balam. "We are truly blessed by the land."

The two of them walked for the rest of the day, heading always deeper into the jungle. All along, Balam taught his friend how to recognize the different trails left by the various preys inhabiting the region. Tupac, hungry for knowledge, was avidly listening, knowing his uncle would be proud. Already, this little trip was proving very profitable to him. As usual, he was learning a lot from Balam.

Night fell quickly, as it always did in the jungle. Despite the afternoon storm which had crossed their path and left the ground damp, the two hunters were now comfortably sitting in front of a fire, listening to the cracking of the burning wood as dancing flames casted grotesque shadows against the orange lit undergrowth of lush plants around them.

"I don't believe I've ever tasted turkey," admitted Tupac, nodding towards the large bird roasting above the fire.

"Really? Never?"

"Never."

"It's one of my favorite. It's delicious with chili peppers and a mushroom sauce."

"Then it's a shame we couldn't find any mushrooms."

"It certainly is," replied Balam. "Although I do have something to spice up the flavor."

He buried a hand inside his leather bag and pulled out a handful of dried allspice pellets.

"I thought you never brought any food with you."

"Food, never, but I always carry a little seasoning to enhance the taste of my meals. I also have some salt if you would like."

There was a short silence during which Balam reached for a stone and grinded the allspice grains into a fine aromatic powder. As he did, he recalled how they both came across the turkey a little earlier. The bird was discretely gobbling around the jungle, unsuspicious of its fate. Seizing the opportunity for a decent evening meal, the Mayan boy had quickly killed it with a single clay pellet shot from his blowgun, and the two hunters had judged the spot perfectly convenient to spend the night.

"You are thinking about her," said Tupac as Balam was staring blankly at the fire.

"What? Who? No..."

He blushed.

In truth he wasn't. For once, his mind was not focused on the Tollàn priestess, but as Tupac mentioned her, Balam immediately saw Xochitl's face in his thoughts.

"Tell me about her. How is it going between you two?"

Balam took a deep breath.

"We've been seeing each other more and more. We sometimes take walks around the city. We've shared a few meals together. I feel like I could tell her anything, you know? Time spent with her always goes by too fast and every time I see her all I can think of is *dear gods, she is so beautiful.*"

"So are you two officially together now?"

"No, no. Not really, I suppose. We haven't done anything, if that's what you mean. However, I believe we do share a special connection, a complicity unlike anything I've ever felt before."

"Sound like it's only a question of time now."

"I don't know. I truly don't know," he answered with a

hint of despair. "You see, while she always seems happy to see me, she is also very..." he tried to find the right word, "...noble!"

He reached out towards the fire and turned the broached bird over as Tupac looked at him with an empty glare.

"Noble might not be the right word," he corrected himself. "She is a priestess of the gods. Of your gods, and she acts like it! Head always held high, looking straight ahead. Unwaveringly walking through the crowd, oblivious to all that is happening around her. Proud. She never lets her feelings show. Nor her desires. Sometimes I think she likes me. When she smiles. When she invites me to stop by the temple to see her. At other times, I feel like she is so high above myself. So unreachable. So filled with holiness, leaving me with no hope. It's as if I was staring up towards a queen, or towards Vucub Kaxiq himself."

"Vucub Kaxiq?"

"Sorry, I..."

"Your celestial bird. The one perched at the top of the world tree, whose roots plunge deep into the underworld and whose highest branches soar amongst the heavens."

Balam looked at his friend with an astonished look, and he marveled at how knowledgeable of the Mayan culture this foreigner had become since his arrival. For a reason he couldn't quite grasp, it made him slightly uncomfortable inside. At the same time, he was also extremely proud of how fluent in the Mayan language Tupac now was.

"You've learned so much since you got here," he said.

"Believe me Balam, she is no divine bird. She is no queen, and she is definitely not a goddess. Xochitl is nothing more than a poor priestess, a shy and withdrawn young woman! I've seen you on the ball court, I know how you are. Proud. Confident. Strong. Be the same with her."

"You think?"

"You should just go ahead and tell her everything," Tupac said coldly. "Have some confidence in yourself!"

Balam raised a hand to his crooked nose.

"Balam, who knows what will happen tomorrow? Mutul is at war. It might not seem like it from inside the palace or even from here, a full day away from the city, but there is a war going on. You should act now while you still have the chance. Go get her as soon as possible. Take my word for it, and enjoy each other's company while you both still have time."

"While we still have time? What's that supposed to mean?"

"Don't worry, it's only an expression. It really doesn't matter. Listen to my honest opinion, and wait no further. Life is too short."

Balam looked at the fire and shivered, suddenly afraid of the dark look in Tupac's eyes. He added branches to the flames.

"I spotted some deer tracks around here earlier," he said after a long moment. "They lead deeper into the jungle."

"Great. Tomorrow, it will be my turn to show you how to hunt an animal!"

A PLEDGE
OF SUPPORT

The scribe expressed a sigh of relief as he finally sneaked back inside the palace's walls. In the east, the stars had long ago faded into the brightening early morning sky.

Soon, the sun would rise and the world would see another day.

In the poorest neighborhoods of Mutul workers were already waking up, preparing for breakfast as their devoted wives prepared them a gourd of maize gruel as their midday meal. They would then kiss their children goodbye before heading out to meet the local crew chiefs, who would randomly assign them to the various fields surrounding the city.

For them, another strenuous day of planting the fields and tending to the irrigation canals was about to begin. For the returning scribe, the approaching morning marked the end of his own task.

A task that was completed uncomfortably close to sunrise.

Once again, there was no legitimate excuse for him being out in the jungle at night, which could have proven extremely hazardous should he have been caught and questioned by a patrol on his way back. The slightest doubt as to his whereabouts might have prompted an overzealous young warrior to search his person, and if he was ever caught carrying compromising documents such as the one currently hidden inside his cloak, he could have been sentenced to death without even having a chance to explain himself.

That is why he needed secrecy and, for that matter, darkness was the best ally he could count on. Unfortunately, even obscurity had abandoned him as, halfway through the night, an almost full moon had appeared in the sky.

For most people the brightness was considered as a blessing. Even deep into the jungle, it was almost impossible to get lost on a well cleaned path when the moon shined brightly. As such, several travelers usually took advantage of these times to travel after sunset, thereby covering more distance in the cooler air.

For him, however, it was a curse that jeopardized his safety, his mission, and his life. Not only was he more visible, but the risks of encountering someone else were much higher.

For that very reason, the meetings with his secret contact were always planned on moonless nights. Unfortunately, this particular message was too important to postpone.

"I am sorry, you must retrieve the message tonight," he had been instructed. "I realize this might compromise the secrecy of our actions. Events are now unfolding rapidly, and I am afraid we cannot wait for the new moon. I need their answer straight away."

"Of course, I understand," he had answered halfheartedly. "You may count on me. I will go tonight, and I will bring the message back."

"Open your eyes. Kabrak'an knows many voyagers will be travelling under the full moon, and so will the enemy. He will undoubtedly dispatch additional patrols to counter any potential attacks from Sian K'aan."

"I'll do my best to be careful."

It was this carefulness that had significantly slowed his progress, making his return dangerously close to dawn. Nonetheless, everything went as planned. The message was waiting for him, well-hidden as usual, and aside from almost coming face to face with two travelers heading in the opposite direction, he hadn't met any patrol.

So now he looked one last time towards the orange colored horizon and stepped inside the safety of the palace. Despite the imminent sunrise, it was still dark inside the stone walls. He grabbed a torch and headed straight for his apartment.

It was only after reaching the safety of his personal quarters that he allowed himself to take a deep breath. His hands were still shaking. His heart was racing inside his chest. His breaths were short and shallow.

Suddenly feeling lightheaded he sat in a corner and tried to relax. The cold stone felt good against his clammy skin. He grabbed a cup of balché and, without hesitation, gulped it down.

He was an ah'tsib. A scribe. A scholar. A man who could spend entire days deciphering ancient texts and codices. A perfectionist who didn't mind spending a lifetime in seclusion, perfecting the art of reading and writing up to the slightest details. He would never be a warrior, nor a hero, and he definitely never had the temper for heart stopping adventures and life threatening missions.

"Could we not ask someone else to carry the messages?" he had asked. "I will do my part. I will write the texts, and I will keep your secret safe, but I lack the strength to face the dangers waiting out there."

The implorations had been fruitless.

"You know we cannot implicate anyone else," was the answer. "The risks are already too high. This must stay between you and me."

"And if I refuse?"

"Do you refuse? Will you not willingly do this for me? For us? Do you not see the greater good that could come out of this?"

The scribe had finally nodded.

"Very well, I accept," was all he'd said.

Already, he had delivered and retrieved several messages. The task was not getting easier. Hopefully, as promised, it would all soon come to an end.

He looked through the small apartment window and noticed that the sun was up. He poured himself another drink before finally daring to pull the folded bark paper document out of his clothes. Without waiting any further, he broke the wax seal and opened the codex, revealing several glyphs as he unfolded the accordion style document.

The scribe anxiously read the short text twice. Although literate, the person who'd written the message was definitely not a scribe. At least not one of royal caliber.

The glyphs were unevenly spaced between themselves. The ink was pale and watery. The lines, unaesthetically shaky and bold as a result of excessive pressure being applied to the brush. Overall, the entire text was grossly written, lacking any artistic sense, randomly mixing various glyphic styles in a totally disorganized fashion.

But the message was clear.

We have an agreement.

You can count on the support of our king and his warriors.

AMBUSHED

The deer was gracefully walking between the trees, stopping here and there to nibble along the way. The animal was perfectly silent, carefully moving his delicate hoofs while skillfully avoiding the many leaves and branches littering the ground, knowing that any cracking would instantly betray its presence.

Suddenly, its body stiffened. The deer raised its head, ears straightened, eyes looking into the jungle towards the noise caught by its sensitive hearing. For a long moment the animal stood thus, perfectly motionless. Finally, satisfied that no danger lurked ahead, it bowed its head down and moved into a large open area.

On the other side of the clearing, lying downwind from their prey, Tupac and Balam watched as the young deer stepped out of the shadows and ventured into daylight. The two hunters were well concealed behind lush bushes and large-leaved plants. Both of them had been waiting for what seemed like an eternity, silently suffering from the thousands of biting insects mercilessly swarming around them.

Balam was well accustomed to staying silently concealed amongst a well-crafted cover, waiting for the unwary prey to appear, lying perfectly motionless. Tupac, on the other hand, was not so accustomed to not moving for long periods of time. His legs quickly started to ache and long for movement as he slowly grew hopeless the animal would ever show up.

It finally did.

The Mayan boy looked aside and silently nodded at Tupac, who very carefully retreated back down the slightly sloped terrain, crawling away from the deer. Once out of sight he stood up, relieved to finally move his aching body. He discretely scratched a few insect bites and grabbed his atlatl.

Since they'd left Mutul, Balam had been particularly curious of the bag hanging across his friend's back. When Tupac had finally unwrapped the mystery package earlier in the morning, the young Mayan had laughed at the sight. Before him were four short spears, each of them almost as long as the distance covered by his outstretched arms. The spears were tipped with a very small flint blade at one end, while feathers were attached to the other extremity. There was also a short stubby stick with a deep notch on one side.

He guessed the stick, which was decorated with symbols Balam had never seen before, might have had some ceremonial usefulness. The spears, on the other hand, looked much too thin to him to serve any purpose at all.

"You expect to kill a deer with that?" he said, pointing at the equipment on the ground.

"Why not?" replied Tupac, insulted. "What's wrong?"

Balam stopped laughing and picked up one of the spears. He'd handled Chava and Kinan's warrior spears several times before. Tupac's spears seemed unnaturally light to him.

"These are much too thin to handle properly. My guess is they will shatter in your hands at first strike, without even piercing the animal's skin. Besides, I've never seen a spear tipped with such a ridiculously small blade before! I personally doubt this weapon could do any significant damage at all. How do you even expect to approach the prey? Perhaps you are hoping to hide somewhere and wait for it to walk right by you!"

Balam laughed mockingly.

"I don't know how animals behave around Tollàn," he added. "Maybe you just lock them up in an enclosure of some sort before going at them. I assure you the ones around here are quite free and especially nervous! They would never let you get within spear reach, or even close enough for any of this to be useful!"

Tupac looked up towards the sky, slightly insulted.

"They're not spears, you ignorant fool. They're called darts! And you don't stab the animal with them, you send them flying into the sky. This is a projectile weapon, similar to your blowgun pellets!"

Balam raised his eyebrows and lifted the dart above his head, testing its weight. Unconvinced, he threw the projectile before him with all of his strength. The dart wobbled into the air and landed shortly without any force.

"Idiot!" yelled Tupac as the dart skidded to a stop.

"Never seen anything like this before," Balam replied. "This is much too light to throw. It simply will not develop enough speed and power to pierce the flesh. Besides, there's no way you can get within throwing distance anyway."

"You don't throw it!" Tupac replied as he fetched the dart and inspected the fragile feathers at the end. "You launch it. With this." He pointed at the notched stick on the ground.

"This little piece of wood? What is it?"

"The atlatl. The spear-thrower. You knock the dart on the notched end and you send it flying into the air. The atlatl increases the throwing efficiency of your arm tenfold."

"Really?" replied Balam, incredulously. "And just how do you aim this thing?"

"Practice. A lot of practice. And experience. You must first evaluate the distance to your target, and then adjust the release angle accordingly."

"So this atlatl will throw the dart with enough speed for the spear point to pierce the animal's skin?"

Tupac looked at him with a smirk.

"Oh yes. When thrown properly, the dart will come down with such speed that it will penetrate through almost anything!"

Balam doubtfully pursed his lips.

"Maybe," he admitted. "I'll be anxious to see that."

Now, half a day later, Tupac silently waited with a dart knocked onto the throwing stick. He watched as the unsuspecting deer stopped and grazed at the ground, estimating his prey at a little less than fifty paces from his current position across the open field.

The perfect distance for a throw.

He could barely see his target through the many leaves concealing his own presence. What little he saw, though, would be more than enough to aim properly.

Tupac patiently waited for the animal to look away. The nibbling deer finally turned around, revealing a white tail against the light brown coat.

The hunter slowly positioned his feet, took a deep breath and, in a single continuous movement, shifted his weight on the forward foot as he swung his arm in a large circle, ending his motion with a snap from the wrist. It was a movement he had practiced extensively again and again since he was old enough to throw a dart. Consistency, critical for accuracy, could only come after thousands of repetitions.

The projectile silently launched into the air, arching high above the clearing. Once again, the deer raised its head, sensing a danger. It was already too late. Before it could react, the dart plunged down with an amazing speed and, with great force, buried itself deep into the animal's body.

The deer jumped under the impact and wobbled back towards the jungle. Mortally wounded, it crashed to the ground just as it reached the apparent safety of the tree line.

Balam immediately jumped out of his cover, unable to believe what he'd just witnessed.

"Yes!" he whispered. "What a shot!"

He looked back towards Tupac, who now stood straight up, a proud smile all over his face.

"You see!" Tupac said. "I told you this was a ... What? What is it?"

In the space of a heartbeat, Balam's face changed from extremely excited to extremely worried as he stared into the darkness of the jungle behind them.

"Balam?"

"Shhtt. Bend low. Now!" he suddenly whispered.

"Why? What..."

"Down!" he ordered with a brusque gesture as he himself dived to the ground.

Tupac obeyed. Once again the two young men found themselves crouching underneath the leaves, hiding in the exact same place they'd waited all morning for the deer to appear. Tupac looked back towards the jungle, listening for anything that could explain Balam's behavior, looking for any sign of the danger apparently lurking into the darkness.

For the longest time there was no movement except for the leaves flowing in the breeze, no sound except for the birds singing in the trees.

He looked at Balam with an inquisitive look. His legs were killing him and he ached to move once again. The young Mayan slowly shook his head, and discretely pointed a finger towards the trees. Tupac looked. He couldn't see anything. Then, suddenly, a shadow emerged from the jungle.

A man. He was very slowly walking amongst the trees, moving almost as silently as the deer had not so long ago. The shadow stopped and raised a hand, signaling others to move forward.

Three other men walked out of the jungle. All of them carried short spears.

Balam could see them clearly now. Their bodies were painted red. Their leader had a large macaw tattoo on his upper arm, leaving no doubt as to their identity.

Sian K'aan warriors.

His heart raced in his chest as he became suddenly aware of their poor concealment. The two hunters had now become the prey. If the enemy warriors were to find them, alone in the middle of the jungle, they'd surely kill them both.

With one hand Balam reached for the flint knife at his waist and, at the same time, looked aside. His blowgun was barely out of reach. *No,* he thought. *I might get one shot as a surprise attack, but the others would kill us before we could do anything else. Better wait and prey they pass us by.*

He looked at Tupac. He, too, appeared nervous as the warriors slowly headed towards their direction. A drop of sweat ran down his forehead and his legs started shivering. *Calm down,* Balam thought as he closed his eyes, breathing as deeply and slowly as he could, trying to remain motionless. The sound of his own breathing seemed so loud he felt the entire world could hear him.

Calm down. Calm down.

The shivering stopped.

With his eyes still closed he felt the enemy warriors walking right next to him before slowly moving towards the clearing, away from them.

It was a miracle they hadn't seen them after killing the dear, a miracle Balam had heard them first. Then the thought struck him. *The deer! The atlatl, the fresh blood. If they see the deer they'll know someone must be nearby!*

He opened his eyes and risked a look ahead. Not wanting to be caught in plain sight, the warriors were walking close to the trees, partially concealed by the thick foliage. Then, just as they were about to reach the dead animal, the enemy party turned north and headed back into the jungle. Balam watched until they once again became shadows within shadows and breathed a sigh of relief.

Both young men waited a long time before they finally dared to move or speak again.

"A Sian K'aan patrol," whispered Balam.

"Are they gone?"

"Probably. I haven't heard anything in a while."

"How did you know?"

"I heard a branch cracking. Animals are rarely that careless." He looked ahead. "I think it's safe now."

Balam stood on his knees and brushed the dirt off his clothes. As he reached for his blowgun he felt the pressure of a spear point against his bare neck. Then, suddenly, spearheads started appearing through the leaves.

They were all around them.

"Stand still boy!" ordered a voice. "Do not move. Identify yourself."

The young Mayan froze. *They must have heard us after all. They saw us and came around towards our back. Damn me, we should have left the instant they disappeared into the trees!*

"Your name!" insisted the voice.

I could lie, and pretend we are from Sian K'aan. Or we could run now. It is probably our only chance. Run.

As he was about to run for it, the warrior stepped out of hiding, his spear point still firmly pressed against Balam's neck. The young man felt a warm trickle of blood running down his throat.

"I will not ask again!"

The warrior was now standing in plain sight and, for the second time of the day, Balam felt relieved. The warrior before him had no red paint over his body, and the tattoo on his arm was not that of a macaw, but of a knotted headdress glyph. These were warriors from Mutul.

"Hun Balam K'ux," he announced with a broad grin. "We are hunters from Mutul. My name is Balam. This is Tupac, my friend."

The man lowered his spear, and three other spearman walked out of the jungle.

"I know you. You are the ball player," he said. "My name is Sukil. What are you two doing here?"

"We are hunting," answered Balam as Tupac also rose to his feet. He then remembered their previous encounter.

"There is a Sian K'aan enemy party nearby!" he said, excited. "They were here not that long ago. Four men. Warriors. They left in that direction."

"We know," replied Sukil. "We've been tracking them for two days now."

"Since when do Sian K'aan warriors venture here, so far away from their city?"

"Sian K'aan is everywhere nowadays. We will be on our way now. You two must be careful."

"What will you do?"

"Hunt them down. See if we can capture one of them alive." The patrol leader turned around and gestured his fellow warriors forward.

"Wait," called Tupac. "We come with you."

"What?" said Balam.

"Absolutely not!" exclaimed Sukil. "You two should return to Mutul immediately!"

Tupac insisted.

"My name is Tupac, nephew of lord Spearthrower Owl,

from the great city of Tollàn. Any enemy activity in this area impacts the safety of our people and of our merchandise. My uncle and I have been mandated by our king to see, first hand, that any threat is removed from our trade routes. If there is a Sian K'aan patrol in this area, I need to make certain you deal with them properly."

He discreetly winked at Balam.

Sukil looked down and sighed. Refusing an official Tollàn request could get him into trouble.

On the other hand, taking the boys with them would jeopardize the success of his mission, as well as the safety of the two young hunters. That was a risk *they* would have to take.

"Very well," he said half-heartedly. "You two can come. But you follow my orders without any questions!"

The two boys grabbed their gear and hurried behind Sukil. They had forgotten all about the fallen deer by then.

Once again, Balam found himself crouching amongst the foliage, well hidden by the lush tropical undergrowth. His eyes were fixed on the narrow path before him, waiting for his prey, as he had done so many times before. Only, this time was different.

This time, the prey was not an animal. It was a man.

Four men, to be exact.

What have I put myself into, he thought.

"Why did you do that?" he had asked Tupac. "Why did you insist on joining them? Do you not realize this is dangerous? And what's the story about this mandate of yours?"

"I was only looking for a little adventure," he'd answered suspiciously. "Cheer up! Let's travel with these warriors for a day or two. Track down the enemy!

Experience the dangers they face! We're here to hunt, aren't we? Who knows, we might even witness a real battle if we get lucky!"

"Or we might get ourselves killed."

"You worry too much. Besides, it is my duty to see to the interest of my people."

So Balam had agreed to follow, at least for a while. Now, waiting for the enemy to appear, he started to doubt the wisdom of his decision.

They'd tracked the Sian K'aan party for half a day before Sukil had stopped the group.

"They are heading north," he said to his warriors. "My guess is they are returning to Sian K'aan."

"Ahau," interrupted Balam. "I've hunted here several times before. I know this area very well. Sach Ch'e and Xibrikil are straight ahead, not too far in that direction."

He pointed north.

Sukil shot the boy an angry look, obviously annoyed at the interruption. On the other hand he, also, was familiar with the area. Balam was right.

Sach Ch'e and Xibrikil were two huge bajos, large seasonal swamps covering a significantly wide portion of the way ahead.

"This time of year, even this early in the wet season, the bajos will extend over a large area, leaving only a small gap between them to cross over to the north side," explained Balam.

"What do you propose?" asked the patrol leader.

"They travel very slowly, careful not to be discovered. I say we hurry around them. We head to the gap and set an ambush for them. If I am right, they'll be upon us not long before dusk."

"If you're wrong," argued Sukil, "we could miss them entirely. I want to catch them. What if they decide to move around the swamps?"

"Then we'll get back on their tails! If we haven't seen them by nightfall we retreat here and pick up their track once again. If they do take the long way around, we'll have plenty of time to catch up with them." Balam looked at the warriors. "You're four against four. Even odds. Your best bet is an ambush!"

Sukil nodded in agreement.

"You have the spirit of a warrior," he said, before turning towards his men. "We move around them, and do as the boy said. Hurry."

So now, for the hundredth time, Balam's hand crept inside the leather pouch hanging at his waist while his eyes remained fixed on the road. The clay pellets were still there, safe and within reach. His blowgun was in shooting position. Dusk was rapidly approaching. If he was right, the enemy party would soon appear. Otherwise, a long nightly walk awaited them, although Balam doubted Sukil would let them come along after leading them through an unfruitful errand.

He waited in silence, perfectly motionless. Hunting a man, he reflected, was exactly the same as hunting a deer. Except maybe that the wind direction mattered very little, which was a good thing since he now hid upwind from the road.

Balam suddenly twitched as he picked up the sound of a body brushing against leaves. He looked in the direction from which the noise came and soon saw them appearing, one by one. The day was coming to an end. Light was quickly disappearing but there was no doubt in Balam's mind. These were the exact same four enemy warriors who'd walked by them earlier in the day. For the second time, they were close to him. Only now, Balam was the one in position to strike.

His heartbeat raced up as he felt the rush so familiar to any hunter who's ever stared down at an approaching and unsuspecting prey. He forced himself to breathe deeply in order to still his hands. The young man reminded himself these were enemies, and his hunting instincts kicked in.

He licked his lips.

His fingers slowly reached for the pouch and grabbed a pellet. He inserted the clay projectile inside the long hollow tube, around which he then wrapped his mouth.

Balam aimed his blowgun at the first man in line, took a deep breath, and blew sharply.

The enemy leader fell to the ground.

Immediately, the four Mutul warriors who'd been waiting along the path jumped out of the jungle and attacked the three remaining men.

The silence reigning over the jungle was immediately replaced by the sound of screams and weapons clashing. The battle was fierce. Being caught by surprise, the Sian K'aan warriors were clearly at a disadvantage.

It was then that Balam saw the fallen leader struggling to stand back up. The thin trickle of blood running down his forehead was barely noticeable against the bright red paint covering his body. The man wobbled forward, holding a dagger as he headed for Sukil's back.

"Sukil!" screamed Balam as a warning, but the Mutul warrior was too busy fighting his opponent to hear him. The boy frantically reached for his bag, searching for another clay pellet. His hand was trembling so much he couldn't find the opening in the leather pouch. For the first time in his life, the young man faced the pressure of battle.

With a still shaking hand he threw the blowgun aside and unsheathed his own dagger. Without hesitation he ran towards the enemy warrior. With a little luck, he might be able to stab the man in the back before his presence was noticed. Unfortunately, as he clumsily ran through the lush vegetation, the warrior instinctively turned in his direction and braced for him as he heard the approaching footsteps.

I'm dead, thought Balam.

He, who had absolutely no combat training, was now running straight at an experienced warrior. No matter how much he tried to stop, he couldn't prevent his legs from moving under him.

In a moment of panic, he stumbled and rolled to the ground. The Sian K'aan warrior limped up to him, raised his dagger, and prepared to strike. Disoriented, Balam waited for death, hopelessly trying to crawl away over the slippery soil.

All of a sudden, the man towering above him closed his eyes and grabbed his forehead where the clay pellet had struck him. He faltered. Driven by pure instinct Balam gathered all of his strength, kicked him hard in the knees, and rolled aside. There was a cry of pain as the warrior's body heavily fell to the ground.

Realizing this might be his only chance, Balam turned back towards the warrior, tightened his fingers around his own dagger's hilt, and repeatedly stabbed the blade into his enemy's chest as blood gushed all over him.

Tupac had been silently watching the whole scene from his own vantage point, safely hidden behind a large stump, well out of harm's way. Balam was a good hunter, very accurate with his blowgun. He immediately knew the boy had once again hit the mark as he saw the leader fall to the ground.

He then watched as the Mutul patrol jumped out of the undergrowth and attacked the remaining enemy warriors. And he watched as Balam foolishly ran towards the stumbling leader. A man twice his size. A trained killer.

Balam should have died on that day, but luck was on his side. Later, he would sprinkle a handful of dried maize kernels over the maize god's altar and offer drops of his own blood, a self-sacrifice to thank his patron god for keeping him alive. For now, he simply stood back to his feet as the Mutul patrolmen ran to him, making certain he wasn't seriously wounded, congratulating him on his first kill. There was laughter and joy on the narrow path between the two swamps as all of Mutul's warriors had survived the battle.

On their way back Sukil would call it an almost perfectly successful ambush, his only disappointment being that none of the enemy warriors had been brought back alive. *But we've stopped a threat,* he said, *and that is always good.*

Tupac waited for all of the Mutul men to hurry around Balam before finally walking out of his hiding spot.

He headed straight for the dead, looking intensely at each of the red-painted warriors lying before him. As he quickly inspected the bodies he noticed that one of them was still breathing. Blood flowed from a large open wound in his chest. Bubbling noises escaped from his mouth as the man laboriously breathed.

Tupac looked around to make certain no one was watching before bowing over the dying man.

The warrior's eyes opened wide as he recognized the young Tollàn man leaning over him. As he opened his mouth in a desperate plea for help, Tupac struck one of his flint-tipped darts deep into his throat, silencing the warrior forever.

A ROYAL VISIT

The rain was falling hard by the time Balam walked out of the city warehouse with a large bundle under his arm. *Damn,* he thought, looking at the drenched roads and the soaked people running for shelter. *These banners will be soaking wet by the time I reach the palace!*

He looked around, grabbed a tarp lying on a chair next to the door, and quickly wrapped it around his precious cargo. The storm would probably be over soon, but there was no time to wait it out. Winaq was certainly impatiently waiting for his arrival.

"I'll bring this back as soon as I can!" he yelled at the warehouse manager before heading out into the rain, leaving the old man behind without giving him an opportunity to protest. He ran as fast as he could, his sandals sending splashes of water in all directions as his feet landed heavily in muddy puddles. While he was soaked to the bones, the precious banners were safely tucked against him, and that was all he cared for.

He quickly waved at the warriors standing guard at the palace's entrance and stepped inside, dripping with water.

"Finally, there you are!" greeted Winaq. "It certainly took you long enough!"

"Oh, you're very welcome!" answered Balam, his wet hair and clothes tightly clasped against his body.

Winaq laughed. "Do you have them?"

The boy showed him the package.

"Great. Come with me."

The old man led the way towards the inner courtyard, where a massive wooden awning had been erected in anticipation of the rainy season. The awning proved itself to be extremely efficient at sheltering the ahauob members from the rain. Even under the raging storm, the thatch roof didn't leak a single drop.

There was, however, a more formal than usual atmosphere to the courtyard. Bright quetzal feathers had been attached to the structure, while the plain basalt stools used by the ahauob had been replaced by eight wooden chairs covered with fancy cushions.

"Here," Winaq said. "I am sorry I must ask this of you, but all the servants are busy preparing food for tomorrow. Could you please hang the banners over the awning posts? When you're done, I'd like you to also re-arrange the seats and add a ninth chair to the circle."

"Why a ninth chair? I was told only seven other states will be attending."

"Because Spearthrower Owl has requested to be present, and the king has agreed."

"He has? I thought this was a Mayan states meeting."

"With Tollàn's undeniable presence in the region, Great Jaguar Paw has allowed him to assist. Now please, install your banners."

With that, the old man walked away.

Balam shrugged, silently wondering whether or not the Tollàns were getting too much attention these days. He dismissed the thought and unfolded one of the rusty red banners, holding it before him at arm's length. He admired the beautiful black trims and the single glyph representing the backside of a man's head with a knot tied across.

Mutul's glyph.

"Good work," he said to himself. "They look better than the old ones!"

About a dozen days ago, the original city banners were

found moldy and totally wasted. Apparently, water had somehow infiltrated the storage room, and last minute arrangements had to be made to fabricate new ones. Time was running short and, out of the fifteen banners ordered, only twelve were ready. That would have to do. The states meeting was expected to start sometime during the following day, and these banners were all that was missing for the palace to be ready.

The young man proceeded with inspecting the banners one by one. Satisfied that all were acceptable, he started installing them around the room, as he'd been instructed by Winaq. It was not unusual for the representatives of neighboring states to meet and discuss various subjects such as trade, conflicts or alliances. This would, however, be the first time so many states would sit together and discuss common issues.

About a month ago, a messenger had arrived from the south, announcing that two of their nobles would be coming north shortly to meet with the king. Then, suddenly, another had joined in. Then three more. Before the ahauob realized what was happening, representatives from seven different cities had invited themselves in Mutul, giving them very little time to prepare.

Balam had just finished installing the additional chair under the awning when the deep sound of a conch horn sounded in the distance. Knowing full well the meaning of the signal, he quickly adjusted everything and ran up to the roof, where Kabrak'an had preceded him.

"Kabrak'an, ahau," Balam said as he approached.

The warrior barely tilted his head, never taking his eyes off the western horizon. The rain had stopped and, already, a late afternoon sun was slowly appearing through the thick grey clouds.

"Good day, boy."

"I heard the horn. The last representative has arrived!"

"Mmm mmm," confirmed the warrior with a nod.

Balam looked in the distance and squinted his eyes, blinded by the sun's reflection against the wet city streets. Far away, he could see a large group of people approaching the palace.

"I didn't know you were back in Mutul, ahau."

"The king asked me to personally supervise the safety of the foreign delegates. Now that the wet season is here, the swamps are well swelled with water, preventing our enemies from traveling wherever they want. Besides, it has been calm at the border lately."

"Who is in charge up there? Wak Xook?"

"Yes, but only with a very limited contingent of soldiers. Most of my men are now in the fields, tending to the crops. I keep only the most experienced warriors with me when the rains come."

"And how was the dry season?"

The warrior looked at him. There was a grave look on his iguana-tattooed face.

"Bloody," he answered. "The worst season yet. I've lost many men. Many shipments were attacked, and we've lost many crops. Sian K'aan has been relentless, coming at us with many more warriors than we'd first anticipated. Apparently, we've severely underestimated their strengths."

Balam lowered his head.

"Speaking of Sian K'aan patrols," continued the warlord, "I was told about your encounter the other day. I heard you pulled yourself out of trouble quite remarkably."

"It was nothing," admitted the young man, nonetheless blushing at the compliment. "I merely reacted instinctively."

"Still, a lesser man would have easily abandoned and would be dead today. Did you have your juch'um yet?"

"The warrior's tattooing ceremony? But I'm no warrior!"

"You are now. You've killed an enemy in combat, haven't you? That makes you a part of us, and it makes you no less deserving than any other warrior in my troops."

"Honestly, it was only dumb luck that kept me…"

"Luck holds a much greater part in hero stories than you might think, so I will hear no more about it. You've killed a man in combat, and you well deserve the tattoo to prove it. I'll talk to Sukil as soon as I see him."

Balam proudly looked away and smiled. He would get a warrior tattoo. He couldn't wait to show Xochitl.

The approaching delegation was much closer now. Balam could see a dozen warriors marching in two ranks. All were dressed in ceremonial attire. All were armed with deadly sharp spears. There were a few other men who looked like rich nobles, and at least two dozen servants carrying cumbersome loads.

The man walking at the head of the group was, however, particularly decorated. He wore an unusually imposing feather-covered headdress on top of his head, and a prestigious seashell necklace dominated his torso.

"The first man," asked Balam. "Who is he? He doesn't look like any common noble."

"That is K'uhul Ahau Ehb' Pakal, holy king of Lakam Ha," answered the warlord in a straight tone.

"A king? The king of Lakam Ha has come? It is a ten day journey to Mutul, and kings never travel!"

"Very rarely, indeed, do kings leave their city, let alone travel beyond their state's borders. Today, the king of Lakam Ha has chosen to personally attend the meeting, and that can only testify to the importance of the matter at stake. It is a good thing, too, that he has come, for he is Great Jaguar Paw's strongest supporter and friend."

"What do you mean?"

Kabrak'an took a deep breath.

"Are you aware that Spearthrower Owl will be present?"

"I am. I've just finished installing his seat."

"Do you know who organized this meeting?"

"I heard the first states who invited themselves were… Wait, do you think Tollàn has organized all of this?"

"Who else? Remember Spearthrower Owl has disappeared for months after his arrival. He was seen traveling abroad, discussing with the southern kings. Then, soon after his return, all of our enemies inform us that they are arriving? That is too much of a coincidence!"

"Enemies? The southern states are not our enemies!"

"No? Then wait a few days and see. I fear Spearthrower Owl will try to rally the other great Mayan states against us, and Great Jaguar Paw knows it. All of the southern states are probably already on Tollàn's side anyway."

"Then why accept the meeting if he already knows it will turn into a bloodbath? Why even attend?"

"Because he must face them eventually, sooner or later. Winaq says they have a plan. That all they need is a little time. That the meeting will be useful to determine true allegiances. I trust them, Winaq and our king. Still, I do not like all of this."

Balam looked down. The king of Lakam Ha and his escort had now reached the entrance of the palace.

"If you will excuse me," added the warrior. "I must see to the safety of this king, and to the safety of all others as well. There are seven Mayan representatives here, all of whom came with their armed personal escort. Since these warriors will have nothing better to do than drink while their masters are arguing inside the palace's walls, I must also make certain that these idiots do not cause any trouble."

Without saying another word the warlord turned around and walked away.

WHISPERS IN
THE DARK

Chava never saw the hand reaching out towards him. He had no idea someone was hiding within the shadows until he was grabbed by the shoulder and swiftly pulled into a corner.

"Hey!" yelped the guard as he was suddenly dragged away. Kinan, his inseparable friend, instantly jumped aside and reached for his spear.

"Who is there!" he demanded.

"Easy! It's only me!"

Kinan stared at the shape before him in an effort to pierce the darkness.

"Balam? Are you insane? We could have killed you!"

"What, here? Inside the palace?"

"You never know," said Chava, still startled, as he carefully readjusted his clothing. "With all these foreigners walking around, one can never be too cautious! You were lucky to catch me off balance. Thank Kinan for still being alive. You'd already be dead if he hadn't intervened!"

Balam pretended not to hear and signaled the two guards deeper down the dark corridor.

"Tell me all that is happening," he whispered. "I want to know everything!"

"Everything about what?"

"The state representatives! What are they doing?"

Chava took a deep breath and put on a serious face.

"Well," he whispered. "If you really need to know, they are having dinner now. I think the man from Ek Tun is having rabbit stew, the one from…"

Balam punched him on the shoulder.

"No, idiot! The meeting! Who is in there? What are they talking about? You two are the king's personal guards. You've spent the last three days barely a step away from him. You must've heard something. So tell me!"

Kinan slightly shook his head in a discrete objection although Chava ignored the silent warning. He looked around to make certain they were alone.

"The king is in there, obviously. So are the scribe, Kabrak'an, Winaq and Icoquih."

"Icoquih? The princess?"

"Yes, the princess. She used to spend most of her time at the temple. Nowadays she seems to be more and more present beside the king. These past few months, she's actually been involved in almost every political decision he took. Now please stop interrupting me!"

Balam nodded silently.

"Other than our people, there is the king from Lakam Ha and his guards. You already know the representatives from Pa' Chan, Wak Kab'nal, Xukpi, Waxak Mo', Iximche, and Ek Tun are present. And Spearthrower Owl, of course. They spent the better part of the first day discussing banalities, really. Export, import, and especially the salt issues. Apparently there is a lack of salt in the west. All of the salt harvesting states along the coast are planning to increase their production and export within the year. You probably don't want to hear the details."

"The southern route," added Kinan, who now suddenly seemed keen on letting Balam know what was happening. "Tell him about the southern route issue."

"Yes, I was getting there. Everyone reiterated how much they hated having to detour so far down south in order to benefit from the guarded route into Mutul. They all admit it's a hassle but then again, most of those who've chosen to use the other paths have been attacked. A lot of merchandise was lost this past season."

"I know, Kabrak'an told me," said Balam.

"In any case, Great Jaguar Paw is being blamed for it all. He is being blamed for the costly detour. He is being blamed for the attacks. He is being blamed for the deaths. And he is being blamed for the lack of safety and order within his own state."

Chava looked around one more time and moved in even closer.

"That's when the interesting discussions started happening. It seems like the war between Mutul and Sian K'aan is having quite an impact over the region. As shipments are being attacked, prices are driven up, markets are plagued with shortages, and people are growing restless! Great Jaguar Paw asked for a little indulgence, he wants more time to solve this crisis. According to him, the end of the war might be closer than everyone thinks. Of course, no one believes him!"

"The warlord was forced to admit that Sian K'aan is more dangerous than it ever was. That they are now stronger than ever, despite all of his efforts!" added Kinan.

"Anyway," continued Chava, "Spearthrower Owl made a strong case that Mutul is the problem, pointing out that Great Jaguar Paw himself should be held personally accountable for all loses. That he doesn't have the will to fight this war."

"And the others listened to him?"

"The western states are on our side Balam. Ehb' Pakal from Lakam Ha, and Pa' Chan. And also Wak Kab'nal and Ek Tun in the east. They all stand by our king. They all agree we should be given more time. But all of the southern states, Xukpi, Waxak Mo', Iximche, they all sit with Tollàn on this issue."

"All of the obsidian producers?"

"All of them. They all support Spearthrower Owl. They all agree Great Jaguar Paw should be replaced."

"Replaced?" Balam was horrified at the thought. "By whom? And how? Are they speaking of war?"

Chava was about to answer when he suddenly stiffened up.

"Someone is approaching," he whispered. "Stay hidden!"

They all crawled deeper into the shadows of a nearby archway, hugging the walls in the hope that darkness would conceal them. By the sound of the approaching footsteps, Balam guessed there must have been three, maybe four people approaching. As the steps got closer, they started hearing a conversation.

"I was expecting at least some of the western states to be on our side."

"So did I."

"Don't worry, they're idiots. It only takes them longer to realize just how much time they are wasting by supporting Great Jaguar Paw. When they see our power, they will side with us."

"About that, I still do not see how you can manage such a victory!"

"I told you not to worry about that. Soon, Mutul will be mine, and the war will be ended. All I need is your support. In the meantime, we should think about our future cooperation."

"Future cooperation?"

"Do you realize we own the world's only two obsidian sources? You in the south and us in Tollàn, we have it all, and we are both driving the prices down because we keep competing one against the other! I've seen the way you manage your operations. It is inefficient and time consuming! You two are well respected amongst your people. Convince your respective kings, give Tollàn the mandate to manage your mines."

"And why would we do that?"

"Because we can transform your obsidian more efficiently, and also because our distribution network far exceeds the boundaries of the Mayan land. We've done it for hundreds of years. Think about it! Xukpi and Waxak Mo' will be rich! Once we work together, there will be no more competition, and the obsidian price will rise!"

"Perhaps, but I know Iximche. They will never agree to such terms."

"Forget Iximche. You two can conquer them anytime you want. We could even help you with that, after we've dealt with Mutul."

As the conversation slowly faded in the distance, Balam risked a look towards the mysterious figures. All he saw were three shadows disappearing into the darkness.

"Who was that?" he asked. "I mean, beside Spearthrower Owl."

"The other two? Ikan and Oyamal," answered Kinan.

"The Xukpi and Waxak Mo' representatives," explained Chava. "The worst scum you've ever met. All they want to hear about is profit from their precious obsidian. They care very little about anything else. They would sacrifice the lives of their own workers for it, and they will war on anyone who gets too close to their precious mines."

"Before these three arrived you were saying the king was about to be replaced," Balam reminded him.

"Don't be a fool, he is not being replaced! Not anytime soon, anyway. It is merely what Tollàn was hinting at. At the end of the day, the southern states threatened to go to war, and the western ones pledged their support to Mutul. The meeting ended with all of the representatives loudly yelling at each other, leaving us guards looking at ourselves unknowing what to do."

"So the meeting is definitely over?"

"Yes, and I fear this could be the beginning of a terrible time. We must go back to the inner courtyard immediately and inform the king of what we've just heard. Spearthrower Owl is obviously planning something."

"The king is still in there?"

"He is, with what's left of the representatives. They were still discussing when we left. You should come with us. The king has asked to see you anyway."

"Me?"

"Yes. You."

"Do you know why?" he asked, perplexed.

"Who knows? Come."

The guards led the way as the three of them headed for the council meeting room in the interior courtyard. As they all walked in, Balam was surprised at the relaxed mood under the awning. After what his two friends had just told him, he would have expected a more agitated atmosphere. Great Jaguar Paw was still there, along with Winaq, Kabrak'an, and at least two dozen others amongst whom Balam recognized the king of Lakam Ha. There was also a large table covered with food.

It was a feast for kings.

There was fish, honey, venison, fresh fruits, breadnut, balché, chocolate and cinnamon drinks, and even crab imported from the eastern shores. His mouth watered at the delicious smell of allspice and chili seasoned meals.

"Ah, Balam!" greeted the king as the young man approached. "Come, meet our guests. Everyone, I present you Hun Balam Ku'x, of whom I spoke earlier. A talented, dedicated, honest young man, and an expert ballplayer!"

Balam turned around to face the crowd. Although he did not personally know anyone, it was easy to identify the provenance and allegiance of the people present in the room. Just as nobles from Mutul had their hair tied in the Mutul fashion, the other states all possessed their own distinctive symbols.

A water lily flint pendant for Lakam Ha's people. A stingray spine hairpin for Ek Tun, a coastal state. Turkey feathers for Wak Kab'nal, and a jade jaguar bracelet for Pa' Chan.

Balam smiled, happy he'd taken the time to dress properly and attach his hair before showing up. First, he was introduced to Ehb' Pakal, king of Lakam Ha, and then to the representatives from Pa' Chan, Wak Kab'nal, Ek Tun. All of the others, he later learned, were merely part of the entourage which accompanied the representatives on their journey.

Balam immediately liked the king of Lakam Ha, whom he found to be a small, jovial man. As they were introduced, the king gave him an honest smile and grabbed him by the shoulders.

"Balam," he said. "I am pleased to finally put a face on the name! King Great Jaguar Paw speaks highly of you!"

"Thank you K'uhul Ahau," Balam simply replied, wondering how he could ever be the subject of a conversation between two kings. It was the first time he faced another K'uhul Ahau, and he was unsure how to react.

"Please, sit next to me," added the foreign king. "I would very much like to know more about you. Do you know my ball champion is here?"

Balam's eyes suddenly lit up.

"He is, K'uhul Ahau?"

"Yes, he made the trip especially to meet you, Balam, Mutul's great ballplayer. Your fame precedes you, young man. Apparently, your name has traveled all the way up to Lakam Ha, and beyond I would suspect. When he learned about this meeting, he insisted on joining me in the hope of facing you in a friendly match. If you agree, of course."

"I would be delighted."

The king clapped him on the back.

"Great!" he said. "Then it is settled. First, let's talk. And eat! It would be a shame to let all of this food go to waste!"

As Balam and Ehb' Pakal made their way towards the food table, Chava and Kinan approached Great Jaguar Paw with a concerned look on their face. The Mutul king was still closely surrounded by Winaq and Kabrak'an.

"K'uhul Ahau, I apologize, but we need to talk," said Kinan.

"What is it about?" asked the king, weary.

"A conversation we've overheard on our way here," explained Chava. "Between Spearthrower Owl and the two southern men."

The king nodded.

"Very well," he said. "In a moment. First, tell me, have you two seen or heard anything about Siyah Kak?"

The two guards looked at each other.

"Ahau?"

"Have you seen Siyah Kak lately?" repeated Kabrak'an.

"No, ahau. We have not," answered Kinan.

"Why?" asked Chava. "Has something happened to him?"

"Siyah Kak has not been seen since the Wayeb," explained the warlord. "No one has seen or heard anything about him in over a month now!"

"Isn't that normal?" asked Kinan. "I mean, for him?"

"What? Disappearing?"

"Wandering away without saying a word to anyone."

The warlord straightened up and looked at Winaq, who slightly raised his shoulders.

"It wouldn't be the first time he hasn't been heard of in such a long time," said Winaq. "I wouldn't be surprised to see him casually returning to the palace with a fresh complement of bones within in his hair. After all, he was asked to patrol beyond the borders."

Kabrak'an looked down and grinded his teeth.

"That bastard needs to be taught a sense of duty," he said. "He should've been here for the meeting."

"Send out the word to be on the lookout for him," interjected the king. "As soon as anyone hears or sees anything, I want to know. He is to report here immediately. I have an urgent matter to discuss with him."

The warlord nodded, and the king turned back towards the two guards.

"Now, you two, tell me what you've heard."

RED PAINT AND
MACAW TATTOOS

The Mutul warrior was humming happily as he attached his sandals and prepared for breakfast. It was a song his own mother used to sing when he was a child. When he would return home crying with a bloody knee, or when he was too scared to go to sleep. At these times, she would gently grab him in her arms and whisper the joyful melody into his ears.

The air had never failed to appease Imix, as it never failed to appease his own son to whom he later sang the same words.

Time had passed so fast. It seemed like only yesterday when he had to wake up in the middle of the night and cuddle his own baby to sleep, singing the melody he remembered from his youth. The baby had grown into a fine young boy who no longer needed his father's comforting lullabies to fall asleep, but it was still a happy song that Imix frequently caught himself humming on happy occasions.

And this was a happy day.

It was his last day of work before a well-deserved leave. His last day before finally returning home to his son. The boy had received a blowgun for his eight anniversary, and he had harassed his father for his first hunting lesson ever since. Imix's duties had kept him away from home lately. With his approaching leave, he would finally be able to take him out into the forest. He couldn't wait to teach him the skills of the hunter. The art of tracking the prey, of shooting the silent weapon.

Only one last day to go.

The warrior sighed and looked at his surroundings. The small barrack had been raised in a hurry after the king had decided to implement a safeguarded route south of the city. Overall, twenty-seven of the small outposts had been built, each of them staffed by four soldiers who, day and night, guarded the protected road. In typical military fashion, all of them were basically identical; small square huts made from whichever trees happened to grow nearby, covered with a crude thatch roof. The branches were so badly stacked together that large openings had quickly appeared through the walls, allowing a sickening draft inside the cabin. It also provided access to all of the crawling bugs and critters which swarmed the jungle during the night.

A warrior's life, he thought, as his eyes wandered from the thatch roof to the dirt floor. Barely enough room for four dried leaves mattresses, a narrow table, and a crowded weapons rack in the corner.

I can't wait to be out of here.

He stood up and headed to the table, where his three barrack companions Manik, Almika and Ebh were already enjoying their morning meal. The four of them had been together at outpost number seventeen since the last rotation, just after the Wayeb.

"Last day?" asked Manik with his mouth full.

"Last day," answered Imix with a smirk.

"Who will be replacing you?" enquired Almika as he pushed a bowl of maize gruel towards him.

"Someone from the northern border, I think. All I know is I'm out of here as soon as he arrives."

"The northern borders!" exclaimed Ebh. "Are you serious? I'm always suspicious when they send us someone from the border."

Imix rolled his eyes. They all knew what was coming. Ebh had long ago earned the well-deserved reputation of master storyteller although, no matter how entertaining, many doubted the veracity of his tales.

"It's true," added Ebh. "Most of the time, they send someone who just needs relief from the combat and the stress they live up there. That's fine with me. I was there last year with Kabrak'an, all dry season long. You wouldn't believe how difficult it is. I've seen my fair share of blood and death. I still do when I wake up at night. If we can give someone a well-deserved break, that's great. The problem is, sometimes, they send us a really crazy one. You know, the ones beyond recovery."

They all laughed.

"I'm serious!" continued the soldier. "Listen, less than two months ago, one fellow, I don't remember his name, he was near the border when his patrol was ambushed. They've all been massacred, typical blood and guts scenario. Anyway, they all die but him. Somehow, he manages to flee and hide in a bajo. He spent the entire night hiding in the swamps, harassed by mosquitoes and hunted by those Sian K'aan savages. He finally made it back to camp three days later, alive. Everyone agreed he was never the same after. He didn't sleep no more. He didn't talk no more. The poor man totally cracked under the pressure!"

"Nothing but stories," replied Almika.

"I heard it directly from a trusted friend," agued Ebh. "They sent him to outpost five or six for a month, so that he could relax a little. Unfortunately, It was already too late. The man didn't eat nor sleep. He didn't speak a single word in four days. They found him dead one morning. He had taken his own life."

"This story keeps getting better every time!" Manik said,

laughing. "Last time I heard it, the soldier ended up as a farmer planting maize in a field somewhere."

"That was a different story," argued Ebh.

Imix stood up and grabbed a maize flat bread.

"I need some fresh air," he said, heading towards the door.

"You won't laugh if they find us all dead, murdered in the middle of the night by some overstressed lunatic!" cried Ebh in a desperate attempt to get his comrade's attention.

As Imix walked out, he heard Manik whispering something which sent Almika bursting into laughter and Ebh cursing at their lack of respect. He took a bite out of the bread and walked the few steps separating him from the road. The famous southern protected route, a narrow winding path now well used by most merchants who traded goods with Mutul.

Imix closed his eyes, faced the sun, and took a deep breath. The fresh morning air carried the smell of the jungle's lush vegetation surrounding them on all sides.

"How is the bread?" asked Almika as he joined him outside.

"Stale. We are running low on provisions."

"I hope we will receive supplies soon. They should have delivered something by now."

"Maybe I should take a walk north and ask K'ib."

"You do that, and bring back some fresh news!"

It was, of course, forbidden for soldiers to leave their post, but the monotony of spending entire days waiting by the road quickly grew on most of them. Although many travelers took advantage of the well maintained and guarded path, very few ever stopped to discuss with them. So, naturally, the soldiers had developed a habit of regularly walking up to their neighboring outposts to exchange news or just to see different faces.

Imix grabbed his weapon, informed his companions

that he would soon be back, and headed north towards outpost number sixteen as it was simply known. He hummed his mother's song as he slowly headed down the path. It was a warm, beautiful day.

Before long, he reached the familiar bend in the road after which, he knew, was hidden the next outpost. Sure enough, he turned the corner and there it was, a small wood and thatch barrack identical to theirs in almost every aspect. Outside, four men were sitting on the ground playing Baq etz'anem, a popular game amongst soldiers involving a dozen small animal bones and a handful of dried maize grains.

"Imix!" greeted one of the warriors as he approached.

"Good morning K'ib," he answered. "How are things around here?"

"Nothing to report so far. How about you?"

"Not much. I needed a walk to change my mind."

"Last day before a greatly anticipated permission, if I remember correctly. Lucky you. Here, let's celebrate!"

One of the other three soldiers handed him a gourd. Imix sniffed the content.

"Balché!" he said. "Where did you find balché?"

"A villager who lives nearby," replied the guard. "We pay him a good price. In exchange, he keeps our gourds filled and his mouth shut!"

They all laughed. Imix grabbed the gourd and took a sip. The beverage was warm.

"So?" asked K'ib. "How are things down at renowned outpost seventeen? Any action lately?"

"Action?" said Imix with a surprised tone. "You must be kidding? We haven't seen any action in a long time, unless you consider villagers walking back from the market with their latest purchase of cotton fabric or pottery interesting. I suppose our presence here has had the dissuasive effect that was expected. We haven't heard from Sian K'aan in a very long time."

The four soldiers frowned and looked at each other.

"What?" asked Imix.

"I suppose we have some news for you then. Outpost eleven was attacked two days ago."

"Attacked? Outpost eleven?"

"No one survived."

Imix's eyes opened wide in disbelief.

"What? How do you know? And why haven't we heard the alarm signal? Why hasn't anyone blown the conch shell for reinforcements?"

"Someone from fifteen came here late last night. He told us everything, and now you know. I suppose you should send the news south. Apparently, the attack was swift. Two of the dead guards weren't even armed, so the enemy was probably over them before they even knew they were under attack. They never had time to call for help."

Imix looked down. This was to be expected. They were at war after all. There had been several reports of attacks on merchandise, mostly on merchants choosing not to use the guarded route, but this was the first reported attack on an outpost. When things are calm for a long time, warriors do tend to let their guards down a little.

Sometimes a little too much.

"Do you remember the guys from twenty-six?" asked Imix. "The ones who were all suddenly replaced?"

"Of course. One day, there's four warriors down there. The next day, all different faces."

"Do you suppose the same thing has happened to them?"

"The commander said they all got sick from something they ate."

K'ib sighed.

"Anyway, eleven was definitely an attack. Consider it as a warning. Tell your companions to keep their eyes opened and their weapons close by. The enemy is most likely still in the area."

Imix nodded silently.

"And cheer up! You'll soon be home enjoying a well-deserved leave!"

"You think? The commander authorized my permission only because the enemy was expected to remain calm during the wet season. If a Sian K'aan warrior group is hiding around here, he could very well order me to stay at my post."

"Don't worry. Last I heard the commander was far up north, along the border. It could be months before the other nobles manage to agree on any decision. There is plenty of time for you to go and come back before they decide to cancel all leaves."

"All right then," said Imix as he stood up. "I suppose all I have to do now is go back and wait until my replacement arrives." He already found the day long and it wasn't even midmorning yet. "Any news on food supplies? We are slowly running low on provisions down there."

"Same here. No news. All I know is a big salt shipment is expected later today, so make sure you are all at your post. You know how salt is scarce these days."

"Don't worry."

"And take some balché with you."

Imix politely declined with a wave of the hand. "I'll let the others know about the attack," he said. "I'll also tell them about that," he added, pointing a finger towards the gourd. "They'll probably come for a drink after sundown."

"We'll be expecting them," answered K'ib.

With these words, Imix waved them farewell and headed back towards his own post, where he found his fellow guardsmen lying in the sun, enjoying a peacefully quiet morning. He joined them, shared the grim news, and waited for the day to pass by.

It was only much later, in the middle of the afternoon, that the salt shipment appeared from the south. At their approach, the warriors of outpost seventeen hurried to their feet and grabbed their weapons in an effort to look sharp and ready before the traveling merchant.

Over a hundred and fifty men came walking down the road, each of them carrying a heavy basket filled with freshly harvested salt on their back.

Imix had once been told about the vast salt pans built by the populations inhabiting the coastal shores. How shallow, artificial ponds were filled with seawater and left to evaporate in the scorching sun. After maize, salt was one of the most important dietary items for the Mayans, used primarily as a preservative for fish and meat.

He returned his attention to the road. At the head of the approaching convoy was a tall man, who was closely followed by five armed warriors. There was another five warriors walking at the back.

"Good day," said the lead man as he stepped off the road to let the caravan through. He was obviously in charge of the shipment. The jade pendant around his neck marked him as a wealthy man.

"Good day," answered Manik. "We were expecting you. No problems on the road?"

"Nothing at all. We actually made good time, the road is in excellent condition. We left Ek Tun barely three days ago. Tell me, do they still have water at the next outpost?"

"They do. There is a small reservoir where your people can fill their gourds."

"Excellent, thanks."

Manik nodded as the man turned around and ran to catch up with the head of the column. Standing by the road, Imix watched as the long line of men passed before them with the heavy burden on their backs.

"What do you suppose they do with all this salt?" Imix

asked. "It sure seems like a lot of salt to me!"

"Not all of it stays in Mutul. Some will be redistributed to local surrounding communities such as Yek and Waka', while a good part will be sent directly to Pa' Chan and the other western states."

"Really? That's another four or five days from here."

"Usually, with the…"

Manik suddenly stopped short of completing his sentence, as something caught his attention in the jungle across the road.

"What is it?" asked Imix, rapidly looking back and forth between Manik and the dense vegetation before him. He couldn't see anything.

"A movement, maybe. I'm unsure," he said hesitantly.

The answer came quickly. Before they both realized what was happening, enemy soldiers started leaping out of the jungle, screaming war cries and wielding deadly spears above their heads. All of them were painted in red. All of them were wearing Sian K'aan tattoos.

With the enemy already upon them, Manik and Imix raised their spears. Three warriors cut their way through the salt-carriers and were now standing in front of Imix. Already, one of their blades had found its way to his left thigh. He desperately maneuvered his spear in large defensive movements, trying to parry the enemy weapons as sharp flint spear heads whistled past his face.

Heavy salt bags were dropped to the ground. Men started running in all directions. Everything around him was now panic and confusion.

Bodies started falling down while his ears were overwhelmed by the familiar screams of pain and agony, although the sounds of death surrounding him were quickly muffled by his own deep, labored breathing. From the corner of his eyes he saw Manik was also struggling against several warriors. He, too, was wounded and bleeding.

Imix could have helped him if he wasn't already overwhelmed by his own opponents. At three against one, it was impossible for him to efficiently block the enemy assault. He managed to avoid most of the attacks but, as he grew tired, more and more blades reached his flesh. Soon, his arms were covered with cuts and his leg burned fiercely as he desperately struggled to limp away from his enemy's weapons.

Then, suddenly, stars appeared before his eyes. The world turned upside down, and he felt himself hit the ground.

Everything went dark.

Imix opened his eyes, only to feel the acute pain of a light shining directly into his face, a brightness so intense he couldn't see through it. His head was hurting, distorted sounds reached his ears, and the taste of blood filled his mouth. For a moment, he couldn't remember what had just happened.

Vaguely, he recalled a blow to the head. Pain. Darkness. He blinked a few times, and realized he was lying on his back, staring directly at the sun. Imix knew he'd probably lost consciousness, and although he couldn't tell for certain how much time had passed, it couldn't have been very long for the sun had barely moved in the sky since the time of the attack.

The attack. It all came back to him in an instant.

As his eyes adjusted to the light, he turned his head to the side and realized the extent of the massacre. Dozens of blurred shapes surrounding him slowly came into focus.

Bodies, all around him. Lying in the dirt, covered in

their own blood, the caravan people had met their fate. Everywhere, salt bags were torn open, their wasted contents dispersed to the winds. Echoes of the attack sounded in his head, playing over and over again. The fighting. The screaming.

The alarm, he thought. *I must sound the alarm!*

He couldn't see anyone alive. He didn't know if his friends had survived. All he knew is he had to reach the conch horn hanging inside the barrack. He had to call for help.

Imix tried to move. There was no feeling in his legs. His arms weren't responding.

He heard sounds behind him.

Help, he thought.

He managed to turn his head in the other direction, only to gasp in horror. Barely two steps away, Manik's lifeless eyes stared at him wide opened in a plea for help that would never come.

He looked around. Ebh and Almika were nowhere in sight.

Then he saw the red warriors walking amongst the dead bodies, the famous macaw tattoo of the enemy city clearly visible on their chest. He counted seven, maybe eight soldiers. There had to be more. Two of them were carrying stolen bags of salt on their backs.

Imix's head was throbbing in pain. He could see them talking. He could hear them laughing. Amidst this massacre of innocent merchants they were enjoying themselves.

Strangely, he couldn't discern their speech, couldn't make sense of their words. That's when he saw a man walking straight towards him.

He tried to move his hand. Surely, his spear must have been lying close by.

Again, his fingers did not respond. His heart raced.

The approaching warrior looked directly into his eyes.

"Quichia! Yoli! " he said loudly.

"Ticmictia, axcanpa! " answered another.

Tollàn! Imix thought. *They speak Tollàn!*

He looked again. The warriors were definitely covered with Sian K'aan markings, and their red bodies clearly identified them as members of the Sian K'aan army, but their language was that of Tollàn!

What is happening? What is this trickery?

"Well, well, well. We have a survivor," now said the warrior in a very poor Mayan. The man spoke with a strong foreign accent. He then exchanged more words in Tollàn with another man.

Tollàn warriors, here! Tollàn is attacking us! Imix looked around, panicked. *The king! I must warn the king!*

His body still refused to move.

"Mann kwalli ohtli," added the man before him, the sadistic smirk upon his face exhibing several missing teeth.

As the disguised enemy warrior raised his spear, his last thoughts were for his son.

And for the hunting lesson that would never happen.

STRANGERS IN
THE MAYAN LAND

Life was calm and peaceful in the small town of Waka'. Surrounded on all sides by a dense jungle and about a four-day walk from Mutul, it was located far enough from the city to stand clear of all the commotion emanating from the metropolis, yet still close enough to benefit from its presence from time to time.

With a virtually non-existent monumental architecture, Waka' was not much more than a village. There were no administrative buildings, no stone-covered roads, and a single stepped pyramid topped by a modest red temple, the only stone construction in the entire town, represented the extent of its ceremonial center.

Years behind developed cities, the village was nonetheless self-sustainable, basically autonomous in all aspects. They grew and harvested their own crops. They weaved their own baskets, sewed their own clothes, and fired their own pottery. They also built their own hunting weapons. It had been as such for generations.

Kneeling behind her house in the middle of her small household garden, Saqirik's expert fingers were rapidly pulling out all undesired weeds growing between the bean plants. She then reached out to the compost box and grabbed handfuls of rich, dark humus, which she generously tossed around the base of the plants. Once the garden properly fertilized, she proceeded to a careful inspection of the many squashes growing on the ground, turning leaves and spreading the crawling plants apart.

A smile appeared on her face as she found a ripe one.

This one will be perfect for tonight, she thought.

With the village's main crop production barely meeting the population's demand, people relied heavily on hunting and on the product of their own gardens to complement their daily meals.

The squash would be perfect to accompany the two beautiful rabbits her brother had brought back earlier in the day. Saqirik was already salivating at the thought of the delicious meal when she was surprised by a pair of hands over her eyes and a kiss on the back of her neck.

"You are home early," she said after recovering her breath. "Is there a special event today?"

"You tell me," answered Pitz'al, her husband "Through the window, I saw two skinned rabbits inside the house."

"That," she replied, turning around, "was supposed to be a surprise!"

"It is a surprise." He gently caressed her cheek. "How is your head?"

"The shaman came this morning. He burned tobacco leaves in the house, and left a small pouch containing a foul-smelling powder."

"Powder?"

"Crushed rattlesnake skin mixed with salt. Apparently, it should help. He said I should take it twice a day, mixed with water."

"Hopefully it will work."

"I hope so. My headaches are getting worst."

"I am sure it will be fine. What else?"

The smile disappeared from his wife's face.

"What is it?" he asked.

"He is here," she said.

Pitz'al looked at her with concerned eyes.

"The warrior," she whispered.

"Oh, him." He feigned an unconcerned look. "It's nothing to be worried about. He only needed more obsidian fragments. He pays quite well, and he even provided his own raw material this time; pitch black obsidian of excellent quality. He said I could keep the leftovers. It was hard to say no."

"You know he frightens me."

"Don't worry. He will be out of here in no time."

He grabbed her head with both hands, delicately kissed his wife on the forehead, and headed straight into the house. As the town's stonemason, it was his responsibility to transform flint and obsidian into tools and weapons for his fellow villagers, but Pitz'al's reputation as a skilled artisan had travelled well beyond the limits of his own village, and people from the entire region sometimes requested his services. It was one such customer who now waited inside his home.

Standing in the doorway, Pitz'al peered inside the dimly lit room. There was a single bed against the wall. A commode in the faraway corner. A table, on which were sprawled two dead rabbits, and two chairs.

A man was sitting in one of the chairs, waiting.

"Ahau, you are a day early," he said.

"I am," answered a sinister voice. "Is it inconvenient?"

"No, of course not. I assume you are here for your order?"

"You suppose correctly. Are the blades ready?"

"They are. Would you like something to drink?"

"No. Your wife has already offered. A lovely woman."

A shiver ran down Pitz'al's spine.

Without a word he headed to the commode, over which were displayed the few religious artifacts he owned. A long and narrow altar cloth sewn by his wife. Three small idols representing Chaak, K'inich and K'awiil. A wreath, made of intertwined maize and tobacco leaves, and two censors. The idols he was particularly proud of, as he had himself carved them out of limestone many years ago.

He could feel the warrior's cold eyes upon him as he bent down and grabbed a small bag, all along struggling to act as naturally as possible.

"Your blades, ahau."

Pitz'al handed the bag to the man, who immediately opened it. Inside were several obsidian fragments, each of them crafted with a sharp edge on one side and a flat surface on the other.

The sound of rattling bones filled his modest house as the warrior reached to the floor, where he grabbed a heavy club indented with multiple fragments identical to the ones Pitzal had just manufactured. He noticed that several fragments were missing.

The warrior selected a blade from the bag and nestled it into one of the empty sockets on the club.

It was a perfect fit.

"Excellent, as usual," he said. He grabbed a pouch from his belt and threw it towards the artisan.

"Fifty kakaw, as agreed."

Pitz'al weighed the pouch, unwilling to open it in front of his customer.

"Thank you ahau. Is there anything else I can do for you?"

"No. That will be all. For now."

The warrior stood up, and fear filled the artisan's heart as the badly burned and scarred face approached him.

"I'll be back when I need more of these."

Pitz'al nodded. He was barely breathing.

"Enjoy the rabbits," added the warrior before he walked away. The stonemason watched him disappear through the door and exhaled a sigh of relief.

"He's gone," he finally said.

"He frightens me," answered his wife as she joined him inside. "With the bones in his hair and his dirty clothes. His wild eyes, his scars! They keep me awake at night! Why did he come here a day early? He is usually always on time."

"I don't know. Like I said, he pays well."

The artisan tossed the pouch into the air.

"You know, with these kakaw, we could easily…"

He stopped. Through the window he could see people gathering on the street, looking towards one end of the village. He immediately hurried out the front door to see for himself what was happening.

Down the road a large group of warriors lined up in two columns was steadily heading toheir way. The earth trembled as they approached, dust raising in the air as they all marched in one single rhythm.

He counted several dozen and still more were appearing in the distance. They all carried heavy packs on their backs. They were armed with short spears and wore large leather helmets. At their head floated a banner representing the feathered snake god, and as they walked into the village people obediently stepped aside, too shocked at the unchallenged intrusion to react otherwise.

"Pitz'al, what is it?" asked Saqirik from inside the hut.

"Shhh!" hushed her husband. "Stay inside, and shut the door behind you!"

The troops marched to the center of the village and stopped at a signal from their leader. The young man at their head looked around.

"My name is Huemac, from the great city of Tollàn," he announced loudly in a very bad Mayan. "Is this the Mayan town of Waka'?"

People silently stared in awe at the heavily armed newcomers. No one answered.

"Is this Waka'?" he repeated.

Still no answer.

"Maybe we are in the wrong village," suggested one of his warriors in the Tollàn language.

"Maybe they don't speak Mayan," added another.

"Maybe you should both shut up," commanded Huemac.

"Where is the city chief? Who is in charge here?" yelled the young commander, once again in a poor Mayan.

"I am," answered a shaky voice, and the crowd split apart.

Through the gap appeared the village's chieftain, who walked towards the Tollàn army accompanied by six men armed with little more than light hunting spears and blowguns. There were no warriors in Waka', only hunters, and the humble display of force was more aimed at preserving the chief's image than at having a dissuasive effect on the Tollàns.

"I am Etmabal, chief of Waka'," said the man, obviously intimidated. Never before had he seen such an impressive group of warriors in his life, let alone in the middle of his own village.

"What is your purpose here?" he added hesitantly as he nervously adjusted a jaguar pelt over his shoulders.

Huemac smiled as he looked at the trembling hunters facing him.

"Do not worry," he said. "We mean you no harm."

"We welcome all travelers who come in peace," said the chief.

"Thank you. We will not stay for long. I have been instructed to meet with a man here. A Mayan warrior from the east."

Etmabal looked at him, dumbfounded.

"Have you seen anyone around here who would be looking for us?" asked Huemac, annoyed at the lack of reaction from the chief standing before him. "He would be a stranger to you, a warrior not from your village."

"The burnt demon," whispered one of the hunters.

The chief looked around.

"There is one who has been seen coming and going for a while now, but he is not a man, and he hasn't said anything about expecting anyone. In fact, he hasn't said anything at all."

"It is me you want to see," called a voice from behind.

Everyone turned. As the modest crowd stepped aside to let Siyah Kak through, a smiled appeared on Huemac's face.

"The last courier told me you were a fierce and scary warrior. I didn't think he meant it literally."

Siyah Kak silently stared at the man.

Huemac met his gaze for a short moment then uncomfortably turned his head back towards the village chief.

"My men will need food and shelter for the night," he said. He then looked once again at Siyah Kak.

"And we need to talk."

Pitz'al, who'd been watching from the side, discretely turned around and hurried back into his house.

"What is it?" asked his wife, concerned, as he stepped inside and closed the door. "What is happening?"

"I must leave for Sian K'aan," he whispered. "Now."

"Sian K'aan. Why?"

"I'll be back in a few days. Go to your brother's house until my return."

The artisan was running inside the house, quickly gathering whatever he would need for the short journey to the city.

"Pitz'al! What is happening?"

The man stopped and looked at his wife.

"Tollàn is invading us!"

A FORGOTTEN TEMPLE

The nights were comfortable this time of year. The day had been scorchingly hot, and although an afternoon storm had provided some relief, the colder nights were welcomed by all. As everyone headed to bed on this dark, moonless night, the cloaked figure of the scribe once again walked out of the royal palace and headed towards the jungle, heavily sweating despite the coolness of the air.

Safely tucked inside his cloak was another folded document containing their last instructions to the rival king. The mere possession of the hidden document was proof enough of his incriminating discussions with the enemy state. It was more than sufficient to accuse him of treason, a crime for which the nacom would have the pleasure of detaching his head from his body should he be caught.

Once again, he would have to be careful.

The night was perfectly silent as the scribe's figure glided around the palace, a shadow amongst shadows. He was being particularly careful, moving very slowly, keeping his body close to the palace's cold exterior wall.

He knew there was barely enough time to reach his destination and come back before sunrise, but this was the most dangerous part of the journey as patrols were frequent in the area. Soon, he would walk by the royal ball court and follow the causeway heading north. From there, he would stay in the shadows of the noblemen's houses until he'd reach the temple dedicated to Ix Tab, the hanged deity. At that point, and not a step before, would he finally dare to significantly increase the pace. Patrols were few in the less reputable northern district.

He approached the walls surrounding the royal ball court. Inside his chest, his heart pounded with a beat reminiscent of a rubber ball striking the ground.

Thump-thump. Thump-thump. Thump-thump.

Fear suddenly gripped him. Would his heartbeat wake the death gods living under the earth? Would they cross the ball court's portal, angered by his disturbance? Would they carry him back to the underworld? He took a deep breath, trying to calm the deafening thumping sound raging inside of him. Despite all efforts he was unsuccessful, and decided it was best not to linger around the stone structure. He hurriedly walked by the two sloped walls and started to relax as every step slowly took him further away from the structure.

The gods are with me, he thought, trying to calm himself. *They are with me. They know and approve of my purpose. Itzamnà knows. He will help.*

Just as confidence was slowly gaining him, he was startled by a voice. *A patrol!* he thought, alarmed.

Instinctively, the scribe looked for concealment, pressing his body even more tightly against the walls as though hoping to merge into the stone.

He quickly recognized the voice echoing throughout the night. It was Icoquih, Great Jaguar Paw's daughter.

Every now and then, after nightfall, she would come out of her apartment and sing for hours in the night. Usually he would settle in a comfortable spot, grab a gourd of balché, and listen to her beautiful voice. Her talent as a singer was well known throughout this end of the city, although it seemed like a shame her songs only brought tears to his face, for always she sang of pain or despair. The scribe often wondered at how someone so young could be inhabited by such melancholy.

Tonight, she sang of a young boy, an orphan who lived by the sea. She sang of his tragic life. Of his many sufferings and ordeals. About his only comfort, which was to sit along the rocky shore under the peaceful light of the moon. Then, she sang of how he tragically drowned one night. How he reached for the water's surface, trying to grab the reflection of the many stars, and fell into the sea. How he had died as he had lived. Alone.

It was a song she'd learned from a salt merchant traveling from the eastern shores. *At night,* he told her, *when the wind is calm and the moon is shining bright, you can still feel the boy's presence as he seeks comfort from the stars.*

The scribe listened to her melody for an instant, captured by the spell of her voice, before cautiously walking away. All anxiety had now gone from his body. As he headed down the familiar path, the beautiful voice faded in the distance behind him.

Soon, he crossed the residential suburbs, reached the relative safety of the maize fields surrounding the city, and approached the border between the cultivated land and the jungle's wilderness.

So far, he'd been lucky enough to avoid Kabrak'an's patrols, but there was a strange feeling upon him on that night. He had the distinct impression that someone was following him, spying his every moves. Several times he turned around to look behind him. Always, the mysterious follower evaded his gaze.

It's all in your head, he thought. *It's only in your head.*

Cautiously, he headed down the main road for a while, ears wide opened in search of approaching footsteps or careless conversation. Then, suddenly, he turned left on an old, long forgotten path.

The path was in such a poor state that anyone not aware

of its existence might have probably walked right by it without even realizing it was there. Even in broad daylight it was practically invisible as a thick and lush vegetation now covered most of the entrance to what was once a wide dirt road. He, on the other hand, had been there often in the past year, and his eyes had no difficulty finding the barely noticeable embranchment.

Once again, he started to relax and breathe a little easier. He felt much more comfortable now, knowing this area was not frequented by the patrols.

Then his heart sank.

Perched on the branches of a nearby tree was the dark shape of an owl, standing perfectly still. Its eyes were wide opened, and it was looking directly at him.

Oh no, an owl, he thought. *Please not an owl.*

Quickly he reached down, grabbed a branch, and threw it at the nightly predator. The owl opened its wings and the scribe stepped back. He then heard a *whoosh* and turned around just in time to see the dark shape flying away into the night.

"Damned birds," he whispered.

Crossing an owl was a very bad omen. They were well known for being messengers of the death lords, spies unleashed into the world of men to observe all that was happening. Soon, the bird would report his trespassing, and the lords of the underworld would be aware of his presence on this ancient sacred site.

He was certain now, he would not survive the night. There were too many eyes upon him. Too many shadows on his footsteps. Nonetheless, he moved forward, determined to complete his mission. There was no turning back at this point.

The message had to be delivered.

The scribe soon reached his destination, the ruin of a small pyramid. The ancient structure, barely half a dozen steps high, was topped by an old temple.

Many generations ago, this sacred site might have been at the center of an ancient village. A holy shrine, where the sick and needy came to offer prayers and sacrifices. These ruins were now the domain of snakes and monkeys.

It was also the secret location of his exchanges with the enemy.

He had discovered the ruins by accident, years ago, when he was a young boy. Since that day, it became his secret hideaway place. At the time, most of the comb roof was still intact. Beautiful murals of red and black illustrating the past glory of ancient kings could still be seen on the interior walls. When part of the structure later collapsed, the painted artworks suddenly became exposed to the devastation of nature. Nowadays, seasonal rains and heavy storms were rapidly washing away the last remnants of the murals which would soon be lost forever.

On the outside, dirt and fallen leaves now covered the major part of the ancient pyramid. Young trees were growing over the soil covered steps. In not so many years from now, one could probably walk right by this place and see only a vegetation covered mound, never expecting a man-made structure to be buried under. Proof, he thought, that no matter how impressive they might be, human structures would never rival against the powers of the gods and of nature.

Silently, he wondered at the foolishness and futility of building ever increasingly high temples and pyramids.

Anyhow, for the time being, this forsaken temple was the perfect location for his secret endeavor. In the dark, he slowly climbed the half-buried steps, careful not to trip against the branches in his path. The pyramid might have been low, but its sides were steep. This was not the time and place to twist an ankle.

As he reached the top, he silently stared into the black,

menacing shadow of the entrance. He looked up into the star-filled sky. Part of him silently wished for the moon to lift his spirit and light his way, while another part knew her presence could only further endanger his life.

He looked back inside the temple.

No matter how long abandoned this place might have been, the entrance to a temple forever remained a sacred place, a portal to the underworld.

His father had taught him, many years ago, how to protect his soul from the evil spirits. He started by reaching inside his clothes for a handful of dried cocoa beans, which he unceremoniously threw across the portal. He then grabbed a dried maize ear and grotesquely peeled off entire rows of kernels with his untrimmed nails. As the ripped kernels fell to his feet, he recited a protective prayer. Finally, as a last line of defense, he left the lifeless body of a bird on the doorstep. The offering was intended as a distraction for any demon who would somehow find a way to slip past his protections.

Satisfied he'd taken all necessary precautions to ensure his safety, the scribe stepped inside the temple and slowly moved ahead with his arms outstretched in front of him. He knew the layout of the temple by heart, yet still he jumped out of surprise as his fingers touched the cold, carved stone of the altar.

An altar which hasn't seen blood sacrifice in generations, he thought. *A temple thirsty for blood.*

He cautiously moved around the flat stone, turned towards the south west corner, and headed straight ahead. His foot fell in a puddle of water.

The underworld!

No, the ground was firm under the thin layer of water.

He took a second step, then a third. His opened hands made contact with the damp wall. He carefully knelt down, looking for the pottery jar. As his fingers found the familiar clay lid, he buried his other hand into his cloak in search of the folded codex message.

Hurry, he thought. *Leave the message and walk out of here. Walk back to the palace's safety as soon as possible.*

At this very moment he heard a cracking noise coming from the opposite corner. It was then that he noticed the heavy, labored breathing behind him.

The demons. The demons have come. The owl has warned them of my presence. Now my time has come.

He closed his eyes and took short, shallow breaths. He felt lightheaded. How would death be delivered to him? Would it come swiftly in a single, lethal blow, or would sharp talons shred his flesh to limbs in a savage, beastly attack? Perhaps he would be taken alive and tortured for eternity in the watery underworld, forever mocked by the death lords for trespassing this sacred portal.

As he pondered about his death, he found himself surprisingly calm.

No doubt because he had already accepted his fate.

Then, suddenly, a voice broke the silence.

"Ah'tsib!"

As soon as the word reached his ears the scribe's shoulders dropped in relief. It was a human voice.

"Ah'tsib. Finally, we meet in person."

His eyes couldn't see past the pitch black darkness, but a strong smell of sweat filled his nostrils.

"Are you here to take the message?" he whispered.

"No, not tonight," replied the raspy voice. "Tonight, I am the one who carries important information. You must take me to your king, ah'tsib. Right away."

PEACE

"Do you know what impresses me the most about the stars?" asked Great Jaguar Paw without really expecting an answer.

"They will always be there," he immediately added. "Always."

Kabrak'an raised his head and looked at the night sky.

"Since the very first day they were thrown above our heads," continued the king, "they have been perfectly predictable. They have been perfectly reliable. They never fail to appear once the sun has set. They are untouchable. We cannot diminish their brightness, nor can we taint their pureness. Stars do not care about our wars and politics. They never get involved in human matters. They simply live up there, in perfect harmony, and thus we stare at them in awe and wonder."

He paused for several seconds.

"The stars are so high above us, my friend. On so many levels."

The warlord sighed discretely. He was in no mood for philosophical discussions or stargazing, for he had much more urgent matters on his mind.

"The harvest will be upon us before long," he said bluntly. "And so will the dry season."

"There!" said the king, pointing a finger at a dark spot where a shooting star had just blazed across the sky, a streak of light lasting but a heartbeat before vanishing forever.

"Did you see? The lords of the night agree with me Kabrak'an. They've sent me a celestial acknowledgement."

"K'uhul Ahau," reiterated the warlord in a serious tone. "We are at war, and there is no reason to believe the next season will be less bloody than the last."

The king looked at him with a strange smile.

"I know," he said. "Trust your faith. The gods will not abandon us."

My faith I trust. I only wish I could also trust the gods, thought Kabrak'an.

"What is the status of our troops?" asked Great Jaguar Paw.

"One thousand five hundred and fifty two men. Including two hundred and ninety recruits who've almost completed their basic training. For now, most are currently dispatched in the fields. They will join me in a few months, after the harvest."

The king lowered his eyes.

"Two hundred and ninety recruits," he whispered. "Two hundred and ninety men..."

"...to replace last year's victims," completed the warlord.

"So many young souls who will never grow old. So many families torn apart. So many grieving mothers. I have seen your new recruits. They are so young. Do you see why we must end the battles? Why we must end this fury?"

"Will it ever end, K'uhul Ahau?"

"I told you, trust your faith. Trust the gods."

The king only saw despair in his warlord's eyes.

"And if you don't," he added, "then believe in me. The end is near."

Kabrak'an looked up to his king and, for the first time in years, he saw hope in his eyes.

He wondered why.

"K'uhul Ahau," interrupted a guard. There was an urgency in his voice. "We've just caught two enemy spies outside of the city."

"Spies? Where are they?" he asked, alarmed.

"They have been brought here, my king. They are inside the palace."

"Then bring them to the throne room immediately," he said. "I wish to see them now."

"It is already done, K'uhul Ahau. They are waiting for you."

Without hesitation, Great Jaguar Paw headed straight inside the palace, closely followed by Kabrak'an.

The many torches lining the walls bathed the throne room in a soft, orange glow. As Great Jaguar Paw's eyes adjusted to the light he realized that, despite the late hour, most of the city's higher nobles were present.

"How strange to see them in their night clothes," he said. "Without their expensive jewelry and with their hair hanging loose, all of them could be mistaken for common citizens."

It was indeed unusual to see the nobles with puffy eyes, yawning, and unshaven.

"News travel fast," he added. "Many have come."

"Pulled out of their beds by the commotion which undoubtedly surrounded the capture of the two prisoners," guessed the warlord. "Apparently, the arrest did not go unnoticed. Many will now want to have a first-hand look at what will happen to the spies."

It was then that the king noticed the pair of cloaked figures standing before the throne, hands tied behind their back. Bloodied hoods covered their heads. Three guards surrounded the prisoners. Wak Xook was amongst them, displaying a discrete but proud grin across his face.

As the king looked at the prisoners, Wak Xook grabbed his spear with both hands and struck the two men behind the legs, sending them straight to the ground.

"Kneel in front of the K'uhul Ahau," he said in a

despising tone. He then swung the spear around and used the blunt end to bring their faces to the floor.

The king looked at the awed crowd for an instant, and then sat on his throne.

"We caught these two spies as they were about to enter the city K'uhul Ahau," said Wak Xook. "I apologize for the early hour. I should have waited for the morning to bring them before you, but this one insisted on seeing you immediately," he added, as he kicked the first man in the ribs.

A faint sound of pain escaped from the hooded figure lying on the floor.

"I should have refused and decapitated them straight away," he continued. "Due to the..." he hesitated, and looked down at the second man "...special circumstances concerning this one's identity, I decided it was best to bring them to you as soon as possible."

Great Jaguar Paw took a deep breath and waived his hand. As he did, Wak Xook pulled the hood off the first prisoner, exposing a narrow dirty face. The man was clearly terrified. His knees were trembling, and blood dripped from his nose.

All noticed the large macaw tattoo covering his left cheek. The mark of Sian K'aan.

The king did not move. Next to him the warlord stiffened.

Wak Xook then pulled the hood off the second prisoner, and the crowd gasped in astonishment. Lying on the cold stone, the bruised and beaten face of the scribe shamefully looked at the king.

"K'uhul Ahau, I..."

"Silence traitor!" interrupted Wak Xook as he shoved him back to the floor with his spear. "I should have killed you in the streets! I swear your body will rot for eternity and your miserable soul will..."

"Enough," ordered Great Jaguar Paw with a calm authority.

Wak Xook immediately turned around and bowed.

"K'uhul Ahau," he said. "This traitor was collaborating with the enemy."

He pulled a folded codex out of his clothes.

"We found this on the ah'tsib."

The warrior handed him the bark paper document. The wax seal had been broken.

"This codex is proof enough of the scribe's guilt, my king. He was plotting with Sian K'aan to attack us. The document instructs our enemy to send three hundred armed warriors at our border two days from now," he said loudly so that everyone present could hear.

The nobles gasped as they shifted in their seats and started murmuring amongst themselves. Next to the throne, Kabrak'an took a step forward.

The firm hand of the aging king held him back.

Great Jaguar Paw raised his eyes and looked at the scribe's bruised face with a sad expression.

"Untie them," he said. "Both of them."

The tone in his voice was such that everyone turned towards him and, as suddenly as they had started, the murmurs stopped.

"K'uhul Ahau," protested the warlord. "He is a traitor!"

"My king," added Wak Xook. "You should read the codex. It is clearly self-incriminating. You will see how..."

"I know what the codex says, Wak Xook," answered the king with a louder voice, suddenly tired of all that was going on. "I know what it says because it contains my own instructions. I have personally dictated the words you've read. *I* have ordered the delivery of this document to the Sian K'aan king."

There was a strong emphasis on the word "*I* ".

Everyone looked at the king, stupefied.

"Now, untie these two men," he added firmly. "Now."

Wak Xook bowed low and, with an expression of disbelief, unsheathed an obsidian dagger and cut the rope binding the prisoner's hands.

"The king of Sian K'aan and I finally came to an agreement," explained Great Jaguar Paw. "This conflict has torn both of our cities for too long. Now, there shall be peace between us."

"Peace?" asked Kabrak'an. "May I ask on which terms, my king?"

"Their fields are depleted. Their children are starving. Their temples are crumbling to the ground. We will start by providing Sian K'aan with food and water for their immediate needs. Then, we will give them access to new planting grounds. We will teach them how to build water-collecting reservoirs. We will assist them in repairing their temples. We will let them trade their goods in our markets, and we shall finally live as brotherly neighbors!"

He would have hoped for cries of joy and support. Instead, he only faced astonished faces, mouths opened wide in disbelief, and the grumbling whispers of disagreement. Apparently, most did not share is enthusiasm for the new peace, although their reaction did not surprise him.

"Do you really mean to share our food and water with those who have stolen from us?" asked the warlord, unable to contain his surprise. His voice was low, as he did not wish to openly disagree with the king.

One of the ahauob administrator stepped forward.

"Forgive me K'uhul Ahau. I believe we deserve some clarifications, for it all seems like a one-sided deal to me! What will they bring us? What could they bring us," he asked, pointing at the Sian K'aan man still standing in front of Great Jaguar Paw. "They have nothing we want. Nothing we need. Nothing to contribute."

The nobles respectfully nodded in agreement.

The king leaned back. This was not how he wanted to announce his new peace, but the events had now forced him down this path. He would have to find the right words to convince them.

"Sian K'aan can help us in a way you cannot even begin to imagine," he said, speaking slowly. "It is not what they can or cannot give us that is important. It is the peace itself that will ensure our survival. Regardless of the costs, the simple fact that we are now at peace might save your lives and the lives of your children. Without it, we are most certainly doomed."

Kabrak'an couldn't believe his ears. "We can win this war my king! We can crush Sian K'aan, and we can keep our maize! And our water!"

"This war has hurt us in so many ways," the king explained. "You can all see it by the many crippled in our streets. You can all count the sons who will never come back. But while your eyes are fixed on our northern border, a much greater threat is approaching from the west. Tollàn has taken notice of our situation. Tollàn has taken every possible course of action to worsen the conflict with Sian K'aan! And now, Tollàn is about to benefit from the war at our expense!"

"Tollàn trades with us," remarked one of the ahauob members. "They, also, have lost significantly. This war hurts them too! It hurts their profits! Why would they want to prolong it?"

Great Jaguar Paw stood up, and the noble immediately looked down, fearing he'd said too much.

"Yes, the conflict might hurt them, but Tollàn's losses are nothing compared to the advantages they are about to gain, for their future profits will be ten times greater if they achieve their goal."

Great Jaguar Paw walked to the bruised and battered

scribe and helped him to his feet. He then walked to the Sian K'aan man.

"Have any of you ever wondered how Sian K'aan was able to stand up to us as they did this past year? How they were able to raid our crops with so much efficiency? How they managed to attack our merchandise and fight our patrols with an apparently never-ending supply of men?"

He looked around.

"Have none of you ever wondered? Their troops are decimated! They are outnumbered. Weak. Demoralized! Yet, they kept coming back at us, always stronger! There is no way they can be responsible for all we accuse them of!"

"If not them, then who?" asked Wak Xook. "Every man we fought clearly came from Sian K'aan. They all had the markings to prove it!"

"There was an attack on a salt shipment lately," explained the king. "One of our warriors was on his way towards his outpost when he heard fighting sounds. He unfortunately arrived too late to help. There was little he could have done, other than get massacred as well, but he saw what happened. The attacker's bodies were indeed painted in red, and they all wore Sian K'aan tattoos, but they spoke Tollàn! They were Tollàn soldiers! They are here, within us, roaming our jungle and attacking merchants disguised as Sian K'aan warriors!"

There were more murmurs amongst the nobles.

"Tollàn has planned it all. Spearthrower Owl has orchestrated everything! The attacks on our merchandise. On our borders. On our people. As far as we know, half the enemy warriors we've have encountered were really disguised Tollàn troops. They have nourished the war between us and Sian K'aan. For what purpose will you ask? To give them an excuse to challenge us. To prevent the other states from opposing them. Spearthrower Owl has already convinced the southern states of our inability to solve this conflict. He has rightfully convinced them that our war impacts the entire stability of the region, a confrontation he has himself aggravated!"

The ahauob members silently looked at each other, beginning to understand.

"You see, brothers, our neighbors from the south have secretly authorized military action against us. They've authorized Spearthrower Owl's troops to cross their borders. As we speak, a foreign army is likely marching upon us. Tollàn warriors are walking on Mayan land, and the southern states will do nothing to stop them! Only peace can help us now. It is not important whether or not Sian K'aan can provide us with anything. We need peace to prove to the other states that we can restore commerce as it was before!"

Kabrak'an frowned, finally understanding. And he was forced to recognize the genius behind this peace. Ending the war eliminated Spearthrower Owl's principal argument for rallying the Mayan kings against Mutul.

"What about the troops?" asked Wak Xook. "The ones mentioned in the message? The three hundred armed Sian K'aan warriors due to arrive here in two days?"

"The Sian K'aan warriors are not coming here to attack us. They are coming here to help us defend this city, for I fear we will soon be under attack. I fear this peace will have come too late."

At this moment, the Sian K'aan man accompanying the scribe took a step forward and confirmed the king's fears.

"K'uhul Ahau," he said. "I came here tonight to send you a warning. And a request. One of our men living in periphery of Mutul has contacted us. The Tollàn army you speak of was seen arriving in Waka' four days ago. It is already here, and Spearthrower Owl has already ordered the attack."

"The Tollàn forces are in Waka'?" asked Kabrak'an,

shocked. "That is less than four days from here!"

"They left Waka' two days ago, warlord ahau, but they are not marching to Mutul. They are headed straight for Sian K'aan. It is my king, K'uhul Ahau, who requests your help. Without the support of Mutul's troops, we cannot hope to defeat them."

Great Jaguar Paw looked at Kabrak'an.

"Why would he be attacking Sian K'aan? It is Mutul that he wants!"

"Which is precisely why he will not attack us," answered a voice from behind.

Great Jaguar Paw turned around and smiled as he saw Winaq approaching.

"My friend," he said, "I am happy you are here."

"Spearthrower Owl does not wish to destroy Mutul," explained the old advisor. "Nor does he want to get rid of its population. He needs the city as it stands today. He wants control of the obsidian, and only from here can he do it. If he destroys Sian K'aan, however, he proves to your opponents that he is a much more capable ally than you are. And with our population terrorized by this new, nearby threat, he will have no problem getting rid of you. If not himself, I suspect his dear nephew would be his first choice as our new king." He lowered his eyes. "I should have seen this coming."

"By the gods, you must be right. He will destroy Sian K'aan and then pressure me into submission. They will not reach Sian K'aan for at least another day," said the king. "Perhaps it is not too late. We can still send troops and catch them by surprise."

Winaq nodded.

"If we could defeat them, we could end the threat once and for all."

"Kabrak'an, prepare your men!" ordered the king. "We will fight alongside our old enemy, for their sake and ours."

Great Jaguar Paw saw the silent looks of approval amongst the ahauob council.

"There is something else you should know," added the Sian K'aan man. "The Tollàn troops have one of your men at their head."

Great Jaguar Paw looked at him inquisitively.

"The burnt lord Siyah Kak, ahau of Mutul, was waiting for them at Waka'. He marches with them."

WAR

"K'uhul Ahau!" said Kabrak'an as Winaq and the king walked out of the throne room. "Why was I not made aware of your peace talks with the enemy?" he asked in a low voice.

"Forgive me, I meant no disrespect to you," answered Great Jaguar Paw. "It was crucial that my discussions with Sian K'aan remain confidential. You were left out because I could have been wrong about their intentions, in which case I would have needed you and your warriors to be fully dedicated to your duties, as you always are. And also because Spearthrower Owl is very cunning. Had he learned of the possible peace, I feared he might have precipitated his attack before an agreement was reached." He paused. "And I will no longer refer to them as *enemies* from this point on. I will ask you to do the same."

Kabrak'an nodded silently.

"Rest assured," he added. "Only Winaq and the scribe knew about this."

"This peace," said the warlord. "How serious is it?"

The king frowned.

"I mean, how dedicated are we to making this happen? Most of all, how dedicated are they? After all, they are the ones who cross our borders and pillage our crops."

"I assure you the Sian K'aan king takes this agreement with the utmost respect and dedication, and so do I. Believe me when I tell you he is significantly more relieved than we are that this conflict is over. His people have suffered immensely during the past years. There will be no more reason for them to raid our borders once we have shared our food supplies. And remember, I believe most of the attacks were actually perpetrated by disguised Tollàn warriors. Sian K'aan admits to the raids, but in a much smaller extent than what we have seen."

The king looked at his warlord.

"Why do you ask? Do you not agree that this is the best way to save ourselves from Tollàn?"

Kabrak'an thought for an instant.

"I believe Tollàn's ambition knows no border. If what you say is true, I believe the Owl lord and his king will never stop plotting against us."

The old warrior sighed.

"I also believe you are right. I do believe this might be the only way, for the moment at least. Still, I need to know I will not risk the lives of my men for a short-lived folly."

He lowered his voice to a whisper.

"How do we know they will not stab us in the back the moment we turn around? How do we make certain we will not sacrifice our men so they can more easily defeat us later? I will not fight their war today just to see them cross our borders again tomorrow!"

"We don't know," admitted the king. "Just as any other deal, this agreement is only as solid as the will of both parties involved. But if we want peace to happen, we need to show some commitment ourselves! Are you not tired of seeing your men butchered? Do you not see that without this peace, it is all the other kingdoms that you will face on the battlefield? You know a war against the southern states is a war we cannot win!"

"Forgive me, K'uhul Ahau. I understand."

"I realize how hard it must be for you. For years, you have fought against an enemy, spilled your own blood, and sacrificed the lives of your men. Today, I must ask you to join them, for the greater good of our city!"

Kabrak'an nodded, as if pondering a decision. While a deep wrinkle across his tattooed forehead betrayed his concerns, his mind was made. He would serve his king, blindly if he was asked to.

"I will take my men to Sian K'aan, and we will stand against the invaders!"

"I expected no less of you."

"The Sian K'aan messenger gave us additional details about the Tollàn troops in Waka'," added Winaq. "According to him, the enemy forces consist of about three hundred warriors."

"Three hundred?" said Kabrak'an, surprised. "That's hardly enough to pose a serious threat. They cannot honestly believe to take the city with such a small force!"

"You think Sian K'aan doesn't need our help?"

"I didn't say that. Their troops are weakened and hungry. Their weapons are in a terrible shape."

"So you believe this should be an easy victory?"

"No. I respect any enemy opposing me in battle. We both know the smallest snakes can deliver the deadliest blow. I only wonder why they haven't sent more warriors."

"We've asked ourselves the same question," said Winaq. "What do *you* think?"

"Obviously, they didn't anticipate our participation in Sian K'aan's defense. Or, maybe, they are expecting support from somewhere else," answered the warlord. "From another Tollàn army in the region perhaps. Or from one of the southern Mayan kings."

He paused, thinking.

"We cannot rule out the possibility of facing battle on two separate fronts. Our city could face a serious threat while most of our troops have been lured away."

Winaq nodded.

"Our conclusion as well," he said.

Great Jaguar Paw closed his eyes and took a deep breath.

"We will honor our agreement with Sian K'aan. However, I do not wish to leave Mutul defenseless. Kabrak'an, you will personally take four hundred men up north to face the Tollàn troops. It should be enough to ensure victory once you've joined with Sian K'aan's warriors."

"We are in the middle of the wet season. I don't even have four hundred men at the border right now. Most of my warriors are busy tending the fields. And what shall I do with the camp?"

"I want you to abandon the border outpost. Grab a few recruits, take all of your men who are up there, and leave. Winaq, send word for all of the warriors currently in the fields to be armed and returned to the city immediately! Mutul will need some protection while Kabrak'an is gone."

"Then I will leave without any further delay," said the warlord.

"Watch your back," added Winaq. "Spearthrower Owl might be a butchering demon, but he is a very clever one."

Kabrak'an nodded, and Great Jaguar Paw wrapped an arm around his shoulders.

"Yesterday's enemy is today's friend," he said. "And yesterday's friend is today's enemy."

The warlord looked at him.

"Soon, we will face the Tollàns, and then what? Will Spearthrower Owl send more troops? Or will the southern states attack us? Is peace even possible?"

The king grabbed him by both shoulders with a firm grip.

"I have to believe it is, Kabrak'an, and you must believe it too. Peace will happen, one step at the time. Otherwise, what are we fighting for?"

The warlord closed his eyes, suddenly feeling very tired.

He raised his hand to his face and ran his fingers along the great iguana tattoo. He was so weary of battle.

"What of Siyah Kak?" he added.

There was a long moment of silence.

"He is a son of Mutul. He has always been a man of action, and I have always admired him for that. I find it hard to believe he has actually turned his back against us. But if he truly did, then what he did is unforgivable."

"If he is there, on the battlefield, I will find him," said the warlord.

"Then I would like you to bring him back here. I will deal with him myself."

"You know him better than that, K'uhul Ahau. Siyah Kak will never surrender. He would die a hundred times before accepting the humiliation of capture. If it comes down to it, it will be a fight to the death."

"Then so be it," said Great Jaguar Paw.

As soon as he parted from the king, Kabrak'an grabbed Wak Xook and Sukil, the warrior who'd stumbled upon Balam and Tupac during their hunting trip. All three were now hurriedly walking along the northern causeway.

"Wak Xook," he said. "How many men do we currently have on the border? Three hundred and fifty eight?"

"Yes ahau."

"Excellent, that will be sufficient. I want you to leave immediately for the border camp. Do not waste any time. As soon as you arrive, recall all patrols and gather everyone at camp."

Wak Xook nodded.

"I want you to prepare all men for the trip to Sian K'aan. We will travel lightly, so make sure they do not carry more than a spear, a shield, and a little food."

"As you wish."

"Leave twenty sentinels behind. I wouldn't want another army to slip through the unguarded border unannounced. Have them patrol the northern and western regions in groups of two. Then wait for me. As soon as I arrive, we go to war."

"What about the wall construction ahau?" asked the commander.

"The king has ordered to stop all work until further notice. Send all the workers back here along with all remaining weapons. I want them in Mutul, ready to defend the city if need be. Now go," added the warlord. "Run. I will grab a handful of recruits, and we will see you soon."

Wak Xook bowed and hurriedly left for the border. Kabrak'an then turned towards Sukil.

"You will personally be in charge of all remaining troops until our return. The city's safety will be in your hands, as I fear the three hundred men marching on Sian K'aan are only a lure. Someone else might be out there, waiting for an opportunity to attack us. Wak Xook will send weapons from the border, and Winaq will send men from the fields. In the meantime, make sure everyone in the city is armed and combat ready."

"Yes ahau."

"Finally, have someone retrieve all the guards along the protected route. We will need all available warriors here."

The warlord finalized the details of the city's defenses with Sukil. He then quickly left and headed towards the recruit training barracks, where he assembled fifty men.

It was almost midday by the time he reached the camp along the border. Once there, he quickly realized his orders had been meticulously followed. Preparations were well under way for his troops to leave the outpost.

His warriors were lined up in four ranks, ready for battle. Each of them carried a spear, a long flexible shield, and a gourd of maize gruel and water. Their spears were decorated with feathers and many wore animal pelts, seashell necklaces, and even headdresses adorned with objects such as animal skulls and deer antlers.

The fifty recruits brought by Kabrak'an were signaled to join the ranks. As they obeyed, they all looked around them, visibly intimated by such a display of savage beautification, their own appearance paling in comparison with the veteran warriors beside them.

Kabrak'an himself was also wearing his battle attire. A jaguar skin over his torso, thick leather forearm protectors, a jadeite bead necklace, and a large iguana headdress covered with quetzal feathers. His prized obsidian dagger hung at his waist, while in his hand he carried a heavy spear tipped with a large razor-sharp flint blade.

The warriors cheered as he appeared in front of them.

The warlord proudly looked at his men for an instant. It had been years since he last took his troops into battle. A real battle, not the petty skirmishes and ambushes they all faced on a daily basis. Large conflicts opposing hundreds of warriors were a rare thing.

He felt the anticipation and the anxiety rising within him as the battle standards towering above his troops left no doubt to the magnitude of the event about to happen. The tall spears, topped with large square shields and banners, were decorated with feathers, bones, jaguar pelts, turtle shells, dead animals, or any other sacred ornament. *The gods are with us,* the standards announced. *Fight us, and face the underworld demons. Fight us, and you shall die.*

"Ahau!" called Wak Xook. The commander appeared from the side. He, also, was wearing his battle attire.

"I was just completing my final inspection of the camp. We are ready to leave at your command," he said.

"Very well, excellent," complimented the warlord.

Kabrak'an turned towards his troops. Other than the fifty recruits he'd just brought with him, most of the warriors standing before him were seasoned veterans, men who possessed years of experience with a spear and several victory tattoos over their bodies.

"Warriors of Mutul!" he yelled with a confident voice. "For years now, we have fought against Sian K'aan. There is little time to explain, but our king has made peace with our northern neighbors, whom I shall now call friends. However, there is a new enemy lurking nearby. Tollàn troops have infiltrated our land and menace our borders."

The men grumbled.

"They believe they can walk here unchallenged. They believe they can threaten our homes! Our families! Our children! They believe they can defy our gods!"

Kabrak'an raised his spear towards the sky. The bright green quetzal feathers adorning the shaft gently flowed in the breeze.

"Today," he added, "we head into battle. Today, we will stand against the foreign enemy, and we will send them back to the land whence they came from! Today, we walk to glory! And to eternity!"

The crowd cheered, calling the battle name of their warlord, the iguana title.

O'on Nimal! O'on Nimal! O'on Kamikal Ahau!

As his name resonated throughout the jungle, Kabrak'an smiled. He made his way to the head of the line, and signaled his men forward.

Mutul's army was on its way towards Sian K'aan.

It wasn't long before he and his troops reached the main road, a path originally cleared generations ago in a time when there used to be peace between the two kingdoms. To their right was Mutul, with its beautiful stone structures and its rich maize fields. That road was well maintained and free of vegetation as it was frequently used to quickly reach the border, to distribute goods amongst the northern villages, and to carry harvested crops back to the city's storage pits.

To their left, however, the road abruptly ended as two fallen trees barred the way to what was once a well-traveled region. Long ago, there used to be a sign nearby, a post planted by the road to mark the border between both states. All that now remained in front of the barricade was a single stela, a warning destined to all unknowing travelers. The symbol adorning its face had been roughly carved into the stone. A skull, perched on a faded flower, looking towards the west. The message was clear; this road lead into enemy territory. Towards death.

Beyond the stela the path was barely recognizable as a lush vegetation had invaded the road. This route had been abandoned a long time ago.

Kabrak'an took one last look towards Mutul and, without hesitation, turned left, walked around the fallen trees, and headed straight into the former enemy land.

As he and his troops progressed deeper past the barricade, a strange feeling slowly grew inside the warlord. A knot tightened inside his abdomen. Everything there felt foreign, strange. The jungle smelled different. The birds didn't seem to be as cheerful as they were in Mutul, and even the sound of the wind traveling through the leaves didn't feel right.

He was a seasoned warrior, battle was his life, but he was now forced to admit that anxiety was now threatening to overpower him, like a demon slowly emerging from a dark pit. He knew the feeling well, the sensation of being on the edge of a cliff, a step away from collapsing into an unrecoverable spiral. From losing control. He fought hard to remain calm, to prevent his fears from getting the best of him.

Kabrak'an subtly looked behind. He could tell his men were also nervous. He could see them looking around and above as they all headed deeper into the unknown.

"Rumors are slowly growing amongst the troops,"

whispered Wak Xook.

"Rumors?"

The commander took a step closer.

"It is being said that Sian K'aan is not in such a state of need and despair as everyone believes. The word is rapidly spreading that Sian K'aan would have actually prospered and done fairly well during these past few years. That their apparent difficulties and small scale raids would be nothing more than a plot destined to make us believe them to be weak, when in fact they have grown stronger."

Kabrak'an smiled.

"They speak of great temples painted in red, temples reaching all the way up to the sky," Wak Xook added. "They speak of great murals, of long white roads, and of citizens lavishing into expensive foreign goods."

"Fear is the greatest trigger of irrational beliefs," answered Kabrak'an. "It breeds stories and promotes imagination."

"Others think the population of Sian K'aan died years ago," continued Wak Xook. "They say their huts are inhabited by wandering spirits who refuse to cross into the underworld. That their temples are filled with blood!"

The warlord raised his eyebrows mockingly, laughing inside. He, also, had his doubts. Yet, he could show nothing less than strength and courage if he wanted to keep his men from to succumbing to their own fears.

"We shall see for ourselves," he said. "Soon we will reach Sian K'aan. Then we shall know the truth."

He looked above at the sun. If all went well, they would be in Sian K'aan before dusk. Then, they would finally see the true face of their longtime enemy.

SIAN K'AAN

"The flexible shields, made of woven reeds covered with deer hide, are quite efficient at deflecting spear blows. Unfortunately, they are significantly too cumbersome to carry into the jungle, and are therefore seldom used during patrols and ambushes. They are, however, perfectly adapted to large scale campaigns, as there is usually plenty of time to deploy them before an important battle."

"Conveniently, they can also be used as a mattress or blanket, and warriors have developed the habit of wrapping themselves in their shield before going to sleep, thereby protecting their body from both the chilly nights and the dampness of the ground. As such, they have become an important addition to any warrior's complement of weapons."

Excerpt from "Weapons and Equipment"
Mutul library, Wars and Conquests section
Dated 12 Kaban, 0 Xul

The road to Sian K'aan was in a much worse condition than Kabrak'an had first anticipated. He'd expected the path to be in an abandoned yet practicable state. Instead, they were faced by a dense and sometimes impenetrable vegetation, turning what should have been a relatively straightforward walk into a perpetual guessing game. In many areas, the road had completely disappeared under the thick undergrowth, and Kabrak'an had to send scouts to figure out the way ahead. Twice they had to turn around after walking into impassable marshes, and to make things worse, an afternoon storm had crossed their path.

So it was much after nightfall that the Mutul warriors finally approached their destination, tired and drenched, where they were greeted by a Sian K'aan patrol. From far away, they all saw the three men standing in the middle of the path. The torches they carried casted an eerie light around the warriors.

"Greetings," said the leader as they came within range. "We've been waiting for your arrival."

"Good evening," answered Kabrak'an. He noticed how the warrior did not offer his hand for the arm shake.

He did not offer his.

"We were starting to believe you wouldn't come," said the man facing him. The other two behind him chuckled in a nervous laugh.

The warlord silently stared at the strongly built warriors standing before him. Although not particularly different from his own warriors, there was something strange about them. The leader had way too many tattoos on his body, to a point where it looked ridiculous. Even in the darkness, Kabrak'an could clearly see the many overlapping symbols and images covering every single parcel of skin, but that was not it.

There was something else.

Then it suddenly dawned upon him. These men were not covered with the red paint he was accustomed to seeing on Sian K'aan warriors. They did, however, wear macaw tattoos, and as his eyes fell upon the Sian K'aan symbol, he suddenly remembered where he was. The three men facing him were all fully armed, and although he was backed by an army of four hundred of his own warriors, he felt nervous.

This was enemy territory after all.

A feeling of anger suddenly awakened inside of him. As his soldier instinct reminded him of the obsidian dagger hanging at his waist, his fingers inched towards the hilt. Despite the warning signal howling inside of him, the warlord gathered all of his inner strength and resisted the urge to reach for the weapon. Instead, he straightened up and looked directly into the eyes of the warrior facing him, where he also saw discomfort and nervousness.

"The road was in very bad condition," he finally said, offering an explanation for their delay. "We were hoping to make much better time."

"This path has been abandoned for years," answered the patrol leader. "You are the first ones to come this way in a very long time."

He paused for a few tense seconds.

"You are welcome here, brothers of Mutul," he finally added. "My name is Jun Akbal."

Kabrak'an relaxed a little, and introduced himself.

"What are our instructions?" he then asked, eager to move on to something else. "Shall we review the tactical situation in the comfort of your city? The night is chilly. My men are cold, wet and hungry."

The warrior shook his head.

"I am sorry, warlord ahau. You will not walk into Sian K'aan tonight."

There was a murmur of concern amongst the troops. Once again, Kabrak'an's hand moved towards his waist.

"My orders are to take you to the plains of Xaqin," explained the warrior. "There, you shall join our troops. Our men have already been deployed on the battlefield."

Kabrak'an looked at him. The Sian K'aan warrior did not wait for the question.

"The Tollàn troops are here," he said. "Their camp is set

not far away."

"They are here? Already?" exclaimed Kabrak'an, surprised. "I thought they wouldn't be here for at least another day!"

"So did we. They travel surprisingly fast. I must take you to your camp site now, ahau. I hope your men are ready. Tomorrow, we go to war."

He gestured forward.

"Please follow me."

Kabrak'an looked at Wak Xook. Things were definitely developing in a strange matter. He signaled his troops to advance, and they all followed the Sian K'aan patrol as their torches guided them through the dark, moonless night.

It wasn't long before they walked out of the jungle. All of a sudden, the black shadows of the vegetation surrounding them were instantly replaced by open skies filled with thousands of stars shining high into the heavens.

"Look!" pointed a warrior near Kabrak'an. "Stars have fallen from the sky!"

Far away, straight ahead on the horizon, hundreds of yellow lights flickered in the night.

"They're not stars," answered the warlord.

"That's the Sian K'aan army," replied Wak Xook.

"Over six hundred men," confirmed Jun Akbal. "All of them ready for battle."

"Six hundred!" exclaimed the Mutul commander.

"And across the plain?" asked Kabrak'an, pointing to more fires burning in the faraway distance. "The Tollàn troops, I assume?"

"You suppose right," answered the Sian K'aan warrior. "Tollàn scum. We will crush them under our sandals in the morning!"

Jun Akbal looked at the Mutul warlord with a smile.

"There's only about three hundred of them. We

outnumber them three to one now that you have come. Maybe you could bring back a sacrifice or two as a souvenir of our alliance's first battle!"

Kabrak'an looked away. He'd learned the hard way never to underestimate the enemy, but if Sian K'aan troops really numbered six hundred men, the odds did seem greatly in their favor.

Six hundred men in front of them. Another three hundred to their left. His own warriors were vulnerable. Such an army could easily dispose of the Mutul troops, especially if they were attacked from both sides at once. He remembered the ambush rumors, and he prayed they hadn't just fallen into a deadly trap. If, somehow, these men across the field were also Sian K'aan warriors, they wouldn't stand a chance.

"Ch'o'j Ahau Sutul Taqan Itzel!" suddenly announced a Sian K'aan man loudly.

Kabrak'an turned his head to meet the newcomer.

"Ahau of Mutul," said Jun Akbal, "meet Sutul ahau, warlord of Sian K'aan."

Kabrak'an nodded, never taking his eyes off the man before him. His counterpart was about his age and stature. A deep scar ran across his right cheek. He was wearing a simple white loincloth and a deer hide covered his shoulders, providing little protection against the cool evening air.

"Welcome," said their warlord with a deep voice. "It is an honor to meet you here as a friend, warlord of Mutul."

"The honor is mine," replied Kabrak'an.

"Your reputation precedes you, warlord. I have heard countless stories about your achievements."

"And I about yours," lied Kabrak'an. He'd never heard of the man before. He had once met another warrior who'd claimed to be the Sian K'aan warlord, a very long time ago. Kabrak'an assumed he must have either died or been replaced.

"I am relieved to finally see you here, on this battlefield," added Sutul. "We desperately need all the good warriors we can muster."

"Jun Akbal seems fairly confident that Tollàn will pose little threat to you."

Sutul took a deep breath.

"Jun Akbal is a very brave warrior. Unfortunately, the truth is most of the men fighting with me are underfed, with many being either too young or too old to fight. They lack training. They are poorly equipped. They might act bravely for now, but you know how untrained people react." He looked at Kabrak'an. "When the enemy comes running towards you, screaming, brandishing their weapons in a threatening manner. When spears clash and shatter. When blood flows over the ground and the screams of the dying fill your ears. When bravery changes into panic. I told my king yes, we might outnumber them. Still, we cannot hope to win without Mutul's help."

Kabrak'an nodded. *What have we gotten ourselves into?* he thought. *Can I trust this man? Who is the real enemy here?*

"Did you take a good look at them?" he asked, nodding towards the Tollàn camp.

"Yes. Three hundred. They came from the west carrying spears. No shields. They should've been exhausted, having traveled for two months straight, and yet they came singing battle songs and carrying war banners. Maybe they expect their gods to do the fighting for them. Anyway, this land will become their graveyard now that you have joined us."

"What about their leader?" asked Kabrak'an. "Have you seen him?"

Sutul looked down.

"At their head was a Tollàn, there is no doubt about that. A young war leader. Next to him was one of yours. The burnt demon, as my men call him. When I saw him, I thought Mutul had broken their allegiance. I thought you had joined the enemy. Honestly, most of my commanders still believe it. They fear we will be caught in a trap between you and the Tollàns. Many believe we would be better off to send you back behind your own borders and settle this on our own."

Damn, thought Kabrak'an. *He fears treachery. We fear treachery. Mistrust between allies is a deadly poison on the battlefield.*

Behind him, Wak Xook subtly cleared his throat. The warlord realized his warriors were still waiting.

"My men have walked all day," Kabrak'an said. "They are tired, and they could use some rest."

"They can all sleep here," said Sutul, pointing to the damp soil. "I am sorry. I would have liked to show you proper Sian K'aan hospitality, but I cannot offer anything better. Jun Akbal will see that you have all that is needed for your comfort. Sleep well. We will attack at sunrise."

He bowed his head and walked away into the darkness.

As the Sian K'aan warlord disappeared in the night, Wak Xook walked up to Kabrak'an.

"Is it wise to stay here?" he asked in a whisper. "I mean, shouldn't we be running home? I have a bad feeling about this place."

"So do I," answered the warlord. "Yet here we are. There is no turning back now."

He raised his voice slightly, so his warriors could hear.

"Prepare yourselves for the night. Take the men one hundred steps in that direction." He pointed towards the east. "Do it as silently as possible. Once there, no one goes wandering around. Sleep closely one to another. Make sure everyone has their weapons within reach. I want two guards on rotation throughout the night. And no fires."

"No fires? But the men are cold," Wak Xook argued in a

very low voice. "And they are frightened."

"No fires my friend. It is probably best to keep our exact position unknown to Sian K'aan for the night," he explained. "I also want to avoid revealing our presence to the Tollàns until the morning."

Wak Xook nodded, and immediately started distributing his instructions to the warriors.

Kabrak'an walked around a little, making sure his directives were followed. Once all of his men were finally lying down, ready for the night, he untied the long flexible shield from his own back and unrolled in on the ground. There, he reached for his gourd of maize gruel, only to find he had no appetite. No matter how much combat experience he had, or how many victory tattoos covered his body, his stomach always seemed to tighten before battle. So he forced himself to a few gulps, closed the gourd, and placed it down on the soil next to him.

It was then that he was startled by a drumbeat. As the sound of sticks beating hollow trunks echoed in the night, he instinctively reached for his spear. The music came from his right, not too far away, where the Sian K'aan army was camped. In the light of their fires he saw warriors covered with deer hides and feathers. They carried their spears high above their heads as they danced and turned around the blazing pits, howling into the night.

"War dances," said Wak Xook as he approached and sat next to him. "Sleepless warriors on the eve of battle, gathering their courage."

Kabrak'an nodded, still looking at the dancers. He silently regretted not allowing his own warriors to perform this customary ritual usually preceding battle. Yet he desperately wanted to avoid attracting too much attention to themselves, from both Tollàn and Sian K'aan.

"How are the men?" he asked.

"Nervous," answered Wak Xook. "And afraid. A fact I

find rather surprising, considering most of them are experienced men. They've all faced death before."

"You find it surprising? Do you not feel the slightest bit of fear yourself? I know I certainly do."

Wak Xook did not answer. There was indeed fear in his heart.

"While on patrol," continued Kabrak'an, "the enemy usually stumbles upon you without any warning. Within an instant, you find yourself fighting for your life. Here, the men are having way too much time to think about everything. Too much time to worry about what could be lying in the darkness across that field. Too much time to wonder whether or not they will awaken in the middle of the night with their throat slit."

Behind him, he could hear his own men mumbling protective prayers in the night. The smell of burning copal drifted from the Sian K'aan fires, where he knew warriors would dance until the morning.

"You, afraid?" asked Wak Xook. "Are you ever afraid of death? Are you ever afraid of what awaits in the otherworld?"

In the darkness, he heard the warlord swallow before answering.

"I do not fear death," answered Kabrak'an. "I am only afraid of dying."

"Isn't it the same thing?"

"No," chuckled Kabrak'an. "Not at all. I have no fear of being dead, for I know that once I have left this world, I will be with my ancestors. I do not fear death. I do not fear for my soul, and I do not fear what will happen once my heart stops beating. But I do fear the instant in which death will come to me. The moment immediately before the dark curtain is drawn over my eyes. I am afraid of being afraid when the enemy spear will end my life. I am afraid of being weak before my last heartbeat, when it is time for me to leave. You see, I wish for a noble death, so my spirit can cross the river of blood and meet my ancestors, but I fear that, in the ultimate moment, I won't deserve it."

Wak Xook nodded, silently understanding.

"It will be a long night," he said.

Kabrak'an looked up towards the sky and smiled as his eyes met Ak' Ek', the turtle, one of the first constellations his father had taught him to recognize. Three perfectly lined up stars, the first one also being part of a triangle at the center of which rested a smoky, cloudlike body.

They were the three stones of the god's hearth. The birthplace of mankind. He, also, offered a prayer to the gods.

He did not sleep at all.

SKULL-FACED
WARRIORS

The sun was still far below the horizon when Kabrak'an and Wak Xook woke up their troops. Most men were pale and shaky. Few had slept, and even fewer had been able to eat anything. Still, all were relieved the night had finally ended without any incident. Although the Sian K'aan drums had beaten all night, there had been no surprise attack. No betrayal.

Now, in the cold morning air, the Mutul warriors prepared themselves for battle. With their warlord's blessing they lit a great fire and sang battle songs as the flames warmed their bodies and spirits. They used cold ashes to whiten their faces and soot to blacken their eyes and noses so that their faces would take the appearance of fleshless skulls. They howled towards the sky, challenging the undead spirits to join them.

Together, they slowly built up their courage.

When they were finally ready, they attached their shields to their arms, they grabbed their spears, and they joined the Sian K'aan troops on the edge of battlefield where, for the first time since their arrival, they finally took a good look at their new allies.

They all suddenly understood why their presence was so desperately needed.

"Look at them," whispered Wak Xook. "Most of them have never before held a spear in their life!"

Standing in three barely straight lines, the Sian K'aan army mostly consisted of peasants, craftsmen, children, and the elderly. Men with barely any tattoos. Ordinary citizens pulled out of their daily chores, handed the first available weapon, and sent to the field of death. They carried clubs, staves, chipped spear heads mounted on broken shafts, and wood cutting ax. The luckiest ones were equipped with wooden shields and actual short spears. All looked towards the approaching Mutul men with intimidated looks.

There were a few true warriors scattered amongst them. Bigger men motivating the peasants who came to join the battle, quickly teaching them how to wield their weapons. There was no fear in their eyes. Their bodies were painted in red and macaw tattoos covered their chests. They carried bowls filled with a mixture of hematite and water, and as they walked amongst the frightened men they dipped their fingers in the paint and smeared their faces and chests with the red oxide paste to mark them as warriors.

"So few," said Kabrak'an. "There are so few of them left." He counted less than two hundred true warriors, and he understood how close to defeating Sian K'aan they'd really came. "For sure, they wouldn't have lasted another season against us."

He saw Jun Akbal, the patrol leader who'd greeted them on the previous night, the man with too many tattoos. He was now chanting war songs, wielding his spear high above his head.

He also saw Sutul, his counterpart, standing in front of his troops. The Sian K'aan warlord looked taller in the daylight. A single, huge macaw tattoo covered his naked back. A jaguar skull sat over his head, and a single quetzal feather hung at his spear.

Dressed in his jaguar hide and with his iguana headdress, Kabrak'an was magnificent on the battlefield.

With the Mutul battle standards perched high above him and his menacing skull-faced troops, he truly appeared as though he commanded the armies of the underworld.

In that instant, he truly was the o'on kamikal, the Iguana of Death.

Both warlords looked at each other and nodded respectfully. The two former enemies were now brothers, united against the invader waiting somewhere across the field, still hidden within the soft blue haze of pre-dawn morning.

Their fires had died sometime during the night. For an instant, Kabrak'an feared that Tollàn had secretely deserted the battlefield, that they'd left in the middle of the night, somehow managing to slip through the tight net of vigils positioned all around them. He feared they were now already within striking distance of Mutul.

He knew that was impossible. His scouts reported the enemy was still there, on the opposite end of the field, lurking in the morning shadows. So they waited for what seemed like an eternity.

Behind him, Kabrak'an heard the sound of a man hurling, openly betraying his nervousness. There were no mocking laughters from his comrades, only discrete words of encouragements and support as the smell of vomit joined the sour smell of sweat, urine and feces already lingering over the field where hundreds of men had spent the night.

The waiting finally ended when came the words they all dreaded to hear.

"There they are!" shouted someone.

As the first rays of the rising sun touched the ground, the Tollàn warriors walked out of the jungle and formed a single line in front of them. Kabrak'an quickly evaluated the enemy strength. The information they'd received seemed accurate, as he counted about three hundred men standing across the field. Even in the distance the warlord recognized the classic Tollàn uniform. Thick leather helmets covering the head, cheeks and lower jaw. Deer hide protecting the torso and legs, and long animal tails hanging from the waist.

They all carried short spears.

Walking through the line came two men. The first was a young warrior who wore the same armor as the others, although his was incrusted with obsidian beads and decorated with black feathers.

The other was dressed as a typical Mayan warrior. The man had a jaguar pelt over his shoulders. A prominent dead macaw headdress on top of his head. Large jade earrings. A seashell necklace. In his hand was an imposing club into which Kabrak'an knew were inserted several obsidian blades. At his sight, Kabrak'an lowered his head, and adjusted his leather wrist protectors.

Siyah Kak, the burnt warrior, had come to Sian K'aan.

"What is it?" asked Wak Xook.

"I almost hoped it wouldn't be true. I almost hoped he wouldn't be here."

"He is a traitor now, ahau. An enemy," said Wak Xook. "Do not forget that, and treat him as such when we meet him on the battlefield."

Kabrak'an nodded, silently agreeing. The nacom had chosen his side. He could no longer be considered a son of Mutul.

The warlord stood motionless for an instant, then raised his spear high above his head. As he did, conch horns were blown. The warriors started shouting. They screamed and chanted as they raised their weapons towards the morning sky. Through the deafening noise, Kabrak'an sent another signal and two new standards were raised to join the ones already present.

The first was Mutul's crimson banner adorned with

their city-state's glyph. The knotted hair symbol clearly identified them as an army from Mutul. The second was Kabrak'an's personal banner. The white iguana over a black background standard, known throughout the land, marked the presence of the famous warlord on the battlefield.

Motivated by the official announcement of their leader's presence, the Mutul troops now cheered even louder, chanting the war name of Kabrak'an.

O'on Nimal!

O'on Nimal!

O'on Kamikal Ahau!

Then also appeared the war standards of Sian K'aan, the macaw banners. Their warriors started shouting as well, carried by the strength of their new allies. They sang and boasted and yelled as if to intimidate their enemy.

Responding to the challenge, the Tollàn troops raised their own battle standard and at its sight, fear invaded the hearts of the Mayans.

Before them was a long serpent entangled around a cross-pole under which were hung half-a-dozen decapitated heads. Blood was still dripping from the freshly severed necks. The snake was alive, for the Mayans could clearly see its head moving, and it's slit tongue flashing through a thin mount. Instead of having scales, its body was entirely covered with feathers.

"The feathered snake!" exclaimed Wak Xook. "May the gods help us if he is here!"

As if materializing his fears, another man appeared through the enemy line, a tall figure entirely covered with green feathers. His bloodied arms carried a small round shield and a spear, and his head was that of a snake, also covered with feathers.

"The snake god!" screamed the Mayans, terrified. "They've brought the feathered snake onto our land! Their gods are amongst us!"

There was no more chanting as the snake-man walked halfway up the field and started dancing ludicrously before them. No music accompanied his steps, only the frightened murmurs of the Mayan troops.

Wak Xook took a step back.

"I fear no storm. I fear no man. I fear no armies," murmured the commander. "But I do fear the old fool dancing on the battlefield, for his soul belongs to the spirits, and the gods are his ally."

"What?" said Kabrak'an.

"An old Teenek saying," he answered. "I heard Tollàn priests always dance in front of enemy troops before battle."

"Why?"

"He is calling the snake god!"

Kabrak'an looked around and saw the look of fear on his men's faces. An enemy god stood against them. They would need help if they were to hope for victory.

Divine help.

So Kabrak'an also summoned a god of their own at their side. He unsheathed his obsidian dagger and raised it towards the morning sun.

"Itzamnà!" he cried. "Itzamnà! Almighty creator god! Today, we call upon you to grant us your protection! Allow us the honor of victory over these foreigners who would invade your land! Who would destroy your people! Please accept this blood sacrifice as a sign of our gratefulness for your protection!"

He swiftly brought the blade down and sliced open his cheek. Blood flowed down his face.

"Here we stand! Your sons, lined up against three hundred Tollàns and one god. Join our ranks and fight alongside your children! Cross the portal to our world and join us in the battle against this foreign god who would take your place in the heavens!"

"Itzamnà!" yelled someone behind him. Then he was joined by another, and another. Soon, the warriors had forgotten all about the dancing figure as they chanted their own god's name. They pulled out their daggers and started offering blood sacrifices of their own. They pierced their nose and ears and lips.

Euphoria and invulnerability filled them once again.

The warlord glanced to the sides, still perplexed as to why there was only three hundred men facing them. He looked behind and all around, expecting more to come. More to appear.

There was no one else. There was no threat of being flanked by the enemy. No threat of being attacked from the back.

So this is it, he thought. *Spearthrower Owl never expected us to be here. This might be an easy victory after all.*

When Kabrak'an felt his men were ready, he raised his spear towards the sky. "Itzamnà rides with us!" he yelled one last time, and he lowered his arm.

Once again, a conch shell horn sounded. The Mayan troops hurried forward shouting battle cries. Kabrak'an noticed the Sian K'aan men had followed his command.

One thousand men were now running towards three hundred.

As the Mayans launched their attack, the snake-man interrupted his dance. He hissed angrily at the rapidly approaching warriors and hurried back behind the Tollàn line.

The Mayans laughed at the fleeing god, intoxicated by a feeling of supremacy, sustained by their undeniable numerical advantage and by the promise of blood. All along, Kabrak'an stared at Siyah Kak, who stared back at him with a deceitful smile. He felt the reassuring presence of Wak Xook close to him and he, too, suddenly lusted for blood.

Then everything changed.

The young Tollàn captain raised his arm. At the signal, his troops dropped their spears and reached behind their back for what looked like short, thin sticks. The Mayans laughed at the sight, insulting the Tollàns as they ran forward.

As they reached midfield, the Tollàn captain dropped his arm.

In perfect unison, the Tollàn troops took a single step forward. Their arms swung in a uniform, circulatory motion, and the atlatl released their projectiles. The sky was instantly filled with darts.

Kabrak'an, terrified, suddenly understood.

"No!" he yelled with horror, frantically waving his arms. "Spread out! Spread out!" he shouted again.

It was too late.

The air filled with the whistling sound of flying projectiles and screams suddenly arose as the first volley of flint-tipped darts fell amongst the tightly packed Mayan troops. They were screams of fear and pain, for many darts had successfully found a target. All around him, Kabrak'an heard the dull thumps of bodies falling to the ground as, across the field, enemy warriors reloaded their weapons.

"Shields!" cried someone. "Shields!"

The Mayans raised their shields above their heads.

The woven reeds were no match for the high velocity darts. Once again, more screams arose as the second volley's flint blades pierced through the flexible shields and embedded themselves deep into the bodies concealed underneath.

Kabrak'an looked around him in disbelief.

It had all happened so fast.

One moment his motivated troops were running towards certain victory. An instant later, most of his men were lying on the ground, thin wooden shafts protruding from their blood soaked bodies. Some were already dead, killed by a single fatal strike, while most of the others lay wounded, crawling for help.

And still the Tollàns were launching their darts in the sky. Again, and again.

He heard Wak Xook's heavy breathing immediately behind him. The few still standing Mutul warriors were in shock, looking at him with eyes wide opened, wondering what to do. To his right he saw that Sian K'aan had also been badly hit. Many were down. Others were aimlessly running in all directions, hopelessly trying to evade the incoming projectiles. He caught a glimpse of Jun Akbal, who was desperately attempting to rally his fleeing troops.

"Wak Xook!" bellowed Kabrak'an, his voice barely audible over the screaming sounds of dying men. His heart was pounding in his chest, and thoughts were racing in his mind.

"Our only hope is to cross this field and engage them in a spear fight!"

"It's too far! We won't make it!"

"We have no choice. Run!" he yelled, as he tightened his grip around his spear. "Attack!"

A few of his warriors moved close to him but as they prepared to run forward, another volley of darts landed amongst them. He immediately felt a burning pain in his thigh as more bodies fell to the ground.

All was now panic. Confusion. Death.

Most of the Mayan troops were now either dead or critically wounded on the blood soaked soil of Sian K'aan while most of the others were crouched on the ground, fear stricken and unable to move, tears flowing on their cheeks.

The battle was lost.

Not a single Tollàn had been killed and already the Mayans were defeated.

With his left hand Kabrak'an covered his wounded leg and took a step towards the enemy line only to find he was too dizzy and disoriented to move forward. He knelt to the ground.

"Wak Xook," he called, breathless.

His commander knelt next to him, eyes wide opened in terror. A dart shaft was imbedded into the warlord's upper back. The prestigious jaguar pelt was now covered in blood.

"Wak Xook!"

"Ahau, I am right here."

"It is over."

"No!"

"It is!"

"Itzamnà will come!"

"The gods have abandoned us!" He dropped his spear and grabbed his friend by the shoulders.

"You must go!"

"What? No!"

"You must leave! Now!"

"I will fight to the death! I will carry you and together we will fight those cowards! We will fight until we are victorious! Or we will fight until our spirits are delivered and sent to the land of our ancestors!"

"Your spirit will have to wait." He grabbed his wounded leg and a pain filled grimace crossed his face. He felt the flow of warm, thick blood running through his fingers.

"You must run to Mutul. You must warn the king!"

"No, I will stay with you. I will send someone else!"

"You will not! Look around you, there is no one else. We have lost. It is over. Mutul will be next if you do not go now. Please, my friend. Run. Save our city."

Wak Xook's eyes filled with tears.

"Please, go."

The commander nodded silently, unable to speak. He grabbed his friend's arm one last time and stood up.

Kabrak'an smiled.

Wak Xook turned around and ran away.

He ran, jumping over the bloodied bodies covering the ground. He ran around the dying men begging for help. He ran towards the great fire they had lit earlier in the morning, the fire around which they had all danced and sang not so long ago.

It was only once he reached the dying flames and the still red hot ambers that he finally dared to stop and look back.

The darts had stopped falling from the sky, but the massacre was not over yet. The Tollàns, spear in hand, were now finishing off the last few survivors. Some of them spotted him in the distance. They laughed and raised their bloody spears in his direction, although he was too far out of reach to hear their insults.

He saw Jun Akbal, badly wounded, fighting a lost battle against four Tollàn warriors. Sutul's body was lying on the field, a dart buried deep into his chest. The Sian K'aan warlord was dead, and so was Pa'k, the young warrior who had earned his first captor tattoo with him not so long ago.

And he saw Kabrak'an, kneeling amongst his dead warriors, looking at him with a smile. Apparently, the warlord hadn't noticed that Siyah Kak was now leisurely walking amongst the fallen corpses, heading straight towards him.

He did not want to see the rest. So again he turned around and ran, his vision blurred by tears.

He ran away from death.

He ran until he reached Mutul.

LORDS OF WAR

In the distance, Kabrak'an saw Wak Xook looking back towards him, and he wondered if his friend would ultimately choose to ignore his order and run back towards the lost battle, or if he would listen to his orders and return to Mutul.

Wak Xook stood there, motionless, for a long moment before finally turning around. With a great sense of relief, the warlord watched the commander disappear into the jungle. He felt relieved because his king would be warned. Relieved because his city and his people would have time to prepare for the approaching menace. Relieved because his friend would live, and although Wak Xook would probably consider his own survival as a curse for a while, Kabrak'an knew the commander would eventually come to accept his fate and understand the wisdom of his decision.

As his friend ran away, the warlord suddenly felt very lonely, more than he ever did in his entire life. He was all alone, surrounded by death. In front of him, the ground was littered with the bodies of his own men. Only a few of his warriors still lived, and those were quickly dealt with by enemy spearman.

There were barely any screams now. There were only moaning sobs, and faint pleas for mercy.

But it was not over yet.

Footsteps were slowly approaching from behind.

Kabrak'an leaned over his spear and forced himself to his feet and grimaced as a sharp pain shot through his entire body. With his weight on his unwounded leg the warlord patiently waited until the footsteps got closer to him. Then suddenly, without any warning, he quickly turned around and swung his spear around him.

Blood gushed as the razor sharp flint blade sliced through his enemy's throat.

The Tollàn warrior, who'd thought the wounded warlord an easy prey, died almost instantly.

Kabrak'an saw three more men approaching with their spears leveled. "Quetzalcoátl!" they screamed loudly as they ran towards him.

With his bright jaguar pelt and iguana headdress, Kabrak'an was clearly a target of high prestige, and enemy warriors rushed towards their goal as they all wanted the honor of capturing the famous warlord.

He once again shifted his weight on his good leg and firmly gripped his spear as he waited for his attackers.

Then the onslaught began.

The first warrior fell to the ground before even realizing he was within Kabrak'an's reach. The second lasted barely a heartbeat longer. The warlord wielded his spear with the strength and fury of a wounded animal, striving to take as many enemies as possible with him to the underworld.

Even wounded, Kabrak'an was a deadly warrior.

With every twitch of a muscle his blade cut through enemy skin and spilled more blood. Relentlessly, he slashed and thrusted his spear, but always more enemy warriors came running to him, and every man falling to the ground was almost immediately replaced by a new opponent.

Soon, he started to feel tired. His body ached. His vision became blurry. Slowly, enemy blades were getting closer and closer to him, until a familiar voice called them back. Immediately, the Tollàn warriors stopped their attack and moved back a step or two.

Kabrak'an breathed heavily. He had lost his headdress during the battle, and his loose hair now dangled in front of his eyes.

"Siyah Kak ahau," he said, exhausted. "You finally dare to join us on the battlefield!"

The nacom approached slowly, the famous obsidian-indented club hanging in his hand. There was no blood on the weapon.

"Ch'o'j Ahau Kabrak'an Aj Waxaklajun Baak," he said, using Kabrak'an's formal title. There was no pleasure in his voice. "The famous O'on Kamikal Ahau from Mutul. You still believe you can win? Do you wish to challenge our undeniable victory?"

"I protest at the cowardly methods you have used!"

The nacom stepped closer, careful to stay out of Kabrak'an's deadly reach.

"These people do lack... finesse," he said. "But you cannot deny the efficiency of their methods."

The warlord spat at him. His saliva was mixed with blood.

"Speaking of cowardness," added Siyah Kak. "I saw Wak Xook running away not too long ago. He looked eager to leave you to your fate. Then again, he always was a little... weak."

Kabrak'an grinned.

"I ordered him back to Mutul. Soon enough, Great Jaguar Paw will learn about your attack and your methods. He already knows you are a traitor. Now, they will be prepared when you make a move against Mutul."

"A traitor? Is this how you refer to me now?" He started walking around the warlord. "Do you really believe our intention is to attack Mutul?"

Several Tollàns gathered around the two men. Siyah Kak knew none of them spoke Mayan, so he spoke truly.

"Do you think I want to see my people murdered by

these foreigners? Do you think I have forgotten who I am? Where I came from?"

"Then why? Why did you lead them here?" He pointed at the Tollàns. "Why are you not on our side? If your heart is truly Mayan, then stand with me and let us fight these invaders together!"

Siyah Kak angrily turned towards him.

"Why? You want to know why? Because Great Jaguar Paw is weak! Because something had to be done otherwise Tollàn would have taken us down!"

He pointed at the red-painted corpses on the ground.

"It was them or us! They are the enemy, but you seem to have forgotten that!"

The nacom took a deep breath. "I never wanted to kill our men. Sian K'aan is the real threat here, the one which had to be eliminated. But who did I see as I woke up this morning? The brave Kabrak'an and his troops, standing next to the enemy! The true enemy, the one we've both known and fought for years. You have joined Sian K'aan! You are the traitor!"

"Great Jaguar Paw made peace with them," explained Kabrak'an. "The real enemy comes from the west. Tollàn plotted against us. For the past two years, they have nourished this war. They are not our allies, and they are certainly not our friends. So tell me, why are you really here? The Tollàns didn't need your help to win this battle!"

"They needed a guide to lead them here."

"Don't take me for a fool! Any hunter could have served that purpose."

"They also needed someone to support the next Mutul king. Someone to endorse the next dynasty. A well-known, trusted, and respected figure to convince the population that Spearthrower Owl's actions are in their best interest."

Kabrak'an straightened up and took a few steps forward. He limped within spear reach of the nacom.

"You think the people of Mutul will respect you after what you did here today?" he asked.

Although fully aware he was now within reach of the razor sharp blade, Siyah Kak did not flinch. Nor did he step away.

"No. They have never respected me, but they will fear me, which comes down to the same thing. They will have no other choice than to accept their new ruler."

"And who is to rule Mutul, if I may ask?"

"Spearthrower Owl's nephew. Tupac. The southern kings have already given their agreement. They will not challenge him."

"Of course not. They will support anyone as long as there is profit in it. But you, what do you gain?"

"Sian K'aan," he answered after a few seconds. "Spearthrower Owl has given me Sian K'aan."

Kabrak'an laughed.

"Then congratulations," he said. "I see you have been true to yourself, nacom. As a new ruler, you have just executed half of your population, most of your labor force, and all of your military troops!"

"You can laugh, warlord. I have here three hundred warriors who will be happy to defend the city and fill the widow's beds! The population will grow again. As for the food, I heard Mutul's new king will feed our mouths. Mutul's maize will fill our storage pits!"

The two stared at each other for a few moments.

"So, what will it be, my friend?" finally asked Siyah Kak. "I have never particularly liked you, warlord. Yet, I respect your abilities. You are a great warrior, and I do not necessarily wish your death. Listen to me, the war is over. Sian K'aan will never again threaten our borders. Join me. Support Tupac's accession on Mutul's throne and the city will thrive under the influence of Tollàn!"

The warlord did not hesitate for a single second.

With the speed of lightning, Kabrak'an swung his spear upwards with a precision such that the flint blade barely cut open Siyah Kak's chin, leaving a thin fillet of blood trickling down the startled nacom's face.

"You have my answer, traitor." He spat on the ground. "I will never betray my true king."

"Then your bones will become part of my collection," Siyah Kak answered as he unsheathed a small obsidian dagger and leaped forward.

The combat was fierce between the two masters of war. Kabrak'an skillfully wielded his spear while Siyah Kak counter-attacked with both club and dagger, but the battle was unfair. Kabrak'an was already tired, and he had lost a lot of blood.

He dodged left and right, successfully managing to parry a few attacks, but his strengths were quickly fading away. His spear felt heavier than it ever did, and each attempt to strike his opponent came with a muffled shout of exhaustion.

He knew it had to end quickly if he was to hope for a chance to win, so the warlord ultimately put all of his faith in one single move. He pretended to move towards one side and then quickly changed direction while thrusting his spear forward, putting all of his weight on his good leg for the push.

Siyah Kak nearly took the bait. Nearly. As Kabrak'an jumped towards him, his reflexes overcame his conscious actions and the burnt warrior lunged to the ground. The warlord's sharp flint blade missed him by less than a hair's width.

And as the wounded warlord's unprotected chest flew over him, Siyah Kak threw his arm upwards and buried his dagger deep into Kabrak'an's heart.

HEIR TO THE THRONE

The midday sun was shining high above the city of Mutul although dark was the mood inside the palace's council meeting room where Great Jaguar Paw and the ahauob members had gathered for an unscheduled meeting.

"I say we attack the Tollàn troops stationed at Sian K'aan without any further delay!" said one of the nobles. "We must send all of our remaining men straight away, while they are not expecting us! We must crush them to the ground as soon as possible!"

"What men?" asked another. "We've just lost four hundred warriors, including some of our most experienced ones. Including our warlord! Would you leave Mutul defenseless?"

"Besides," replied a third. "Who is to say they would not fall into the same deadly trap as Kabrak'an did? How do you know Tollàn is not already on their way here? Tell me, then, where we would stand?"

"What other choice do we have? Would you have us sit here, patiently waiting for death?"

"Tollàn will not attack us," interrupted Winaq, calmly. "Not immediately anyway. They would have already done so. They would have attacked us in the first place. I believe they wouldn't have wasted any time with Sian K'aan if Mutul had been their objective all along."

"So you think we are safe?"

Winaq looked at the noble.

"Oh no," he answered. "Far from it. It is clear Tollàn will attack us if they have to. They will comfortably wait in Sian K'aan for the proper time to march here, perhaps until reinforcements are sent from their capital. Or they might simply wait for the southern kingdoms to do the dirty work for them. In any case, Spearthrower Owl is not a fool. He wants to rule Mutul, the trade capital. Mutul, the economic center. Not Mutul the phantom city. I believe he would much rather keep Mutul's workforce and troops intact than see the city sacked by Xukpi's warriors."

The ahauob silently agreed they were probably under no immediate threat from the invasive army who'd just decimated a third of their troops.

"What do you propose then, advisor ahau?" asked one of the nobles. "For it seems to be only a question of time before we meet our doom. Spearthrower Owl will come, most likely sooner than later. He will try to take advantage of this fresh wound in our mind. If we resist, Tollàn will take Mutul by force. What should we do? I cannot foresee us simply handing him the throne!"

Winaq looked towards the battered warrior sitting in the corner.

"Wak Xook ahau, you are now Mutul's most experienced warrior. What do you think?"

Every face now turned towards a man who hadn't said a single word since his description of the morning's events in Sian K'aan. He silently sat on the Kabrak'an's seat, which Great Jaguar Paw had proclaimed was now his and waited, his eyes empty of any expression. He was tired. He was depressed. So many friends had died, and it had all happened in an instant.

There wasn't anything intimidating about the painted skeleton face anymore. On his cheeks, tears had left two clean streaks through the smeared traces of ash and soot, but now that everyone looked at him, Wak Xook stood straight and answered.

"I do not see any obvious solution," he said, "although the problem is simple. The enemy waits at our doorstep. They have apparently allied themselves to the southern kingdoms, who outnumber us several times, so we cannot hope for any help from their part. If we attack, we risk our troops and the city. Mutul could stand defenseless. Or, we could take a stand here and send ambassadors to our remaining allies."

He turned his eyes towards Great Jaguar Paw.

"You still have the respect of many states, K'uhul Ahau. Ek Tun. Wak Kab'nal. Lakam Ha. Some might come to our help. With their support, we could manage to oppose a significant resistance to Tollàn and their allies, although we could also plunge the entire Mayan world into a war. A long, bloody war, but I do not see any other alternative. We need to gain some time. And we need to train warriors. Many of them, although most of the remaining men are little more than peasants and commoners."

Great Jaguar Paw closed his eyes. *War,* he thought. *Always war. And I had hoped for peace.*

"It is true we do not have enough spears to hope for victory. Unfortunately, I do not believe the other states will help us," the king said. "They didn't help us against Sian K'aan, they won't help us against Tollàn. Why would they? This is our war, not theirs."

He stood up and walked silently for a few paces before finally coming back to his seat.

"My father once told me that power, real power, does not lie within the hands of a king. Nor does it reside within the cutting edge of a few hundred spears. And it is definitely not secretly hidden inside our temples either," he said, waving one hand towards the High Priest. "The gods cannot be blindly counted on as they follow their own will. So, to whom shall we now turn for help?"

He closed his fist.

"A single drop of rain cannot quench the thirst of an entire population, so we have learned to dig great reservoirs. By doing so we have turned insignificant droplets into a powerful water reserve. In the same way, man can build a city, or they can destroy one. They can make a kingdom prosper, or they can rise against a king. Even the gods need us. They need our sustenance. They need our sacrifices. So it is the people who hold the true power, as long as you can make them work as one. We have thirty thousand citizens living here!"

A triumphant smile appeared on his face.

"You see, a good leader doesn't have control over his subordinates, he only finds a way to make them work together, towards a common goal. We are here to lead, although we are nothing without the people. If they disapprove of us, they will find a way to replace us. But if you lead them as they deserve, they will give you their life. Wak Xook is right. We need to protect ourselves. We need to train our people. I have seen common laborers turn into fierce warriors to protect their family. People only need a little motivation to regroup, to grow beyond their own selves. So, how do I give my people the motivation to stand up against the enemy in numbers so great that it would forever discourage Tollàn from attacking us? How do I turn our seemingly meaningless population into a significant advantage?"

He looked around. No one answered.

"The answer is simple," said Great Jaguar Paw. "It lies within a king's most fundamental role. It is written in our most ancient texts. It is part of our oldest traditions."

There was still no reaction from his small audience.

"Tonight," he explained, "I will enter the water."

"No!" shouted Wak Xook. "You cannot!"

Some of the youngest nobles looked towards Winaq

with a puzzled look.

"He will sacrifice himself," explained the advisor.

The ahauob members suddenly looked terrified.

"A long time ago," continued Winaq, "when an aging king felt his time had come, he would commit the ultimate sacrifice in order achieve the highest state amongst his ancestors, allowing his eldest son to pursue the cycle of kingship. The stories of these kings and of their sacrifices can still be read on the oldest stelas displayed throughout the city's ceremonial center. As far as I know, no king has purposely entered the water in several generations. K'uhul Ahau," protested the advisor. "You must..."

"Winaq!" interrupted the king before lowering his voice. "My friend, I have thought this through. We both did, and you know this is the only answer. Just as in our myths, as in the stories of our gods, victory can only come through sacrifice and death. You know this is the only solution. As your king, it is my duty to shed my own blood for you."

"K'uhul Ahau," said Wak Xook. "That would still leave us with a significant problem."

"Does it?" asked the king, who knew what was coming.

"You have no son. No heir. Who would take your place after you are gone?"

The king looked around him, and waited a moment before answering.

"On several occasions I have thought about this issue. Many times I have asked myself the same question. At first, I thought Kabrak'an could have been the ideal choice. Strong and famous, although maybe a bit old." He smiled. "Unfortunately, the warlord is dead now, but someone else has recently emerged. Someone I have come to trust and admire."

He took a deep breath.

"Balam will be king after me."

The ahauob all threw him a look of disbelief. All except

Winaq, with whom the king had previously discussed this possibility, were obviously abashed by the announcement, not expecting the young man's name to come out of the king's mouth.

"Balam? Why him?" asked one of the young nobleman. "Why not someone else? Why not one of us?"

"Someone like yourself?" asked the king. "You mean to say I should consider you as my heir?"

The young man half nodded and half shook his head, taken by surprise. Unable to answer, he lowered his head under the discrete smiles of everyone else watching.

"Balam is a fine young man," explained Great Jaguar Paw. "He grew up at the palace. He understands the political arena. Yet, he somehow managed to remain pure, free of the corruption so often seen in nobles. He has demonstrated strong leadership skills amongst many other talents. He is modest, fair. Most importantly, I trust his judgment. I trust his values. Winaq will stand by his side, as he always stood by mine, so I know he will be a great king. Our allies have already met him. They will support his nomination."

"Besides, the people will not accept just about anyone," added Winaq. "They will want someone they can look up to, someone they can admire. A leader who has no fear. Tell me, what are heroes made of in the eyes of our people? Mmmm?"

No one said anything, although they all knew the answer.

"People admire warriors and ballplayers. Balam is both. He has always been known as one of our greatest players on the field and, more recently, he has been tattooed under the juch'um. He has proved his worth as a warrior by killing an enemy in battle. Give him the opportunity. You will see that people already love him!"

"He is not of your blood K'uhul Ahau!" replied one of

the nobles. "He is not of royal lineage! Do you really want to break your ancestor's dynasty?"

"The dynasty will not be broken," explained Great Jaguar Paw. "Balam will marry Icoquih."

"Is this even legal?" asked another man. "Is it allowed for a king to transfer his power through his daughter?"

"There is a precedent," he answered, looking towards the ah'tsib.

The scribe, with his face still heavily bruised from the beating he'd received after his capture, nodded in agreement.

"Your great grandmother Ix Une' Balam K'uhul Ahau," he said. "Sole child of her father, she has allowed the continuation of our founder's bloodline Ehb' Xook K'uhul Ahau, your direct ancestor. The ancient laws clearly state that when a king has no male heir, any man of the king's choosing may be married to his eldest daughter. This man shall become the K'uhul Ahau, ruler of the state, with the same rights as a king's own son."

"My king," added Tewiq'nel, the high priest, "I must also protest. You know very well that the first duty of a king is to communicate with the gods. To interact with the deities. He is untrained!"

"Icoquih will teach him. You, more than anyone else, know she is ready. Since the day she was born, she has been thoroughly prepared for the eventuality where I would have no sons. She has performed the sacred rituals several times before as your assistant. Now, she will perform them as your queen."

All of the nobles looked at themselves, and all were forced to agree it all made sense. Every single argument was in favor of this course of action.

The king would sacrifice himself.

And Balam would be king.

A BLOOD-
COVERED ALTAR

It was a little past midday when Balam walked back into the city, empty-handed. He had left Mutul three days before with no food, his blowgun, and a pouch full of clay pellets. The young hunter had hoped to bring a deer or a large peccary back with him, but other than a small quail which ended up serving as the previous night's meal, he hadn't seen anything worth mentioning.

It had been a miserable hunt, and now even the weather was threatening to further darken his mood as the sun, which had shined all morning, was now rapidly disappearing behind dark, menacing clouds.

His disappointment quickly turned into curiosity as he entered the usually busy streets of Mutul. Instead of being surrounded by noisy crowds of people going about their daily business, his return was only met by silence and loneliness.

For an instant, he felt as if he'd stumbled in Mutul during the Wayeb, the deadly month. They were now well into the month of Mak, the month of the Itzamnà festival, and people should have been busy preparing the feasts accompanying the celebrations. Even the lively marketplace seemed desolate, which was definitely odd.

Despite the darkening afternoon, the market should have been crowded with customers looking for food. Children should have been running up and down the streets. Instead, he only saw a few people hurriedly walking here and there with a strange look upon their face. He also saw patrols. Many patrols.

He walked along the streets with a puzzled look as he headed straight to the palace, where he finally met familiar faces. Chava and Kinan, the inseparable guards, were standing watch at the entrance.

"Balam!" greeted Chava, apparently relieved. "Finally. Where have you been?"

"Hunting," he answered, pointing towards his blowgun. "What is going on here?"

"What do you mean?" asked Kinan, surprised. "No one told you?"

"Told me what?" replied Balam, irritated.

The two guards looked at each other.

"Tollàn has sent an army against us," answered Chava.

"What?"

"They've attacked Sian K'aan this morning."

Balam was confused.

"They've attacked Sian K'aan or us?"

"Both. The king has made peace with our northerly neighbors," explained Chava.

"We are allies now," continued Kinan. "Great Jaguar Paw sent Kabrak'an and four hundred warriors to help defend Sian K'aan."

Balam listened carefully as the two guards told Balam everything about the scribe's secret missions, Kabrak'an and Wak Xook's departure for war, and Siyah Kak's treachery.

"Kabrak'an left with four hundred men? Then there is nothing to fear," said Balam after Chava and Kinan had completed their story, not knowing the famous warrior was already dead. "Kabrak'an will defeat this army and return victorious before long."

Kinan shook his head and lowered his voice.

"A few of Kabrak'an's warriors have been seen coming back. The battle has unfolded this morning at sunrise."

"This morning? And they are back from Sian K'aan already? They must have ran as if demons were on their tail for them to get here so quickly. How many were they?"

"A handful, no more. Rumors are quickly spreading throughout the city," said Kinan. "Rumors of defeat, Balam. Painful, unequivocal, absolute defeat."

"They barely escaped with their lives," added Chava. "They spoke of the snake god sending thousands of darts through the skies, and of a thousand deaths. They said a river of Mayan blood flowed through the battle field!"

"What about Kabrak'an?" asked Balam.

"Nobody knows, but I heard Wak Xook himself was seen entering the throne room earlier."

Balam couldn't believe his ears. Rumors were always exaggerated. Always. Besides, Kabrak'an was the greatest warrior of the kingdom. He would come back victorious.

He had to.

"Where is everyone?" he asked.

"The king is in the council meeting room with the ahauob. Most of the population is waiting in the acropolis plaza, praying."

Balam thought for an instant.

"What do the Tollàns have to say about this? Surely the king has questioned Spearthrower Owl?"

"No one has seen the Tollàns since yesterday."

"Well if you can't find the Owl lord, at least ask their high priest. He is always inside that pyramid of theirs," suggested Balam, exasperated. His stomach was grumbling for food, and he was tired. "Or ask Tupac. One of them must know something! Someone must have an explanation as to why their king would send troops all the way over here!"

"Balam, no one has seen *any* Tollàn since yesterday!"

said Chava. "They all seem to have suddenly vanished from the city."

"Not a single one?" asked Balam, concerned.

"Not one," answered Kinan. "We suppose they fled Mutul in anticipation of the attack."

"The treachery runs deep, my friend," added Chava.

"They knew, Balam. They knew. They were all part of this. Even your friend, Tupac, must have played his part."

"Tupac? No, I can't believe it. He is my friend."

A cold, westerly wind suddenly picked up. The day grew darker and thunder growled in the distance as a storm approached.

Chava looked at the ground.

"The last we've seen of them was their high priest and your young priestess, Xochitl."

"You saw her? When? Where?"

"Last night. It was odd. I didn't recognize the priest at first because his face was entirely painted in black, but it was definitely him. They were both heading up the Tollàn pyramid."

Balam's legs suddenly felt weak. Xochitl had once warned him to be cautious when the high priest was masked in black, and although she'd never told him why, he knew something bad had happened.

"So? Did you check the pyramid?" he asked anxiously. There was now fear in his voice.

"There doesn't seem to be any sign of life up there," answered Chava. "No one will go up the monument, Balam. This damned pyramid is a foreign land in the middle of our city. A portal to their underworld. A breeding ground for evil. No one can..."

Balam ran away before he could complete his sentence.

"Wait!" yelled Kinan. "The king wants to see you right away!"

It was useless. Chava and Kinan could only watch as the

young man disappeared down the causeway, and they knew he was heading towards the Tollàn monument.

Balam ran as fast as he could, as if his own life depended on it. A great anxiety surged from deep within his body at the thought of not knowing where Xochitl was, as if a big hole had just opened within his stomach. He feared that he would never see her again.

So he ran. He ran until he reached the base of the Tollàn pyramid, and only then did he stop, breathless.

The stepped monument looked even more menacing in the somber shadows of the stormy skies. Balam looked all the way up towards the small temple at the summit. There were no movements, no signs of life, nothing except the darkness of the small entrance guarded by the two idols standing a silent watch on each side of the portal.

"Xochitl!" he called from the ground. "Xochitl!"

The grumbling sound of the approaching thunderstorm was his only answer. A gust of wind blew his hair in his face, and the air suddenly smelled of rain.

"Priest!" he yelled. "Lord Spearthrower Owl! Anyone!"

Again, no answer.

Gathering all of his courage, Balam slowly undertook the ascent. He raised his right foot and carefully rested it upon the first step, as if testing the pyramid's sturdiness. He then raised the left foot and did the same.

He'd been up there once before, on the day he met Xochitl. He had climbed all the way up to the temple and survived. So he took another step, and then another. His legs started moving fast under him as he ran up the steep stairway.

He hurried up to the summit where he came face to face with the wooden idols of Tlaloc and Quetzalcoátl. Both statues were covered with a fresh coat of blood. Balam avoided looking directly at the foreign deities, focusing instead on the dark entrance before him.

He hesitated for an instant.

"Lord Spearthrower Owl?" he asked, hesitantly. "Anyone?"

His call was only answered by the wind blowing around him.

Balam took a deep breath and walked inside the dark chamber. A strong smell of burnt flesh immediately filled his nostrils. He resisted the urge to run back outside and waited as his eyes adjusted to the dim light.

Slowly, he started to discern his surroundings. A torch holder against the wall. A small hearth in the middle of the room. A table at the far end. *An altar,* he thought, as he noticed the dark shape lying motionless on top of the flat stone.

He took a few steps closer, fearing what his heart already knew. A sudden flash of lightning momentarily lit the dark temple chamber. The deafening sound of thunder echoed within the temple.

Brightness had lasted only an instant but his vision blurred with tears and he felt as if a heavy weight had been dropped over his chest.

"No," he whispered sobbing as he immediately recognized the beautiful face of the one he loved.

"Please no."

There was no doubt. It was her.

He looked at Xochitl's cold body on the altar. She was lying on her back, naked down to the waist. On her head rested a sacrificial headdress of black feathers.

Her chest had been cut open.

Next to his feet, lying in the cold hearth's ashes, was an odd charred mass about the size of his fist. Balam knew her still beating heart had been offered as a sacrifice.

He walked up to her body.

With the back of his hand he whisked away the headdress and looked at her beauty one last time. None of her pleasant vanilla aroma remained. Instead, she now smelled of smoke and sweat. With a trembling hand he touched her hair. Her forehead was cold. So cold. His whole body suddenly started shaking, and he fell to his knees.

There, kneeling in a pool of dried blood, he sobbed uncontrollably while outside the rain started falling.

It was pouring heavily by the time Balam finally walked out of the temple and stood on the slippery edge of the wet platform. Rivers of water flowed down the pyramid's stairs. He looked sideways towards the Tlaloc statue where Xochitl's blood was slowly being washed away by the rain.

In a sudden burst of rage, he grabbed the wooden idol and threw it down the stepped pyramid. He then turned around and grabbed the feathered snake statue. He looked directly into the serpent's eyes. Without hesitation, he spat in it's face and also sent it flying down the steep stairway.

He watched as both statues tumbled down the pyramid, bouncing off the stairs. He watched as the severely mangled images of the two gods finally stopped their descent at the bottom of the structure, half buried in a pool of mud. Balam then raised his arms towards the sky.

"Tlaloc! Quetzalcoátl!" he yelled defiantly in the Tollàn language.

"Tollàn gods! I challenge you! I defy you! I have destroyed your image! I have violated your temple! Now strike me down if you can! Strike me down if you have any power over this land!"

He stood there with his arms raised as rain poured down his face. He waited for a long time as lightning flashed all around him, but no divine spear pierced his skin. No Tollàn god retaliated against his insolence.

There was only rain falling down over his body and he felt Chaak, the Mayan rain god, embracing him.

He fell down to his knees, drenched with water. He was

crying and laughing at the same time. The rain mixed with his tears and washed away the blood from his hands.

He cried because he'd lost Xochitl forever. Because she would never truly know how he felt about her. Because he would never again see her beautiful smile.

And he laughed because he now knew Tollàn's god were powerless in this land.

He had challenged Tollàn's gods, and he had won.

So now he would challenge Tollàn's men.

FRIENDS NO MORE

The storm had been brief. The rain had stopped, the clouds had cleared away, and a late afternoon sun was once again shining bright amidst a deep blue sky over the royal acropolis where the entire Mutul population had spent the past hours praying. Many local chieftains had also come, leaders of small Mutul-dependent villages on the outskirt of the city whom the rumors of the attack had reached. All were now totally drenched, their clothes and hair still dripping wet, but none had left. Despite the violent storm all were still waiting for their king or for any other form of authority to come. Fear had settled in their hearts, and the people now badly needed guidance and comforting.

Great Jaguar Paw answered their call. He was dressed very soberly, without any fashionable headdress or jewelry other than a simple obsidian necklace hanging around his neck. He slowly walked out of the southern temple, stood at the top of the acropolis stairway, and stared at his people. He saw fear in their face. Concerned fathers. Frail elders. Desperate mothers holding crying children.

The king looked upwards for a good omen. He desperately searched the skies for a sign from the gods that he was on the right path, that all would be fine. He saw none, and so he addressed their fears as he should. As he had always done. Truthfully.

"People of Mutul," he said loudly. His voice echoed throughout the plaza. "What you heard is true. Tollàn has turned against us. They've sent an army into our land. This morning, they have attacked Sian K'aan and most likely taken possession of the city. They have deceitfully defeated Kabrak'an and part of our troops. And now, Mutul is threatened."

Sensing his people's apprehension, the king raised his hands.

"Do not fear! The gods have not yet abandoned us, and neither will I! Most of our warriors are still here, patrolling the city, prepared to defend your families!"

Murmurs of panic erupted from the assembled crowd as the king's words were repeated to the people standing in the far back.

"What will we do?" asked an angry voice. "What will we do when Tollàn comes? They will kill the men, and they will take our wives and children as slaves!"

People were desperate. Years of skirmishes, raids and war had affected their morale. And with this new threat looming over them, most feared the end was near.

Great Jaguar Paw nodded, understanding, but just as the king was about to proceed with his carefully rehearsed speech, a voice echoed in the distance.

"Yes, holy king. What will you do?"

Everyone immediately turned towards the back of the plaza where a small group of men emerged from the crowd. As they slowly approached the acropolis went silent. People stepped aside to let them through, and the king gasped as he recognized the figures.

Spearthrower Owl and his nephew, Tupac, had returned to Mutul. They were accompanied by half a dozen armed Tollàn warriors.

Wak Xook, standing at the bottom of the pyramid, immediately turned towards Great Jaguar Paw. Despite having washed his face clean, he still wore his battle uniform. His clothes were still stained with Kabrak'an's blood. He took a step forward, ready to send his men against the enemy who'd foolishly walked towards them, ready to get rid of them forever. Ready to avenge his friends.

With a gesture from the hand the king dismissed his intentions. The Tollàn troops were likely dangerously nearby, and the death of the foreign lord would only postpone the problem as the enemy king would only send a new leader to attack them. This would have to be a battle of words, not a battle of spears. Besides, he wanted everyone to know, first hand, the true nature of the Tollàn lord.

"Spearthrower Owl ahau," he said. "I am surprised of your presence here, especially after the events which have unfolded today in Sian K'aan."

"It is I, king, who is surprised that you dare present yourself before this population!"

People started shouting insults at the Tollàns, but Spearthrower Owl dismissed their cries.

"Your king has abandoned you!" he shouted. "Great Jaguar Paw has made Mutul weak! For years now, you've been at war against Sian K'aan. For years, you've suffered their attacks. The theft of your crops. The murder of your children. All this time, what has he done? Nothing! And who has finally delivered you from their threat? Tollàn!"

He turned around.

"Tollàn has delivered you, but it is not over! The southern states have seen what is happening here. Soon, it is they who will turn against you, for they have lost confidence in your king. They want him out! There is no future for you with Great Jaguar Paw. He will lead you to your doom!"

He smiled, waiting for his words to sink in.

"This very morning," Spearthrower Owl added, "the great Kabrak'an himself fell at the hand of Siyah Kak ahau!" The crowd gasped. "His head will now stand over my new temple in Sian K'aan! And you, all of you, what will you do now? How will you protect your children when Xukpi's troops cross your borders? When the southern states besiege your city? Believe me, they will! You have no choice. You must get rid of Great Jaguar Paw!"

His finger was now pointed towards the king.

"Get rid of him, and put Tupac on the throne!"

He waved his arms towards his nephew.

"Tupac has the support of the southern Mayan states. He has the support of Siyah Kak, who is one of yours, and who understands what is best for Mutul! Most of all, he has the support of Tollàn! Put a Tollàn king on your throne, and gain Tollàn's protection. Put Tupac on Mutul's throne, and ally yourself with Xukpi and Waxak Mo', the strongest states in the entire Mayan world!"

He paused, happy to see the population reacting exactly as he had anticipated. Unsurprisingly, there were no supporting cheers. The Tollàn lord never expected people to simply accept their fate. His speech, however, had not been met by silence. People were now looking all around, discussing amongst themselves.

Spearthrower Owl was standing in the middle of the Mutul mob with very little protection. Despite the fact that many of his most loyal men hid amongst the crowd, ready to take him to safety at the first sign of trouble, he had taken a huge risk, a calculated risk. That he had not yet been lynched meant he now stood a decent chance of convincing them. Fear, he knew, had always been a prime motivator.

For years, he had secretly sent his warriors into the Mutul jungle. Disguised as Sian K'aan warriors they had started a war. They raided their borders. Tupac's idea to attack their shipments proved to be brilliant. Then, it had been child's play to convince the southern kings that Mutul was weak, that he was their only hope to end the war. Now, his great scheme would finally unfold.

Great Jaguar Paw walked down the acropolis stairs.

"See," he said. "See how Tollàn manipulates you. Today, you have just witnessed for yourself Spearthrower Owl's true nature. Now you can see how deceitful he his. You can see how his only motivation is profit and power! How could you ever trust someone like that? How could you ever trust him to protect you and your families, for he will not hesitate to sacrifice every single one of you if and when it suits his purposes."

He smiled as the crowd nodded.

"I am your king!" he added. "I have sworn to protect you, and protect you I will! Tollàn's troops will never set foot on our land. Tonight, at sunset, I will go to our ancestors myself. I will cross the great river of blood and rally all of our gods against the invader. I will gather Itzamnà, Chaak, K'awiil and Ixchel. I will find Kabrak'an's soul and bring him back with me. I will lead them through the heavens and we will stand by your side! You are not alone! Tonight, I will enter the water!"

The crowd erupted in cheers, acknowledging their support to Great Jaguar Paw. They recognized his promised sacrifice. They trusted their king's ability to travel to the otherworld, and they trusted their gods to help them.

Tupac then addressed the king.

"K'uhul Ahau Chak Tok Ich'aak, your time is over. It is your people who will pay with their lives if you stubbornly remain on your throne! I am Tupac, nephew of Spearthrower Owl, future king of Mutul!"

The king raised his head and smiled at the young man's impetuous foolishness.

"Do you dare challenge me, Tupac, nephew of Spearthrower Owl?"

"It is I who challenges you, Tupac of Tollàn," answered a voice coming from behind the crowd.

Once again, everyone turned around towards this new

protagonist, and all immediately recognized Balam, the famous ball player. In his arms was the lifeless body of Xochitl. She'd been draped in a white cotton sheet.

Tupac was momentarily angered and surprised at the intrusion, but at the sight of the Mayan young man and his dead beloved priestess, he only laughed out loud.

"I see you have found the remains of your priestess," he said. "Unfortunately, her sacrifice was necessary to ensure our victory at Sian K'aan."

He laughed even more.

"I told you to hurry while you both still had time ahead of you," he added.

"I thought you were my friend," answered Balam in Tollàn. "How could you?"

"Friends? Never, but I am grateful for all of your precious knowledge. It shall prove very useful as I rule over Mutul."

Balam stared at the two Tollàns standing amidst the Mutul crowd. Earlier, there had been a great empty hole in the middle of his being. This hole was now completely filled with hate. In his head, he saw the two mangled Tollàn idols lying in the mud at the bottom of the pyramid, and he knew Chaak would grant him his revenge.

He started speaking Mayan for all to hear.

"I am Hun Balam Ku'x, a son of Mutul! My blood is Mayan! My heart is Mayan! So I hereby repeat my challenge. Tupac, will you face me in a ball game, or will you cowardly turn away?"

The crowd gasped at the challenge, but it was Spearthrower Owl who reacted first.

"The boy matters very little, nephew. What matters is that victory is close. Our troops will force these weaklings into submission. All you need to do now is wait and the throne will be yours!"

"I can beat him, uncle. I know I can."

"No," hushed Spearthrower Owl. "Were you not listening to the king? He will leave this world by his own hand. Nothing can stop us now! There is no need for you to needlessly expose yourself!"

His nephew brushed him aside.

"I will meet your challenge whenever you want," he said in Tollàn between clinched teeth. "And then, I will take Mutul's throne for myself!"

Balam smiled.

"Then the Kik' tz'enem shall decide. To the royal ball court!" he announced loudly.

Great Jaguar Paw looked at Winaq with a smirk. Although unexpected, Balam's fortuitous intervention couldn't have come at a better time. If he was to win, this would undoubtedly strengthen his status before the population. Great Jaguar Paw would have absolutely no problem convincing everyone that Balam had the strength to be their next leader.

Should he lose, however, the consequences would be disastrous for his plan. In any case, there was nothing he could do. The challenge had been issued in accordance with their traditions, so he could only watch as the events unfolded. Their fate was now in Balam's hands, and he silently prayed that he would prevail.

As for the population, they raised their arms and cheered loudly for there would be a ball game, and the gods would be present.

They all hurried towards the royal ball court.

THE TRIAL
OF BLOOD

Although slightly bigger than the practice courts, the royal ball court was basically identical to its commonly used counterparts. Two sloped side walls atop a waist high embankment, an open-ended central alley, and stone rings vertically mounted on each side.

However, it was not the structure itself that made the court particularly beautiful, but the many elaborate carvings adorning the stone walls. Images of deities playing ball, of kings involved in religious rituals, and of priests performing sacrifices, all of them engraved within the stone in a beautiful complement of myth, legend and history.

Three giant markers also stood atop the eastern wall, circular stones rivalling in height with the tallest man, each of them representing one of the three principal deities worshipped in Mutul. The first marker represented Itzamnà, creator god, shown as an old toothless man sitting with his legs crossed. The second marker illustrated Chaak, the rain deity, dancing with an axe in his hand. The third stone depicted Ah Mun, the maize god, shown as a beautiful young man sprouting from the earth. The markers were used to mark the three points required to win the match.

So it was under a scorchingly hot afternoon sun that people rushed to the royal ball court, pushing and shoving their way as they all knew the good spots were spare. The fastest ones quickly hurried up the sloped walls, massing themselves atop the monument while others gathered at both ends of the playing field. Some climbed on the surrounding structures while children sat on their parent's shoulders, causing the anger of whoever had the misfortune of standing behind. All were struggling to get a decent view of the court and although very few succeeded, many even offered money to move closer to the game. Everyone wanted to see the match, regardless of the cost.

The entire city center was suddenly animated by an unprecedented frenzy. People chanted, bets were exchanged, horns were blown and drums were beaten as the energized crowd waited for the Kik' tz'enem, the ritualistic dual, to begin.

First came the priests, who had to struggle their way through the rowdy crowd. They sprinkled water and swept maize leaves all over the court as one of them stood in the middle of the central alley, playing a bone flute. They lit copal incense at each end of the field, sending dark clouds of smoke towards the deep blue sky. They also recited prayers although their words, along with the music from the flute, were lost in the overwhelming cacophony of noises generated by the people all around them. When the court was finally judged ready for the ceremony, the priests walked away and cleared the field for the two opponents.

Tupac first arrived from the north, escorted only by Spearthrower Owl. He was wearing the battered ball gear he usually wore during his matches against Balam. He also carried a large ceremonial shield engraved with the image of Tlaloc while on his head rested the ceremonial Tollàn headdress. Beautifully crafted from wood, entirely painted in black, and adorned with hundreds of obsidian beads, the elaborate head gear covered the head, cheeks and lower jaw. As they tried to move forward, people huddled around them, booing and insulting the foreigners. Mutul warriors finally had to intervene to let the Tollàns through.

"Balam! Balam!" chanted the impatient crowd with little regard to the Tollàn challenger as they waited for their champion. They waited for what seemed like an eternity before conch horns were finally blown, announcing the entrance of the local favorite.

Balam slowly approached from the south, alone. Other than for a blood stained white sash tied around his left ankle, he wore nothing but his own ball gear. The crowd split apart to let him through, all along encouraging him. Through this clamor of cheers and music Balam made his way to the southern end of the court, all the time his eyes remaining fixed on Tupac.

There, the two of them waited, face to face, separated only by two dozen steps or so.

Finally Tewiq'nel appeared through the crowd. He walked to the center of the court, closely followed by a child carrying a rubber ball.

The crowd went silent as the Mutul high priest turned towards the three markers, his hands raised into the air.

"Itzamnà! Chaak! Ah Mun! Gods of Mutul, and spirit of our ancestors! We call upon your presence! We beg you to cross this portal linking both of our worlds. Join us today, on this blessed ball court, to witness the battle between these two men whose fate will be subjected to your judgment."

While he performed the ritualistic prayers, Tupac nervously shifted his weight from one foot to the other, anxiously waiting for the match to begin. Balam, on the other hand, looked perfectly calm as he smiled and looked around.

Behind him, the nobles had gathered atop the palace walls. He saw the king, Great Jaguar Paw, flanked by Icoquih and Wak Xook. Next to them stood Winaq, the ahauob council, and many of the higher nobles. He also recognized the silhouettes of Chava and Kinan, the royal guards, who nodded their support.

He nodded back.

Tewiq'nel finished his prayers, ceremoniously pulled an obsidian dagger out of his clothes, and slowly ran the blade along his own forearm. After letting several drops of his blood fall to the dusty ground he signaled both players to move forward. Without a word, Tupac removed his cumbersome headdress and walked towards the court center, where he was joined by Balam.

"You both know the rules," said the priest. "They are the same rules as usual, the only difference being that you need to send the ball through the ring three times to win, as a hit against the ring itself will not score a point. May the gods be your witnesses and influence the outcome of this match in whichever way they see fit. Are you ready to begin?"

Balam nodded, while Tupac turned towards the high priest.

"You have forgotten to spray the field with maize grains, priest," he said with a disdainful grin.

"Forgotten?" Tewiq'nel answered, laughing. "I don't think so. The portal has now been opened."

"Maize kernels are never used on the royal ball court," explained Balam. "Today, we expect the death lords to come. And when they cross this portal and materialize into our world it will not be in vain, for they will not return to the underworld empty-handed. One of us will go with them."

Tupac's smile disappeared from his face. The two young men who'd faced each other so many times before would now play for their lives.

He spat on the ground and nodded towards the bloodied sash tied around his opponent's ankle.

"You think Xochitl will help you?" he asked in Tollàn. "You will join her sooner than you thought."

"She is with me, now and forever," answered Balam in the same language. "And she will help me avenge her own death."

"Her soul is trapped inside the Tollàn pyramid, where it belongs. It is well guarded by Quetzalcoátl. She cannot help you."

"I've thrown your idols down the pyramid. I've buried them in mud and filth, and they were powerless to stop me. Your gods are not here!"

Tupac's eyes widened with anger. He did not reply.

"May the gods be your witnesses," said the high priest.

With these last words the child handed Tewiq'nel the rubber ball. He then stepped onto the embankment and held the ball high above both players.

Conch horns sounded. Once again the crowd started cheering. From atop the palace's walls where he stood, Great Jaguar Paw looked down at the scene. As he raised and dropped his arm., Tewiq'nel threw the ball high into the air.

The match had begun.

Under the crowd's encouragements, both players jumped as high as they could, their body armor clashing together as they fought for possession of the ball. Balam, although physically smaller than his opponent, managed to pull out of the confrontation with control of the ball, which he quickly started bouncing off his right knee. He moved back a little, and immediately sent the ball flying back into the air.

The two players had faced each other several times in the past. They knew each other well. Tupac, used to Balam's feints, crouched low and prepared to jump to the side, ready to counteract the move he anticipated from his opponent.

But the young Mayan did something unexpected.

Contrary to his usual feint, Balam jumped a second

time. With a strong hip movement he sent the hard rubber ball directly into Tupac's face. The Tollàn boy fell to the ground in pain. Balam then jumped on his opponent's shoulder and, using him as a springboard, he propelled himself forward. He skillfully regained control of the ball before it struck the ground and leisurely headed towards one of the rings, easily scoring the first point.

Up on the eastern cornice, a black and red flag was raised in front of the first marker. The crowd's reaction was immediate. They cheered and chanted as Balam walked back towards Tupac, who was now slowly getting back up. Blood was flowing massively from his broken nose, and his eyes were filled with tears.

"A new move," he managed to say through the pain.

"Did you really think I taught you everything? I showed you how to play as friends. Now, you shall learn how to play in the trial of blood."

"At least now I know where your crooked nose comes from, my friend."

"There is no more friendship here, Tupac. The gods do not play for pleasure. Welcome to the royal ball court."

Balam smiled as he headed back towards the center of the court, where Tewiq'nel waited to send the ball back into play. Tupac spat, sending a mixture of blood and saliva on the ground. "Then so be it," he murmured.

Once again, both players jumped as the priest threw the ball above their heads. Only this time, Tupac viciously elbowed Balam under the ribs. The young man came crashing down flat over the dusty alley, the wind blown out of his lungs, but the move had unbalanced the Tollàn who was unable to properly recover the ball in midair. Tewiq'nel stopped the play as Tupac inadvertently touched the ball with his hand.

The crowd booed Tupac as Balam stood back up, clenching his right side with his hand. Both of them now knew there would be no quarter. This was a fight to the death, and only the strongest would survive. Once again, both players returned to the court center, and the ball was thrown back into play.

It was a tough and vicious match between the two boys who'd practiced so much together. The ball was bitterly disputed as both players anticipated very well each other's feints and reactions. All along, the crowd chanted and cheered for Mutul's champion, their cries overpowering the thumping sound of the rubber ball bouncing off the stone, for never before had they witnessed such a fierce and unforgiving match.

Tupac eventually marked his first point, and a white flag joined Balam's flag in front of the first marker. This was followed by a long series of aborted plays which always ended with the ball landing on the ground or touching a player's hand or foot. Many times, the ball struck the ring's edge without going through.

It was Tupac who marked the following point. Spearthrower Owl clenched his fist as his nephew was now only one point from victory, but almost immediately after Balam managed to send the ball through the ring.

So it was with an even score that the two players now stood in the middle of the court, both of them bloody, sweaty, and exhausted. The afternoon sun was unbearably hot. The air was dry and dusty. The surrounding walls, shielding the players from any breeze, turned the ball court into an oven.

Tupac limped back into position, licking his dry and crusty lips. Water was not allowed for the players. The Kik' tz'enem was as much a test of skill and courage as it was a trial of strength and endurance. His face was bruised. Two of his fingers were broken, and his chest armor was covered with the dried, caked blood which had finally stopped flowing from his broken nose.

Balam's face was also heavily bruised. He had a few broken ribs and at least one broken tooth. Pain shot throughout his entire body every time air flowed over the exposed nerve, and so he forced himself to breathe through the nose, allowing barely enough air to fill his depleted lungs.

He looked up towards the eastern embankment. There were two flags flowing in front of the first marker, and two in front of the second. Only the third marker, the one engraved with the image of the maize god, remained flagless.

The next point would be the victory point.

For the last time, both men stood face to face before Tewiq'nel who once again sent the ball flying high above the court.

Tupac jumped to seize the ball. Balam, who still had a few more moves to teach his former student, remained on the ground. As Tupac's body flew before him, he grabbed his opponent's feet and forcefully swept them sideways, toppling the Tollàn in midair. Tupac fell sideways on his hip. Unfortunately, he just managed to trip Balam as he was about to recover the ball.

The hard rubber ball flew to the side, bounced off the sloped wall and fell onto the embankment.

Thump, thump-thump. Thump.

Both Balam and Tupac jumped back to their feet at the same time. As they ran toward the side wall, Tupac tried to trip Balam once again only this time, the Mayan leapt over his sweeping foot and, with all the strength he could muster, sent his elbow flying towards his opponent's jaw. Tupac's head swerved back as a chipped tooth flew out of his mouth.

Balam then jumped onto the embankment and recovered the ball, while Tupac positioned himself between him and the ring. Both men intensely stared at each other, their body armor shifting up and down under their heavy breathing.

Then, with a smile, Balam suddenly relaxed. He took a deep breath, dropped his tense shoulders, stood straight, and started bouncing the ball between his hips and the sloped wall beside him.

Thump-thump-thump-thump-thump.

The thumping sounds of the bouncing rubber ball echoed throughout the ball court. Everyone looked at the two opponents, holding their breath, sensing the end was near and still, Balam bounced the ball off the wall.

Thump-thump-thump-thump-thump.

"They are here!" he finally said. "Can you feel their presence?"

"What?" asked Tupac, exhausted. "Who?"

"The Death Lords! The bouncing angers them. Now, they have come to claim their due!"

Without thinking, Tupac leaped forward.

Balam sent the ball high above him. He then jumped sideways and, using the sloped wall as leverage, he violently kicked Tupac down the embankment.

The Tollàn player came crashing hard to the ground.

The ball came back down, struck the edge of the ring, and bounced back towards Balam. The Mayan boy jumped high into the air, struck the ball with his hips and redirected it straight through the ring, scoring the final point. The match was over.

Balam had won.

The crowd went wild as the final black and red flag was planted in front of the maize god marker, and the news of Balam's victory quickly traveled to the people standing too far to see the action. Horns were blown, drums were beaten, and the crowd started chanting Balam's name.

Through it all Balam, still standing on the embankment, simply stared at the ground where Tupac sat bewildered, his right arm bent in an unnatural way. He was suddenly overwhelmed by a great sadness.

Following the orders of the high priest, guards stepped onto the field and grabbed the loser by the arms, forcing him to his knees. They immediately stripped him of his ball gear and tied his hands behind his back. Tupac winced as pain shot through his broken bones. One of the warriors drew an obsidian blade and roughly cut off his long black hair, leaving a series of bloodied cut marks all over his pale scalp.

From where he stood, Great Jaguar Paw looked at the victor. Balam was already regarded as a champion, but with this single victory gained on the royal ball court, the young man had just elevated himself to the status of hero in front of the entire city-state.

Excellent, he thought. *Now everyone knows the gods are with him, for he has achieved victory on their own battle field. Today, Mutul loves him as their champion.*

Tomorrow, they will love him as their king.

"K'uhul Ahau," whispered Winaq. "Tewiq'nel is waiting."

The high priest was standing in the middle of the court, expectantly looking up to the palace. Siyah Kak was the city's executioner, the nacom. It was his duty to send the souls of the sacrificed on their way to the otherworld. In his absence, Tewiq'nel did not know how to proceed.

"Wak Xook," said Great Jaguar Paw. "This one is yours."

The warrior looked down and smiled. The victory was not his but on this bloody day, he would at least have the satisfaction of parting one enemy's head from its body.

Without a word, Wak Xook headed down to the palace where he grabbed the ceremonial flint axe and immediately made his way towards to ball court.

The death lords of the underworld had come.

It was unwise to keep them waiting.

SACRIFICE

The sun was low above the western horizon when Great Jaguar Paw arrived at the sacred reservoir, and although the place was surrounded by thousands of his people, he felt absolutely alone in the world.

It was a beautiful evening. The day's heat had been replaced by a comfortable warmth. Birds sang in the trees. A gentle eastern breeze caressed his face. The king looked at the shimmering surface of the water and knew this was a good omen. The gods approved of his actions.

Yes, it was indeed a beautiful evening, and Great Jaguar Paw was happy about that because he knew it would be his last in this world.

"K'uhul Ahau," greeted Winaq.

"Winaq, old friend. How are you?" They shook arms.

The old advisor nodded in silence. He would have wanted to start a long discussion. He would have wanted to try, at least one last time, to convince the king from going ahead with the ceremony, but the words wouldn't come out. Somewhere, deep within, the old man knew this was the only option.

"Okib'," he finally said, using the king's birth name. "Okib', do you really want to do this?"

Only the closest members of the royal family were ever allowed to call a king by his child name, and even then, it was considered so impolitely informal that no one ever did. Yet, Great Jaguar Paw did not take offense. On the contrary, he shed a tear at the name which instantly brought back memories of his youth. They were happy memories. The strength of his father's presence. The warmth of his mother's touch. Friends. Love.

"Thank you," he whispered, discreetly sniffing. "Balam will need you. There is no doubt in my mind that you will support him as you always supported me."

There was so much more to say. So much more to discuss, but time had come. So he rested his hand on his friend's shoulder one last time and stepped forward. His daughter and the high priest were waiting for him.

There was no music on that evening. No drum beat. No horns blowing. No singing. They had all celebrated earlier, after Balam's victory on the ball court. Now, there was only a perfect and absolute silence, a silence through which Great Jaguar Paw shined by his appearance.

His legs, forearms and torso were entirely covered by massive jade pieces meticulously crafted into the images of Mayan gods and other supernatural beings, the white-green stone contrasting sharply with his dark skin. At his waist were attached several heavy basalt idols. He also wore an imposing obsidian necklace, large ear spools, and a wide nosepiece. On his head rested a highly complex headdress of bones, seashells and feathers, while in his hand he carried an eccentric flint scepter representing the sun god. Although he was so heavily burdened by his attire, it was effortlessly that he now headed towards the water's edge.

"K'uhul Ahau," greeted Tewiq'nel.

"Father," added Icoquih.

The king nodded silently.

Copal incense was lit. As Tewiq'nel started a long prayer, Icoquih reached down towards a pottery bowl. A strong smell of cinnamon and allspice emanated from the thick maize paste it contained. Using her bare hands, she applied the odorous concoction all over the king's body.

Great Jaguar Paw looked at the twirling clouds of black smoke rising towards the sky, he looked above him as the burning sap was dematerialized and sent into the heavens, and he felt peaceful. Soon he, too, would join his ancestors in the otherworld, where he knew his father and his grandfather patiently waited.

There was no need for great speeches today, no need for explaining his actions. The population of Mutul knew.

They knew the purpose of his sacrifice. They knew why he had to cross over to the other realm. It was, after all, a king's duty to see to the welfare of his citizens, to interact with the gods, and to provide the necessary sustenance of sacrifices allowing life to move on. So, they knew what it meant when Balam arrived and stepped onto the small stone platform erected by the water's edge. When Icoquih bowed to her father one last time and walked over to stand by her future husband.

They knew they were in the presence of their new king, of their new queen. Silently, they approved.

They approved because they trusted Great Jaguar Paw's judgment. Because they knew Icoquih could communicate with the gods as well as her father did. And they approved because Balam was now their hero. He was the man who had challenged the enemy on the playing field of the death gods and had lived.

He was a man who would not hesitate to sacrifice his life for them. A man who would be respected by all nations.

So, as Great Jaguar Paw took his first step into the water, their hearts were filled with hope.

Balam remembered how nervous he had felt earlier, before the ball game. That nervousness was nothing compared to the anxiety he felt in the instant he was officially presented to Mutul's population.

His face and body were still heavily bruised from the afternoon's game, although the king's servants did their best in cleaning him and clipping his nails short. They'd washed his hair and fashioned them in the Mutul way. Winaq had also insisted that Balam should wear the Tollàn headdress previously worn by Tupac before the ball game, so that everyone would remember how he'd single-handedly defeated the enemy on the field of the gods.

It was also Winaq's idea to have the shaman immediately tattoo him, before the ceremony, with the royal ball court glyph commemorating his victory over Tupac. Plain for all to see on his upper arm was the freshly tattooed skull and rubber ball symbol, it's still bloody outlines imprinted right next to the juch'um spear point tattoo he'd been awarded after his first kill on the battlefield.

So it was as a warrior and as a hero ball player that he stepped onto the platform. As he did so, Balam looked at the staring crowd and wondered. Barely a day ago he was still a normal boy, a hunter with little ahead of him other than his youth and his hopes for a foreign priestess.

Now that all of his dreams had died, he was to be king. He was to be a ruler. When Great Jaguar Paw told him his intentions after the ballgame he was shocked. His first instinct was to say no, to run away and hide forever. To never come back.

They'd both talked for a long time and, finally, he had decided to accept his fate. At first, he did not fully grasp what it all meant. Now that he looked towards the faces staring at him, he started to understand.

And he was afraid.

There were so many people standing around the reservoir, so many faces. Fathers. Mothers. Children. So many lives would now depend on him. All of a sudden, he felt overwhelmed, as if he should have known the name of everyone surrounding him. As if he should have known their stories, their struggles, their successes. They would, after all, soon become his people.

"How am I ever going to be able to rule them all?" he mumbled. "How can I ever succeed?"

Someone grabbed his hand. Cold and delicate fingers interlaced with his. For a moment he thought of Xochitl, of the bloodied sash still tied around his ankle. He thought about her and he knew he would never be alone, not as long as he carried her memory within him.

And so he smiled.

Winaq looked behind him and was pleased with the sight. He saw Balam, the future king, standing hand in hand with Icoquih. Proud and pious Icoquih. Strong and victorious Balam. Both of them were smiling, and Winaq knew all would be well.

As a direct heiress to Great Jaguar Paw she would bring stability to the kingdom, she would provide interaction with the deities. As for him, his newly gained notoriety would provide most useful in gaining the support of foreign states. Winaq knew their best protection against the hostile southern Mayan kings would be to maintain peace in the region, and to ally themselves with the powerful western cities. There was a lot to be done. He would see to it as soon as possible.

Okib' took a step forward. His foot dug slightly into the silt as cold water reached his ankles.

Happiness suddenly filled him. In his heart, he was no

longer a king, he was no longer a ruler. He felt the innocence of childhood growing within him. The joy of being a child, of looking forward to a brighter future. Of growing up. Of being reborn.

He took another step. The weight of his heavy attire pulled him deeply into the muddy reservoir bottom.

He giggled as cold water reached his belly, instinctively raising his arms above the water level. He remembered his childhood games. He remembered playing in the water with his late younger brothers as their mother watched from the shore. Soon, he would be with all of them once again.

All he could now see through his half-closed eyes was the intense brightness of the setting sun amongst a blood red sky. There, waist deep in the water, he stopped for an instant to admire his last sunset.

It was a red sunset.

A true Mayan sunset.

Everything before him was now a bright ocean of red.

He had done it. He had reached the great river of blood separating the world of the humans from the world of the gods.

Without hesitation, he took another step towards the otherworld. Towards his destiny. Towards his ancestors.

He felt the water level rising to his neck.

He held his breath and took another step.

Then another.

And another.

DEFEAT

Siyah Kak was sitting on Sian K'aan's throne, absentmindedly playing with Kabrak'an's obsidian dagger. His eyes remained fixed on glassy blade as he turned the weapon between his fingers. It had been a full day since the death of the warlord, a full day since they'd walked unchallenged into Sian K'aan and, already, he was bored.

As promised, Siyah Kak was now king, or at least he would be as soon as the priests would complete the preparations for the investiture ritual. It had taken some significant convincing on his part for Sian K'aan's religious authorities to recognize his claim as their new ruler. In the end, they had accepted to officialize his new position, a decision no doubt motivated by the decapitation of the several elders who'd initially opposed him.

Knowing he was about to become Sian K'aan's new king should have made him happy. After all, they had defeated the enemy city. They had avenged years of robbery and murder. Strangely, victory left a sour taste in his mouth. Despite the fact that he now wore the late warlord's finger bones within his long dark hair, Kabrak'an's death did not bring him the satisfaction he usually felt after dueling. He'd never expected to come face to face with his Mutul brothers.

Now there he was, lying victorious within the sacred hall of his defeated enemy, and yet never before in his entire life had he felt so out of place. With an obviously disinterested look on his face he silently waited as the

Tollàn lord nervously paced back and forth before him.

"Mutul will pay!" Spearthrower Owl murmured angrily with a clenched fist. "It was all so perfectly planned! So carefully executed! I swear, Mutul will pay!"

He was still mumbling when the Tollàn high priest stormed inside the room, out of breath.

"Lord Atlatl Cauac, I was just informed of your arrival. What happened? And where is Tupac?"

"Dead!" he answered. "He is dead! The Mutul bastards killed him!"

"What! When?"

"Yesterday."

He told the high priest everything about the confrontation in Mutul.

"Our plan was flawless. Everything was perfect until Tupac, foolish boy, decided to accept the young Mayan's challenge. I slipped away from the crowd as soon as the game was lost. I knew there was nothing I could do to save his life. You should have heard these savages cheering when the warrior approached with the axe. They didn't even take his heart! They simply knelt him in the middle of the ball court and decapitated him like a vulgar criminal!"

The priest looked down, unable to find any words.

"I watched from a distance as his head rolled in the dust. As his blood stained the court. As they celebrated on the very emplacement of his debacle."

"I don't know what to say, my lord."

"There is nothing to say. Tupac is with Quetzalcoátl now. He is dead, although he should have been sitting on Mutul's throne!"

"Not as long as Great Jaguar Paw lives."

Spearthrower Owl looked at him with a strange smile.

"Ooh, but the king of Mutul is dead!"

"Dead? How?" he asked.

"Yesterday evening Great Jaguar Paw, in a great lack of

lucidity, committed suicide! He called it sacrifice, but I have never before witnessed a bloodless sacrifice in my entire life."

"You have seen this with your eyes?"

"I stuck around, wanting to see what was going to happen next. Disguised as a traveler I watched the ceremony from far away."

"So the boy will be king?" asked the priest. "He presented himself before the population mockingly dressed as a Tollàn lord?"

"They called him *Spearthrower Owl's son, future ruler of Mutul*, and they laughed! They cheered as he removed Tupac's headdress and threw it to the ground!"

"You said Great Jaguar Paw willingly walked into the great reservoir?"

"Yes! The fool killed himself, probably out of fear! And fear they should feel, for retaliation there will be!" He smashed his fist into his open palm. "Siyah Kak! Prepare your men! We will attack Mutul as soon as Waxak Mo's and Xukpi's troops arrive. With the southern states on our sides, we will crush Mutul once and for all!"

"Waxak Mo' will not participate in an attack against Mutul," echoed a voice coming from an adjacent room.

"And neither will Xukpi," added another.

Spearthrower Owl immediately turned around, offended by the unannounced intrusion.

"Who is there?" he bellowed. "Show yourselves! Immediately!"

Two men appeared through an archway and slowly walked inside the throne room. Spearthrower Owl immediately recognized them.

"Oyamal! Ikan!" he said, addressing the two southern states representatives. "We had an agreement! Your respective kings promised me the support of their troops! They promised to help me get rid of Mutul!"

"No," said Oyamal as he stepped forward. "My king has promised support to get rid of Great Jaguar Paw, and it is my understanding that the king of Mutul is no more."

"A new king will take his place. Nothing has changed!"

"Everything has changed," replied Ikan. "The deal was simple. We let Tollàn troops march through our borders, we do not condemn the presence of your warriors in this land, and we support a new king on Mutul's throne. In exchange, you end the war with Sian K'aan, and you restore peace to the region so that obsidian shipments can once again travel freely. All of these conditions have been met, have they not?"

He looked towards Siyah Kak, who shyly nodded.

"It might seem as though, but..."

"There is no but," interrupted Ikan. "You wanted someone else on the throne, you have him. What more could you ask for? I was at the ceremony. I've seen the new king. I have spoken with Lakam Ha. They, also, recognize Balam as Mutul's new leader, and they have accepted him as such."

"*I* do not recognize him as their legitimate king! I want you to attack Mutul, in respect of our agreement!"

"Fortunately, you opinion carries very little weight in this land, Tollàn ahau. Do you think we are stupid? Do you think we do not see that all you really want is our obsidian?"

Spearthrower Owl looked down, his face red with fury.

"The war is over," said Oyamal. "We are satisfied with the way things are now. The balance of power has been restored within the region, the obsidian trade can proceed as before, and we can now all return to our profits. For profit is all we really care about, is it not?"

The Mayan representative smiled.

"Should there be any unforeseen hurdle from your part, the southern kings would be very disappointed. Do we make ourselves clear? Now, since you have basically decimated Sian K'aan, we will tolerate the presence of your men already here, so this city doesn't die. But be warned. The southern states will allow no more Tollàn warriors across their frontiers. Any foreign soldier seen crossing our border will be mercilessly hunted down and killed, and we will not tolerate any attacks on Mutul or otherwise, it is you we will turn against."

"We wouldn't want you to become too powerful here," added Ikan. "We are, after all, competitors."

With these last words, the two southern representatives turned around and left.

Spearthrower Owl clenched his teeth as they walked away. Great Jaguar Paw had brilliantly outwitted him. The king knew he had to disappear, he knew his image was tainted beyond recovery and so he'd promptly removed himself from power, knowing the southern states would no longer be a threat to his people once the war was ended with Sian K'aan. But not before finding the perfect successor. Not before leaving behind a local hero on Mutul's throne, a man who's defiance of Tollàn's power would inspire other Mayan cities to do the same.

"Great Jaguar Paw has won," he admitted.

"Patience," said the priest as he headed outside. "Come with me."

Spearthrower Owl sighed and followed.

They both walked out of the corbelled arch and onto the streets of Sian K'aan.

Spearthrower Owl looked at the people around him. Mayan woman and children, for the most part, but there was also many Tollàn men. Warriors, most of whom were still wearing their battle clothes.

To his right, an altar had been quickly erected in the center of the small city plaza. He saw the Quetzalcoátl battle standard planted next to the modest monument.

Copal incense was burning. Fresh blood covered the flat stone.

The Tollàn lord felt the presence of his gods once again.

"The former Sian K'aan ruler," explained the priest as he gestured towards the dark stain.

He raised his chin and smelled the air.

"I sacrificed him this morning at sunrise. I burned his heart to the feathered god and I danced around Quetzalcoátl's altar with his skinned flesh draped around my shoulders. Siyah Kak took care of his family and children."

Spearthrower Owl looked all around. The city was in a pitiful state. The infrastructures were crumbling down, filth littered the muddy streets, and the many stelas and murals which had once embellished the city with images and tales of previous kings had now been crushed and ravaged into unrecognizable rubbles.

Good, he thought. *There will be no reminder of the conquered king. No image of it's now extinct dynasty will survive the conquest. Soon, no one will even remember that the fallen king and his ancestors have ever existed.*

"Should I get rid of Siyah Kak?" discretely asked the priest. "He is useless to us now that Tupac needs no supporter. There is no need for us to keep him alive."

"No, Siyah Kak can still be useful. We should keep him a little longer."

"As you wish. So what shall we do now?" he asked.

"We wait," answered Spearthrower Owl. "Mutul is too powerful for now. Stelas of Great Jaguar Paw will be erected. People will celebrate his memory. The boy might rule the city, but with the old counselor standing by his side, it might as well be Great Jaguar Paw himself sitting on the throne. One day, our time will come. We must be patient. The southern kings will not easily be fooled, they will not hesitate to attack us should we walk against Mutul, but they will let us be as long as their interests are safe.”

“The southern kings... There must be a way to appropriate ourselves the riches in the south!”

“There is always a way. I still believe Mutul is the key to this region. Somehow, we must appropriate ourselves that city! In the meantime, we still need them. We need their business, as they need ours. It is therefore imperative that we maintain a healthy trade relationship with them. Tollàn’s obsidian must be distributed through Mutul, as their cocoa and feathers must reach our land.”

The Tollàn lord breathed deeply. All was not lost.

“I will ask Siyah Kak to support their new king, so that our commercial relationship with them remains undamaged.”

“And you? What will you do?”

“I will not return to Tollàn. Not yet, and neither will you. From here, we can better plan our next strategy.”

He turned around. The sun was slowly setting above the jungle.

“Look out there, priest. The entire Mayan world is waiting before us. There is a fortune to be made in this land. It can all be ours if we plan carefully!”

Spearthrower Owl opened his arms and laughed. He looked at the Mayan city, at his own warriors walking the streets. He thought of all the Mayan obsidian hidden deep within the southern mountains. He thought of all the goods and riches traveling the many roads within the jungle.

His king had given him one clear directive. He wanted more power. More profit. And he had no intention of disappointing him.

Endless possibilities were out there, waiting to be grabbed.

EPILOGUE

On the day following the king's sacrifice Icoquih ordered the body to be recovered from the murky water depths. For a full year, no one was allowed to drink from the sacred body of water. With great ceremony, the deceased king was washed and buried amongst his ancestors within the sacred acropolis tomb.

Soon after the king's death Balam was married to the princess. Nine months later he accessed the throne of Mutul. For himself, he chose the name Yax Nu'un Ayin, while Icoquih was thereafter known as Lady K'inich. Present to the investiture ceremony was Siyah Kak, the burnt king of Sian K'aan, who came to support the new king and reinforce the image of their allegiance. Also present were Ehb' Pakal, king of Lakam Ha, and Oyamal and Ikan, the southern states representatives.

Balam successfully ruled Mutul for the following thirty years, bringing the city to an unprecedented level of prosperity. Every single year, on the anniversary of the famous ballgame, he organized festivities where he played ball against an opponent dressed as a Tollàn. After his staged victory, he always presented himself in the center of the court wearing Tupac's old headdress, so that no one would ever forget the events leading to his kingship and the divine battle they'd won against their enemy.

Xochitl's body was secretly buried deep into the jungle, under a vanilla tree. For the rest of his life, Balam regularly visited her grave, always leaving flowers over his lover's tomb. She was never forgotten.

Wak Xook was immediately named warlord of Mutul. Not trusting the Tollàn troops stationed in Sian K'aan, his first act was to rebuild his army. He then immediately reinstated the border patrols and trained his troops in preparation for the eventuality of a war against Tollàn, devising efficient defensive strategies to counteract the atlatl so that never again Mutul warriors would be caught unprepared by the treacherous aerial attack. The defensive wall, however, was never completed.

For a while, there was peace between the two neighboring states, but it was a peace marked by tension and animosity. Despite Great Jaguar Paw's dream, the two sister cities were doomed to a life of war punctuated by short periods of tolerance.

Spearthrower Owl remained in Sian K'aan, where he spent the rest of his life plotting against Mutul and the Mayan world, attempting to gain ultimate obsidian trade control. He never succeeded. Spearthrower Owl died an old man, alone and far from his home.

As for the Tollàn high priest, he was sent back to Mutul so that Spearthrower Owl could have a trusted ally inside the city. He hauled the damaged wooden idols back up their pyramid and sacrifices were once again performed inside the temple, but the Tollàn gods had lost all power in Mutul. Balam, now known as K'uhul Ahau Yax Nu'un Ayin, personally saw to it.

Less than two-hundred years later, the Tollàn Empire had practically vanished from the world, leaving behind little more than the ruins of one of the greatest cities of its time. Tollàn's influence was forever eradicated.

As for the Mayan civilization, it flourished for almost a thousand years after these events.

AUTHOR'S NOTES

Although being a work of fiction, this story is set around actual historical events. Some of the main characters presented throughout the book have actually existed. The locations are real, although I have strived to call the various cities by their ancient Mayan names instead of their modern names. Mutul, for instance, is the famous Guatemalan site of Tikal. Sian K'aan is today known as Uaxactun. Tollàn is Teotihuacan, near the current day Mexico city.

By our calendar, the story begins on October 21st, 376. Great Jaguar Paw, the actual king of Tikal, performs the k'atun ending ceremony marking the end of a twenty year period. This event is commemorated on Tikal stela 39, where the king can be seen victoriously standing over a prisoner, a sacrificial axe in his hand. The text accompanying the stela specifies that the king actually did perform the bloodletting act on that day.

As the story unfolds, the reader is introduced to the many interactions occurring between the different Mayan kingdoms. The Mayans have never formed an empire. On the contrary, their land was divided in numerous states, each of them dominated by a single city. The kings ruling these city-states were more often than not at war one against each other. For the purpose of this story I had to dramatically simplify the number of these kingdoms, as remaining true to the dozens of city-states which actually existed would have unfortunately proven unmanageable in only a few hundred pages.

I did, however, try to represent the extent of the commercial relations between the various states. Goods were traded all over the Mayan territory, and products originating from as far as modern-day Mexico city were common in Belize and Guatemala at that time.

On January 16, 378, the city of Uaxactun is attacked and overturned by an invading force. At the head of that force is a Mayan warrior long referred to as 'Smoking Frog' due to the appearance of his name glyph, a glyph later deciphered as 'Siyah Kak'. This warrior is shown on Uaxactun stela 5 holding a club with obsidian insets.

On the very same day, Tikal stela 31 registers the death of Great Jaguar Paw. The late king of Tikal was eventually replaced by a man named Yax Nu'un Ayin, who is referred to as 'Spearthrower Owl's son' in the texts and shown wearing a Teotihuacan headdress.

It is well known that Teotihuacan had a significantly disruptive political influence in the events surrounding the Tikal – Uaxactun war. And there truly was a Teotihuacan king or lord named Spearthrower Owl in the Tikal region at these times, although the true nature of his purpose remains unknown.

The exact sequence of events leading to Uaxactun's conquest and Great Jaguar Paw's death is still nebulous, but archeologists and historians generally agree that Teotihuacan likely overthrew both Tikal and Uaxactun on that day with the help of a Mayan warrior, and that Mutul's new king Yax Nu'un Ayin truly was of Teotihuacan descent.

Despite the generally accepted theory, you've read how I chose to incorporate the various facts surrounding this event into my story.

Regarding the ball game, it is clear from the several artistic depictions and by the many ball courts found throughout the archeological sites that the game was of significant importance to the Mayans. Although the exact rules remain unknown to this day, it is popular belief that either the winner or the loser was usually sacrificed upon the outcome. I choose to believe that the game was as popular then as is modern day hockey in North America, or as football/soccer is throughout the world. I'd like to think that great tournaments were regularly organized. That every city had their star players worshipped by the fans, and that sacrifices following the game represented the exception rather than the norm.

I clearly remember the first time I've walked onto a Mayan ballcourt, on the famous archeological site of Chichen Itza in Mexico's Yucatan peninsula. As I stepped onto the field, I was taken abash by the immensity of the court, and I could only stare in wonder as to how the game could ever be played on such a large terrain. I later learned that Chichen Itza's oversized ballcourt was likely never intended to be played upon, that it was likely used for ceremonial purposes only.

I then visited Cobà, where the ballcourt is of much more modest dimensions. There, standing in the middle of the playing alley, I was finally able to see how skilled players could bounce rubber balls off the sloped side walls and through the vertically mounted side rings.

The Mayan culture is still very much alive today. Millions of Mayans still inhabit the land of their ancestors. I invite anyone who travels to the popular Riviera Maya, or to any other location in the vicinity of any Mayan ruins, to take the time to visit these wonderful archeological sites. Hire a guide, and let yourself immerse into this ancient culture.

You will be amazed at what you will discover.

J.G. Nadeau